The Landlord's Dead Body

TERRY JOE GUNNELS

Gunnels Publishing

Inquiries and Book Orders should be addressed to:

Gunnels Publishing
Email: terrygunnels51@cox.net
Phone: 757-930-1596

ISBN: 978-1-960605-90-0 (sc)
ISBN: 978-1-960605-91-7 (ebk)

Contents

Acknowledgements

To my wife, Shirley Jean (Cookie),---for encouraging me through 45 years of marriage in all projects I have undertaken. And for spending untold hours proofreading this manuscript for errors.

To all my BETA readers who gave me valuable feedback,

1. To Sterling Norris Monk,---for reading, giving feedback, finding errors I missed and providing a male point of view.
2. To Debby Groome Wilkerson,---for her insight on characters, and story line.
3. To Brenda DePaula,---who pointed many errors and short comings in my writing. Her honest opinions made the rewrites to the story a definite improvement to the book.

I must give a special thanks to my Editor, **Donje Putnam,** who could be titled "co-author" in many areas since she constantly encouraged me to make changes to update into today's world and current generation. She pointed out things that may be used or valid in real-life situations, but in a book, the setting is repetitious and tedious to read.

To all others,---for exciting me to move forward with the story and encouraging me to publish.

I give my heartfelt THANK YOU to every person involved with this book.

Terry Joe Gunnels

Prologue

About six weeks ago:

In the middle of the night, at the darkest hour, they got out of a car at the recently cleared land behind the Senior Village apartment complex owned by the Christianson Company.

The driver opened the trunk and took out the light bulb to keep the area dark while unloading the body.

"Hurry up and get her out," he grunted as he dragged the body out of the trunk of the car.

"I'm doing the best I can," she answered. "I never realized a body was so heavy. They don't have this much trouble in the movies."

"Right, because they aren't real dead bodies in the movies, you twit. Be quiet and help me."

"You did this by sleeping with her, so don't blame me!" she snapped.

"She said she was on birth control, and besides, I didn't kill her, you did. So don't blame me!" he said, dragging the body away from the car. "Get the shovel."

She reached inside and took out a tool.

"No. Not that one. That's a garden spade. Get the shovel. That's the one with the long handle, and come over here and help me."

"I don't know one tool from another. They all dig, don't they?" she said.

"Keep your voice down. Someone'll hear us."

"It's dark. We're all the way across this empty field from the closest building, and if someone did see us, they couldn't tell who we are or what we're doing," she answered.

"Just dig, okay?"

"How deep?" she asked.

"I don't know. Most graves are six feet deep."

"I'm not staying out here all night digging this stupid grave," she exclaimed as she picked up the spade and handed him the shovel.

"How about four feet? We want to cover the body, so no one finds it, but I agree. I don't want to be here all night."

They dug in silence until they were several feet deep. Then they pushed the body into the shallow grave along with her purse. They piled the dirt in the grave covering her body, gathered their tools, got in the car, and left the field.

As they slowly drove away from the open field, she turned and asked him, "When are they going to start construction? They took months to clear the land."

"I don't know. But they're still trying to secure the financing. They still need some investors for the down payment and then banks for the rest of the money. Commercial real estate is a complicated business. The Christianson's have come a long way in the past few months. When Daniel, the old man, was in the hospital, they thought he might never recover. Now, he's good as ever. His son, Mickey Ray, has joined up with his father, and they're roaring ahead. A few months ago, it seems that Mickey Ray was a kid. Now he's Daniel's right-hand man. He's become a shrewd businessman for his age."

"Do you think they'll find the body?" she pondered.

"Probably not. It depends on where all the underground things like utilities and building foundations are located. I guess it's possible, but there's always lots of open space in apartment complexes. Maybe they will, maybe not. Still, it'll be decomposed in a few months. They may not even be able to identify her, so we should be in the clear."

"Maybe, but, you idiot, we buried her purse with her. If they dig her up, they'll know who she is!" she exclaimed.

"Oh my God, you're right. We need to go back and dig up that purse," he sighed heavily as he began to slow down.

"You go back. I'm not getting out of this car until we get home. I've done enough digging to last me a lifetime. You're one sorry human being," she said, sitting back in the seat. "If you behave and keep it in your pants, we can put all this behind us and go on with life. I'll say this. If I ever catch you doing something like this again, I'll not help, nor will I ever forgive you! Do you understand me on this?" she said with finality.

"I understand, now let's go," he said as he pulled back onto the road.

CHAPTER 1

Monday, The First Day of Construction, and a Dead Body

Two men, business partners, father and son, Daniel and Mickey Ray Christianson, looked over the vast field, cleared and ready to break ground for the next real estate project. It would be the largest residential project in Bridgeton, and it had been a long, tedious road to get to this point.

They had hired engineers, architects, land use, and environmentalist experts. They had spent endless hours wining and dining potential investors, talking to city officials, and attending numerous city council meetings. Last, they had presented the project proposal to bankers to get the forty million dollars needed to build the project that was beginning this morning.

The land was cleared. The equipment was beginning to dig the footings for some of the buildings marked out on the map attached to the wall in the construction trailer parked on-site behind them.

Daniel's arm rested on Mickey Ray's shoulder while he steadied himself by holding a cane.

"Son, this is the proudest moment of my life," he said while looking over the site.

"Yes, Pop. It's mine, too," Mickey answered.

"I wish your mother were alive to see us working together on it."

"That would be the icing on the cake, wouldn't it, Pop?"

"You bet. The men know where to start, don't they, son?"

"Yes, I talked to the site foreman yesterday afternoon. He didn't like talking to me on a Sunday, but I explained that we needed to start on Monday, today. We got it all straight. They're going to start on building five digging the footing. The plumbing company will follow them as well as the underground electrical utilities. Let's go inside the trailer and look at the construction schedule," said Mickey Ray.

The project they were starting was on the edge of the township of Bridgeton, a small town between Williamsburg and Richmond, Virginia. Daniel had grown up in the town, left the area when he went into the Air Force and met a young lady, Eleanor, and got married. When he had served his term in the military, he returned to Bridgeton and began investing in rental real estate.

Eventually, he sold his single-family homes and began investing in apartment buildings and later building apartment complexes. As his two kids, Darcy Jean and Mickey Ray, grew up, Darcy got married, had two kids, and later divorced. When Mickey got old enough, he helped Daniel with the maintenance responsibilities of the properties.

Darcy Jean and the kids moved into the family home to help care for their father when he got out of rehab following an automobile accident. She married James Bower, a war veteran and Mickey's best friend, a few months later.

Mickey was in his mid-twenties at the time of Daniel's accident but quickly matured, dealing with problems and maintenance situations while his father was recovering. Mickey was handsome, had a trim physique developed from his regular visits to the gym, and rich. Daniel and Mickey Ray paired up and organized this project when his father recovered. Mickey Ray attended almost all business meetings and became quite familiar and popular with the town's officials. The young ladies were coming out of the woodwork, hoping to be noticed by Mickey. He was considered the "most eligible bachelor" in Bridgeton.

As they walked to the construction trailer, Mickey said, "They got the trailer set yesterday afternoon and hooked up all the utilities."

They walked up the steps to the office trailer and went inside. Even though it was early morning, it was hot, and the morning sun was already heating the trailer, so Mickey turned the air conditioning on to keep it at a comfortable temperature while they had their first meeting of the day. He put on a pot of coffee to be ready when everyone showed up.

Daniel looked around the office for the first time. He knew that for the next 18 months, he and Mickey would be spending a lot of time right here. On one wall was the map of the layout of the new complex. On another wall were artist renditions of the interior of the units and exterior showing the proposed landscaping and renditions of the interior of the restaurant, senior clubhouse, and pool area showing the cabana-style concession stand. On the other were pictures of him and Mickey Ray standing with the town mayor, the local bank president, and some of the investors and people they couldn't even remember. Another wall had filing cabinets, a blueprint storage cabinet, and a drafting table. A door led into another room that was Mickey's office.

Daniel didn't have an office here, but Mickey insisted that they also put Daniel's name on the door. In Mickey's mind, it was still Pop's dream, and Pop was the inspiration, and he was only his father's helper.

As they sat in a couple of the chairs in the main room of the trailer, Daniel and Mickey talked.

"Pop, we've come a long way, haven't we?"

Daniel looked around the room, sighed, and answered, "Yes, Mickey Ray. I remember that night about six weeks ago when we had that investors meeting, and I officially announced that you would be the new CEO of the Christianson Company."

"Yeah, I was nervous as a long-tailed cat in a room full of rocking chairs!" They both roared in laughter at Mickey's comment.

"You didn't show it, son. You were cool, calm, and answered every question they threw at you. And who was that black lady that asked you what would happen if the housing market crashed?"

"Oh, yeah, I think her name was Mrs. Claybourne. She was the well-dressed lady from that investment firm in New York. I remember her. I answered that this project wasn't like buying into the stock market where you make or lose money only when you sell. I told her that historically real estate values went up. Even if values did fall, the investors would be getting monthly checks from rented units and the additional services we'll provide here."

Daniel laughed and commented, "That was the perfect answer, and that's what she wanted to hear. We got all the additional financing we needed that night, and it was all because of you, Mickey. You handled yourself very professionally."

One by one, men filed into the trailer and paused to look around at the decorations on the wall. There were even a few family photos of Darcy

Jean and her kids with James. Mickey stood behind a table sitting in the middle of the room covered by a cloth. Finally, he called everyone to order.

He began by saying, "Guys, this will be the first of many meetings we'll have here. I hope that we'll discuss the future progress, not problems. With every project comes some problems. When you come here with a problem, please try to come up with a solution. We'll discuss every detail and work it out."

Mickey pulled the cover off the table, revealing a three-dimensional architectural model that showed the entire project.

He pointed to one corner of the model. "You already know that we're starting in this corner. The backhoe was unloaded just minutes ago and has already started digging the foundation on this building," he said, pointing to one of the tiny buildings on the model. "As that progresses, others will be working on the underground utilities in this area. We have to run power, water, sewage, and natural gas lines through the entire area and under the roadways throughout. I think you've all met Randall. He's the site supervisor. He'll coordinate the work with all of the line foremen. There'll be several different contractors working on various jobs, and he'll hopefully keep things running smoothly and each of you out of the other's way. You report to him. He reports to me or my father here, Daniel. We have a schedule and barring any unforeseen circumstances, we should get this entire thing complete in the next eighteen months. Let's go to work, men!"

They all looked at the model and discussed various job topics amongst themselves. Randall made the rounds introducing himself to those he didn't already know. As one would ask him questions, he would sometimes go to the map on the wall and discuss their questions and give them an answer or make notes to get back with them later.

As Mickey and Daniel talked to one of the line foremen, the door to the trailer opened, and a burly man stepped inside. "Mr. Christianson?" he called out.

Daniel and Mickey both turned and answered the man. "Yes, can we help you?" they said almost in unison.

"The backhoe operator has run into a problem."

"How can he have a problem? He's only been digging for ten minutes."

"I'm sorry to tell you this, but he dug up a body."

"Oh, crap!" said Mickey. "This isn't a good way to start a construction job. Pop, if you'll stay here and answer any questions the men might have, I'll go check this out."

He followed the man across the field and over to the backhoe. About three feet deep, there were some clothing and body parts in a hole. The operator stood several feet away from his machine, pale and throwing up. Mickey walked over to the man. He looked to be in his early forties and very upset.

"I've been doing this for all my adult life. I've never had anything like this happen. I didn't know what to do when I saw it," he said.

Mickey placed his hand on the man's back. "Are you alright? Why don't you go over there and sit down? You didn't do anything wrong. You stopped and reported it. You did good. It's okay. Take a breather. What's your name?"

"Al. My name's Albert," he said.

"I'm Mickey Ray. My Pop and I own the project. You calm down. Take some deep breaths. Go sit down. We'll call the police and let them take it from here. You just sit. I'll have someone bring you a bottle of water. Would you rather have a cup of coffee?"

"Yes, sir, that would be good," he said.

"Just call me Mickey Ray. Coffee or water, Al?"

"Water's fine, sir," he said. "I thought I would pass out when I saw what I did."

"You don't have to call me 'sir.' Call me Mickey Ray, or if you prefer, Mickey. You didn't know anyone was buried here. No one knew. It's fine." He looked over at the burly man. "Would you get Al a bottle of water? We have some in the construction trailer."

"Yes, sir," he said, turning around to walk away.

Mickey called out, "And call me Mickey...not sir!"

The man put his thumb up in acknowledgement as he headed for the trailer.

Mickey took out his cell phone and called the police. In a few minutes, the man returned with a bottle of water and handed it to Mickey.

"What's your name?" Mickey asked as he extended his hand to shake the burly man's hand.

The man put out his hand and said, "I'm Bob."

Mickey gave Al the water and told him he needed to stay until the police arrived and tell them what had happened. And then he could have the rest of the day off.

"Bob, I told Al he could leave after giving the police a statement. It shouldn't take long. All he did was put the bucket in the ground and find the body. And Al gets a full day's pay. He's had a pretty big shock. Don't let anyone around this area, and don't touch anything. Tell the police I'm over there in the trailer," he said, pointing to the trailer as he walked away.

Everyone had gone except Daniel and Randall when he returned to the trailer. Mickey walked in, and both men looked at Mickey for answers.

Mickey said, "I need a tall cup of coffee. This's going to be an awful day."

"Tell us about it, Mickey," said Daniel.

Mickey walked over to the coffee pot, poured a large cup full, grabbed a doughnut, put it in his mouth, and chewed it up along with a few sips of coffee. Daniel and Randall stood patiently waiting for Mickey Ray to speak.

"I can't add much to what Bob, the foreman that came in here, said. The backhoe operator dug up a body. I called the police, and they should be here in a few minutes. Needless to say, that area will be shut down until the police release it. Randall, if you get another operator to run that machine after the police leave, I'd appreciate it."

"Sure thing, Mickey Ray. I'll have them move over to the next building. He might be able to get that one dug today, and we'll continue around the ring. Then we'll get back to that one," Randall said, then left the trailer to find another operator.

A few minutes later, there was a knock on the door, and Detective Peter Reynolds walked in. "Hey Dan," he said. "You haven't got started, and we get a call from you."

Daniel smiled at the detective and waved his hand toward Mickey. "Peter, this is my son, Mickey Ray. He's the one that called it in, and he'll be handling things here."

He shook hands with Mickey and introduced himself as Detective Peter Reynolds, who had been assigned to this case.

"Nice to meet you, Detective. What do you think of it?" asked Mickey.

"I called a forensic team to get on it. They'll take most of the day, and we need to cordon off the area for a couple of days to make sure we don't miss anything," he said.

"I understand. Do you think we can get back to it by Wednesday?" asked Mickey.

"I don't know. Can you give us the rest of the week? I can see you have a lot to do, and it really isn't getting in the way. Can you go with me back over to the site so we can talk about it?"

"Sure, Detective. Can Pop come along?"

"Both of you can come. You're more familiar with the site and maybe can shed some light on what's happened the past couple of months. How're you doing, Dan?"

"Doing great, Pete. I see you're still limping from that wound you got a while back," said Daniel.

"Doctor said I may always have this limp. Getting shot in the leg just didn't heal as good as new like they said it would. I see you're still using that cane."

"True, but I believe that I should be able to throw it away in a couple of months. At least that's what I'm hoping. Let's take a look at the dig site. Mickey told me about it, but I haven't seen it yet."

The detective opened the door and held it while Daniel carefully descended the steps. He held it open for Mickey. The detective again took the lead to the backhoe. They lined up and looked into the shallow hole when they got there.

Detective Reynolds shook his head then pointed at the body. "It's female. She had on a dress. I think the ladies call it a sundress. The backhoe operator tore it and her body, so I can't tell much beyond that. We'll know more after an autopsy. My guess is she hasn't been here very long, only a few weeks, because of the level of decomposition. It looks like a young lady, but I can't say.

"I know that you've had heavy equipment in this area for months, but as I said, the decomp's not too extensive," said the detective.

"Yes. We started clearing the land months ago. We've cut down many trees, graded the land, turned up a lot of soil to dig out stumps, and leveled the entire acreage. We would've dug her up sooner if she'd been here more than a few weeks ago. Do you think someone wanted us to find her body?" asked Daniel.

"No, I doubt it. If someone wanted the body found, they wouldn't have buried it in the first place. They would have left it somewhere or dumped it without digging a hole. My guess is the soil was easy to dig.

They just picked a spot where you happened to dig. There are a lot of areas that you'll not disturb during the entire construction. Bad luck for somebody. The problem is, identifying the body and clues. When you bury somebody, you lose a lot of clues along with it. Nature erases a lot. If there was physical trauma, that might be difficult to separate from the damage done by the backhoe. Sad. It really is so sad. We'll do what we can, but in all honesty, chances are, we'll never find her killer. I wish I could be more positive, but you understand. I'll do my best to find the SOB that did this. Sorry I have to shut the site down. I hope you understand."

"Of course, we understand, Pete. You have a job to do, and we don't want to interfere. We have a lot of other areas we can work on right now. Take your time. We'll work around it. Let us know when your people are finished. We have a schedule and an order that we have set to make the job progress efficiently," said Daniel.

"Thanks, Dan. We'll do our best to wrap it up and get out of your way," said the detective as he reached out to shake hands with Daniel, then Mickey Ray.

As Detective Reynolds limped back to his car, Mickey turned to his father and shook his head. "Pop, he seems like a pretty decent cop. I hope he's true to his word about working to find that lady's killer."

"He will, son. Pete's one of the best in the Bridgeton police department. If he says he'll try, you can count on him to do it. I've known him since he joined the force."

"Well, Pop, let's have a real breakfast. I'm starving."

"Where do you want to eat, Mickey Ray? You do know you're buying, right?" Daniel said.

"I wouldn't have it any other way, Pop. How about the old stand-by, the diner? My truck or your car?"

"Let's take the Rolls, boy. We've been working so much, we haven't had time to buy a new truck for me to drive."

They got into Daniel's Rolls Royce Silver Seraph that he had bought while still in the hospital recovering from an accident. James, Mickey's best friend, had said that Mickey wanted a Rolls Royce. A mechanic, Logan King, that they used on occasion for unique jobs, had found this one, but Mickey wasn't ready to commit to it, so he bought it for his father instead. Daniel had loved that car since he first saw it. Years before, Daniel and Mickey Ray had purchased an old Corniche, a 1970's era Rolls Royce convertible, and restored it to showroom condition. Someone had set fire to it, and it was damaged beyond repair. Mickey had taken the insurance money and put it in the bank. He hadn't decided on what he wanted to buy, so he drove Daniel's work truck until then.

They pulled into the diner and picked out a booth in the far corner. Pauline came to the table.

"Hello, Daniel, you're looking better every time you come here. Soon you'll throw that old cane away," she said as she took their order.

Daniel and Mickey talked about the construction while they ate. After leaving the diner, Daniel took Mickey back to the project site to pick up his truck. Mickey needed to go back to the other apartment complexes to check the vacant rental units. He told Sam, the maintenance supervisor, that he planned to hire two more men to help him with maintenance. Sam was retired military and had been the maintenance man back when Daniel was running the business.

Mickey had decided to promote Sam to foreman and head of maintenance since they'd be hiring more men and having an actual maintenance department.

"Hey Sam, I'm going to interview two men this afternoon, and if they're even remotely qualified, I'm going to hire them to work with you. As luck would have it, one of the men, Jesse Clayton, just knocked on my door at the construction site and asked for a job."

"That's great, Mickey Ray. I need help. I've got several units that need work and a handful of service calls. I can't keep up with it all."

"I understand, Sam. I hope they'll take a load off you if you train them."

"Whatever you say, Mickey Ray. I still have four units to get ready and only two people to help me right now. Until you get someone for me, I'll do the best I can."

"I know you will. Just hang loose for a few more days. I've interviewed several people, but they want too much money for too little experience," said Mickey. "I've got some errands to run now, but I'll try to get back later."

He got back in the truck and headed to Darcy's house to talk to James. When he pulled around to the back of the house, James was in the garage working on a project.

"Hey Mickey. I should have this area done in a few more days. We can store tools in here, along with business records and spare auto parts," James said.

James was working in an oversized garage that Pop had built behind the main house. Pop had bought, restored, and maintained a dozen cars. The garage was vacant since their aunt had stolen them and sold them to an unknown buyer. When James and Darcy were married, James moved into the main house with her and her kids. James started to remodel the garage if Daniel, his new father-in-law, wanted to restart his old hobby of collecting classic autos.

Mickey's father lived in the guest suite of the house where Mickey and Darcy had grown up. Mickey had moved into Darcy's former townhome. He might build a home of his own one day, but right now, he was single, and the townhome was adequate for his needs.

James was a friend from high school. He was a former military veteran who was on total disability because of scars he had gotten while he and his team were on a special secret mission. He was burned over a large percentage of his body, including his face, which made him very self-conscious around people in public. Before he had fallen in love with Darcy, he would dress up as a clown and go to the mall and do magic tricks for the kids because he knew if they saw his real face, they'd run away in terror. Darcy's kids, Joel and Cyndi, had accepted his disfigurement and loved him.

"James, I have a lead on a 1930 Model A Ford. It needs some work, but it's a simple car, and Pop might have a great time restoring it. What'd you think?" Mickey asked.

"I'd bet he'd love it. It's a project the two of you could work on together."

"His birthday's around the corner. I might get it for him. It's priced right. Want to go look at it with me?" asked Mickey.

"I'd love to. It could be a surprise. If you think it's something you would be interested in getting for him, could I go in halves with you? I don't know what to get him from Darcy and me. That would solve that problem."

"Sure, you can go in half. We'll look at it tomorrow. I'll set it up," said Mickey. "Have you seen Pop today?"

"No. Why?"

"We started construction on the senior expansion project today, and one of the backhoe operators dug up a body. It's a female. We called the police, and Detective Peter Reynolds came over. He shut that portion of the site down for the rest of the week."

"I haven't heard anything about it. Your dad was there when all this went down?" James asked.

"Yeah. He knows the cop and says he's a straight arrow. I hope I can get some info from him. You know how people can be. Some people wouldn't move into the complex when it's complete because they're superstitious. People can be weird like that. I don't want word to get around. I'll give it a couple of days, and I'll stop by the station and see what he'll tell us."

"Sounds interesting. Want some company when you go?"

"I could always use the company, and an extra hand, James. I just had an idea. This place is so big. How about putting in some gym equipment in the corner until we get a few cars in this place."

"Hey, I like that idea. It wouldn't take up too much room, and right now, we've got two thousand square feet of empty space. I'll look into it."

Mickey went into the house to see Darcy for a few minutes. She was washing clothes and getting ready to go to the office.

"Hey, Dee, what's up?"

"Hey Mickey, what're you doing here?" she answered. "A few more minutes, and you'd have missed me. I've got a ton of work to do today at the office," she said, moving clothes from the washer to the dryer.

"I thought I'd stop by for a few minutes. You'll never guess what happened first thing this morning at the jobsite," said Mickey.

"What?" she said.

"A backhoe operator dug up a dead body."

Darcy's mouth dropped open with surprise. She stopped, standing with a piece of clothing in her hand and looked at Mickey. "My, gosh, Mickey. What happened to him?"

"Her. It was a woman. We don't know yet, but the police came to start an investigation. It was Detective Peter Reynolds. Pop knows him pretty well. He says Reynolds' a good cop."

"Oh, no. How long will that hold up the construction?" Darcy asked as she went back to loading the clothes into the dryer.

"It won't hold up anything. There are plenty of other areas we can work. But it was a shock. The newspaper will get ahold of it, and we'll be swamped with reporters."

"No doubt about that, Mickey. How will we handle that?"

"I don't know right now. We've never had anything like this happen. I'll deal with it when it happens."

"What's James doing? I've got to get to work," she said, closing the dryer door.

"He's out working in the garage," answered Mickey.

"He enjoys that. I mean the garage, and he seems excited to get it fixed up for Pop to start working on cars again."

"Yes, he likes doing things for Dad," Darcy said, grabbing another load of clothes. "I believe he's looking as forward to fixing up cars as daddy does. Dad seems to be happy here. I wasn't sure when we first moved in a few months ago, but he's accepted it well. He gets out and walks every morning about sunrise, then comes in and fixes breakfast for everyone. The kids are happier than I've seen them for years. Dad and James both dote on them. Sometimes I'm afraid they're spoiling them, especially Joel. Have you heard from Valerie lately?"

Valerie and Mickey were engaged to be married. She was kidnapped, and James and Mickey rescued her, but as a result, Valerie had suffered some severe emotional issues. When she felt she couldn't deal with it any longer, she enrolled in a culinary school in Oregon and moved. Mickey and Valerie still kept in touch, but they both knew it was over.

"Yes," he said with a sigh. "She called me last night, and we talked for almost half an hour. She's doing fine. She loves school and is taking a class on baking. Can you imagine taking a class just to bake a cake?" Mickey said.

"Oh, Mickey, there's more to baking than just cakes, but I know what you mean. Well, little brother, I have to get to work. I have a new secretary starting today, and I need to be there to get her started. I love my new office. It has been a real adjustment since I went to work full time for the Christianson Company. The attorneys in the firm I used to work for were good to me. But they understood that I needed to leave when I gave notice. I talked to them yesterday, and they said they're open to letting us do some of their research for cases. I can still get in a few hours to bring a little business to the office. It isn't real estate, but if we can bring in some cash doing off-site research and paperwork for law firms, that sounds good," she said as she gathered up a load of clean, dry clothes.

"Great. I've got to get back to the jobsite myself. See you later."

As he pulled through the gate to the jobsite, he saw a city vehicle sitting where the backhoe had found the body. He parked his truck and walked over to see two people in the hole with brushes brushing dirt away from the body. He stood there watching for a few minutes before one of the workers looked up and saw him. The man stepped out of the hole and came over to Mickey.

"Good morning," he said.

"That depends on your viewpoint, I guess," Mickey answered.

"I guess that's true," he responded. "Are you Mr. Christianson?"

"I'm one of them. I'm Mickey Ray. My father's over there in the construction trailer. And you are?"

"I'm Baker, Clyde Baker, but everyone calls me Baker. Sorry, I can't shake," he said, showing his gloved hand.

"I understand. What can you tell me?" said Mickey.

"Not much, sir. The ongoing investigation, you understand."

"Yes, I understand; however, I see that you found a handbag. It's lying right there next to the body. Can you tell me her name? There was identification in the bag, wasn't there?"

"I'm sorry, but..."

"Baker, I'm not asking for anything that might jeopardize an investigation. It'll be all over the news in a few hours anyway. All I'm asking for is her name."

"Um, I guess that might be acceptable. Let me look in the bag and see what's in there," he said, turning back to the body in the shallow hole.

He picked it up, opened it, rummaged around, and took out a case containing several credit cards and a Virginia driver's license. He came back and held it up for Mickey to see. Mickey looked at it, and his mouth dropped open.

Baker looked at Mickey and said, "Do you know her?"

"Holy crap! Yes, I do, or did know her! My sister and I went to school with her, and she lived in one of our apartments. We weren't friends or anything, but you know how it was when you were in school."

"Yeah, I remember how school was. Sorry, I can't let you touch the evidence, but is there anything else I can help you with?" he said.

"Can you take the items out of the bag and just hold them up for me to look at?"

"I don't know if I should do that."

"Come on, Baker. I promise not to touch, and what I see is between you and me."

Baker took an evidence bag and poured the handbag's contents into it, then sealed it up with tape. He then handed it to Mickey.

"Don't open it up. You might contaminate it. You can look at it with me standing here. Then I have to get back to work," Baker said, noticing the others had stopped working and looking up at him.

Baker took her jewelry, her watch, a hair clip or barrette, and put it in another bag.

Mickey took a quick look and snapped a picture of each clear bag with his phone, then turned them over and snapped a picture of the other side. He then made a motion of zipping his lips and nodded.

"Between you, me, and God. Thanks. I'll put in a good word for you if I have the chance," said Mickey as he walked back to the trailer.

Daniel called out from the office when he entered, "Is that you, Mickey?"

"Yeah, Pop. I stopped by the hole to check the progress there. Pop, the dead body is Betty Duncan. She was buried with her handbag," he said as he walked into the small trailer office and sat down in the chair across from his father.

"What else did you find out?" asked Daniel.

"In her handbag was her driver's license. Dee and I went to school with her, and she lived in one of our apartments. Pop, she is or was a real sweet girl. If Detective Reynolds doesn't find her killer, we have to," Mickey said sadly, shaking his head.

"Pete will do his best, Mickey, because he's the best. We need to stand back and let him do his job."

"I know, but I just can't understand what anyone would have against her to want her dead. She was in the same graduating class as Dee. She lived in one of our apartments with her mother. When Dee and I were in school, she worked at a grocery store in town.

"Her father was a mechanic and worked on city vehicles at the motor pool. She had two brothers. When they all grew up and graduated, one brother joined the service, the other got married and moved out of town, somewhere out west, I think. Anyway, Betty wasn't particularly pretty and not popular in school. She worked and helped support her mother when her father died a few years ago of cancer. She and her mother were quiet and never caused any problems. I had forgotten all about them until now. I know the detective will work on her case, but we should do something also."

"Mickey, Pete's good at his job. Let him do it. Don't get in his way," Daniel warned.

"Pop, when the news gets out, it will hit the fan. The media will be all over it."

"It's not our problem, Mickey. Leave it alone. We have an apartment complex to build."

"I know, Pop. You're right, but we need to get ahead of this thing so it doesn't affect potential tenants or future investors. Several people are still working on marketing and selling our company stock to investors. We don't need bad press right here at the git' go!"

Daniel shook his head. "I disagree, Mickey. We, no, you need to leave it alone. Let the police handle it."

Mickey reached across the desk, picked up the phone, and dialed Darcy at her new office. "Hey, Dee, it's me. How's the new girl doing?" he asked.

"I don't know yet, Mickey Ray, I just got in. What do you need so soon? I just saw you a few minutes ago?" she said.

"Hey, we have an ID on the female that was dumped on our construction site. You'll never guess who it is!" he said.

"Right, I'll never guess. Tell me," she said.

"Betty Duncan."

"Really? The Betty Duncan we went to school with?"

"Yes, the same one."

"She helped you with a couple of your math classes, didn't she? You were friends?" asked Darcy.

"Yes, she did, but we weren't what you'd call friends. I paid her to help me," he answered.

"Yes, I see. You don't charge friends. She was a nice girl."

"Right, she was nice and didn't deserve to be killed. Someone killed her and buried her with her handbag and ID in it. She and her mother moved into one of our units a few years ago. Are they, or I should say, is her mother still living there?"

"I don't know, but I can find out. Give me a few minutes to make a couple of calls and dig into our rental records. I'll call you right back."

Mickey hung up and asked Daniel to call Detective Reynolds to see if they could notify Mrs. Duncan.

Daniel called Detective Reynolds and explained the situation to him. The first thing he did was ask how Mickey had found out before he did.

Daniel tried to smooth his ruffled feathers. "Pete, your people didn't do anything wrong. I know it's an ongoing investigation, but it happened on our property, and all they did was give Mickey Ray the girl's name. That isn't a crime and doesn't release any confidential information. Clyde Baker, the forensic man, was very good, polite, and professional, so don't take it out on your team."

Mickey could hear the detective on the other end of the phone was very upset that Mickey had interfered with his people.

Daniel kept talking and trying to calm the detective. "Do you want to tell that lady her daughter is dead? Mickey knows her and can help her through this, and she'll be more prepared to answer your questions. So, you see, we're doing you a favor, Pete. Fine. If you don't want to let Mickey go alone, why don't you and Mickey go together?

"We don't want this on the news, do we, Pete? You and I both want to keep this quiet. We'll do that. We don't want the world to know that someone was killed on our property, and you don't want reporters getting in your way. We'll help you if you just keep us up to date with the investigation. You have my word. We'll not get in your way. Thanks, Pete," Daniel said and hung up.

Daniel sat back in the seat. "I hope this doesn't turn into a media circus. This is a small town, and nothing newsworthy happens, so all hell could break loose when something like this happens. Pete said that if you meet him there, you can go together to break the news to her. Maybe that would make her mother feel a bit more at ease."

"Dee and I'll do our best to placate the news and keep it calm," said Mickey.

"I've got some errands to run, Pop," Mickey said, walking to the door. "I'll see Mrs. Duncan later. When Dee calls back, will you give me a call and leave a message? I've got to interview two people to help Sam with the maintenance situation. It's gotten so he can't keep up, and things are getting behind. I've got to go to the other office."

"Sure, Mickey. I'm going to hang around here for a while longer until everyone else leaves. Then, I have to go home and play with my grandkids," he said, putting things away and straightening things on the desk.

Mickey was already feeling overwhelmed. Starting a new project, trying to keep the existing property running smoothly, and now a murder on the new site. Sam, his maintenance foreman, needed help. He had several jobs and more responsibilities each day. Mickey drove to the office of Black Forrest Village, where he told the two job applicants to meet him. He talked to each of them for about half an hour and decided to hire them both on probation to test their suitability for permanent employment. He then called Sam and updated him on the new hires.

25

CHAPTER 2

Telling Mrs. Duncan Her Daughter is Dead

Mickey went by the office and got the message that said Betty's address was still at the same location in Black Forrest Village. However, she's listed as delinquent in rent and on the list for court proceedings and possible eviction.

Mickey pulled into the Black Forrest apartment complex, parked, and waited for Detective Reynolds. Together they walked up, and the detective knocked on the door. After a few minutes, a haggard-looking woman opened the door. He could see the resemblance to the young girl Betty from his high school days.

"Hello, Mrs. Duncan?" the detective asked.

"Yes, that's me," the lady answered.

"How are you, ma'am? I'm Detective Peter Reynolds, and this is the property owner, Mickey Ray Christianson."

"I bet you're here about the rent. I'm trying to get it for you. I hope to get it paid up by next weekend," she said apologetically.

"No, that's not why we're here. May we come in, please?" he asked gently, "if you have a minute."

"Did I do something wrong?" she asked.

"No, of course, you didn't. But we need to talk."

"Alright, I guess so," she said and opened the door wide for them to enter.

They walked inside and looked around. It was sparsely furnished but spotless and tidy. The furniture was old and worn but clean, with little throw pillows in the corner of each arm of the couch. He walked over to the sofa and sat down, motioning for Mickey to follow. She moved to a lounge chair and also sat. As he continued to look at the living room, he saw a picture on the wall of Betty and her brothers. Lined up side by side were each of their high school graduation pictures. At the very end was a large family portrait with everyone smiling. Knowing what he had to say, he felt sad to break this horrific news to this lady.

"What can I do for you, gentlemen?" she asked.

"Please, call me Mickey Ray," Mickey said.

"We came to talk to you about your daughter, Betty," said the detective.

"I haven't seen her for a while," she said.

"Do you remember the last time you saw Betty?"

"It was last month. She was going out with a friend of hers, but she didn't say who. She just got in her car and left. She was kind of private about her friends."

"I understand. Do you remember the exact date?"

"I think it was around rent time, so I guess it was the first or so of the month. She usually dropped the rent off at the office. She didn't do it that day. She went out and never came back. Why? I really am trying to get the rent. Mickey, I know you own this place, and you're due your money. Right now, I don't have any place to go…"

Mickey interrupted her, "Don't worry about your rent at this time, ma'am. We're not here about that."

The detective cut in her apology and said, "I'm sorry to give you this news, but Betty's body was found yesterday in another area while construction was going on."

"You mean that other area, where they've been cutting down all the trees to build new stuff?"

"Yes. That area," he said.

"Her body, you say? What do you mean by her body?" she stuttered.

Mickey cut in at this point. "We mean that Betty is dead. We're so sorry that we have to give you this news. I came with Detective Reynolds because I knew Betty and she was such a nice girl. We went to school together."

She broke into tears and cried out loud. Mickey had anticipated this and brought some tissues. He took some out and gave her the small tissue pack. He sat silently until she had cried out and settled down.

"Yes, I remember you, Mr. Mickey. You brought her home from school a couple of times." She looked at Mickey and said, "How did she die?"

"I don't know, but we suspect she was murdered. The police don't know yet, but they'll let you know as soon as they find out more. Detective Reynolds is a very competent investigator. He's been assigned to her case. He'll have a lot of questions to ask."

"Why would someone want her dead?" she said almost in a whisper.

"We were hoping you might be able to help us with that, Mrs. Duncan," the detective said.

"Can you find out for me, Mr. Mickey? After all, it's your property," she asked.

"Please, it's just Mickey. Not Mr. Mickey. That's the police's job. That's why Detective Reynolds is here. I'll help them wherever I can, but they are trained to do this."

"You knew her, Mickey. You own this property, so aren't you responsible for what happens on it?"

"Only to a point. Murders are the jurisdiction of the police. As I said, I'll help them if I can. Betty and I weren't close. We were in a couple of classes. She tutored me a couple of times with some of my classes, but that's about it. I haven't had any serious contact with her since we graduated."

"Oh, God, I don't know what to do. I don't even have enough money for rent. I had a stroke a few years ago, and I'm on disability, and my check is barely enough to buy groceries and not enough left to pay rent. How am I going to get money for a funeral? I don't know what I'm going to do." She rose and stood completely still as though she was in a trance.

Mickey rose and moved to her side. "Mrs. Duncan, don't worry about any of that. Your rent will be taken care of, I assure you. My family will take care of the funeral expenses. If you let me, I'll pick you up in the morning, and I'll take you to the police station or wherever you need to go. Is that okay with you?"

"Mr. Christianson, I can't ask you to do that. I can drive there myself," she said, looking up at him.

"Again, it's Mickey or Mickey Ray, and you didn't ask. I volunteered to do it. It's the least I can do for you right now. It would be my honor to help you. I'll pick you up around nine in the morning, and we'll do whatever needs to be done." He hugged her as she broke out in tears once again.

She put one arm around his neck, and the other arm hung loose. It was a result of her stroke that she couldn't raise it. He stood and held her until she had again cried herself into exhaustion. She sat back down and sadly hung her head.

"I thought that she had just given up supporting me and left to make a new life. I never even dreamed that she was dead. I feel so ashamed of thinking that about her."

"You didn't know. I'm sure Betty would never have left a mother as wonderful as you. If you need anything, anything at all, you just call this number," he said as he handed her one of his business cards.

Detective Reynolds stepped up and also handed her a card and added, "I'll need to come back later and ask you more questions so we can find the person who did this to your daughter."

Mickey hugged her and whispered in her ear, "Don't worry, Mrs. Duncan, we'll do our best to find Betty's killer, and I'll help you make arrangements for her funeral."

When they went to the car, Detective Reynolds turned to Mickey and said, "That was very generous to help with the funeral. I'm glad that you realize the jurisdictional boundaries in this case. I'll handle it, so stay out of my way."

"Pop told you we wanted to help, and as you clearly heard, Mrs. Duncan wants me to help, so why can't we work together on this?"

"Because it's my job. Let me do it."

"Pop gave you his word that I won't get in your way, but this could be a media nightmare for the Christianson Company. We have millions of dollars invested in this project, and something like this could potentially put a huge wrench in the works. Like I said to Betty's mother, I knew Betty. We weren't close, but I knew her. Right now, she wants me involved, so for her comfort and my business, I'll help you."

"I don't care as long as you stay out of my way and don't impede my investigation. Got it?"

"Got it, Detective," Mickey said.

Mickey left and called his father at the construction office. "Hey Pop, how're things progressing today? Everything going smoothly?"

"Yes, Mickey Ray. So far, so good. The forensic team still has the yellow crime scene tape up, and they said it would need to stay up for a few days if they need to come back again. I see that you came by and picked up the message I left for you. Did you talk to Betty's mother? Did she tell you anything?"

"Yes, I met Detective Reynolds there, and we talked to her together. We didn't talk to her about Betty's murder. Reynolds said he would talk to her later about that. I told her I'd pick her up and take her to the police station in the morning. She was pretty messed up today. We understand that. She should be more settled down tomorrow, and I'll talk to her more then. If you call Detective Reynolds to tell him, I'll bring her by the station, that would be a big help to me."

"Consider it done, Mickey Ray."

He called James and told him about Betty's mother.

"I remember her, Mickey. She was a sweet girl. She was always nice and friendly even though she didn't have many friends at school. Sorry to hear about someone killing her. Who would do something like that?"

"I don't know, but we'll look into that. The cash we have stashed away, I think we should help her mother out with some of it. What do you think?"

Mickey was referring to several million dollars he and James had found in a storage unit a few months ago that had belonged to a smuggler. They knew that if they turned it over to the police, it would get lost in the system and even sit forever in an evidence locker or warehouse. They had agreed to use it to help people in dire straits, and this seemed like a perfect use of some of the money.

"I agree. What do you want me to do?" James asked.

"First, take enough money to the rental office to pay the rent up to date. Then go to the bank, set up an account, and deposit money in it to last about six months. Tell Dee to set up an automatic payment directly from that account to the rental office and deduct the rental amount from it every month. Then, get a prepaid card for one thousand dollars and deliver it to her. Tell her it is from an anonymous source, and you can't divulge the donor. As time goes by, we'll add more money to replenish her account. And reload that card. There are a lot of social programs to help people like Mrs. Duncan, so we can look into that too. Also, I said that my family would pay for Betty's funeral. She doesn't have the money for rent, so she can't pay for a funeral. Is that agreeable to you?"

"That's a lot of money to pay to someone we don't even know, Mickey," James said hesitantly.

"I agree, but she's on disability, and that's barely enough to pay groceries. We agreed to help people with that money."

"Good point, bro. I'll do it. Do you want company when you pick her up in the morning?"

"That might be comforting to have other people that cared about Betty. I'll swing by and pick you up."

"Hey, you going to take the Rolls?"

"Sure, why not. We'll switch from the truck to the Rolls when I come by to pick you up," said Mickey.

Mickey stopped by the field office at the construction trailer. Pop was there, and he asked him if it would be okay to use the Rolls tomorrow. They talked about the construction progress, and Daniel told him that they had planned to get several of the footings dug. The plumbers and electricians would be laying power lines and water and sewage lines as soon as they could get the building inspector's approval.

He left there and went over to Black Forrest Village to see Sam and the newly hired men he had interviewed last week and showed up for work this morning.

Sam stood outside the building, talking to Mickey about them and their skills.

"Well, Boss, they're okay. One seems to be pretty good at painting. The other is a good plumber. Both of them are totally ignorant about electrical things. They're afraid of it even when the power is cut off. One day isn't a good indicator of their trainability. Give them at least a week, and we can tell if they are good enough to keep and train."

"I see. Keep an eye on them, and I hope they work out. I know you need them, but we'll let them go if they aren't good, and I'll keep looking. We want to find out quickly to replace them and move forward, if necessary. I also interviewed two others that can start tomorrow. Only about 50% of the people I interview even bother to show up for work."

Mickey left, stopped by the local Pizza parlor, and got a pizza to go. When he got home, he started the answering machine. There were several hang-ups, and one that a concerned recording told him their records showed that the extended warranty was about to expire on his vehicle.

The last message was of mild interest to him. Another of his old schoolmates informed him that he was invited to their annual fundraising event at the Bridgeton Country Club. He had gotten one last year that he had thrown in the trash. Word had gotten out that since Valerie had canceled their wedding and moved away, he was fresh meat around town for the single ladies group. He was always invited to attend some fundraiser or luncheon, even sometimes as a speaker at some social group.

The girl that left the message was Francine Braydon. She and her twin brother, Francis, were social climbers. Their father, Franklin Braydon, was a former Mayor of Bridgeton. Francis was married with two children and a lawyer in town. Francine and her mother, Donna, had a small business as event planners. Francine had been divorced twice at only 30 years old, and each time, she took her maiden name to reclaim her innocence to unsuspecting suitors and a weak attempt to erase those past mistakes. Francine was childless and considered herself a prime catch for the right person. She also felt her previous husbands were unsuitable for her imagined social prominence. Francine was still a stunningly attractive woman, and she knew that she could bend most men to her desires. Therefore, she was always on the prowl for rich and handsome suitors.

Francine said into the machine that Mickey should have received an invitation to the event. As of yet, he hadn't responded to the invitation, and an RSVP was expected. The event was being held in only a few days, and she pleaded for him to attend even if he hadn't had time to respond.

He usually went through his mail every two weeks because he didn't get a lot, and most of what he did get was junk and advertisements. He checked his mail, and just as she said, the engraved invitation was in the stack. He threw it away but then reached into the trash and withdrew it. He thought that he might as well go. He had nothing else to do that night, and why not? He might have some fun playing her game.

He saw the date and realized that the event was only one day away. He guessed he should get his tuxedo out of storage. Okay, he thought, it wasn't really in storage. It was stuffed in the back of his closet. It might still be a fun evening, even if it was a stuffy snobbish affair.

CHAPTER 3

The Newspaper, Alice Duncan, and Funeral Home

A foghorn rang out in Mickey's head. Over and over, it rang out. Finally, he woke up and realized the foghorn was the phone beside his bed. He reached over and knocked it off the bedside table. He got up and reached to the floor and saw on caller ID that it was Darcy, so he returned the call.

"Yeah, what is it, Dee?" he grumbled into the phone.

"Have you seen the newspaper headline this morning?" she said to him.

"No. I haven't even got out of bed yet. Even if I was out of bed, I don't get the daily paper. What's the problem?"

"The headline is, 'Dead body found in the construction site of the newest Christianson building project.'"

"Oh, crap. That just happened yesterday morning. How did the news find out about it so soon?" Mickey asked as he cleared his head.

"I don't know, but this kind of bad press can hurt the stock sales," she said. "Investors don't like bodies turning up in a building site."

"I know. Can you handle it? I've got a dozen things to do today. Who's listed in the byline on the article?"

"Let's see," she hesitated as she looked at the paper. "It's Carter Evans. I've never heard of him. Have you?"

"Nope, but we need to get in touch with him and get him and the paper to back down until this is solved."

"Newspaper reporters can be like pit bulls, especially in this new digital news world," sighed Darcy.

"What time is it anyway, Dee?" Mickey asked, yawning.

"It's 5:30 A.M. I've been up for an hour and a half and already had two cups of coffee," Darcy stated.

"Well, I don't usually get up until 7 A.M., but I won't get back to sleep now with this news. If you can, run a background on this Carter Evans, and see how easy he is to work with."

"Will do, Mickey. I'll talk to you later," she said, and the phone disconnected.

He got up, put on a pot of coffee, and took a shower. He then headed to the diner for an early breakfast. This was going to be a long day.

James met Mickey and they pulled up to Alice Duncan's apartment in his dad's Silver Seraph.

"Good morning, Mrs. Duncan," said Mickey. "We're here to pick you up. We'll take you to the police department, and when you're finished there, we'll go to the funeral home and help you make arrangements for Betty."

"Okay, let me get my purse," she said as she opened the door and invited them inside. She disappeared into the back room, and in a few moments, she came back out holding a small purse.

She looked up at James and asked, "Aren't you the one that came by late yesterday and gave me that credit card?"

James gave a slight bow and said, "Yes, ma'am. I'm the one."

"Did Mr. Christianson send you?"

He glanced at Mickey, and he shook his head, no. "Well, Ma'am, he did tell me to stop by here, but I'm not allowed to divulge the person that sent the money. Mickey did tell me that his family is taking care of the funeral arrangements. Mickey, myself, and my wife all went to school with Betty. We all want to help you during this time."

"So, you also knew Betty?"

"Yes, we all knew her. I'm James Bower, by the way. Mickey didn't introduce us. He's my brother-in-law," he said, putting out his hand to shake hers.

"Thank you for coming, Mr. Bower."

Mickey spoke up, "Now, Alice... May I call you Alice?"

"Of course," she said.

"Fine, let's go. Detective Reynolds will be waiting for us."

As they walked to the car, Alice stopped and looked at it. "Wow, what a fancy car."

"Thank you. It isn't mine. It belongs to my father. James insisted that we drive this one today. I have a truck. He said that you deserve it, and I agree."

James opened the back door for her. As he did so, he added, "Alice, the back seat is the place of honor in a Rolls Royce. The ones in the front seat are only passengers in service of those in the rear. Today we honor you and Betty. We're at your service."

After she got in, James got in the front passenger's seat. He gave a quick wink to Mickey, who smiled in agreement with him.

As they drove, Mickey began to talk. After some small talk, he got down to business. He wanted to sound friendly and helpful, not like it was an interrogation like the police would be doing as soon as they brought her to the station. "Did Betty have any close friends? You know, someone we should notify that she has passed?"

"I guess that would be a good idea. There was Laurel Cunningham, and maybe Carla Briggs."

Mickey said, "I remember Laurel. She used to be Laurel Rayburn, didn't she? I don't know Carla. Isn't Laurel married to Wallace Cunningham?"

"Yes, that's the same, Laurel. Why? Do you know her?" she asked.

"James, Darcy, and I went to school with her. Bridgeton's a small town. When you only have two high schools, if people don't leave town, you get to know almost everyone after a while," chimed in James.

"I guess you do. I never thought of it that way. Carla was a girl she met at work. Carla wasn't married, well she was divorced, but I don't remember her maiden name. Do you know her too?"

"No, I don't think so. Where did Betty work?" asked James.

"She worked at the grocery store."

"Which one?" asked James as he wrote notes on a small tablet.

"The one right down the street, the one on the corner. I think it's called The Pop-In Grocery. Betty was the assistant manager," she said. "I haven't gone to the store since Betty disappeared. I was too embarrassed."

"You have no reason to be embarrassed, Alice," James said.

"How about boyfriends?" asked Mickey.

"No, not really. There were a few several years ago, but none recently. She just mostly hung around with her girlfriends and her book club."

"What kind of book club?"

"Just a few friends that got together once a month and talked about the latest books they read. It was mostly an excuse for them to get together and have lunch at a restaurant."

"Do you remember any of the men she dated?" Mickey asked as he drove.

"Not really. I think Betty went out a couple of times with the mechanic that worked on her car. He worked at the garage down the street."

"Can you tell me his name? We'd like to talk with him," asked James, as he continued to write.

"I'm not sure. I think his name was Ralph. The shop's name was Carlson's Garage. That's all I know about him. The other guy she dated was one of the men that worked at the Main Street Bookstore. His name was Mike Reece. He came over for dinner at the house a couple of times. He seemed really nice. I don't know what happened between them. She just quit mentioning him, and he quit calling her." Alice looked down at her lap.

Mickey could tell all this was beginning to upset her. He felt he should back off, but he wanted to ask a few more questions. "I don't mean to upset you, Alice. If you answer a couple more questions, that might help us. We'd also like to look into her death if you don't mind."

"Isn't that why we're going to the police station. Aren't they going to look for her killer?" she asked.

"Yes, the police will look into it, and my father knows the detective assigned to her case. Pop says that Detective Reynolds is the best in the department. Since we knew Betty, we have had a bit of personal interest in it. We know what a wonderful and kind person she was, so it's just our contribution to help," said Mickey. "We'll stay out of it if you want us to."

"I want you to help the police if it speeds things up. I don't know what else I can tell you," Alice said.

"I can't say it'll speed things up, but we'll do whatever we can if it makes you feel better. You said Betty had a car. What kind was it, and where is that car now?"

"Now that you mention it, Mickey, I don't know where it is now. I just thought that when she left, she took it."

"Did she have any money problems?"

"None that I know about."

"Good for her. Money's always a motive for murder," he said, pulling into the parking lot of the police station.

"Okay," she said quietly.

James got out and reached a hand out to take hers and escort her into the station. All three walked in with Mickey and James on each side of Alice. Mickey walked up to the front desk and asked for Detective Peter Reynolds.

When Detective Reynolds came out, he looked at James and Mickey. As he shook hands with all three, he told Mickey and James they could leave. He would take care of her from here. Mickey told the detective that they would wait because they promised to take her to the funeral home to make arrangements for Betty. Reynolds said it might be an hour or more, but they agreed to wait for her.

After almost an hour and a half, she came back very distraught. Mickey knew that they had grilled her like she was a suspect. He also knew that it wasn't personal. Detective Reynolds was trying to get enough information to start the investigation. She asked Detective Reynolds when Betty's body would be released so she could finalize the burial. He said that possibly in about two more days. They could plan the burial for this Saturday.

As they walked to the car, James suggested they take a few minutes to get lunch. Mickey drove Alice to the nicest place in town. They spent almost an hour and a half at Giovanni's Italian Restaurant. James and Mickey tried their best to treat her like royalty. They both had family deaths and knew what she was going through, so they tried to find pleasant topics to discuss to help her through this time. They also knew that it would hit home when they went to the funeral home, discussed the arrangements, and picked out a casket.

They took her to the funeral home and assisted her with suggestions, and she picked out a basic but nice casket. She understood that it would be a closed casket service because of the decomposition, damage done by the backhoe, and the autopsy. As they left, she was understandably melancholy, and Mickey and James didn't talk much as they drove her back to her apartment. They felt her sadness and respected her desire for quiet as they rode.

They escorted her to her door and once again expressed their condolences. She insisted on hugging them and thanked them profusely for their attention to her needs and Mickey for the wonderful treatment and the funeral.

CHAPTER 4

Carter Evans and the Printed Newspaper Media

Mickey answered his cell phone when he saw it was Darcy calling. "Hey, Dee. You got back to me a lot earlier than I thought."

"I got in touch with Carter Evans. He wants to talk to you," she said.

"I don't want to talk to him. I want him to back off until all questions are answered! And the case is solved," exclaimed Mickey.

"He's not going to back off. If you don't at least talk to him, he'll ramp up the story. He threatened to follow you and or the police twenty-four-seven until they call it a cold case or until it is solved, whichever comes first. You need to talk to him, Mickey. He could help us or hurt us. It all depends on how he writes the story."

"Oh, crap. Okay. When and where?" Mickey sighed.

"Believe it or not, he is doing some phone research on you in his office. I can set up a meeting immediately right there if you want."

"No. I am not going to him. Have him come to me. James and I will be at the diner. Mr. Carter Evans can buy us lunch."

"Okay. That should be easy enough. When?" Darcy asked.

Mickey thought for a moment, "Let's see, it's almost noon. How about one-thirty? James and I'll be there waiting for him."

Later as they sat at a corner table in the diner, James said, "Where do we start? I've never done anything like this."

"How should I know? I haven't either."

"Then why are we doing it, Mickey?"

"It took a lot of public relations to get people to forget the trouble we had when we started this project. All the public outcry about developing this property. All the tree huggers and people wanted that area to stay as it was. The people in this town want it to stay small and sleepy. They wanted it to stay undeveloped. Now someone gets murdered on the property just as construction begins. It could be a PR nightmare," said Mickey. "We have a vested interest in finding her killer."

"No, we don't. It's not any of our business. Leave it up to the police. Besides, I distinctly remember you saying that all you wanted to be was a landlord! You said that you were not getting involved with other people's problems. Do you remember, Mickey Ray?"

"I remember. So, what's your point?" asked Mickey.

"My point is…IT IS NONE OF OUR BUSINESS!"

"Fine. I'm curious. I want to know who did it, with your help or not. I'm going to ask a few questions. Are you in or out, James?"

"I don't know why I let you talk me into stuff like this! I guess I'm in. So where do we start?" James said resignedly.

As the man entered the diner, he brushed his hair back and put his costly cellphone into his shirt pocket. Looking around, he spotted Mickey and sauntered toward him. He put out his hand to shake Mickey's hand and introduced himself.

"Hello, Mr. Christianson, I'm Carter Evans."

"I gathered that. Sit down," said Mickey motioning to a chair.

"It's a beautiful day, isn't it?"

Mickey leaned back in his chair and folded his arms. "Why did you print that story, Carter?"

"Right to the point. I like that. I ran it because it's my job to find newsworthy stories for the Bridgeton Times. Being a small town, we don't get a lot of murders and juicy stuff like this to print. It's sad when the front-page story is the new addition to the library building downtown. Library additions don't sell a lot of papers, but murder does."

"I'm sure it does. It also upsets grieving family members. That mother needs her privacy, time, and space to grieve for her deceased daughter," Mickey said gritting his teeth.

"I feel bad for her. I really do, but I have a job to do. You should understand that!" Carter said matter of factly.

"How did you find out about it so fast?" asked James.

"As we news reporters say, I have my sources."

"I thought you'd say that. Also, James and I agreed to talk to you if you bought our lunch. Before you arrived, we each ordered the biggest steak the house has on the menu. Do you want the same?"

"Nope. I already had lunch. And I assume the gentleman sitting there is James? Great to meet you," he said, putting his hand out to shake James's hand.

James just sat silently without offering his hand in return.

"Okay," he said, retracting his arm. "I guess those are war wounds? If so, thank you for your service. I appreciate our men who served. My father was a Vietnam veteran. He was KIA."

James, without emotion, said, "Sorry to hear that."

"Look, guys. All I'm doing is my job. I didn't ask for this assignment. It was given to me by my boss. Okay, I admit I wanted it because a front-page story looks good on my resume, but someone will cover it, and it might as well be me."

"I'll concede that you are doing a job, but if you present it wrong to the public, it will hurt the victim's loved one and damage our business," said Mickey.

"I understand the hurt you mentioned, but I don't understand how a murder could hurt your business. That is unless you killed her. I don't believe that for a minute."

"Would you want to live next to a cemetery?" asked James.

"No. Definitely not," Carter answered.

"Why?" asked James.

"Because that's creepy."

"No, it's not. There are bodies of loved ones, mothers, fathers, sons, and daughters. Even children are buried there. Most of them wouldn't hurt you when they were alive, and they certainly wouldn't hurt you dead!" James expounded.

Carter looked at James seriously with creased brows, "What's your point?"

"My point is, for some time, a person was buried on his property," James said. "That property is being developed for apartments and other amenities. People may be put off when they find out about a body buried there, just like you're put off by living next to a cemetery."

"Well, she isn't buried there anymore. Problem solved. Let's move on. When is the funeral?" Carter asked.

"Who said it was female?" asked Mickey.

"Same source that told me about the body. I also know it was a certain Betty Duncan, and you went to school with her. Did the two of you have a thing going? Is that why you're so interested in who killed her?"

"No, we barely knew each other. We need you to back off for just a few days until the police find Betty's killer. Then, we'll sit down with you and help you draft a story that doesn't drag her or my company through the mud. Deal?"

"No. Not even close to a deal. At this point, I don't know about any 'mud,' as you call it. If there is none, and you are clean, my story will not reflect any. If there is mud there, I will find it and report every grain of slime I can find. Deal?" Carter countered.

"No deal, Carter.

"There's no mud for you to find on my family's company or me," said Mickey.

"Then you don't have anything to worry about, but let me warn you, I never trust anyone involved with a victim on any level."

"What about the victim's family?" asked James.

"At this point, I don't know anything about her. As time goes on, I'll find out about her and her family. There's a reason she was killed, and I'll report it to the newspaper readership. Be sure to keep up with the story as it develops. Maybe you'll see your name on the front page. Thank you, gentlemen. I'll see my way out," he said, standing up to leave.

Mickey called out, "Be sure to pick up our lunch check on the way out. You promised! And be sure to give the server a generous tip."

They watched as he stopped at the cash register on the way out.

Pauline brought their steaks, and as they started eating, James said, "I think he could cause a lot of problems. And the police department has a huge leak."

"Yep," said Mickey as he took a bite of his meal.

When they finished their lunch and got in the truck, James asked, "Where do we start?"

"Let's start by talking with her girlfriends. They can probably tell us more about Betty than her mother. After all, did you tell your parents everything you did?"

"Nope, and I know you didn't either. No kid does that, and you sure don't when you grow up and want to stay out all night!"

"Why don't we start with Ralph at the garage?" said Mickey. "If we go by your house, you can pick up the Vee, and then we'll split up. We can cover more ground that way."

The "Vee" as James called it was a civilian Humvee that James had modified with basic armor, a turbocharged engine, run-flat tires, and stiffened suspension that had gotten him out of trouble on several occasions.

"Sounds like a plan," said James. "I'll take Ralph. You take Mike."

When they got to James' house, they switched back to their own vehicle. Mickey pulled the Rolls back into the garage and got in his truck. Darcy would be at work, so they knew she wouldn't be at home.

Mickey knew the bookstore that Alice had mentioned. James also knew where Carlson's Garage was located, so he drove in that direction.

Mickey pulled in front of the bookstore and parked. Inside he saw a woman stocking a shelf with books.

He walked up to her, "Excuse me, could you tell me if Mike's working today?"

"Yes, he is. He's in the basement level stocking books. That's our bargain area. May I help you find something, perhaps a particular book or author?" she asked.

"Thank you, but no. I just need to talk with Mike for a couple of minutes."

"Okay, just follow the yellow arrows on the floor. They'll lead you to the stairs going to the bargain section. If Mike can't help you, I know almost every book in this store. Just come back and see me."

"I'll do that. Thank you again," he said, looking at the yellow arrows and walking toward the stairs.

When he got to the bottom of the stairs, he saw a short, stocky man standing on a stool, putting books on the very top shelf. Mickey walked over to him.

"Hello, are you Mike Reece?" called Mickey.

"Yes, I am. How may I help you?" the man said.

Mickey put out his hand to shake the man's hand, but he had both hands full of books and clearly wasn't going to put them down, so Mickey began talking.

"I'm Mickey Ray Christianson. I'm a friend of Betty and Alice Duncan," he said.

"Okay."

"I was hoping that I could ask you a few questions about Betty."

"It depends on what you want to know," he said icily, then continued placing books on the shelf.

"When was the last time you saw her?"

"I don't know, about two months ago. Why?"

"I understand you, and she dated for a while. True?"

"Yes, we did. But we just weren't suited for each other."

"Yes, I understand. I'm single, and I've dated ladies who felt the same way. Can you tell me what made you feel that way? I mean, did you not get along, no common interests? What was the problem?"

"What is this? Why are you asking all these questions?" he asked, becoming even more cautious with his response.

"We're doing some background checks on her, that's all, Mr. Reece."

"Who did you say you are? And why are you doing a background check on Betty?"

"I'm Mickey Ray Christianson. I'm her landlord, and we are just getting some background."

"I don't understand. You're her landlord. Don't you check people out BEFORE you rent to them, not after? Why're you checking her out now?"

"Because, Mr. Reece, her body was recently dug up on my property, and I want to find out who buried her there," Mickey said.

"What do you mean her body was dug up? I didn't even know she died. Don't you people keep records on who buries the people in your cemetery? Why did they exhume her body?"

"I didn't say they exhumed her body. I said it was dug up on my property."

"Don't you own the cemetery where she was buried?" Mike asked.

"If you don't mind, stop for a moment and listen to me," said Mickey.

"Fine. Talk. I'm Listening."

"Betty was killed and buried on some property that I own. It's not a cemetery. It's now a building site. I am interested in finding her killer. I was hoping you might be able to shed some light on what may have happened to her," Mickey said slowly.

"I don't know anything about that. And if you aren't the police, I don't have to talk to you."

"You're correct. You don't have to talk to me, but they will be here soon enough. If you don't talk to me, you will talk to them."

"Okay, I'll take my chances with them. I must ask you to leave this shop right now! I have nothing else to say to you. If you come back in this shop asking questions, I'll call the police myself."

"You may not have to do that, sir. I'm sure they'll be around asking you even more questions than I've been asking. I am only trying to find out who killed Betty. If you ever cared anything about her, you would want that person found."

No response from Mike.

Mickey stood looking the man straight in the eye. Mike didn't flinch. It was a mental stare down, and neither man looked away.

Finally, Mike spoke. "I have nothing else to say. Now leave before I call the cops."

"That sounds like a plan. Why don't I wait here while you make the call," Mickey suggested.

"Look, she and I don't see each other anymore, and I haven't heard from her in over a month, so go away and leave me alone. For the record, I didn't kill her, and I'm sorry she's dead."

"I told you, call the cops as you threatened. I'll wait," said Mickey calling his bluff.

"Whatever," Reece said and picked up more books to put on the shelves.

After several minutes of watching Reece stock books, Mickey turned and went back up the stairs to the ground floor. As he passed the lady stocking shelves, she smiled, and he smiled back at her.

"Was Mike able to help you, sir?" she called out to him.

"Not one bit," he answered, walking out the door.

While Mickey was getting nowhere with Mike Reece, James talked with Ralph at the garage.

"So, you and she kind of hit it off, Ralph?" said James.

"Yeah, we did. Betty is a really sweet young lady. We got along great. We didn't date long and not often for the most part. She would bring her car in here for service. You know, oil change, a brake job, state safety inspections, minor stuff. We dated maybe three months. Usually, it was dinner and a movie. You know how most dates go. She likes romance movies. I like action. She wanted fancy restaurants. I like pizza and beer. We just don't have a lot of common interests. Still, she is nice, and we get along. If you like someone, you know you find things to do and ways to connect. We didn't officially break up or anything, and sometimes I'd call her. Other times, she'd call me. We just kind of called each other less and less until we didn't call each other at all. I should give her a call sometime, just to catch up."

"Sorry, but you can't call her anymore," said James.

"Why not?"

"Because she's dead. That's why not."

"Oh, no, man! Are you serious? How did it happen? I didn't know that." He had been working on a car, but when James said that, he dropped his wrench and stared at him in disbelief.

"Yes, I'm serious. Someone murdered Betty and buried her body in a shallow grave at a construction site," James stated.

"Oh, no. I'm so sorry to hear that. Even though we didn't get along, she didn't deserve for anyone to hurt her. We were still friends and all. I hope you catch the person that killed her."

"When was the last time you heard from her?"

"I don't know. A month. Maybe two. I haven't kept track, and you know how time flies," Ralph said.

"Do you remember what you talked about the last time you saw her?"

"Nope," he said. "Why should I?" Ralph reached for the wrench he dropped.

"Thanks, Ralph, for your help. Hey, have you ever worked on a Rolls Royce?"

"No, but if it's got an internal combustion engine, I can find a manual or software to repair it."

"I have a friend that bought a used one, a Silver Seraph. And he's looking for a competent mechanic to work on it. Maybe I'll send him to you," said James.

"Oh, I almost forgot, I heard that Betty was dating someone else. I don't know anything beyond that. I think she even went away for a weekend with him. I guess that's not important now if she's dead."

"It might be if he killed her. Do you know his name?"

"Nope, I can't tell you anything more. I just heard it. Maybe it was just a rumor. Who knows?"

"I know what you mean. Thanks, Ralph." James got in his Humvee and completed his notes before forgetting anything.

Mickey went back to the main house, and James was waiting for him. "What'd you find out," Mickey said as he got out of the truck.

James had the big door open to the garage and was washing the Rolls. He looked up and squinted as he looked into the sun as Mickey approached. He continued washing then rinsed the suds off the car. He threw the wet soapy cloth into the bucket, and Mickey saw a little head pop up on the other side of the car, followed by his own father's head.

"Hey, Uncle Mickey," the little fellow called out. It was his nephew, Joel.

His father called out also, "Hey, son. How about some help here. James has just about worn out this old man and his grandson!"

"Old man, my foot, Pop," Mickey laughed. "You're just barely sixty. That isn't even old enough to retire. Get back to work. Both of you!" Everyone laughed, and Joel and Daniel disappeared behind the car's front fender again.

Mickey heard the slam of an old-fashioned wooden screen door on the back of the house. Turning, he saw his little niece running toward him. He reached down and scooped her up and swung her around him in a circle while she screamed in pleasure at the motion. Mickey put her down and kissed her on the cheek. He quickly thought this was the way life should be. The only thing missing was his mother.

"Where's your mother, Cyndi?"

"She's in the house, Uncle Mickey. Are you stayin' for dinner?"

"I don't know. I'm pretty hungry, and you may not have enough food for this cowboy."

"You're not a cowboy, Uncle Mickey," she giggled.

"I'm not? We'll what am I?"

Cyndi looked thoughtful for a few moments, then said, "You're a landlord."

Mickey laughed and said, "I guess you're right, little one. That's exactly what I am."

She ran over, picked up a cloth, and began wiping the car dry.

James told Mickey what Ralph had said, including he heard a rumor that Betty had gone away for a weekend with some unknown man.

"Back in high school, we were all different people," said Mickey.

They all grabbed a dry cloth and dried off the Seraph, and James pulled it into the garage and closed the door for the night.

Mickey stayed for a homemade meatloaf dinner. And all was well with the family.

CHAPTER 5

Autopsy Results and a Surprise

Mickey went to the jobsite to check the progress the following morning. Pop was already there, and he was in a meeting with the plumber and the electrical contractor.

As Mickey walked into the office, he heard the electrical foreman saying and pointing the finger at the plumber. "It's his screw-up. He would have seen it if he had only looked at the Jobsite prints."

Mickey asked, "What's going on here?"

"One of Raymond's men cut through our line. This pea brain let one of his men run a trenching machine cutting through the line. Now we have to dig it up and re-lay a new one. It puts us a day behind work. The cost isn't coming out of my contract."

"We looked at the site plans, and no one noted that the work had been done," the other man answered angrily.

Mickey said, "Is that true, Donald? If your men finished, they should have noted it on the master sheet. Since you didn't mark it off, no one but you knew about it. Come on now, Donald, no one here's a mind reader."

"We just finished it two hours earlier. I didn't have time to come in here and mark it as done," said Donald.

"I'm sorry, Don. You should have been here as soon as it was complete. I have to take Raymond's side on this. We all make mistakes, and whoever is responsible must pay. It's on you. Be more careful in the future. Now go back to work and get us back on schedule," said Mickey.

Mickey turned and walked over to his father. "Hey, Pop. How is everything else going so far?"

Daniel watched the foreman walking out of the door. "Mickey, you handled that like a real Christianson. That was so good to see you in action."

"Thanks, Pop. Last night at the house was great, wasn't it? I enjoyed myself so much, and I hated to leave."

"It was good, Mickey. We'll do that more often."

"You didn't mind that I took off yesterday to help Mrs. Duncan with her daughter's funeral, did you?"

"Nope. Not one bit. I'll hold down the fort here. You do what you feel's right for her. She needs someone like you right now since she has no one else."

"Thanks, Pop. I have a list of names I need to send to Dee, and ask her to do some background checks on them."

"What kind of background checks, on who?"

"Some friends of Betty. The dead girl. Remember James, Darcy, and me, all went to school with her. We want to know what happened to her as much as her mother."

"Take all the time you need. Anything I can do, let me know."

"There's one thing you can do, Pop. Think you can get the results of the autopsy?"

"I don't know, but I'll try. I'll call Pete and try to convince him to tell me. He may not. It's part..."

"I know. It's part of an ongoing investigation," said Mickey sarcastically.

"You got it, but I'll twist his arm, maybe call in a favor or two."

"Detective Reynolds owes you a favor?" asked Mickey.

"Quite a few. You didn't know this, but I gave Pete's son a job one summer helping to keep the grounds mowed and trimmed when you were a little kid. I helped him out. His son had broken into one of our vacant apartments and done some damage. Instead of pressing charges, I let him work out the cost of repairs. He grew up and turned out to be a very good, responsible person. He has three kids and works in city hall as a plan's examiner. I used to see him occasionally when I needed to get building permits. Anyway, as I said, Pete owes me a few. I'll call him when the office opens."

"Great, Pop. I've got to call Dee and let her run this list for me," Mickey said as he picked up the phone on the desk.

He talked with Darcy and read out the list of names.

"Sure, Mickey, things are slow in the office, and I can run those checks now. I did run a background check on Carter Evans. He came from a small New York newspaper."

"I didn't know New York had a small anything," Mickey interrupted Darcy.

"Yes, NYC is big enough many small businesses can survive. And dozens of small newspapers are one of them. Anyway, he was an up-and-coming reporter until something happened. I haven't found what it is yet, but I can tell you, he is a pit bull reporter. Don't get on his bad side. He's got a writing style in that he can phrase things in a way that makes someone look good or bad without actually saying it and manage to stay clear of scandal or libel lawsuits. I'll get back to you as soon as I have something for you."

A while later, at Black Forrest Village, Mickey met with Sam on the new hires.

"Mickey, I think the one that I told you would be a good painter, he's good, but already he was late for work both days. Late the first two days of a new job is not good. The other guy is working out a bit better. He seems to pick up faster and is interested in learning. Let's give him a couple more days. Do you have anything at the construction site? One of them mentioned that he liked working around new construction."

"Which one, Sam?"

"Jesse Clayton," answered Sam.

"He's the one that came knocking on my door. I would have thought he would be better. He did say that he wanted to work at the new construction site. I'll check with Pop and see if we can transfer him over there," Mickey said.

"Right now, the only thing I think he can do is be an errand-runner. We need more maintenance staff. We have to have more people as we add more units. I'll do what I can. Keep me in the loop." He left and met James at the diner for breakfast.

Pauline had already set the table and filled their cups when she saw them roll in the parking lot. When they came in, she pointed to the corner table and let them know that their coffee was waiting for them.

Mickey and James both sat down and started dressing the coffee. James always drank his black. Pauline came over and took their order.

"What's up for the day, bro?" said James.

"As soon as Dee calls me back, we can start where we left off yesterday. She did run a check on that reporter. He can hurt us if we aren't careful."

"Hurt us how?" said James, a bit concerned now.

"Dee said that his writing style can infer things without actually saying them, so he can put us in a terrible light if we aren't careful."

"How's that?" James asked.

"I don't know how yet, but if we don't watch out, it could hit the fan," exclaimed Mickey. "Let's just concentrate on the job at hand. We'll deal with Mr. Carter when he does something. We have to interview the ladies on the list and find out what they know.

"I got an invitation to Braydon's annual fundraising event tonight," said Mickey.

"I didn't get one, but that's no surprise. Who would want a monster like me at the social function of the year," James said.

"Don't say that. First of all, everyone in this town knows you're a hero. Second, they don't know the exact things you've done to save this town. And unfortunately, we can't tell them. Besides, the only reason I was asked is they want some of the family money. I'll give them enough so they can't complain, but they're all a bunch of snobs, and I'm not too fond of a single one of them. Especially our former-illustrious mayor, Franklin Braydon. They all think way too much of themselves."

James looked Mickey in the eye. "No matter, that daughter of the Braydon's is a real babe! Wow, she could have any man she wants in this town. Don't let her get her hooks in you, Mickey Ray. She'll eat you up and spit you out. She's already done that to two other guys. She took everything they had, and that crooked lawyer brother of hers helped her do it. Somehow, he got the last guy's prenuptial agreement thrown out and took him for every dime he had. She's a black widow for sure."

"I've heard all the rumors. I agree she's evil but maybe not as bad as they say," Mickey said, picking up his coffee to take a sip.

"Maybe not, but I'd carry a first aid kit with snakebite anti-venom in it before I even said hello to her."

They both laughed as they each processed that statement. They ate in relative silence. Just as they were taking their last bite, Mickey's phone rang. He saw it was Darcy and answered it.

"Mickey, are you ready to hear about the names you gave me?" came her voice over the phone.

"Yes, you're on speakerphone, but I've turned it down low so only James and I can hear."

"Oh, James is with you? Hi, honey!" she said.

"Hey, love," James answered as Mickey rolled his eyes in mock sarcasm.

"All right, Ralph Clark. He's 38 years old and spent three years in jail for stealing, stripping, and reselling stolen auto parts. He shot the owner of one of the cars he was hijacking. Put him in a wheelchair for life. He's a bad guy."

James was taking notes on this as she talked.

"Next was 35-year-old Mike Reece. He was married previously and had three kids. He was charged with spousal abuse and had a permanent restraining order against him taken out by his former wife. Another bad one."

James said, "Sounds like Betty liked older, violent, and generally all-around bad men."

"That's my assessment also, James. Give me a bit more time to run the girl's background. I hope we don't find a connection between them and these men." With that, she said goodbye and clicked off.

"Okay, I would never have guessed that Ralph was that kind of guy, but according to what you said about Reece, I wouldn't put it past him," said James.

Mickey's phone rang again. This time it was Daniel.

"Hey, son, I just talked to Peter, and he read the autopsy report to me over the phone. Most of it isn't relevant, but I thought I should pass on a few points to you. First, death was caused by blunt force trauma to the head. She was struck repeatedly. Whoever did it wanted to make sure she was dead. The coroner determined the backhoe didn't damage her head.

"Her last meal was seafood. It was probably a seafood platter since she had clams, oysters, fish, and even lobster in her stomach. The most interesting thing is she was five weeks pregnant. They don't have a DNA sample of the fetus yet, but they hope it isn't too degraded to get some. They won't know the results of that for several more days. At this point, that's all I have for you. Hope it helps."

"Wow, Pop, this is gold. We need to figure out how it helps us. Thanks a lot. Are they making the repairs to the electrical and plumbing lines yet?" Mickey asked.

"Yes, they are digging the lines up as we speak. They worked overtime on it to get back on schedule," Daniel responded.

"Good, that's what I wanted to hear. Later, Pop," he disconnected and laid the phone back on the table.

"Did you hear that?" Mickey said to James.

"Yes, I did. Now we could have a motive for murder."

"Yes, but 'who' is what we need to find out," Micky said thoughtfully.

They got up, left some money for the check and a tip for Pauline, and went out to James' Humvee.

James said, "I'll drive today. You can follow me back to the house and leave the truck there. You can take the Rolls to the affair when we get back there later."

Mickey laughed, "What? You don't think they'll appreciate my truck at the gala?"

"As long as you bring money, I'm certain they won't care what you drive, but you'll fit in with the snobbish crowd with the Rolls."

Mickey sat back as James drove to Laurel Cunningham's house. Mickey looked up her address on the computer and programmed it into James' GPS in his Humvee. All he knew about Laurel was that she was married and had two kids. They drove to her address on 14 White Oak Lane. It was the last one on the street. James pulled up front and parked at the curb.

The house was freshly painted and had a beautifully manicured lawn with many flowers and bushes. Around each bush was a ring of fresh mulch. It looked immaculate. As they walked up the driveway to the sidewalk, they looked past the house into the backyard. They saw a little building that was, by its looks, the garden shed. By the door of the shed, several mulch bags were waiting to be spread on the flower beds.

Mickey and James rang the doorbell. After some time, a disheveled woman with wispy brown hair up in a messy bun answered the door. She stuffed a pair of yellow gloves into the house-cleaning apron bunched around her waist and pushed the fallen strands of hair back. She smiled weakly and was embarrassed at her appearance.

Mickey stepped forward. "Laurel Cunningham?"

"Yes. May I help you?" she asked.

"Yes, I'm Mickey Ray Christianson, and this is James Bower. May we come in for a few minutes?"

"Why. What's this about? Has something happened to Wallace? Is my husband okay?"

"Yes, he's fine. It's not about him. It's about a friend of yours, Betty Duncan. I'm sorry, we didn't mean to scare you. We just want to ask you some questions about her. That's all."

"Mickey Ray Christianson? Where have I heard that name before? Oh, my goodness, I remember you. Your sister's Darcy Jean, isn't she? How is she doing?"

When she realized who they were, she became more relaxed, and she invited them inside.

"I'm sorry, sir. I don't recognize you. What did you say your name was?" she asked James.

"I'm James Bower. I understand you don't recognize me. I didn't look like this in high school," he said, pointing to his scarred face.

"I'm so sorry. I didn't know. Please forgive me."

"Don't worry about it. I'm used to it. It happened a long time ago. If you remember, Darcy Jean, I'm married to her now."

"How wonderful for you. She was such a pretty girl in school."

"I think she's still pretty," James said.

"Well, you're both fortunate people. Please, forgive the way I look. I was just beginning to mop the kitchen floor."

"You look fine, Laurel. We just want to ask you some questions about one of our high school friends," said James.

"I guess I have a few minutes to talk. Who is this about?" she asked. "Forgive my lack of manners. May I offer each of you something to drink? A soda, perhaps? I guess it's a bit too early for anything stronger."

"No, that's okay. We don't need anything but thank you," Mickey said.

"Do you remember Betty Duncan?" James asked.

"Yes, I do. We were very good friends. That is until she disappeared. Why?"

"She's dead," said Mickey speaking up.

She turned to look at Mickey, "Oh, please…wait. What did you say?"

"I said she's dead," Mickey repeated.

"Oh, my. How'd she die, Mickey?" she asked.

"Someone killed her," he answered.

She raised her hand to her mouth with a shudder and gasped. James and Mickey sat quietly, watching her, gauging her response.

After a few moments of awkward silence, Mickey said, "She was struck in the head with a blunt instrument. The police have labeled it a homicide."

She turned and looked from Mickey to James, then she spoke with a coldness that was a complete surprise to them. "We were good friends for many years, but the last couple of years, she changed. She started seeing questionable men if you understand me."

"No, Laurel, we don't," said James. "Neither of us has seen her since high school. That's why we're here talking to you now. We're looking into it. We were hoping you could give us some insight into her personal life. It might tell us a reason why someone would want her dead."

"No, I don't know any reason why someone would do that. She stopped coming around here a bit over a month ago. We both were members of a book club. She had some friends there."

"Do you have any information on the club?" asked James.

"It is called the Bridgeton Benevolent Book Club," she said. "I can give you the name and phone number of the club's director if you think you might need it," she said as she stood up and walked toward a small table next to the couch.

"We would appreciate that, Laurel," said James.

She opened the drawer on the end table, rummaging through some papers, and finally withdrew a business card.

"This is the name and number of the club director. She also works at the library. They meet once a month at a restaurant. I don't know which one. I was a member for a while, but things got busy here at home with the kids and all. I quit going to the meetings. They change meeting places every couple of months. Sometimes they meet at someone's house," she said, handing the card to James.

"Was there anyone Betty was particularly close to or date whom she recently broke up with?" asked Mickey as Laurel handed the card to James.

"No, as I said, we didn't see each other very much when she started dating Ralph, that mechanic. Then they broke up, and she dated some other strange guy. I kind of lost track of her after that," she said to Mickey.

"At these book club meetings, is it exclusively a ladies club? Do the members bring dates?"

"Oh, no. A couple of the ladies bring their husbands or boyfriends. Everyone's welcome. It's a good place to meet people. Why? Are you thinking of going to a meeting?"

"No. Not really. We want to talk to as many people as possible to better understand Betty's circle of friends. That's all," said James.

"I see. Well, you should talk with Irene Blalock. She's the one who organizes the meetings," Laurel said. "Maybe she can help you."

"Thank you, Laurel. Can we call you or come back if we think of something else?" asked James as he smiled at her.

"Yes, of course, you can. Anytime, James," she said, smiling back.

Mickey handed her his business card. "Isn't your husband a financial planner?"

"Yes, he's sold a lot of shares in your company to some of his clients. He really believes in it. We bought some shares ourselves based on the pitch you gave to the group of people at your investors meeting six weeks ago."

"I'm surprised that you'd remember something like that," said Mickey.

"Oh, yes. Wallace came home very excited that day. He said he wanted to get in on the ground floor of that project and started immediately telling his clients what a great opportunity it was to get in early. I remember it because it was the day after our anniversary."

"I see. You've got a good memory. Please call us if you remember anything," Mickey said, pointing again to the business card in her hand.

"Okay. I'll do that." She then turned to James, "I still say that Darcy Jean is one lucky girl."

They got up, shook hands with her, and she followed them to the door and let them out.

As they walked to the car, Mickey said to James, "I think she was quite smitten with you, sir."

"Yeah, just like those women that are smitten, as you say to men in prison. They are attracted to broken-down losers."

"You're not a loser, James, and you know that. My sister would NEVER be attracted to a loser," Mickey said sternly.

"I know. You're right, I'm not a loser, but I am broken down," James answered as he got into the Humvee.

"What did you think of her, James?"

"I don't know. She was nice enough, but something was creepy about her. She acted a bit strange when you asked her about Betty. I can't quite put my finger on it. She was just a bit off."

"Yeah, I agree. Her tone totally changed when we mentioned Betty. Hey, we have to get back. I have to get ready for the hoop-de-doo tonight. I've got to put on my penguin suit and attend that stupid fundraiser," Mickey said.

"Yep. I guess I'd better get you back to your vehicle, and you be sure to come by the house and get the Rolls," said James as he pulled out of the driveway of Laurel Cunningham's house.

56

"Yep. I guess I'd better get you back to your vehicle, and you be sure to come by the house and get the Rolls," said James as he pulled out of the driveway of Laurel Cunningham's house.

CHAPTER 6

The Fundraiser and Francine

Mickey took a shower and put on his tuxedo.

Standing in front of the mirror, he took a look at himself and nodded at his reflection. He had to admit to himself, he looked pretty darn good. He admired his reflection as he turned side to side and struck different poses. One was the famous picture of Napoleon with his hand inside his jacket. Mickey knew that originally that practice came from ancient Greece. It was improper in some circles for a man to speak with his hands outside his clothing. He turned again to the side, put up his fingers with a gun-like pose, and said out loud, "The name's Bond. James Bond." He laughed at his own joke.

He took a comb from his pocket, took one more swipe through his thick dark hair, and walked out the door. When he got to the family home, he switched vehicles and drove away in the Rolls Royce, proceeding to the hotel where they held this fundraiser every year. He pulled up to the front entrance. Handing the valet his key to the Rolls, he walked into the lobby and followed the sign to the ballroom.

When he got to the ballroom, he was greeted by Franklin Braydon and his wife, Donna. As he walked up to Mr. Braydon, he shook his hand.

"Why, Mickey Ray Christianson, how are you? I'm so glad you decided to come this year. As you know, you are invited and most welcome every year," Franklin Braydon said with a smile.

"Yes, sir, Mr. Braydon. It seems that I already had plans in the past and wasn't available."

"I understand, Mickey Ray. You know my wife Donna, I'm sure?"

"Why, yes, I do, sir…ah, Franklin. And she's just as lovely as I remember her," Mickey said with a slight bow toward her.

A stunning blonde who'd clearly had work done, Donna Braydon displayed a broad and genuine-looking smile at Mickey and put out her hand to shake his. "Thank you, Mickey Ray. Francine will be so pleased that you're able to attend our little gathering this year."

As Mickey shook her hand, he nodded back at her and flashed her a smile. She was a stunning lady. Age had been kind, and her plastic surgeons had earned their money.

Mickey walked further into the large room and looked around. Everyone who was someone in town was here. The bank president who had loaned them the balance of the money they needed for their expansion project was talking to a circuit court judge. Talking to someone he didn't recognize was the police chief and commissioner in the corner. The present mayor and his wife were also speaking to someone Mickey didn't know. There were too many lawyers to count, including Francis, Francine's twin brother. The room was filled with people with money and influence. Servers were flitting from person to person, taking empty glasses and replacing them with full ones.

He knew how these events worked. People organize them, in this case, Donna and Francine Braydon. They rented a huge ballroom, a small orchestra, a high-priced caterer who serves expensive foods like caviar and fancy canapes. It was always a formal affair requiring men to wear tuxedos and women to buy an expensive evening gown. Near the end of the evening, they auction off something like a luxury cruise or fancy vacation at an all-inclusive resort. And, of course, this doesn't include the outright donations to the cause of the year. Usually, after all the expenses, very little of the money collected goes toward the named charity. The charity may only get ten percent of the donations, while everyone involved, especially the organizers, are well paid.

Mickey took a drink to look social and walked around the room, nodding and speaking to those he knew. Once he stopped, someone called to him from behind. He turned around, and a stunningly beautiful young lady reached out to him.

"Mickey Ray Christianson, I'm so glad you made it this year," she softly called out to him.

When Mickey saw Francine Braydon, his heart skipped a beat. She was more beautiful than he remembered. The bright red gown she wore was cut low in the front, revealing just a peek of firm voluptuous breasts cinching a tiny waist and ending just a couple of inches from the floor. Long blonde hair hung over each shoulder and framed her face and silky, smooth skin. As she moved her head, he could see large diamond earrings dangling from her ears down to her shoulders and a matching necklace that accented her throat. Her piercing crystal blue eyes could bring a man to his knees with a casual glance.

He looked at her and couldn't respond. He remembered how pretty she was in school, but she was an upper classmate. She was so out of his social class that he never thought she would talk to him. She had gotten more beautiful with time. Francine was captivating. Now he knew why James had warned him about her. She was utterly stunning. His knees began to get weak. He needed to sit down. He had never seen someone so beautiful in all his life. He just stared.

"Mickey. Mickey Ray. Are you alright? You're absolutely white. Let's go sit down." She took his hand and led him to the edge of the room. Guiding him to a chair, she sat down beside him. He shook his head to clear it.

"I'm sorry, Francine. I don't know what happened. I just got confused for a minute."

"It's fine, Mickey. I understand. Take a few deep breaths. You'll be okay. What happened?"

"Um, I don't know. I'll be okay in a minute or two. How are you?" he managed to croak.

He thought to himself. "YOU happened." But he couldn't say that. He felt like a fifteen-year-old kid at a school dance.

She touched his face and brushed the hair out of his eyes with one swift motion. He shuddered. He needed to clear his head. Get a grip. She's a black widow, he thought. Do not, and repeat, do not let her get into your head.

He sat up, straightened his shoulders, and said to her, "How've you been?"

"Oh, I'm okay, I guess. You know how it goes. Life goes on," she said, looking at him and smiling. "Why don't we get some fresh air."

"Where to?"

"We can just step out to the balcony. No one's out there. We can be alone and talk."

"We can do that," Mickey got up and started toward the rear door.

As they walked, they talked about the past years. Francine told him about her first two marriages and told Mickey that the last two husbands just weren't suited to her. They were too controlling, she said. He knew the first one, and he knew that he was a doormat and not controlling at all. He didn't know the second, but he had heard that he wasn't ambitious enough for her. She wanted to move forward. Her second husband was satisfied with a tiny little law practice. Francine wanted the world. He could tell, she may not be lying, but she was warping the truth. They went onto the balcony and sat in one of the outdoor upholstered chairs put there for this event.

Mickey told her about his parents' accident in which his mother was killed, and his father almost died. He deliberately left out what he and James had done to solve it. He didn't tell her about finding the little girl in the wheelchair and rescuing her mother and father. Again, another element in his life had to remain a secret from the world.

"Well, Mickey, it sounds like you've had a life full of excitement with your parents' accident and Darcy's divorce then marriage to James," said Francine feigning interest.

He knew the kind of person she was, but he couldn't help the effect her beauty had on him. As he talked, she reached over and took his hand. He looked deep into her blue eyes, wondering what was going on inside her head. Her sexual magnetism drew him even deeper.

She met his gaze, reached out to him, took his hand, and squeezed it.

He felt afraid and comfortable at the same time. Her eyes were steady like a snake probing its prey, hypnotic and piercing. He was electrified at the touch of her hand in his. He felt his breath getting more shallow as he tried to conceal his hyperventilating, and he began to get light-headed.

As her hand slipped from his and their physical bond was broken, his mind became clear again. He knew he needed to get up and move around. To get his heart pumping oxygen back to his numb brain. He stood up.

Looking around for an escape, he looked back down at her, cleared his throat, and said, "I've had a wonderful evening, Francine, but I have a busy day tomorrow. I think I should be leaving now."

"You can't be leaving just now. You just got here," she said.

"Since you were kind enough to invite me, I felt I should at least make an appearance, Francine."

She smiled coyly. She stood and reached up, put her arms around him, and kissed him.

Backing away from him, she said, "You can't leave yet, dear boy. Let me take you around and introduce you to some of the other guests. Since the Christianson family is the premier family in Bridgeton now, you should get to know all the powerful people here."

With that, she took his hand again and led him back inside the banquet room. They went around the room for the next hour, and she introduced him to lawyers, investment bankers, and even a state senator. She worked it into every introduction that Mickey Ray Christianson was the CEO of Christianson Company, the largest developer in Bridgeton. He slowly began to understand.

She was using him as her arm candy. Even then, she was promoting him as one of the up-and-coming people in the growth of Bridgton.

After making the rounds of all the guests, he said, "Francine, I must be getting home. I appreciate the invitation and for you taking the time to introduce me to everyone here, but I'm exhausted."

They walked out to the Lobby and sat on one of the double-sized lounge chairs. She kissed him with even more passion than before, completely disregarding passers-by.

"Are we going to see each other again, Mickey?"

"I don't know. Do you want to?"

"Of course, I do! Why do you think I asked?"

"I don't know. I haven't dated a lot of girls. None since Valerie left."

"I know. I heard about her leaving. She's the one that lost out. I think it's all for the best. Maybe her loss is my gain. What do you think, Mickey?" she said with a coquettish smile.

"I don't know. We'll see, I guess," he stammered.

"Don't forget to leave us a donation, or maybe you could just bid on one of the prizes. We're auctioning a seven-day cruise for two to the Caribbean. It's one cabin, double occupancy. That would be perfect for us, don't you think, Mickey?" she said with a sparkling smile and leaned over against him.

"Yes, that would be nice, but I'm busy with the new construction project right now, but I'll write you a check as I leave. Is that acceptable?"

She gave him a little pouty face and said, "I guess it'll have to do this time, but maybe we could have a short weekend getaway sometime. Just you and me. I know you don't work weekends, now do you?"

"No. I try not to. We'll see," he said, rising from the seat.

"Okay, Mickey Ray. I'm looking forward to it," she said as she rose from the chair and walked toward the door back inside the ballroom.

There were little envelopes on tables all over the room. People were to put their donations inside, and a person collected them at each exit door. He put a donation in one of the envelopes and left.

As he drove home, he thought back over the evening. He felt so stupid. Now that he was away from Francine, her spell on him was broken. How could that happen? He had never been that way around anyone in his life. He felt in her control, and he didn't like it. He needed to see her again. Mickey knew he shouldn't, but he also knew it was the only way he could permanently break that spell. As the adrenalin swore off, he felt exhausted, totally drained.

He drove around until he was calmed down. His shaking stopped. He was his old self again. He went back to the family home place, picked up his truck, and went home.

He got home, and the light on his answering machine was blinking. When he pressed the play button, the sweet soft voice of Francine floated out of the tiny speaker of the device.

"Hello, Mickey. I just wanted to give you a call and tell you how much I enjoyed our time together tonight. I'm looking forward to spending more time with you. My private number should show up on your caller ID. Use it. Call me. Soon. Hugs and kisses, Mickey." Then he heard the distinct sound of lips kissing over the phone, and she disconnected.

He felt his blood pressure rise again. Then he walked away to take a cold shower and go to bed. He had a long day tomorrow. He had a murder to solve and an apartment complex construction to oversee.

CHAPTER 7

The Librarian

Again, his phone rang the following morning, awakening him from a sound sleep.

"Hello," he said into the receiver, brushed his hair from his eyes, and looked at the clock at his bedside.

"Mickey, get up. We have a new problem."

"What now?" he said, instantly recognizing Darcy's voice. "Couldn't it have waited a little later?"

"No. You need to start getting the daily paper. There's another headline by Carter Evans. This time he's alluding to the Christianson Company as having something to do with Betty's death. And he even noted that she was pregnant!"

"How could he know that? I just found out yesterday?"

"I don't know, Mickey, but we need to do some damage control before it ruins the reputation of the project before we even get started."

"You're right. If people get wind of this, they wouldn't buy our stock, or even worse, those that have already put money down could pull their money back out."

Mickey could hear paper rustling at the other end of the line.

Darcy spoked, "Further down, he says we even called him and tried to cover it up by asking him not to print the news."

"That statement alone could make us look bad," Mickey sighed. "I'll get on it. I'm meeting with James at the diner a bit later. We'll put our heads together and figure something out. Hey, why don't I come over to your house, and you fix breakfast for all of us?"

"You know by now, little brother, I don't do breakfast. Not for you, or James. He'll meet you at the diner like always."

He heard the phone disconnect. He thought she has two kids at home, and Dad, and her husband, James has to meet him at the diner to get breakfast. He loved his sister, but she had her limits. He got up from the bed, dressed, and drove to the diner.

He was still a bit bleary-eyed when he sat down and took a sip of the coffee already sitting in front of him. He looked over at James sitting at the other side of the table.

James spoke. "Dee already showed me the newspaper headline. What do you want to do about it?"

"I don't know."

"We need to do something to keep your reputation clean," James noted, looking down at his coffee.

"I know. Any suggestions?"

"Nope," answered James.

"We need to have another meeting with Carter. I'll have Dee call him again and set another meeting."

"What do we say to him this time, Mickey?"

"I don't know. I'll think of something. I'll let you know as soon as I know. I have to go by the trailer office at the construction site. We'll decide what to do then."

"Okay, I've got some errands to run. I'll meet you in an hour, at the trailer," James said, dropping some bills on the table as he got up to leave. "Coffee's on me today."

Mickey nodded and continued to sit to sort things out alone. Finally, he got up and headed to the trailer office and stayed a few minutes to catch up on the progress and spend a few minutes with Daniel.

When he went inside, Detective Reynolds was sitting talking to Daniel. He turned toward Mickey when he came into the trailer.

"Good morning, Mickey Ray," said Detective Reynolds.

"Good morning, Detective," he answered.

"I hear that you've been asking questions around town about Miss Duncan?"

"A little bit, sir, I wouldn't do anything to get in your way."

"Good. That's what I want to hear. We, the police department, tend to get a bit upset when people interfere with our job."

"I understand, but if I hear something that might help you, I'll give you a call," said Mickey.

"Thanks. We'll also try to stay out of your way. You have quite a project going on here. It'll be a great thing for our town," he said.

Mickey turned to Daniel, "Pop, James and I have a few things to take care of today, so I may not be here. Is that okay with you?"

"Sure, son. I'll hold down the fort," Daniel said. "Hey, how did it go at that fundraiser last night?"

"Same old crap. Same old people. It is all a bunch of hype, and not many real people get the help they need. Darn it, Pop, ex-mayor Braydon's wife and daughter probably made more money than will go to the people that need it."

The detective was sitting, listening to Mickey talk. He chuckled and said, "Mickey, you got those people pegged right. They're all in that together. The organizers, caterers, bands, and all the others are involved in that scheme. I've never been invited because I don't have enough money to get an invitation. Only the rich and well-to-dos get invites. And the Christianson gang's in that group," said the detective.

"Yes, sir. I agree. Pop and I believe it's a scam. It is a way to legally generate money and let people think they're helping the down and out. All they're helping is themselves.

"Hey, Pop. One more thing. Do we need any people at this site to help with anything? I hired someone a couple of days ago to help Sam at one of the other sites. He said he works okay but would like to work at this site."

"An all-around type of 'Man Friday' might be suitable. Someone running errands and walking the site several times a day might be good. Minor stuff like that. We did have someone break into the supply trailer the other day. I'll call Sam and get him to send him over."

"Thanks, Pop. We'll need a whole new team of people when this project is complete."

"Got it, son. I'll get him transferred over and start looking for more people," Daniel said as he made notes on a pad.

"Well, Detective Reynolds, I guess I better get going. Nice to see you again."

"Same here, Mickey Ray. Remember, stay out of our way, and we'll stay out of yours! I came by to tell you, you can have that site back now and start the digging again. We've got all the info we need now."

"Got it," said Mickey as he closed the door behind him.

He got in his truck and waited for James. When James got there, he locked up his Humvee and got in Mickey's truck.

"We need to interview Carla now. That about does it, unless we check out her book club people," said Mickey as he started the truck.

"I agree, but since we don't have anything to go on from here, we should check her club. Hey, how did the fundraiser go last night?"

"It went okay, I guess. I spent most of it with Francine Braydon. Wow, you were right. She is gorgeous. She took my breath away. I felt like a clumsy little school kid. I tell you, James, I was a total idiot around her."

James laughed, almost spitting out a mouthful of coffee he had brought in an insulated mug. "Did she get to you, little bro?"

"Yes, darn it. Don't laugh. I haven't felt so stupid since I was a kid. I was so nervous I could hardly speak. And she told me to give her a call, and we could go out again."

"Are you gonna call her?"

"I don't know. Maybe, maybe not."

"What do you mean, maybe not? The most beautiful woman in town, and you don't know if you want to have a date with her? Did she hit you upside the head or something?"

"She came onto me hard, you know. She took me completely off guard. If I do decide to go out with her, I need to get my head on straight first."

"That part, I fully agree, but you still need to remember, she's a black widow. She'll knock you off your feet and then stomp on your dead body. As long as you don't forget that, go for it. Turn the tables on her."

"I don't know if I could do that. I don't have a lot of experience with the ladies. The only girl I ever dated was Valerie. It would be like going from a tiny little kitten to a mean hungry lion."

"Yep, she's fast as a racecar, but boy, look at that bodywork!" said James.

"Alright, let's get serious. We need to get our head around Betty's murder."

"Her previous boyfriends could be on the suspect list, especially Mike. He got irritated almost at the mention of her name. Ralph may have been friendly, but he doesn't have a stellar past either," said James.

"Let's go to the Pop-In Grocery Store where Betty worked and talk to Carla. Maybe she can give us some insight or at least a lead."

"We can stop back later and get the Vee."

They drove to the little grocery store. Seeing a woman in a booth surrounded by shoulder-high partition walls, they knew that it was the manager's office type of cubby.

The lady looked at them and smiled as they walked up to it. "How may I help you gentlemen?"

"Is Carla working today?" Mickey asked.

"I'm Carla," she said.

"I'm Mickey Ray Christianson, and this is James Bower. If you have a few minutes, we'd like to speak with you about Betty Duncan."

"I'm sorry, but Betty doesn't work here anymore," she said.

"Yes, we know. That's why we need to talk with you. We won't take up much of your time."

"How can I help you? She just disappeared. She didn't give notice or anything. Just gone. She didn't even come back for her last paycheck."

"Yes, I'm sorry to inform you of this, but she won't be coming back. She's dead, Miss Briggs," Mickey trailed off.

"Oh, my," she said, bringing her hand up to cover her mouth. "I didn't know that."

"Yes, we just found out a few days ago. I own the apartments where she lived. We started an expansion project near there, and her body was unearthed as we were digging a foundation trench," Mickey said.

"Oh, my God! How awful!" she said, sitting in the swivel desk chair behind her.

"We're so sorry to bring you this bad news, but we were hoping you could help us," said James.

"I don't know how. I don't know anything. Are you policemen? Have I done anything wrong?"

"No, of course, you haven't done anything wrong. And no, we aren't the police. You see, my friend here, Mickey Ray, not only owns the apartment where she lived, but he also owns the land where her body was found. We want to make sure that whoever committed this heinous act against Betty is found. We want to find her killer. That's all."

"I don't know what I could do to help," Carla said.

"Did you and Betty ever talk? I understand that you two were good friends."

"Well, we were friends but not what you'd call good friends. You know, we just chit-chatted like people do when they work together."

"Did she have any problems with anyone else that worked here?" asked James.

"No, we are, or were both managers, so at times we would have to call someone on the carpet, but that's part of being a manager. We didn't have any serious problems with anyone."

"Did she have the authority to hire and fire people?" asked James.

"We both have that authority."

"Had she fired anyone around the time she disappeared? Someone that might be upset about it. Upset enough to kill her, maybe?"

"Yes, she fired two people a few days before she disappeared. She found them in the back in a, umm…compromising position, you might say," she said. "Even with that, I don't think that it would be enough to kill her over."

"People do horrible things for the smallest reason. Can you give us the names of these people? We'd like to talk to them also."

Carla opened the desk drawer and took out a tablet and pen. She turned on her computer monitor, scrolled down a few pages on the screen, and jotted down their names, phone numbers, and addresses. She handed the piece of paper to James.

"I hope this helps, but I can't imagine either of those people doing something like murder," she added.

"Maybe they didn't, but you never know people, do you, Carla?" said Mickey Ray.

James again spoke and asked, "Can you give us the exact last day Betty came into work?"

Carla Briggs turned back to her computer and punched a few keys. As a screen popped up, she looked at it and said to James, "It was the first Thursday of the month before last. It was also the last day of that pay period. That was almost seven weeks ago."

Mickey Ray looked away from the store manager. He looked through the huge plate-glass store window and saw Detective Peter Reynolds and another man he assumed was his partner getting out of a plain black car and walking toward the store.

"Well, thank you, Carla. We appreciate your help. I hope that if we need something else, you'll let us stop by again," Mickey said and motioned for James to follow him. He headed toward the produce section as he heard a voice call out to him.

"Mickey Ray Christianson. Stop right there," said the voice.

Mickey turned and smiled at Detective Reynolds. "Good morning, Detective."

Detective Reynolds walked up to Mickey and James. "And what're you doing here?"

"Shopping for produce?" Mickey said.

James turned to attempt to hide a stifled laugh.

"Don't get smart with me, Mickey Ray! I know why you're here. You're here for the exact reason we're here."

"Let me introduce you to my friend, James Bower. He's married to Darcy Jean."

"Don't try to distract me, Mickey. I told you not to get in my way!"

"We're not getting in your way, Detective. Betty's murder happened on our property, and I want to know who and why someone killed Betty Duncan. By the way, are you going to introduce your partner?" asked Mickey.

"This is Detective John Peters. We've been partners for many years. Now, back to this situation. I don't like you going around getting into something that's not your business. It's a police matter."

"Wait a minute," Mickey said, then pointed at the other man. "This is John Peters, and you are Peter Reynolds. That makes you Peter and Peters. Can I call you the Peter Twins?"

Right then, James couldn't hide his laugh and tried a cough to stifle it, but it came as a combined cough and laugh, and both detectives glared at Mickey and James.

"Listen here, Mickey Ray. You both may find this funny but murder is serious business, and I'll not have either of you getting in my way. Do you understand me?"

Mickey and James straightened up and got serious.

Mickey said, "Our apologies, detectives. We understand and have the utmost respect for you. We want to help, and we'll do our best to stay out of your way. In all fairness and honesty, I can't drop this. It happened on our land, so we're making it our business. We'll do our best to stay out of your way, but we are proceeding with our investigation."

As they got into Mickey's truck, James said to him, "Do you think it was wise to get so cocky with the police?"

"I guess we should have been a bit less flippant. They do have a job to do, and all they're doing is what they're being paid to do. If we find something that may help, I'll give them a call and fill them in. You know, go along to get along," Mickey said.

"So, are we going to back off?"

"Nope, not one bit. We'll be more discreet in our investigation. We'll try to watch ourselves and stay out of their way." Mickey's phone rang, and he took it out of his pocket and answered it.

"Hey, Dee," he said.

"Yeah. Got it. I understand. Yes, James is here. We're at the Pop-In Grocery right now. Okay, tell him to meet us at the park in the middle of town. We'll talk there. Okay, I'll tell him," Mickey said and pressed disconnect on the phone.

Turning to James, he said, "She talked to Carter Evans, the reporter. He's right around the corner at the newspaper building. As you heard, I said we'd meet him at the park. Oh, Yeah, Dee said to tell you she loves you. When will you two get past that mushy stuff?"

"I hope never. Let's walk to the park. Were only a couple of blocks away," he answered. "What're you going to say to him?"

"I haven't a clue."

"Ah, a man with a plan…I love it," James snickered.

"Shut up, James," Mickey said as they walked.

They got to the park and continued to the center area, where a statue of a civil war soldier stood in the middle of a fountain. Sitting at a concrete picnic-style table, Mickey looked around and commented, "I can't remember the last time I came and just sat to enjoy the beauty of this park."

"I do," said James. "I was in elementary school, and the class came here as a field trip, and the teacher told us all about the story of the statue and how it represented the soldiers from Bridgeton that went to war but didn't return."

"You remember that far back?" Mickey said.

"Yeah, I thought that no matter which side you were on during that time, there were people at home that were praying for your return. Even as a kid, I was moved by it. The entire story made me sad."

Carter came up to the other side of the table, sat down with a backpack and recorder, and laid it onto the table between them. "Good afternoon, gentlemen."

"Turn off the recorder, Carter," said James.

"Why? Afraid of something you might say will get out to the public?"

"I said turn it off. Now!" he repeated.

Carter didn't move.

James reached over and picked up the recorder, dropped it on the ground, and stepped on it with the heel of his boot. He then stood up, reached into his pocket and took out his wallet and placed a hundred-dollar bill where the recorder had been on the table. He then silently sat back down.

"Now, we can talk," James said.

"Hey, there wasn't any need for violence. You can't just destroy my property like that," Carter said angrily.

"I'm sorry," said James. "I told you to turn it off. I think that Benjamin on the table should cover the cost of the recorder."

Mickey put out his hand in front of James. "Back off, James. You too, Carter. We just want to talk. Off the record. If we can reach an agreement, we can do our job, and you can do yours."

"I AM doing my job, and you can't stop me from doing it," Carter fumed.

"Fine, my friend here apologized and paid for your recorder. Now let's all settle down and come to an equitable agreement to work together. You can get a great story, and we can find out who killed Betty Duncan."

Carter leaned back and folded his arms across his chest. "And what do you suggest, Mickey Ray?"

"First, how did you find out so quick that Betty was pregnant?"

"Private source and I don't need to tell you," he answered.

"Fair enough," said Mickey. "Here's my suggestion. We're working on this case, the police are working on it, and right now, you are using information to spread innuendoes about me, my family, and our company."

"Yeah, well, as long as I don't make actual accusations, threats, or deliberate lies, you can't stop me. I am keeping you honest. We, the public, don't know if you had anything to do with her death or not, do we? The public, my readers, have a right to know the truth. My job is to give it to them."

Mickey took a few deep breaths. This reporter was getting to him. He wanted to reach out across the table and punch him. He wasn't a violent person, but Carter was definitely pushing his buttons.

"Okay, Carter, let's say I agree with you. Here's what I don't like. We didn't have anything to do with her death. Why would we work so hard to find her killer if I had anything to do with it?"

"To divert attention from yourself. Maybe you buried her in the wrong place, and finding her body was an accident. Now you're running damage control by pretending to work with the police to cover it up."

"That's not true, and you know it!" said James.

"No, I don't know it. True, I don't think you had anything to do with it, and eventually, as all comes out, I can always print the truth or a retraction. Until then, my readers are buying papers and eating it up. Readership has been up twenty-six percent since the story came out. They will keep buying papers to see what is next until it is solved."

"In the meantime, it will hinder the construction and weaken our reputation in the community," said Mickey.

"Not my problem," said Carter smugly.

"So, you don't care who you destroy when you're writing a story?" asked James.

"Now, you're getting it, my good man," he said, smiling at James. "If you're not guilty of any wrongdoing, it'll come out, and I'll let my readers know who is guilty. It is all part of the excitement."

"You know the old saying, where there's smoke, there's fire?" responded James.

"Sure, that's an old saying, and most of the time, true," Carter added calmly.

"There are times when it isn't true, but there are always people that will believe that, no matter what comes out, the Christianson Company had something to do with it," said Mickey.

"Yeah, I know. Sorry about that, but it's the cost of doing business. No one's completely blameless," Carter said.

"Carter Evans, you are a real sniveling snake. I was hoping we could work together. We could share information. We could help you get a good, true, accurate story, and we could avoid bad press. But with your attitude, I don't see any way to work with you."

"Look, I'm looking to sell papers. If I do, I get a feather in my cap, maybe a raise. If it is good enough, I might even get a job offer from a newspaper in a real town, not this little mudhole you call home. I don't care about you, your company, or to be honest, I don't care about this town. So don't get in my way. I don't need or want your help," he said as he grabbed his backpack and stood up.

James looked at him with his steel-gray eyes and said, "I will not speak for Mickey or the Christianson Company, but I can speak for myself. I will personally make sure that if you say anything that will hurt my family, I will see you fired and living in the street. I will do it by telling the cold hard truth and making sure that you are unhireable anywhere in this country. Do you understand me?"

"Ooooo, Mr. Scar-faced man. You scare me. I'm shaking in my boots. We'll see who goes down. You and the Christianson Company or me." Carter turned and walked away.

Mickey turned to James, "I don't think you should've said that, James."

"Maybe not, but I meant every word. He's going down."

"James, I'm serious. Do not lay a hand on him. Do you understand me?"

"Yes, and I didn't mean him physical harm. I'll ruin him financially and all his job prospects. If he hurts you, I'll see him unemployed for the rest of his life."

"Okay, did you get all that?" Mickey asked.

"Every word. If we need to use it, I'll edit out what I said," he said, pulling his cellphone out of his pocket. "We have a recording. He doesn't."

"Still, you shouldn't have destroyed his recorder."

James stood up. "I don't care. I'd do it again."

"Next on our list is to call the leader of that book club. If you'll call her and ask if we can stop by and talk with her, we'll go by the construction site on the way and check on progress."

When they got back to Mickey's truck, he pulled out of the grocery store toward the construction project as James took the card with the Bridgeton Benevolent Book Club's phone number and name of the group's director.

As Mickey drove, he heard James say into the phone, "Mrs. Blalock? How are you today? That's good to hear. Mrs. Blalock, this is James Bower. Did you have a friend named Betty Duncan in your book club? No, ma'am. I'm not selling anything. No, I'm not taking a survey. Yes, my friend and I...No, ma'am. I'm honestly not selling anything. I want to talk with you…about Betty. Are you at work right now? Will you be there for a few more minutes? My friend and I would like to come by and talk with you about…No, we're not salesmen, Mrs. Blalock. I assure you we are not. We're investigating a murder. Yes. Correct. No, we're not the police. No, Betty Duncan isn't in any trouble, at least not anymore. Please, ma'am. We'll be there in about ten minutes. Thank you. Goodbye."

James hung up and shook his head. He laid his head back on the seat's headrest and closed his eyes. "Wow, I thought a couple of times, she was interrogating me. She almost hung up the phone twice. I don't think she believes that we're not going to try to sell her something when we get to the library. We need to talk fast and win her over if we're going to get anything out of her."

Mickey looked over at James and laughed. "I could tell she wasn't buying your story. Hey, we need to get you some business cards. People seem to think you're more legitimate when you have a business card."

"You're right, and why is that, I wonder?" James said with his eyes still closed.

"I don't know, but I've noticed that, even when they throw it in the trash as soon as you leave. At least they take the card and answer most of your questions."

As they continued talking, they finally pulled into the Bridgeton Library. Mickey reached into his pocket, took out a business card from his wallet, and put it into his shirt pocket.

At the Library's main desk, they asked for Mrs. Irene Blalock. The woman behind the counter picked up a phone and dialed. When the person on the other end answered, she told her that two men were inquiring about her at the front desk. She pointed to a door at the back of the large room and told them that Mrs. Blalock would see them back there.

Mickey and James walked back and knocked on the door. They heard a female voice call out, "Come in. It's open."

A heavyset woman was sitting at a desk that seemed much too small for such a large person. She looked exactly as many people would picture a librarian to look. She had a bun on her head and wore a frumpy-looking print dress. Mickey smiled at the lady and introduced himself. She sat stoically, saying nothing.

"We won't take up too much of your time, Ma'am. We want to ask you a few questions about Betty Duncan, and we'll be on our way."

"What kind of questions, Mr. Christianson? Is Betty in some kind of trouble?"

"May we sit?" Mickey asked.

Mrs. Blalock nodded assent and gestured toward the two chairs in front of her desk.

Mickey continued. "Ma'am, Betty's body was found on my property a few days ago. She was struck in the back of the head and was buried in a shallow grave a few weeks ago. When construction began in that area, a backhoe unearthed her body, and we're looking into her death. We were hoping you could give us some insight as to why someone might want her dead."

She looked confused at Mickey's statement. "Why would you think I should know something. Do you think I had anything to do with it?"

"Oh no. On the contrary, we believe you had absolutely nothing to do with her death. We're looking into her life so we can find the person who would harm her. If you know someone that can fill us in on her whereabouts and contacts about seven to eight weeks ago, maybe we can put together a timeline. I'm sure with all these books in this library, you, of all people, can understand how these things work. This type of investigation, I mean."

She leaned back in her chair, looked toward the ceiling, and put her hands together in a prayer-type position. She sat silently with a thoughtful look on her face. Mickey and James looked at her, then at each other. They looked up, hoping to see what she was looking at on the ceiling. They saw nothing but plain blank ceiling tiles, whose primary purpose was to dampen sound in the library's office.

After almost thirty seconds, she lowered her head and looked alternately into Mickey's and then James' eyes. "Show me some identification, gentlemen!" she said calmly.

Mickey took out his business card and put it on the table.

"I said, identification. I didn't ask you for a business card," she said, looking straight at Mickey.

He reached in his pocket, took out his wallet, took out his Virginia driver's license, and laid it beside the business card.

She looked over at James. "And you too, young man."

James took his driver's license out, and as he laid it beside Mickey's, she reached out and took his hand. As she held his hand and looked at the scars on the back of it, she asked, with a softer, kinder tone, "What happened to you, Mr. Bower?"

"War injury, ma'am," he said.

"Afghanistan?"

"Yes," he answered.

She squeezed his hand slightly, then let go and said, "Thank you for your bravery and service to our country, James. I constantly pray for our men in service in all parts of this world. I hope God blesses you in a special way for your sacrifice."

James, self-conscious, now put his hands in his lap and looked down at them.

She continued talking to them. "Mickey?" she asked.

"Yes," he said.

"I recognize the name. You're the son of Daniel and Eleanor Christianson. I was so sorry to hear about your mother's passing."

"Thank you," Mickey said.

"How is your father, Daniel, doing now?"

"He's doing fine now, Mrs. Blalock. He's back at work now."

"Good. He's done a lot of good for this little town. Didn't your company begin a new project of expansion on one of your apartment complexes recently?"

"Yes, we started earlier this week," Mickey said.

She turned toward James, "I read in the paper years ago when you returned to this area, you had a very tough recovery period, but it seems that you have recovered very well. It was a very touching piece that the local paper did for you. I wish you continued success."

"Thank you, ma'am."

"Alright, first things first, you must call me Irene. Now, what can I do for you?" she said.

James started. "As we said, we're looking into the death of Betty Duncan. We're told that she was a member of your book club. We're trying to put together a timeline of her life around the time of her death. Can you help us?"

"I'll do whatever I can to help you."

"May we have a list of your members to interview? That'll give us a start," asked James.

"I'll do better than that. Our meeting this month is tomorrow night, at seven o'clock at Luigi's. You are welcome to attend."

"Thank you, Irene. We'll be there. And by the way, Mom and Pop had just left that restaurant on their way home, and they were run off the road, causing their accident," said Mickey.

"I'm so sorry, Mickey Ray. I didn't know that. I hope it isn't too painful for you to attend our meeting tomorrow night," she said kindly.

"Oh, no. It isn't too painful. Valerie, my ex-girlfriend, and I, used to go there often."

"Fine, I guess I'll see you there. Can you both come? You may bring a guest if you wish. Everyone's welcome. James, I see you're married. You may bring your wife if you wish."

"Thank you. My wife's Mickey Ray's sister, Darcy Jean. I'm sure she'd love to come. What will you be discussing?" James said with a warm smile.

"Usually, we discuss one of the latest bestsellers, but we thought we'd try some classics for a few months. We'll be discussing Edgar Allen Poe and a couple of his most famous poems, '**The Raven**' and '**Annabelle Lee**.' Are you familiar with those poems, James?"

"Yes, I love Poe. I'll be ready to discuss your ears off, Irene!"

She laughed and added, "I love your laugh, James. It'll be a pleasure to have you join us. How do you feel about sharing some of your knowledge and insight about Poe?"

"I would love to, but I don't think it would be proper for me to be a public speaker. I mean, look at me. I look like the Frankenstein monster. If I speak, we should talk about Mary Shelly, the author of the Frankenstein novel!"

"Please don't say that to me, James. Your looks don't bother me a bit, and if I know our club members, no one will care. If you have some insights, we'd love to hear them. Please speak to our group," she almost pleaded.

"If you're sure that they won't mind, I would like to do that," James said.

"Alright, tomorrow night we usually have dinner first, I'll bring the meeting to order. I'll give a short background of Poe, and then introduce you to the group, and you can have all the time you need. We usually give a short synopsis of the work or works we're discussing and then take questions. Can you do that?"

"Yes, of course, I can. It would be my pleasure," James said.

"Good. Now, if you don't mind, I must get this work done, or I won't be able to come tomorrow," she said as she began straightening the papers on her desk.

Mickey and James got up and left feeling quite pleased with themselves with that visit.

As they walked out to Mickey's truck, James said, "Hey, Mickey, how about coming over for dinner tonight?"

"Sure, big brother, but don't you think before you ask guests, you should ask the boss?"

"Darcy may be the boss, but I NEVER have to ask her permission to ask you over for anything, little bro."

Mickey got to James and Darcy's house early that afternoon.

CHAPTER 8

The Funeral and
the Book Club

Saturday morning Mickey washed the Rolls he had driven home from the family home last night after dinner. The entire family would be attending Betty's funeral, and he planned to pick them up. Darcy, James, and the kids would be riding in Darcy's car. Mickey and his dad were riding in the Rolls, and they were chauffeuring Alice Duncan from her apartment to the church, then to the gravesite.

James would be discreetly snapping pictures of the people attending the service for future reference. All went well. Mickey recognized some people, including Carla Briggs from the store, Laurel and Ray Cunningham, Irene, the librarian. As he expected, there were several others he didn't know. The one that surprised him the most was Francine Braydon. He knew she went to school with them, but he didn't understand why she would attend the funeral of a schoolmate. Mickey didn't know if Francine and Betty were friends in school.

After the services were over, Alice, Betty's mother, tried to talk to each person that attended, but as in many cases, people slipped away.

Mickey went over to Francine as she was walking to her car. "Francine, I didn't know you and Betty were friends," he said.

She looked at Mickey and smiled, "There are a lot of things you don't know about me, Mickey. If you'd give me a call, we could get to know each other a lot better."

"Come on, Francine, it's only been a couple of days."

"Hey now, Mickey Ray, that's a couple of days lost."

"I've been very busy with work."

"Yes, I understand, and you've been asking a lot of questions around town too."

"That's true. Does that bother you?" Mickey asked.

"No. Of course not. But that isn't your job. You should be leaving that up to the police," she stated firmly. "You're a developer, not a lowly cop!"

"Come on, Francine. Cops are keeping us safe in this town!" he retorted.

"I guess it's all in your perception, dear Mickey," she said with a sly smile.

"All I'm trying to do is get some closure for Betty's mother. That's all, Francine. Give me a break!"

"Okay, but if you persist in asking around town, remember everyone's not what they seem. Everyone has something to hide, and Betty was no different."

Mickey was taken aback by her attitude. He didn't understand why she was acting this way toward him. Especially since she thought enough to come to Betty's funeral. He thought that Francine would be pleased that someone would care enough to try to find Betty's killer.

"Oh, Mickey. Let's not get into that at Betty's funeral. Call me, let's go have some fun together?" she said coyly.

Fun? thought Mickey. What kind of way to describe a potential date for two people their age. They were grown-ups, not a couple of high school teenagers.

"Okay, Francine. How about tonight?" he asked.

"I'm sorry, I am busy tonight. I'm having dinner with my brother Francis and his wife tonight, but I'm free tomorrow evening."

"Tomorrow it is. What time should I pick you up? We can have dinner and just spend some time catching up."

"Sounds marvelous, Mickey. I love seafood. Why not try that little seafood place over on the Eastern Shore?"

"Sorry, I'm not familiar with it, and the Eastern Shore is a long drive for dinner."

"Yes, it is a long drive, but we could stay the night over there. I know a quaint little privately owned hotel where we could book a room," she said with a smile.

"I'll pick you up at seven, and we can find a place to have dinner a bit closer to home. I have some long days at the construction site all next week. I can't leave town right now. You understand, don't you?"

"You can't even take a day off for me?"

"Sorry, but I can't. I need to be on-site," he said with finality.

"Okay, but you don't know what you're missing," she said with a wink as she turned and walked away.

"What's your address?" he called out.

She stopped and turned. "I'm living at home with my parents while my house is being remodeled."

"See you tomorrow, Francine," he said as he turned and walked away.

When he got back to the car, Daniel sat in the front, and Alice sat in the back seat. Daniel looked at him and winked.

"It's not like that, Pop. Nothing is going to happen," said Mickey.

Daniel said, "She's a beautiful young woman, Mickey."

"Yes, Pop. She is, but she's not what I want in a woman. We're going out tomorrow night, but it's just one date. I doubt if it'll continue. There's something about her I don't like."

"What do you mean?" asked Daniel.

"I don't know. I can't quite put my finger on it. At least not yet," he said, turning around to address Alice.

"Alice, are you buckled in?" he asked.

"Oh, yes, Mickey. I'm all ready to go. I heard you say that you're going out with Francine Braydon."

"Yes, ma'am."

"Watch out, Mickey Ray. She's not a nice person. Especially for such a nice person like you," she said.

"I'll be careful! Don't you worry. Now, let's get you home."

When they arrived at Alice's apartment, Mickey got out and escorted her to the door. "Is there anything more we can do for you?"

"No, Mickey Ray. You've done so much already. All I can say is be careful of that Francine and her twin brother. They're bad news. I know. Trust me!"

"Thanks for the warning. I'll watch out. I promise."

He got back in the car and buckled up. "Well, Pop. It's way past my lunchtime. Would you like to go by the diner and grab a bite?"

When they got to the diner, they got out and walked inside, and Pauline seated them in the back. She took their order and brought their drinks.

As Daniel sat, he asked, "Mickey, what progress have you made in the investigation of Betty's murder?"

"James and I are asking a few questions. That's all. I wouldn't call it an investigation."

"Son, I'm right in the middle of it. First, Detective Reynolds called me and asked me to get you to step back. Then, James and Darcy talk about it at home. Last, you check-in at the jobsite, then you and James run off playing like amateur private eyes all day," Daniel said.

"I never thought about that, Pop. I guess you are right in the middle. What did you tell Detective Reynolds?"

"What do you think I told him? I told him, you're a grown man, and I have no control over you. But I also added that since the body was found on our property, we had a right and a responsibility to know who defiled it."

"What was his response?"

"I can say he wasn't happy with my answer, but he understood my position since he also has a grown son. I told him I'd speak to you about it, but you're on your own on this one. You have my blessing to keep on with your private investigation. Just try to keep out of Pete's way. I don't want any trouble with the police."

"Got it, Pop. We'll try to be more, under the radar?"

"Thanks, at least that gives me plausible deniability with Pete. I hope you find her killer," he said as Pauline put their food on the table. "We need to get a murder board," he said.

"What did you say, Pop?"

"I said we need to get a murder board."

"What do you mean, a murder board?"

"You know. One of those boards that you can pin pictures, and information about a case, so you can get a clear picture of the suspects of a case and how they connect," said Daniel.

"Are you joining us in trying to solve the case, Pop?"

"Not really. I can't get out and interview people. Darcy can do the internet research for you, and I can pin the information up and maybe come up with some ideas. If I see something, I can give you and James an update to help you."

"Pop, that is joining in the process."

"Okay, so it is. James, Darcy, and I are right here in the same house, and they talk about this stuff all the time. How can I not join in?"

"Fine. Can I borrow the Rolls tonight? James, Darcy, and I are going to a book club meeting at seven? I can't believe I just said that. As a grown man, I just asked my dad to borrow his car."

They both laughed out loud, and the surrounding customers looked over at Daniel and Mickey. Mickey looked back at the diners and shrugged his shoulders, and gave them a smile in return.

Mickey felt so happy at that moment. He and his father, working together and enjoying each other's company. If only his mother were here, it would be perfect.

They finished eating, and Mickey drove Daniel home. He knew that Pop would take the truck, and that evening, there would be a whiteboard on a stand sitting in the corner of the den ready for them to gather around and look at the clues to this mystery. As Mickey drove off, he noticed James' Humvee sitting in the driveway in front of the garage. Mickey instinctively knew James was inside the house, reading the poems "**The Raven**" and "**Annabelle Lee**" and studying them for his presentation tonight.

Mickey went home and began making notes on what they had found out on the people they interviewed. He wrote down what they had told them and added personal notes about how they reacted to their questions. He took notes on their attitudes and backgrounds to not get them mixed up when they looked at them later.

He put each person in a different file folder. He gathered information and personal thoughts and placed everything in a pile. He knew that soon they would be standing in front of the whiteboard that Daniel called a "murder board" and would be trying to make good connections from one person to another.

After looking at the names and notes for almost two hours, he stacked everything in a neat file and walked away from it. He was ready for Pop's "murder board."

Mickey drove to Luigi's, and saw Darcy's car. He pulled the Rolls beside their car and parked. Darcy and James were sitting near the front of the meeting room next to a podium. Next to them was Irene. Irene directed him to sit next to her. He sat down, and the server taking their orders handed Mickey a menu.

"Good evening, Mickey Ray. I'm so glad you came," said Irene. "Your sister and James are a wonderful couple. We've been talking while waiting for you to arrive."

"I hope you haven't been talking about me, Irene. That would be a boring subject."

"Yes, we were talking about you, and truthfully, it's been a fascinating conversation. Darcy here was telling me that you were quite a little stinker when you were a child," she laughed.

Mickey laughed along with them and answered, "Trust me, I could tell you some stories about Dee also."

"I'm sure you could," Irene said.

The server walked around to Mickey and said, "Good evening, Mr. Christianson. It's nice to have you with us this evening. May I take your order?"

"Thank you, Gabriella. It's nice to see you also. I would like the chicken piccata with a glass of rose wine, please. And a bottle of your finest white wine for the table."

"Of course, sir." She looked at each one at the table, and asked "a glass for each of you?"

They all nodded.

Mickey looked around the room. "My, it's quite a nice group of people tonight, Irene. Is it usually this large?"

"No, it isn't, but I did make a few calls and put out the word that our town hero was going to be a guest speaker this evening."

"Oh, no," James lowered his head in embarrassment. "I didn't know you would do that."

"Please don't be shy, my dear James," Irene said. "Everyone's looking forward to what you have to share with us tonight. Poe and his works are so fascinating."

Mickey saw Darcy smile with pride at her husband. She placed her hand on his back, leaned against him, whispered in his ear, and gave him a gentle kiss on the cheek. He raised his head and smiled back at her.

Irene was interesting and quite funny. A very different person from the one Mickey and James first encountered at the library. Irene was taken with Darcy and quickly caught on calling her Dee, like most of Darcy's close friends. It turned out that a lifetime ago, Irene also worked at a law office and ran many errands to the local law library for her employers. She had Darcy openly laughing at some of the silly things people would hire attorneys to do for them. They both laughed when Irene told Darcy about the woman, no names given, who would write songs and hire the attorney to apply for a copyright for each song. The author was deathly afraid that someone would steal her songs, publish them, and make millions of dollars off her work. Irene assured Darcy that no one would touch any of the songs. They were horrible works of poor prose set to bland music. It was a grand time at the table during dinner.

Once everyone finished eating, Irene stood and moved to the podium and introduced James. She told a bit of his background in the military. She briefly covered his injuries, letting the group know that they had a true American hero in their midst. James stood and moved to the podium to thundering applause.

"Ladies and gentlemen, I'm honored to be here, but this evening is not about me. It is about the author, Edgar Allan Poe. So, I will begin by giving you a brief background of this literary genius.

"Poe was one of the most influential writers of the 19th century. He was a poet. He was the creator and master of the horror genre of literature. He is considered the father of the detective story and was an inspiration to the famous Sir Arthur Conan Doyle, the creator of Sherlock Holmes."

James continued to the most famous of Poe's poems, **"The Raven."** At the end, he said that he would take questions.

He had so many questions about the poem that they ran out of time to read or discuss the poem **"Annabelle Lee."**

At the end of the allocated time, he again received grand applause. And several openly called out for his return at the next meeting. He held up his hand in appreciation of the warm welcome and took his seat.

Irene stood again and thanked James for coming and giving them such an exciting talk. Irene dismissed the group and invited them to stay and get to know James and his family.

Soon a group of men and women gathered around James. Some asked for his autograph, and others wanted their pictures taken with him, especially the ladies. While James was catering to his new following, Darcy and Mickey Ray circulated through the crowd, seeking out some of the people they recognized on the membership list given to them by Irene. They would mention Betty and ask if they were friends and when they saw her last. Many of the crowd didn't even know Betty. Others did but weren't interested in talking about her. All they really got from most people is that Betty wasn't very well-liked.

Mickey Ray did corner one couple that was willing to talk, so Mickey continued talking with them.

Jack and Denise knew her. Jack shook his head as Denise talked. "Betty could be a handful sometimes. She would ask for the strangest favors."

"What kind of favors?" Mickey prodded.

"Did we know anyone that was traveling to Richmond, so she could ride along? I mean, who does that? You know, just ask a stranger for a ride to another town."

Jack spoke up, "Yes, she even asked me once to take her to Virginia Beach so she could walk on the beach barefooted. That doesn't make sense. That's out and out weird. Like Denise said, who does that? She got rude about it when I refused to take her. She didn't ask for Denise and me to go. She only wanted me to take her. I didn't like her. Too out there for me. We were kind of glad when she stopped coming to these meetings."

"Yes, that's a bit out there," agreed Mickey. He needed to move on. Yes, Betty was strange, but this didn't help him, so he thanked them and moved on around the room.

Darcy talked with a single lady named Susan.

"Oh, gosh, yes. I knew Betty, and she was a witch of the first order. I met Mike Reece at the Reader's Corner Bookshop. We started dating, and he started coming to the book club meetings, and Betty moved in like a tiger. She started flirting with Mike, and as you probably already know, they went out. You know, that little tart asked him out. She approached him, not the other way around. If she hadn't asked him, we might still be together. Anyway, I don't know exactly what happened, but after a few months, she threw him aside. If he would leave me for someone like her, I didn't want him back. He can go pound sand for all I care."

"I see," said Darcy. "I don't blame you for not wanting him back again. You made the right decision. It's been enlightening talking with you. I need to get back to my husband now."

Susan smiled at Darcy, "You are a wonderfully lucky lady. You have a fantastic husband, girl!"

"Thanks, I know it," Darcy smiled back and walked back to James.

After making the rounds and spending time with James, the crowd began to leave.

Irene came over to Mickey, James, and Darcy. "James, you were a big hit. A real shot in the arm for this group. We haven't had this many people at a meeting in months. I do hope you'll come back next month," she pleaded.

James smiled, "I don't know about being a big hit, but everyone was so nice and friendly, I'd love to come back again."

Irene insisted on paying for James and Darcy's dinner, and Mickey paid for his own and the bottle of wine for the table.

Irene told them that they could call her office if they needed anything. She gave them her private number and said she did a lot of research years ago and would love to help them with this case. After the goodbyes, they went out to the parking lot, and Mickey got into the back of Darcy's car.

James turned to Darcy in the passenger's seat and Mickey in the back seat. "Did you guys get any information from anyone that might give us a lead?"

"I found out that Betty wasn't such a great person. She wasn't well-liked as a person," said Mickey.

"Yeah, Mother Teresa, she wasn't. She stole Mike from the bookstore away from Susan in the club, and they had it out. We know why Mike wasn't so pleasant to you, Mickey," said Darcy.

"That could put both of them on the suspect list," said James.

"Is stealing someone's girl or boyfriend a good motive for murder?" asked Mickey.

"Yes, it is," chimed both James and Darcy.

"I guess I'm outvoted on that one. Fine, Mike and Susan both go on the list. Now, what else do we have?" said Mickey.

"We need to get back to the house and talk about it. Wanna go back there?" asked Darcy.

"Not tonight, Dee. I'm wiped out. I'll come by in the morning."

"Come by after church, Mickey. James and I are going to church with the kids in the morning. Do you want to come? After that, we can go back to our house, put up the murder board, and discuss the case."

"Yeah, I guess I'll come. Has Pop already got a whiteboard?"

"Yes, he does, and he already set it up in the den. It is a perfect place for it," said James.

"Fine. I'll see you at church in the morning. Dinner is at your house. What are we having?"

"Does it really make a difference to you, Mickey?"

"Nope. Any kind of food, especially free food is fine with me!"

"I thought so. Now get out of my car and go home. I'll see you in the morning."

Mickey got out of their car, in his, and drove home. He felt good. He was glad that Dee was having a positive influence on James. As far as that goes, she was a good influence on him. He hadn't been to church in years.

CHAPTER 9

Sunday, Afternoon at Darcy's, a Date with Francine

Early Sunday morning, the phone rang on Mickey's bedside again. He reached over once again, knocking it onto the floor.

Picking the phone off the floor, he called into the receiver, "What?"

"Mickey, wake up. Get a cup of coffee and call me back. You need to hear this." It was Darcy, and she disconnected the phone.

Mickey wandered into the bathroom, washed and got dressed, and warmed up a cup of coffee that he took from the refrigerator. He reached over and dialed Darcy.

"What do you need at 0 dark hundred on a Sunday morning?"

"Mickey, I thought you had talked to that reporter, Carter Evans," she said angrily.

"We did," he answered, still in the fog of sleep.

"I don't know what you said to him, but he went on the warpath again on the front page of the newspaper," she spouted.

"What did he say," Dee?

"He said that in an interview with a representative of the Christianson Company, he was told to back off, and when he refused, he was threatened by one of our bodyguards. He insists that we're working with the police to cover up a murder. He specifically named you, James, and Detective Peter Reynolds. He vowed that he wouldn't back off until someone was indicted, and he firmly believes it is you. He said that you paid Mrs. Duncan off and even paid for Betty's funeral to keep her quiet. He added that it is his opinion that anyone that does business with the Christianson Company is doing business with a corrupt bunch of people."

"Can he say things like that?" Mickey said, now also angry.

"Everyone has a right to their opinion and has the constitutional right to express it, as long as he states it is his opinion and is NOT stating it as fact. If he says that we are crooks or says that we ARE corrupt and can't back it up, then that is libel, and we could sue. We can't sue for printing an opinion."

"But some people will believe it. And the Sunday paper has the largest number of readers of the week," he said, almost shouting.

"Did you threaten him, Mickey? He also said that your bodyguard destroyed his recorder so he couldn't produce proof."

"No, I didn't threaten him. Yes, James smashed his recorder, then apologized and paid for the damages."

"James was with you? Oh, I get it. He's the bodyguard that Carter was referring to."

"Yes, to both. We do have recordings of it. James recorded it on his cellphone. Yes, he threatened him, but only that he would get Carter fired. He never threatened him with bodily harm, and that we can prove."

"What do we do, Mickey?" she asked.

"Nothing today. It is Sunday. Let's just go to church and enjoy the day, and Pop and I will get with the attorney tomorrow."

"Okay. We'll go to church, but I guarantee I won't enjoy church or the rest of the day. I probably won't sleep tonight," she said, sounding dejected.

"I'm right there with you, Dee. Don't mention it to James or Pop until after church and dinner, and then we'll talk about it when we gather for the murder board meeting."

"Okay, bye," Dee said and clicked off.

It was finally beginning to get light outside. He was wide awake and knew that it was going to be a stressful day. He finished his coffee and dressed for church.

Even with all the trouble, Mickey felt it was good to be in church again after so many years. He felt so at peace there. So many people he knew didn't even believe in God. He did, and he always would. He knew that he hadn't always acted like it, but he knew that God was always in his corner even then. The pastor preached a sermon on hope and forgiveness.

Even James seemed to be paying special attention to the sermon. He took notes and wrote in the margins of his Bible. James said he believed in God when he was a child but lost the belief when he saw the atrocities of war.

James needed something, someone to believe in again. When he came home with his body scars, he withdrew within himself. When he wanted human company, he wandered the malls dressed up as a clown making balloon animals to entertain the children. They loved his silly jokes and stories. James had become a different person since he connected with Darcy and her kids and then got married. He began to believe again. He felt the love of a family.

People accepted James as a broken, wounded man and loved him despite his scars. James was internally and mentally healing. As Mickey's best friend and brother-in-law, Mickey was proud and humbled. Mickey knew he needed to start coming back to church.

After the service, they met at Darcy's and James' home. Mickey got out the notes and clippings he carried in a small pouch and placed them on the board with tape. Darcy was in the kitchen warming up vegetables to go with the take-out chicken they picked up on the way home. Soon they were all sitting at the dining room table eating and laughing as a well-adjusted, loving family would do on a typical Sunday afternoon.

They took their dishes into the kitchen, and Darcy loaded the dishwasher as Mickey, James, and Pop went into the den to arrange the notes on the murder board. In a few minutes, Darcy came into the room and told the children to play outside.

James, Daniel and Darcy sat in front of the murder board. Mickey stood beside it. "Before we get to this business, we need to discuss a more pressing matter."

Daniel and James got a quizzical look on their faces.

"What business," asked Daniel, "I thought things were progressing along as planned."

"Have you seen this morning's newspaper, Pop?" Mickey asked. "No. Why should I?"

"Take a minute to look at it. You, too, James," he said as he handed each one a copy of the Sunday paper.

Daniel read it, then folded it, placed it in his lap, and sat quietly until James finished.

"This is a load of bullsh...I mean, it's all lies! None of it's true!" he said, getting red in the face as his anger increased.

"That's correct, James," said Mickey, "but look at how he wrote it. He says things like, 'In my opinion,' and 'I believe,' and 'You could assume,' and so on. He doesn't come out and say that we are crooks or murderers. He lets the readers draw their own conclusions based on partial truths and innuendos. Pop, you're being mighty silent. What do you think about it?"

"First, we don't need to get all fired up over it. You're right. I don't know what to do the way he's written it. I'll call our attorney first thing in the morning. Maybe we can get a gag order until the investigation's complete. I've never had anything like this happen. I'm sure that we'll be getting calls from our investors wanting to hear our side."

"I didn't think of that, Pop."

"Don't worry about that. I'll take care of it. I'll field those calls. You and James get out there and sort this out, and for goodness sake, either work with Reynolds or stay out of his way. We don't want the police breathing down our necks."

Darcy spoke up, "Dad, what do we do until then?"

"We carry on as usual. I know, saying not to worry is easier said than done. James and Mickey will continue to investigate and report everything to Peter Reynolds. I'll take care of the legal and run interference with the banks. Mickey, how's it going with that Braydon girl?"

"Pop, I don't want to talk about her to everyone here. We haven't even had a date yet," he said uncomfortably and blushing.

They all laughed at Mickey's embarrassment.

"Let's get back to the murder board, people," said Daniel.

"Well, all those notes, and they look like a total jumbled mess. We still don't have any clues who killed Betty," Darcy said.

"We do have two people, maybe three, as suspects," said Mickey. "We have Mike at the bookstore and Susan at the book club. They used to be dating until Betty broke them apart."

"Yes, but as compelling as that could be, we don't have any proof. Or any facts to even present that might look like they did it," said James.

"We need to find out where they were on the week that she was killed. We still don't have an exact day," said Daniel.

"I'll look into that," said Darcy. "That was almost two months ago. That might be hard to pin down."

"The others, Laurel and her husband Wallace, aren't suspects. Wallace's only connection to anything is he sold company stock to his clients. Laurel and Betty had been friends since high school. That's no crime."

"Carla Brigg's was a work friend, that's a connection, but that's about all," said Mickey.

"What about the couple that Betty fired for, you know, 'doing it' in a back room at the store?" said James.

"Doing it? What do you think we are here, children? No one says, 'doing it,' James," laughed Mickey.

James was clearly embarrassed at Mickey's comment.

James cocked his head and said, "Hey, man, my wife, father-in-law, and you, my brother-in-law, are here. I don't talk about stuff like that around any of you. It's not appropriate. So just keep your opinions to yourself. Got it?"

It was Mickey's turn to be embarrassed.

Darcy spoke up, "Okay, we now have that straight. We know what James meant, and yes, someone should check them out. Who's going to volunteer to do that?"

James spoke up, "I will."

Mickey said, "I don't mind, but I need to check on some suppliers for the building contractors. So, I won't be available very much all next week."

Daniel chimed in, "Mickey, I can take care of it. We'll work together at the site to free up more time, so you and James can interview more people. Also, I'll call Peter and try to get more information from the autopsy report. It might help if we can pin down a more accurate date and time of her death."

"I guess that about wraps it up with what we have to work with now. We'll get back together when we have more information," said Mickey.

Darcy put some leftovers in a bag for Mickey to take home.

When he got home, he turned on the television, and it was all over the news that a body was found on the Christianson expansion project. The anchorman said that the police had listed it as a murder and an investigation was underway.

He had a few hours before he had to pick up Francine for their date tonight.

Mickey pulled into the driveway of the previous Mayor of Bridgeton, the Braydon's home. He looked at the huge house and admitted to himself he was impressed. Mr. Braydon was a retired lawyer and had served as the town's Mayor for almost 30 years. He had made many influential friends during his time in office, and because of his connections, he had acquired a fair amount of wealth. He seemed to invest in certain ventures at just the right time and, by miraculous strokes of luck, knew just when to get out when some were ripe for failure. He had done well for himself and his family.

Mickey got out of the Rolls Royce, walked to the front door, and rang the doorbell.

"Hello, Mr. Braydon, I've come to pick up Francine," said Mickey after Franklin Braydon answered the door.

"Welcome to our home, Mickey Ray. I don't think you've ever been here before, have you?" Francine's father asked.

"No, sir. I haven't."

"Wait, didn't you come to any of Francine or Francis' parties when ya'll were in high school?" he asked with a furrowed brow.

"No. I wasn't part of their group when we were in school," Mickey answered.

"Oh, I see," he said. "I understand. For some people, high school was an awkward time. But you made it through. Good for you, Mickey. I'll let Francine know you're here," he said and walked over to an intercom on the wall near the door. "Francine, Mickey Ray Christianson is here to see you."

Francine's voice returned over the intercom, "Thank you, Daddy. I'll be right down."

"Sometimes she can take a few minutes, Mickey. May I offer you a drink while you wait?" he said.

"No, thank you."

"It's 30-year Scotch. Some excellent Scotch, if I say so myself," he said, nodding his head toward a doorway.

Mickey followed him. "I appreciate the offer, but I'm driving, and I'm not much for hard liquor. I occasionally have a glass of wine, but that's pretty much it. So, the superior flavor of your Scotch would be wasted on me."

"Ah, I see. Thank you for being forthright and considerate of me and my daughter, Mickey. At least have a seat while we wait."

Mickey took the nearest seat and looked around the room. It had floor-to-ceiling bookcases. "Are those old leather-bound books in your bookcases, first editions?"

"Why, yes, they are, Mickey. Very observant of you to notice," Mr. Braydon answered with pride. "I purchased them as investments. They look good, but each year, because of their scarcity, they increase in value."

"Your carved desk, I also imagine, is hand-carved," commented Mickey.

"My, my, you notice everything, don't you, my young friend? Yes, I commissioned it to be carved and shipped here from India many years ago when the wife and I visited there on a business trip. That's where we also purchased the oriental rug on the floor. It was handwoven. Those people from India are very talented. Now, I must admit, the old globe in that corner," he said, pointing to it, "isn't anything special. I thought it went well in the room," he added.

Mickey was admiring the deep red Oriental rug, and he was sure it cost a small fortune when Mr. Braydon said, "At least have a glass of brandy. I'd be insulted if you didn't."

"Fine, just a small bit," said Mickey, and he thought to himself. This old fart was trying to impress him by playing the part of some old southern gentleman.

Playing the role was the operative word. He wasn't that old, although he looked old. A gentleman, he definitely was not. When he was in office, he had a reputation for being offensive, rude, vulgar, and extremely vengeful when he didn't get what he wanted. Now he was acting like a kind father figure. He wanted to get up and get out away from this vile man, but he had a job to do. He needed to find out why Francine was really at the funeral yesterday.

Mickey took the brandy snifter and took a tiny sip. It's okay, he thought.

"An occasional drink calms the nerves, I always say, Mickey."

"Yes, I guess it does."

"I spent many hours in here, going over plans for the city. Before that, when I was practicing law, I'd spend late night hours going over a case that I'd try in court the following morning. I won most of my cases, you know," he said with a sardonic smile.

"Oh, really, I didn't know that," Mickey said.

Francine walked into the room and stopped. "Is Daddy boring you with stories of some of his old cases, Mickey Ray?"

"Never, Francine, I found your father's stories quite interesting," Mickey said, giving his own sardonic smile as he spoke.

Mr. Braydon's smile disappeared as he looked at Mickey straight in the eye, "Take care of my daughter, Mickey Ray Christianson."

"I'll heed your warning, sir."

"You better."

"Oh, Daddy. Don't be so melodramatic. It's only a date. We'll be back in a few hours. Don't wait up." She reached out to Mickey. He got up from the chair, set his glass on the table, and reached for her hand.

"I stopped doing that many years ago, Francine. Take care. Both of you."

"We will, Daddy," and they walked out to his car.

As Mickey opened the door for her to get in, he said, "Your father is quite the showman, isn't he?"

"Yes, he is. He did offer you a drink before the brandy, didn't he?"

"Yes, he did."

"And he told you it was 30-year Scotch?"

"He did that also."

"Let me tell you a secret. It isn't 30-year Scotch. He does that to people he knows or thinks they don't know the difference. Oh, it's a good Scotch, but not the really expensive stuff. He saves top-shelf brands for people that he feels are important. If they refuse, he gives them a medium price brandy. Again, assuming they, or in your case, you, won't know the difference."

"Thanks for letting me know. Next time, I'll take the Scotch and compliment him on a fine drink," Mickey said, getting into the driver's seat and starting the car.

"Do you mind if I call you Fran?" he asked.

"Did someone tell you to call me Fran?" she asked.

"No, it's just easier than saying, Francine."

"No one has ever called me that. I guess it's okay. Now that I think of it, it sounds kind of sweet. I would like it if you called me Fran."

"Okay, then Fran it is," he said, driving out of the driveway.

She laughed, "Okay. I'll let you call me that, but only you."

"Thanks, I appreciate that. If I'm the only one, then that makes me special!" he said, laughing.

"I guess it does," she said and laughed with him.

Mickey was feeling much better as he drove on. He had been nervous in her house, and he had butterflies in his stomach when she came out. The simple dress with dangling earrings and flat shoes she wore helped make him feel more at ease. It was more down to earth that the flowing evening gown she wore at the fundraiser. The dress also accented her long shapely legs. His heart was still racing, but at least he could breathe, and his mind wasn't going blank as she sat beside him.

"I heard that your girlfriend broke up with you and left town. What happened?"

"She didn't exactly break up with me. She decided that she wanted to go to culinary school in Oregon. She might come back when she graduates. It's only eighteen months. We keep in touch."

"Has she found another boyfriend yet?" she asked, reaching over and placing her hand on his thigh.

"No. She's concentrating on school. You said you liked seafood. Is it okay if I pick a nice place?"

"I told you, that little seafood place on the Eastern Shore, but you can pick the place if you insist."

"I know one right here on the other side of town. We can go there. The food is excellent, and it's fresh. They buy the seafood from the market right on the docks in Hampton. They also have fresh oysters there," he said with a wink.

"Now you're talking, Mickey Ray," she said, returning the wink.

"If we get along, we can get to know each other with more dates in the future. You're a very beautiful lady. Let's enjoy each other's company tonight. Okay?"

She sat quietly looking out the window the rest of the way to the Seafood Palace. He asked for a private table away from other people if possible. Being the perfect gentleman, he held the chair for her when she sat down. If he didn't think of something to talk about, it would be a long night.

The waiter brought them a menu and asked for their drink order as he sat down.

Mickey asked for a glass of white wine and ordered the same for Francine.

"What makes you think I want white wine?" she said.

"We'll be ordering seafood. White wine is the obvious choice for seafood," he said.

"It'll be okay. Are you going to order for me also?"

"No, I'll let you do that since I don't know what you like."

She gave him a coy smile. "You can order for me, Mickey. I'm curious what you think I might want."

The waiter came back with their wine. He poured it, put the bottle on the table, and took their order for oysters on the half shell as an appetizer.

Mickey ordered two lobsters and a large side order of spaghetti squash for them to share.

Fran lifted her glass and said as she clinked her glass against his, "Here's to us and our new relationship."

"Not too fast, Fran. We're on a date, not in a relationship."

She smiled, "Not yet, Mickey Ray."

"Well, I must admit, as I told you in the car, you're beautiful, and what man couldn't resist a woman like you," he said.

She laughed and drank the wine in one gulp.

As the last few drops trickled into her mouth, Mickey took the glass from her hand. "Not so fast, Fran. Save some room for the lobster. We don't want you to numb your tastebuds to the point that you can't taste the culinary delight of the meal that the chef is preparing for us tonight," he said mockingly.

"Oh, Mickey. You're so funny. I know why you ordered the oysters. They're an aphrodisiac."

"I didn't order them for that reason. I ordered them because I like oysters. I hope you do too."

"What am I going to do with you, Mickey Ray?"

"First, you can tell me, what was your relationship with Betty Duncan?"

"How did Betty Duncan's name come up? And what do you mean by relationship? I had no relationship with her. I barely knew her."

He reached over and filled her glass with more wine. "If you had no relationship with her, then why did you come to her funeral?" he said and took a tiny sip of his wine. Then he picked up an oyster, put a few drops of hot sauce on it, and dropped it in his mouth.

"I went to her funeral out of respect. We went to school together, for heaven's sake."

He picked up an oyster in the shell. "Do you like hot sauce on your oysters?"

"No, a little salt is all." She held her mouth open as he poured the oyster from the shell into her mouth.

She swallowed the oyster and said, "Let's not talk about Betty. Let's talk about us."

"Ok, but we both already know about us. Let's talk about something we don't know," he answered.

"Like what?"

"For starters, when you put on one of those fundraising events, how much actually goes to the organization that you are sponsoring?" he asked.

"That's a strange question, Mickey."

"No, it isn't. If I donate one hundred dollars, how much goes to the organization?"

"That's a loaded question. First, you have to consider the costs to put on the event, and the amount that's raised, and then…."

"Wait. It's simple. If one hundred people each donate a thousand dollars, how much is given to the sponsored charity?"

"I was trying to answer that, Mickey Ray. You have to rent the event location, then hire the entertainment like a band or orchestra, and hire caterers. Usually, some type of drawing or prize must be purchased as a giveaway, and of course, the one who organized the affair deserves to be paid. If it is a public event, there are advertising costs like television or radio. It cost a lot to put on one of those events."

"I see. Everyone gets a cut, so in the end, the charity only gets a small percent of the proceeds. Am I correct?"

"Well. I guess so, but if we didn't do fundraisers like that, the charity wouldn't get anything. Using your example, it could cost sixty thousand dollars based on your figure of one hundred thousand dollars. The charity receives forty thousand. It's better than nothing. Everyone has a good time, and the charity's happy."

"I guess that's one way to look at it," he said.

"Fran," he reached over and covered her hand. "Why didn't you come to my mother's funeral? We went to school together too."

She took the glass in her other hand and took a drink. "Because I was out of town when she died."

He knew that wasn't true. Not that she was wasn't out of town, but he knew that Fran had no clue when his mother died. At that time, he wasn't on Francine's radar.

He gently lifted her hand and kissed it. "Please don't be upset with me. I am just curious. Betty's mother is so upset about her daughter's death. I just wondered."

"So, we're back on that subject again. Mickey, just let it go!" The wine was beginning to settle in and affect Francine's judgment by this time. She looked at Mickey with a smirk. "Did you know her, Mickey Ray?" she asked.

"In school, I knew her somewhat."

"What do you mean, 'somewhat?'" she asked.

"She was in my math class. I'm not good at math, so I paid her to tutor me for a while. That's all."

"You didn't date her?"

"No, we never dated. She was my math tutor. When I passed my math requirements, I never saw her again, other than to pass her in the hallway. I swear."

She looked at Mickey and pushed a bit of hair hanging down on his face. "You keep saying I'm beautiful, but you know you aren't so bad-looking yourself."

Mickey blushed and felt his heart race again.

"She must have done a great job tutoring you. After all, you're running a multi-million-dollar business now."

"I don't have to do the math to do that. I oversee jobs and make sure things go as they should. There isn't a lot of math in that. We have people to handle that."

"You must have had some reason to want to help Betty's mother. Have you had any contact with her since high school?"

"No. I know that she rented one of our apartments. I haven't seen her since high school."

"She was a slut," Fran said with a slight slur.

Mickey knew the wine was affecting her now. But things weren't going the way he wanted. She was interrogating him. It was supposed to be the other way around.

Mickey saw the waiter coming toward them with a large tray with their meal on it. The waiter put the tray on a stand next to their table.

He put the plates on the table that held their lobsters and a single large dish with the spaghetti squash to serve themselves.

"May I help you with your lobster bibs, sir?" the server asked.

"Yes, you may help the lady. I can do my own, thank you," answered Mickey.

After attaching the plastic bib around Francine's neck, the server reached over, filled their glasses, and left.

Fran again lifted her glass and toasted to the slut she knew as Betty Duncan.

"Why do you say she was a slut, Fran. What do you know?"

"She went around with married men. That's what I know," she said as the wine loosened her tongue even more. "Are you sure that you didn't date her, and that's why you feel obligated to pay for her funeral, Mickey Ray?"

"I think I would remember if we dated, Francine. And what makes you think I paid for her funeral?"

"I can read, Mickey. It is all over the newspaper and even on the television news. She was a slut," her slurring getting more prominent as the wine took more effect.

"Who did she go around with, Francine?"

"I can't say anymore, Mickey Ray," she said. "I'm hungry."

Mickey helped her with the lobster, and he had the waiter take away the rest of the wine. He ordered each of them a slice of double chocolate layer cake for dessert and coffee to wash it down. He hoped that the caffeine in the chocolate and coffee would take the edge off the alcohol. He wasn't afraid of her father, but he didn't want to get on his wrong side either. They sat and talked as they slowly finished their meal.

As the wine took more effect, she talked about her charity work. She was quite passionate about it. She told Mickey how her last fundraiser had paid for the entire playground equipment at the city park and how the previous one had sent one hundred and twenty children to summer camp last year.

After dinner, they rode around to talk more and let the alcohol get out of her system. He tried to get her to open up more about Betty, but she refused to give any names. Most of what she had to say mainly was hearsay and not helpful to their investigation.

They rode to the park, sat on a bench in the moonlight, and talked. She could be a lovely person, and he felt that he could easily fall under her spell. He needed to take her home.

As they walked to her door, she reached out and took Mickey's hand.

When they got to the front door, she reached up and put her arms around him. She pulled him close, placed her lips against his, and kissed him gently but firmly. They kissed for what seemed to Mickey like an eternity. Finally, he pulled away, panting as his heart raced in his chest. Since Valerie, he hadn't kissed a woman and never one as beautiful or sensual as Francine. He was shaking as he looked into Francine's deep blue eyes that seemed as bottomless as the ocean, and he slowly backed away.

"Am I going to see you again, Francine? I enjoyed tonight," he said, looking into her eyes.

"It was very nice, and yes, I hope we can see each other again," she answered.

He cocked his head and smiled. "There's a concert of the Bridgeton Orchestra tomorrow evening. May I take you?"

"I think I can make time for that," she said.

"What time should I pick you up? The concert starts at eight. If I pick you up at six, we'll have time for dinner before the show. It should be over around ten, and we can go for dessert afterward."

"It's a date. See you at six," she said.

She turned to the door, opened it, then turned back to him, blew him another kiss, and slowly closed it. He stood there, feeling the breeze blowing gently around him. He took a deep breath. It was a long ride home.

CHAPTER 10

Another Interview with Mike, then Susan

He opened the door of the construction trailer and since he was the first one there, started a pot of coffee so it would be ready when Pop showed up. He sat down at the desk and looked at the schedule for the week.

Everyone had reported in last week, and things were on schedule. But as with any construction job, that could change at any time, any day. There could be unforeseen problems. There could be delays in delivering supplies or mistakes that had to be corrected before construction continued.

He and Pop were constantly working to keep the different trades working together as a team and not against each other. Things had to happen in a particular order for construction to proceed without slowdowns and corrections. His job was to make sure things were done correctly and that city inspections were performed and approved before the next phase.

He sat looking at some of the building blueprints when the door opened, and Daniel stepped inside.

"Hey, Pop, grab a cup of coffee and pull up a chair," Mickey said.

"How was your date with Francine Braydon, son?" Daniel asked.

"Pop, how did you know about that? Never mind. Living with James and Dee has its disadvantages…for me, anyway!"

"Yes, son. This family has no secrets."

"I've got to remember that from now on. Even James can't keep his mouth shut, can he?"

Daniel laughed heartily and said, "He's a fine young man and has really come out of his shell since he married Dee."

"Seriously, Pop, Francine is a beautiful woman, but I don't trust her, so other than having some company, it'll never go anywhere."

"Does she know that?"

"I'm trying very hard to keep her at a distance, but she can mesmerize a person just being around her. Right now, she thinks she can sink her hooks into me."

"All I can say is that she is a real charmer and is used to getting anything and anyone she wants. Just watch yourself," Daniel said.

"We're going to a concert tonight."

"For a person that wants to keep someone at a distance, you sure work fast, son."

"I know," he said. "I admit, she's hard to resist, but you're right. I'll be careful. Now, let's take a look at these blueprints. I need to show you something," he said, standing up and sliding the prints across the desk to his father.

"Okay. I see them. I don't see anything wrong," Daniel said, scanning them.

Mickey explained that even though it meets minimum codes, problems will surface in the future.

"Good catch, Mickey Ray. I see it, and I'll call a meeting about it tomorrow to make sure that we have the proper materials and labor cost changes."

"Thanks, Pop. Can you call the contractors in, and I'll show them the changes we want to make. I'd like for James and me to take some more time to investigate Betty's murder," Mickey asked his father.

"Sure, Mickey. Take all the time you need."

Mickey and Daniel went over a few more details in the schedule for the week. Then Mickey left to pick up James.

When Mickey pulled up to James' house, James came out and told him to come in and eat breakfast there instead of going to the diner.

When Mickey walked into the kitchen, Joel and Cyndi were sitting at the table eating pancakes. Darcy was at the stove frying bacon.

"Hey, Uncle Mickey!" said Joel.

"Hey, little Joe. And how's my favorite niece this morning, Cyndi?" Mickey said with a huge smile at both of them.

Cyndi looked up at him, wrinkled her nose with a mouthful of food, and said, "I'm your only niece, Uncle Mickey!"

They ate and talked. The kids went outside to leave the adults alone to talk about business while Mickey sat at the table with James and Darcy.

"Dee, can you run background checks on Francine and her brother, Francis Braydon. I want to know what they were up to around the time Betty was killed," Mickey said.

"Do you think she had anything to do with Betty?" asked Darcy.

"No, not really, but I want to cover all the bases. She called Betty a slut on our date last night. She wasn't drunk, but she had enough wine to be tipsy and a loose tongue, but not quite loose enough to tell me who Betty was sleeping with that had made her say that," said Mickey as he sipped coffee.

"We need more information on the couple that Betty fired. Their names were Howard Hudson and Riley Gentry. Find out what you can about them. Do they have a relationship outside the workplace? While you're doing that, James and I can interview them. Also, I want to talk again with Mike at the bookstore and Susan, the one he was dating until Betty came into the picture. He knows something. We need to find out what it is he isn't telling us. Can you give us a call as you find out the details? Maybe we can meet back here to arrange the murder board," added Mickey.

James said, "Let's roll. I'll drive."

Mickey and James headed for town and the bookstore. They walked in, and again Mickey spotted the same lady that had directed him to the downstairs area where Mike was working.

"He must spend a lot of time down there. That's where he was the last time I was here," Mickey said to her.

She smiled. "Yes, Mike spends most of his time down there. That's kind of his kingdom. He's not really a people person."

"We'll go down and talk to him. Does he work here full time?" Mickey asked.

"Yes, he works every day, even on Saturday, his day off. He is a bit strange like that. He doesn't even get overtime for doing it," she said.

"But that's the law. Any employee that works over forty hours a week must be paid overtime. Even I know that," Mickey said.

"I know. He's salary, so they don't have to pay him for it. It's okay with him. He doesn't care. His whole life is here. I don't understand him. He doesn't have any kind of home life. He lives alone, I think."

"He doesn't have a girlfriend?" Mickey commented.

"No, he had one for a while. She was very nice. Then he started dating another lady. She was so different than the first one. She could be bossy sometimes."

"What were their names? Do you remember?" asked James.

She thought for a minute, then said, "I think the first one was named Susan. Mike met her at some book club meeting where he was a member. Then he stopped dating her and started dating another woman in the club. I don't remember her name," she said.

James nodded his head in understanding. "Was the second lady's name, Betty Duncan?"

"Yes. That's her name. Did you know her?" she asked.

"Sort of. She's dead now, and we're investigating her murder," said Mickey.

"Oh, no! Did Mike have anything to do with it? I hope not. He's strange, but I would hate to think that I work with a murderer."

"We doubt that he did, but we need to ask him some questions to find out if he knew someone who might want her dead. You understand we aren't accusing Mike of anything," James said to her.

"Oh, good. You scared me for a minute."

"I doubt if you have any reason to be concerned. Oh, I'm sorry, I'm Mickey Ray Christianson, and my partner is James Bower," he said, putting out his hand to shake hers.

She reached out to meet his hand, "I'm Patricia Handly."

"We wouldn't want to get you in any trouble with Mike, so we won't mention that we talked to you, Patricia. Thanks for taking a minute to help us out. Can we come back and talk to you if we need more information? Again, we won't tell Mike," Mickey said.

"Oh, sure. I'm here every day between opening and closing time. Except on Mondays and Sundays. We have a part-timer that works weekends."

"We'll head downstairs to find Mike." He put a finger up to his lips in a sign of silence.

Mickey and James went down the stairs, looked around for Mike, and saw him in a corner with a vacuum cleaner in his hand and a dusting nozzle on the end.

As Mike saw them approach, he turned off the vacuum. "I thought I told you not to come back," he said scornfully.

"Yes, you did say that, Mike. I came back anyway, and I have more questions," Mickey said.

"You're not the police, and I don't have to answer any of your questions. Now get out, or I'll call them and report you for harassment."

"Oh, please do call them. Ask to speak to Detective Peter Reynolds. He's investigating the murder of Betty Duncan. We have some information about your relationship with Betty that you might want to share with them," said Mickey.

"You have nothing on me, so leave."

"Correct, but we can give them enough information that they can detain you at police headquarters until they can confirm what we tell them. You had a pretty rocky relationship with Betty. We could make it sound serious enough to charge you with her murder."

"I didn't kill her, so you can't have any information that would prove that I did."

"All we have to do is tell them what we know, and they can book you on *SUSPICION* of murder. Then the police can hold you until they decide whether you did or not."

"I didn't hurt her. Okay, I slapped her once. That's all, and she had it coming."

"Why did you slap her, Mike?" asked James.

"Who are you? You look like a freak!" Mike said, trying to get James rattled.

"I am a freak, a crazy freak that would just as soon take your head off and feed it to the fish you have in that tank in the corner," James said, turning his head and nodding at the sizeable 50-gallon fish tank in the corner of the room.

"You lay a hand on me, and I'll have your badge, you monster."

"I don't have a badge, so I don't have to play by police rules. We are on a first-name basis with the police, so I advise you to talk to us or spend a few days in jail until we get this mess sorted out. Now, do you want to talk to us here or the cops down at the station? Your choice," James said as he folded his arms.

Mickey and James stood there in silence while Mike considered his options.

Finally, Mike Reece spoke again. "Okay, we can talk here. Then you'll leave me alone and keep the police out of it?"

"Yes, we'll leave. We'll not report you to the police if we believe that you didn't kill Betty, but we can't promise the police won't find out and come here to talk to you," Mickey said.

"Who is Mr. Freak here?"

James moved closer to Mike, grabbed his collar, and slammed him against one of the bookcases. He then stepped closer to him until he was nose to nose with Mike. "I was injured in combat in the military defending people I don't even know. I know you, and I don't even like you. DO NOT ever mention my injuries to my face again, or I'll feed your head to the fish," said James. "I'm James Bower, and I'm his partner," said James pointing to Mickey.

Mike's eyes grew large with fear. "Okay, I was out of line about that. I'm sorry," he said to James.

James glared at Mike for a few moments, then let him go and backed off. "Talk to us," said James.

"Alright," Mike said as he rubbed his hands down his clothes nervously to smooth out the nonexistent wrinkles. "I met Betty at the Bridgeton Benevolent Book Club. In the beginning, we kind of hit it off. I thought we had a lot of things in common. Books and reading was not one of them. She liked the nightlife. We would go out to eat, then hit a nightclub or two. She was on the hunt for someone better than me.

"She spent a lot of nights at my house. She lived with her mother, so we couldn't go to her house. I found out she was also dating two other guys while going out with me. In all honesty, I don't know how she could go out as much as she did and still work a job."

"Did you know she was pregnant when she was killed?" James asked.

"Yes. She tried to blame it on me. She said it was my child."

"Was it?"

"I don't know. I didn't know she was dating other men when we started going out. When I found out, I confronted her. We got into a huge argument. That's when I slapped her."

"When was this?" asked Mickey.

"About two months ago. She cried, said she was sorry and promised not to date anyone else. That's when she told me about the baby and told me it was mine."

"Did you believe her?"

"Yes, I even offered to marry her to give the child a father. She refused my offer and insisted that I give her money to raise it. I refuse that offer. I told her that if I supported the baby, she had to come along with it. She said she would get a paternity test and go to court to force me to pay child support. That's when I told her to get out and never come back. I thought that maybe she sent you to collect money from me."

"Did she get a paternity test?" asked Mickey.

"I don't know."

"How long ago was it?" asked James.

Mickey and James were almost taking turns asking questions. "About two months ago?" asked Mickey.

James took his turn as he took notes in a small pocket notebook. "Can you give the exact date?"

"No. I can't. Can you remember exactly when you did something?"

"Somethings, I can. If I killed someone, I'd remember the date and the exact time," James said.

"I didn't kill her. I swear. All I did was slap her. She was alive and quite well that last time I saw her," Mike said.

"It doesn't matter if you're the baby's father or not. What matters is who killed Betty. We'll keep our word and not notify the police unless we determine that you did kill her. If you did kill her, we'll personally bring the police here to arrest you. As you say, if you're innocent, you have nothing to worry about. Would you be willing to give a DNA sample to determine if you're the father?" asked Mickey.

"As you said, at this point, it doesn't matter, so I will not give a DNA sample. I think I have said all I have to say."

"Okay, if we need more information, we'll be back," said James.

"I'm sure you will," Mike said as he bent over to turn the vacuum back on and picked up the dusting nozzle.

Mickey and James walked back up the stairs and waved to Patricia as they walked out the door.

"Hey, you're going to get us locked up if you do that to the wrong person, James," said Mickey as they got in the Humvee.

"Do what?"

"You know what I'm talking about. You can't grab people and throw them around like that. You could go to jail for assault. At the very least, we could be sued."

"He deserved a lot more!"

"Maybe he did, but you still can't do that! You assaulted him. And he could still call the police and file charges."

"I'll deal with that if he does," said James. "He's a jerk of the first order. I don't like him," answered James.

"I don't either. And I can't figure him out. He isn't telling us everything. What he's **NOT** telling us may have triggered him to kill Betty," said Mickey.

"My thoughts exactly," said James.

"Should we talk to Susan? Susan might have gotten so mad she killed Betty because Betty took Mike away from her."

James thought on that one for a minute. "Call Irene at the library so we can get Susan's address."

As James drove, Mickey called Irene and talked to her for a few minutes and got Susan's home address and her employer and phone number. Mickey called her employer and asked if Susan was working today but didn't ask to speak to her. She worked at a local real estate office as a secretary and would be in the office all day. Mickey and James decided not to warn Susan they were coming to talk with her. They wanted to catch her off guard. Mickey also told James that Irene wanted to schedule him to give another talk to the book club. She asked that James give her a call so they could schedule it.

James laughed at that. He never expected such a warm welcome. He had gotten so used to being almost a recluse because of his disfigurement that it was a huge adjustment for him to be so widely welcomed by people.

James drove them to the real estate office where Susan worked, and they went in and asked for her. When she came out, she put on a wide smile and offered her hand for them to shake.

"Hello, James and Mickey. It's such a surprise to see both of you again so soon. How can we help you? Would you like to speak to an agent? Is one of you looking for a house, perhaps?"

James took over at this point by shaking her hand with a smile. "No, Susan. Neither of us are looking for a house. We want to talk to you privately for a few minutes if you don't mind."

"Why, of course, James. That was a wonderful talk you gave to the club. I hope you plan to come back to discuss Poe's poem '**Annabelle Lee**,'" she said, motioning for them to follow her.

"If the club wants me to come back, I'll see what I can do," James said. "I've been swamped lately," he answered as they walked to a back room.

When they walked in, she gently closed the door behind them. "Now, what can I do for you?" she asked.

Mickey started by asking, "We have a few questions about Betty Duncan and Mike Reece."

Susan rolled her eyes. "That's old news. Why? What did they do?"

"That's what we are trying to find out. We understand you dated Mike for a while until Betty came along?" Mickey said.

"Yes, I did. At first, Betty was friendly and personable in the club. Then as she got comfortable with people and activities, she tried to take control."

"We know she could be bossy, but what we are interested in is what happened between you and her when Mike left you and started dating Betty," James asked.

"At first, I was furious. I could have killed her. I hated her, and I wanted her to die a horrible death."

Mickey and James looked at each other. Had Susan just confessed to them? They didn't expect that. It came as a complete surprise to them.

"Well, she did die. That's why we're here," Mickey said.

Susan visibly shuddered. "Oh, no! I didn't mean that. How did she die?"

"Someone killed her," said Mickey.

They all stood there, with Mickey and James looking directly at Susan.

After a few awkward moments, she spoke again.

"I read that they found a dead body in that project you're building. Was that Betty?"

James looked at her with his steely eyes, and shook his head.

She stuttered. "Oh, my. I shouldn't have said that. I didn't really mean I wanted her dead. I had nothing to do with it. I didn't even know she was dead. Who killed her?"

"That's what we want to know. We're hoping you can help us. Do you know anyone that hated Betty enough to kill her?" said Mickey.

There was a conference table in the room. James could see that Susan was shaken. He took her arm and guided her to a chair at the table. He sat her down and sat down beside her, then turned his chair to face her. Mickey sat down on the other side of the table. They sat for a few moments to give her a chance to compose herself.

"She was killed by a blow to the back of her head. Her body was buried on one of my properties, and we discovered it during some construction work," Mickey said.

She sat quietly, looking at the floor. She was wringing her hands. "When did she die? I mean, I haven't even seen her for weeks, probably over two months. By this time, I had forgotten about her."

"She was killed six to eight weeks ago."

"I shouldn't have said what I did about wanting her dead. I didn't kill her. I really didn't. Please believe me. I didn't kill her. Do I need an attorney to prove I didn't kill her? For a while, I hated her, but I wouldn't kill anyone."

"Calm down, Susan. We aren't the police. We aren't accusing you of anything, but if there's any evidence that might make you look guilty, then maybe you should call an attorney," said James.

"No. I don't think there's anything. I didn't do it so, there isn't any evidence to hide or be found. Yes. I hated Betty for a while, but I got over it. I mean, I got over Mike. We haven't seen each other in months. I'm dating someone else. The guy I'm dating now I might even marry if he asks me. Mike leaving me for Betty was the best thing that ever happened to me. It just took me a while to realize it."

"I met this guy I'm dating now when I was in the hospital two months ago," she said.

"You were in the hospital two months ago? For what?" asked James.

"I had my appendix taken out. I was only in the hospital a couple of days, but I was out of work for six weeks."

"Do you remember the dates you had the operation and your time off work?" Mickey asked.

She gave them the dates while James made notes, then they waited for her to get herself calmed down enough to go back to work. They left with her still sitting in the chair in the conference room.

"Wow, that was intense," said Micky. "What do you think?"

"She's either not a killer or gave an Oscar-winning performance."

"I agree, but we still need to check out her alibi. The dates she was out of commission should clear her," Mickey added.

James pulled out into traffic. "Where to now?" he said.

"Let's try Howard Hudson and Riley Gentry," said Mickey. "They have different addresses listed, but they're in the same area."

There was a car in the driveway of Howard's house. A young man with shaggy blonde hair answered the door when they rang the bell. He was wearing ragged jeans and a torn t-shirt. They saw a girl sitting on the couch in the background.

"Howard Hudson?" asked James.

"Yes, can I help you?" he asked.

"I'm James Bower, and this is my partner, Mickey Ray Christianson. May we talk to you about Betty Duncan?" James asked.

"Sure, come inside," he said, stepping aside, making room for them in the house's living room. "Have a seat. Can we get you something to drink? Water or a soda. I don't have anything any stronger. This is Riley, my girlfriend."

Mickey and James each took a seat in the two wing-back chairs in the living room but declined the drinks. Howard sat on the couch beside his girlfriend.

"What's this about Betty?" Riley asked.

"First of all, we'd like to know if either of you has seen Betty in the past month or two?" said James.

"No, why?" said Howard.

"Have you talked to her since she let you go from the grocery store where you worked?"

They both laughed. "No," they said in unison. "That was a bit embarrassing."

James was uncomfortable with this line of questioning, so Mickey took over. "I'm sure it was. But we needed to ask."

"Are you the police?" Riley asked.

"No, Betty's body was found at one of the properties I own, and we're investigating her death," said Mickey.

"Sorry to hear that. How did she die?" Riley asked.

"She was murdered."

"Sorry. Was she shot?" Howard said.

"No, why would you ask that?" said Mickey.

"I don't know. Being shot's the first thing that came to mind, I guess. At least that's what I think of when I hear someone's been murdered," Howard said.

James looked at them. "Way too much television," he stated.

"She was bludgeoned to death. How do you feel about that?" cut in Mickey.

"Sounds gross. But to be honest, I don't care one way or the other," Riley said.

"That's a bit cold-hearted, don't you think?" said James.

"I didn't mean it like that. You know, when you hear of someone being killed on the radio or television, you're sorry about it, but you really don't care because it doesn't affect you one way or the other."

"I guess that makes sense," said James.

"Look, guys, if you aren't the police, why are you here. We didn't even know she was dead," said Howard.

"I care," said Mickey. "She was found on my property. Now, since she fired you, I assume you may have wanted her dead, at least by your own admission, don't care what happened to her."

"We didn't want her dead, and we don't have any hard feelings about her. We're both collecting unemployment now, so we're doing okay. Riley and I met on our morning walks. Then she got a job working at the store where I worked. She lived right around the corner with her last boyfriend. We had talked about moving in together but hadn't got around to it yet. When we got fired, she told her last boyfriend she couldn't pay her half of the rent, and he made her move out. She moved in with me. With our unemployment, we're doing fine. When our checks run out, we'll find jobs."

"How did you feel about getting fired?" James asked.

"We didn't care. We didn't really like working there anyway, but we wouldn't qualify for unemployment if we quit. Betty did us a favor by firing us."

"So, no hard feelings, then."

"Not one bit. Betty said that if we listed her as a reference, she'd give us a good report. She understood how we felt, but company rules said she had to fire us. So, as I said, it's all good."

"When did all this happen?" Mickey asked.

"Let's see. I think it was about two and a half months ago. We still have a lot of time on our unemployment benefits, and we're going to get every last check we can get out of the government. After all, it's one of our rights," Howard added.

"I see. I understand. I think we have everything we need from both of you," said Mickey.

As they got up to leave, James said to them, "Unemployment is not a right. It's a benefit that businesses pay for."

Howard said, "Hey, man. She fired us. We weren't doing anything wrong! Are you going to report us to the employment office or something? Maybe I shouldn't have said that stuff about not looking for a job."

"Don't worry. We're not from any branch of the government, state or federal. Your secret's safe with us, Howard," said James, walking to the door.

"Thanks, James. I don't mean to be disrespectful or anything."

Mickey held up his hand, "Don't worry about it. Here's my card. If you think of anything or anyone that might have wanted to hurt Betty, give me a call. Will you do that for us, Howard?"

Howard took the card and thanked Mickey and James for not reporting him. He promised to call them if he thought of anything.

As they got into the Humvee, James looked at Mickey and said, "I think we can safely cross them off the list of suspects. I don't like Howard. I don't like people that scam the system. He's lazy and is just milking it. He even admitted to it."

"That's true, but he isn't a bad person. He isn't any different than most people that get laid off or fired. It's a sad part of our society. People used to be ashamed of being laid off or fired, but he's proud of getting free money."

"I don't like it," said James.

"It's the way of the country now, James. Get used to it, my friend." Mickey got out his phone and saw that Darcy had called, so he returned her call.

"Hey, Dee, what's up?"

"I got some of the info you asked for. Want to hear it?"

"Yes, I'm putting you on speaker so James can hear it."

"Okay, I looked up Francine. Other than her last two messy divorces, where she got most of her ex's money, she's clean. That's a warning to you, Mickey. She's a black widow. Watch your back around her."

"Everyone calls her that! I get the message loud and clear. Now, what about her brother?"

"Legally, he's clean also, but as you know, he's a lawyer like his dad. He seems to be relatively competent but not quite the shark his dad was until he retired. He's been known to be a philanderer. He owns a small plane to take on short business trips and has a slight interest in a couple of restaurants in Raleigh, North Carolina. Rumor is that he also takes his flavor of the month girlfriend with him on some business trips. He likes fast cars and loose women. He's married with two kids. His wife knows about his infidelity but puts up with it because of the social and financial standing in the community. Rumors and scandals are two different animals.

"Last, they got their names from their father, Franklin, because it was as close as he could get without having a Junior in the family.

"Since I was researching the family tree, I looked up their mother, Donna. She was a state beauty queen many years back and puts up with her husband's indiscretions also for fame and fortune. As you already know, she owns and operates an event and fundraising business and does quite well at it."

"Thanks, Dee. That's great information. I don't know how it helps us right now, but we'll try to piece something together later this evening when we gather around the murder board," said Mickey. "We'll be back in a few minutes. I have a meeting at the construction site this afternoon, so I need to pick up the truck and get back to the office."

Mickey disconnected and laid his head back on the vehicle's headrest as James drove home. "James, I'm tired. I wish I could go back a few years and spend some time there."

"Don't we all, little bro," James responded.

James pulled into the driveway at home. Mickey then left for the construction site.

When he opened the door to the construction trailer, two men were talking to Daniel. He spoke and shook hands with Raymond and Donald as he walked in. He pulled a blueprint off the shelf and asked Raymond to look at the prints.

After explaining the problems and how he wanted them fixed, Raymond left, and Donald stepped up. Mickey went into a detailed explanation on the wiring that needed to be upgraded. They reached an agreement, and he also left.

When the two foremen left, Mickey sat down across from his dad in the chair.

"That was great, Mickey. You handled that like a pro," said Daniel.

"Thanks, Pop. I guess right now, I am a pro. I never realized how exhausting this really is."

"It can be extremely exhausting, son. No one knows how much until they walk in our shoes."

"We're having a murder board meeting tonight to gather all the information James and I have collected today."

"Darcy's been pretty busy with the kids and all the paperwork for this project," said Daniel.

"Wow, Pop, I forgot. We can't have a murder board meeting tonight. I've got a date tonight with Francine. Maybe we can do it this afternoon," Mickey said.

"That's okay, son. I'll close the office early and call Dee to set it up for this afternoon instead."

"Great, Pop," said Mickey as he walked and closed the door behind himself.

CHAPTER 11

Afternoon Murder Board Meeting at Home

They again sent the kids outside while they went into the office where the murder board was set up.

They all gathered around and looked at it. Betty's name was pinned in the middle of the board. The other suspects' names were taped around Betty's name, forming a circle. Ralph the mechanic, Mike at the bookstore, Carla at the grocery, Howard and Riley, Laurel Cunningham, Susan from the book club, and Francine all had strings attacked from Betty's name tags in the middle. It looked like a giant spider.

Mickey spoke up, "I think, for now, Howard and Riley can be disconnected and moved to the bottom of the board. Unless they're lying to us, they seemed to benefit from being fired by Betty. I don't think they did it."

They nodded their heads, and Darcy began moving the pictures down across the bottom of the board.

James pointed to Ralph's name and said, "I don't know about Ralph. He didn't seem to hold anything against Betty. People date and break up all the time. I don't know that he had any reason or motive to kill her or even wanting her dead."

Darcy asked, "Why's Francine Braydon's name on the board? She didn't have anything to do with Betty."

Mickey said, "I put her name there because she was at Betty's funeral, and when we went out the other night, she called Betty a slut. I don't know why she said it, but we leave her name there until I find out what Francine meant."

"Sounds reasonable to me," said James.

"Moving on," said Mickey. "We can take Laurel Cunningham's name and move it down to the bottom, but Susan, we can connect to Mike and Betty."

"Pop, have you heard anything about the DNA test on the fetus?" asked Mickey.

"Yes. The coroner got the test results, but it doesn't match anyone they have in the database. Even if they did find a match, it wouldn't be conclusive that the father is the one that killed her. It doesn't give a motive unless she tried to hold it over the father's head to give her some financial support," Daniel said.

"So, what do we know at this point?" Mickey asked the group.

"Nothing that points to the possible killer," James said. "All we have is possible motives and not particularly strong ones."

"Dee, we need more information about timelines. We know that Betty was five weeks pregnant. We need to know everyone's whereabouts at that time."

"That could be impossible to find out," said Darcy. "Do you know where you were at that time? I can't tell you where I was at that time. She was killed about two months ago, and she was five weeks pregnant, so that puts the conception timeline over three months ago."

"I'll see what I can do, but that eliminates all the women," Darcy added.

"Not really. If there was a jealous girlfriend or wife, that would be a motive to kill Betty," said Daniel. "Women can be vicious people."

"Yes, Dad, if James ever slept with another woman, I'd kill him and her!" she laughed.

"Don't worry, Dee. That's one problem you'll never have to worry about," said James.

"I better not!" said Darcy.

"Guess that's all we can settle now," said Mickey. "What about the reporter, Carter Evans? Pop, did you call the lawyer?"

"I put in a call to our attorney, but he hasn't returned it yet. I told the receptionist that he needed to call back.

"I got a call from Detective Reynolds. Mickey, you and James need to talk to him and smooth his ruffled feathers.

"I got a call from Mrs. Claybourne from New York. Mickey, if you remember, she was the woman that represented The Great Northern

Investment Group. She attended the last meeting we had just before starting construction. She was concerned about our dead body problem."

"Yes, Pop, I remember her. She asked a lot of questions. She was a very intelligent woman. She kept me on my toes in that meeting." Mickey stated. "She suggested a graduated investment schedule. A version of 'pay as we build.'"

"Yes. She's concerned that if we get enough bad press, it'll affect the property values, and they'll suspend their investment buy-in payments. That could give us a cash flow problem. We don't need that right now," Daniel said seriously.

"What can we do about that, Pop?"

"I need to get with the lawyer to see if we can get Carter Evans to stop the stories until he gets better information and stop this slander campaign, he's launched against us. Then I can arrange for a meeting and assure Mrs. Claybourne that it's lies and inuendoes."

"Pop, I hate to back out, but you can deal with that easier than I can. I don't have enough experience to handle that kind of problem."

"Yes, Mickey. I'll handle it. I was hoping that the police would solve it and we could get back to the construction. Before it gets worse, I think you and James need to step it up and work with Pete."

"Anything else?" asked Mickey.

Everyone shook their head.

"Fine, everyone, let's get on with business," said Mickey as everyone got up to leave. "James, why don't we go and talk with Detective Reynolds. Maybe we can come to an understanding."

They called the police station and talked with Detective Reynolds. He agreed to meet with them. He had given the front desk sergeant permission to let them come back to his desk after signing the visitor's log.

When they walked into his office, he was on the phone. He motioned for them to sit down. He hung up the phone and said, "Well, boys, what brings you here?"

"First, we want to apologize for being disrespectful to you at the grocery store the other day."

"If Daniel and I didn't have some ties a few years back, then maybe I wouldn't be so understanding. I know your family and Dan didn't raise you like that," he said, leaning back in his chair.

"Look, Detective, we want to work with you, not against you. We don't want to get in your way," Mickey said apologetically.

"I know. I'll forget it this time. Now, what's on your mind? I know you didn't come all the way here to apologize. You want something. What is it?"

"We want to work with you," said James.

"No," Detective Reynolds said.

"My family has a stake in this case," said Mickey.

"No. It's a job for the police. Not you, Mickey Ray."

"Have you read the paper or seen the news the past few days?" James asked.

Reynolds looked at James for a few moments, then answered. "I'm not an idiot, nor am I uninformed. Yes, I have read the paper. I know what the reporter is trying to do, and by gosh, he's doing a great job of turning the town against your company and the police. He's making all of us look bad. He's made us look like we're conspiring with you to cover up a murder."

"So, you understand why Mickey and I need to find Betty's killer. Darcy is my wife, so I am part of their family too. No one slanders my name or my family." James' voice rose as he talked.

Mickey reached over and placed his hand on James' arm to calm him down. "James, Detective Reynolds is on our side."

"It doesn't sound like it. He probably believes that we did have something to do with Betty's murder."

"Mickey's right, James. Calm down. I've known Daniel since both of you were kids in elementary school. I know he's straight as an arrow. But Carter Evans is stirring the pot, and none of us want to give him any false leads."

Mickey spoke up. "How about this? We'll share information with you. We'll call you each day with an update. I know that you can't share information with us. Technically you can't share, but if you can steer us in the right direction, that would help."

"I can't do that. That'd be sharing information. That could get me fired. And if Carter Evans saw us together even if we weren't sharing info, he would assume that we are and make it look like a conspiracy."

"Correct, but we'll call you. No in-person visits from here on out. If we interview a person, we'll let you know and tell you what we found. If we're onto something, you can tell us to look into it further or tell us that we're barking up the wrong tree. You have to admit, we can get into places that you can't. At least for now. Who knows, everyone might shut up when and if they believe that reporter."

"I'll run it by the captain. Now, what are you willing to tell me now, as an offering of good faith."

Mickey leaned back in the chair and started talking. "Okay, first of all, we've interviewed Carla, the store manager where Betty worked, so you know about her. Wallace Cunningham's wife, Laurel. She gave us a lead to the Bridgeton Benevolent Book Club and..."

"The what?" Reynolds interrupted.

"The Bridgeton Benevolent Book Club. We got some leads there and..."

"How did some book club get into this?" he interrupted again.

"Respectfully, Detective, will you let me explain?" said Mickey, slightly exasperated.

"Go on," Reynolds said.

Mickey spent the next half an hour telling them everything they had found out. And Peter Reynolds sat quietly making notes.

When Mickey finished, Reynolds raised an eyebrow in surprise. "The two of you have covered a lot of ground in a short time. I must admit, you got significantly more than we did, and if you repeat that, I'll deny it.

"Yes, we did interview Howard and Riley that Betty fired. We also interviewed Mike Reece and Ralph, the mechanic. But we haven't talked with anyone from this book club you mentioned. I'll see if the captain will go along with you helping us, off the books and under the table. If it gets out, we'll all be in trouble."

"Thanks, Detective. We won't let you down. I can add that sometimes we may need a bit of information, so we don't go off chasing rabbits," Mickey said as he rose and extended his hand to Reynold's.

James did the same, and Mickey and James walked out of the police station in a triumphant mood.

Mickey called his father to get an update on his meeting with the lawyer. "Pop, what did the attorney say?" he asked when Daniel answered the phone.

"He wasn't promising. He said that as long as he didn't make any real accusations or point specifics, there wasn't a lot we could do. He will talk with a judge and try to get a gag order until the investigation is complete, but he wasn't too positive.

"I talked to Mrs. Claybourne in New York. She's going to be trouble. She's already sending out written warnings to some of her clients to stop further investments in our project until the investigation is concluded and our company is cleared of any involvement or wrongdoing."

"How is that going to affect the construction schedule?" Mickey asked, getting concerned.

"We have enough available funds to last another month, and if it isn't closed out by then, we'll have to shut down. After sixty days, the banks can call the loans, and we'll be out of business. We'll be insolvent in 90 days. Mickey, this is getting bad quick."

"Thanks, Pop, I'll talk to you later."

"It's bad, isn't it Mickey?" asked James.

"Yes, it is, James. I've got a screaming headache. Take me back to the house, so I can go home and lie down, please."

"Don't you have a date with Francine tonight?"

"Yeah, but I may call and cancel," he said, leaning against the headrest with his eyes closed.

CHAPTER 12

Another Date with Francine
at the Symphony

Mickey took some pills to soften his headache. Just because some out-of-town butthead wants to get a better job, he is financially trying to destroy his family. Why does someone do that! He couldn't understand it. Evil, pure evil. That's the only reason for it. As the pills took effect, he finally drifted off into a fitful sleep.

After a couple of hours, he bolted awake. Looking at the clock, he saw that it was too late to cancel his date with Francine. He didn't want to go, but good etiquette and general manners require that he go. He dragged himself off that bed, showered, and dressed for the concert.

Mickey drove to the ex-mayor's house to pick up Francine. As they rode to the restaurant, he reached over and took her hand in his.

He glanced over at her and smiled. "You look ravishing this evening, Francine."

"So do you, Mickey Ray," she answered back. "What have you been working on today at the jobsite?"

"Nothing that would interest you. A lot of boring construction stuff."

"Are you still trying to find Betty's killer? I mean, how do you go about doing something like that?" she asked.

"James and I are working on it, but we haven't found out anything positive yet."

"Well, tell me what you did find out?"

"We talked to some of her friends to retrace her activities two months ago. That'll tell us a lot about what or who she was involved with."

"What do you mean, who she was involved with?"

"You've seen movies where they take someone down to the station and ask them: 'Where were you on the night of the 15ᵗʰ of May?' Questions like that. By the way, where were you, on the second week of the month before last?"

"Oh, yes, you ask questions like they do in the movies."

"Yes, and where were you?"

"Are you serious? Are you asking me seriously?"

"Sure, why not? You can answer me, can't you?" Mickey said.

"I can't believe you just asked me that, Mickey Ray Christianson!" she said as she pulled her hand from his and turned to look out the window.

"Don't take it so seriously, Fran. I'm asking everyone the same question. You know, leaving no stone unturned. Don't take offense to it. Come on now, let's enjoy our dinner and evening at the Symphony. You'll have to forgive me. I've had a headache most of the day. I'm in a foul mood this evening."

She huffed and continued to look away from him out the window. "Come on, don't be mad. You're too pretty to be mad," he said.

She turned back and looked at his profile as he drove. She smiled at him and again reached over and took his hand in hers. "Why are you in a foul mood, Mickey Ray?"

"As I said, I'm sure it would be boring for you. After the day I've had, I came home, laid down on my bed, and fell asleep with a headache. If I hadn't slept so late, I would have called and canceled our date tonight."

"Why would you do that? What happened? Please tell me," she pleaded.

"Do you read the newspaper?" he asked looking straight ahead at the road.

"Very rarely. I mostly get my news from the television. I did see that they reported you found a dead body on your property. That's about all I saw. Is that what's bothering you?"

"It is much worse than that." As he drove, he told her all about the reporter and the story he wrote in the daily newspaper.

"Oh, no, Mickey! That's horrible, but you'll get past it. I know you didn't have anything to do with her murder."

"Thank you for believing me and not that slime ball," he said softly.

"You're right. Let's just forget the world and focus on each other tonight," she said, reaching over and wrapping her arm around his.

They ate and laughed at each other's silly jokes at the restaurant, and Mickey hadn't had such an enjoyable evening in months. He thought that all the rumors about this young lady couldn't be true. She was so attractive and could be so funny and warm. He was beginning to like her.

As they talked, he told her about the people they had interviewed and their conclusions about each one. After a wonderful dinner, they went to the Symphony.

Their seats were in the sixth row, in the center. They could see and hear everything. The concert was titled "An Evening with Chopin."

Francine had feigned attention during the first half. After the intermission, they were seated again. Francine took his hand and moved it to her lap. After a few moments, she leaned against his shoulder and drifted off to sleep as the pianist played Chopin's greatest music. Her hair draped onto his shoulder, and the fragrance of her hair mixed with the delicate scent of her perfume intoxicated him. He tried not to move so as not to disturb her. He gently shook her at the end of the final number as the audience rose to their feet with applause. She groggily arose and joined in the clapping of hands, not fully aware of what had happened. She quickly shook her head and looked sheepishly at Mickey.

He smiled down at her and said, "It was a wonderful performance. I'm sorry you missed it." He turned and kissed her gently on the cheek. "Let's get you home. It's almost ten o'clock."

"No, Mickey. I don't want to go home yet. Please, let's go out for coffee and dessert," she pleaded.

"How could I resist? There's a little coffee shop right down the road. We can detour by there on the way home."

They walked out of the concert hall into the crisp outside air, Francine hanging onto Mickey's arm. He gave his ticket to the Valet, and they patiently waited for the Valet to bring them the Rolls.

As they found seats at a table at the coffee house, Mickey ordered two coffees and one large dessert to share.

"Oh, Mickey. I'm so embarrassed that I fell asleep. I guess I'm more tired than I realized."

"Let's face it, Fran. You don't like classical music, do you?"

"It's okay, but not my favorite."

He grinned and said, "I asked you, thinking that you might be impressed with my refined taste."

"You don't need to impress me, Mickey."

"I should be pleased that you would come with me. I enjoyed the concert, but the best part was being there with you," he said, looking into her eyes searching them for approval of his efforts. "I took piano lessons as a kid and was good enough to play some of his music."

"Really?"

"Yes. I haven't touched a piano in years, and if I tried to play now, I'd butcher Chopin's works of musical art, but it was a wonderful concert. Thank you for coming with me. Next time, I'll pick a different venue. Deal?" asked Mickey.

"Deal. That sounds great. I guess that means we'll have at least one more date."

"I guess it does. By the way, I'm serious. You look beautiful in the dress. Did you buy that dress just for the concert?"

"What? This old thing?" she said, laughing. "No, but I will say that I have only worn it once, so it's good as new. Do you like it?"

"On you, anything you wear would look good, Fran," he answered. "Would you answer one thing for me?"

She leaned in and placed her elbow on the table, and rested her chin on her hand. "Anything you ask, Mickey Ray," she said, batting her eyes at him with a smile.

"Where were you the first week of the month, two months ago?"

She sat bolt upright. "Are you serious, Mickey Ray? After tonight, you still consider me a suspect?" she glared.

"No, of course, I don't. I'm asking everyone that same question to put everyone in place. I don't suspect you of anything. Will you answer me?"

"I will NOT! Take me home."

Mickey smiled again. He then reached over and scooped up a bite of the huge piece of cheesecake in front of them, and moved it to her mouth.

She glared at him for a few moments as he waited with the utensil at her mouth. Finally, she smiled and opened her mouth, and Mickey gently placed the dessert into it. She took a sip of her coffee.

"Did I tell you that Betty was pregnant when she was killed?" he asked.

"No, but I don't want to talk about her anymore."

"Okay. Let's finish this dessert, and I'll take you home. By the way, what's your favorite dessert?" he asked.

"Francis and I both like the same dessert. We both like cherry pie with ice cream on top. What's yours?" she returned the question.

"Banana cream, with heaps of whipped cream. Now that's a dessert for kings!" he laughed.

"Banana cream or pudding?"

"Either one, as long as it has whipped cream on it," he said laughingly.

"No, my luscious man. You don't put whipped cream on banana cream. You put meringue and bake it in the oven. Come to my house someday, and I'll make you a banana cream pie to kill for!"

"Now, you have a deal, Fran. Your house for dessert one day."

"I told you. I like that you call me Fran. I didn't at first, but since you are the only one, that makes a special thing between us. Kind of like a pet name. What shall I call you?"

"I don't know if you could find a pet name for Mickey," he said thoughtfully.

She smiled and leaned into him and whispered, "How about lover boy?"

Mickey blushed, "Maybe someday, but I like my name right now. Mickey's fine."

"Okay, Mickey. Just let me know when you feel comfortable with 'lover.'"

Still feeling uncomfortable and blushing, Mickey backed away slightly, cleared his throat, and changed the subject. "Are you and Francis close."

"As you may know, we are twins, and twins are usually very close. We like a lot of the same things. We like many of the same foods. We like the same kind of music, but classical music is not one of our favorites."

"Twins. I thought that was an old wife's tale about twins liking the same kind of things," he said.

"Nope, it's true. We even go shopping and help each other pick out clothes."

"Now, that's creepy. Francis helps you pick out your clothes?"

"Yes, and I help him pick out his. I can dress him better than his own wife," she laughed. "If you would like to go shopping with me, I would let you pick out some of my clothes, and I'll help you."

"Nope, I'll do my own shopping, thank you very much, and as for you, Francis does a wonderful job of dressing you," he said as he got up from the chair. "I guess I had better get you home before your father calls out the National Guard to rescue you."

She stood, and as they walked out the door, she grabbed his arm. "I think we're going to have a wonderful time together, Mickey Ray."

CHAPTER 13

Back to Reinterviewing
Some Suspects

James came out and told Mickey to come into the house. Darcy had found out some information she wanted to tell him. Going back into the house, Mickey grabbed a cup of coffee and sat down.

Darcy came in and sat across from him. "I was up half the night last night working on this. Once I got going, I couldn't put it down."

"Yeah, I never could figure out how you can work half the night and be up bright and early the following morning. What did you find out?" asked Mickey.

"You asked me to run checks on everyone. I started with Betty. I found some interesting stuff about her."

"And?" Mickey said, leaning forward in his seat.

"Pulled up her bank records. There are some strange deposits there."

"How did you do that? Wait, don't tell me! James knows someone that can hack into back records, right?"

James spoke up, "Yes, and don't ask me any questions about him either."

"I know the drill, James. Anyway, he did it for you?"

"Yes, and Digger told me how to do other useful things, too," Darcy added.

"This guy's name is Digger?" he said as he turned to look at James.

Darcy continued, "It's not his real name, but take a look at these deposits." Darcy showed them print outs of several months of Betty's bank accounts. "Look at these deposits, Mickey."

"I see several deposits of various amounts, but that isn't unusual, is it?"

"Look at these," she said, pointing to two deposits of one hundred dollars a week, another for one hundred and fifty dollars. "There was a single deposit of five thousand dollars and another one for twenty-five thousand. They're all made just a few days apart."

"I don't see it. I mean, I don't understand. What does it mean?" asked Mickey.

James said, "Simple. Blackmail." Then he took another sip of coffee.

"Blackmail? Who blackmails someone for one hundred dollars! Sure, I see the five and twenty-five thousand, but one hundred?" Mickey argued. "And what would she have on them that they would be willing to pay blackmail?"

Darcy said, "I'll look into some of our other suspects, but blackmail is a motive, no matter how little. All things are relative. What's a lot to one person is nothing to another. Go back and talk to Mike at the bookstore. See what he has to say."

"I see. One hundred isn't much, but the total could add up. If she got one hundred dollars from several guys, then it's a nice little sum each month, and tax-free, I might add," said Mickey.

"Now, you're catching on, dear little brother," said Darcy.

James said, "Mike did admit that she told him about being pregnant, and he offered to marry her, but she didn't want it. He might admit to blackmail, but not murder."

Mickey took one final gulp of coffee. "We need to talk to Mike again. And a hundred dollars a week could be a lot to him. He doesn't make a lot of money working at a bookstore. Let's go, James."

"You bet," James said, putting his coffee cup in the kitchen sink and turning toward the door with Mickey in tow.

"Is Pop up yet?" he asked as they walked to the truck and drove to the jobsite.

"Yep. Up and gone already."

"How, he isn't supposed to be driving yet," said Mickey.

"I know, but Sam's been coming by and driving your dad to and from the construction site. Since you promoted Sam to foreman, he's arriving at the maintenance office early every day," James said.

"Sam's Pop's most senior employee. He's been a gem for many years."

They walked around looking for Daniel at the site. Mickey got out of the truck and walked up to Daniel talking with the plumbing foreman.

"Sure, I can do that, but then it'll sit for a while until it gets inspected, and then they pour the footings in the trenches, Dan," Raymond, the plumbing foreman, was saying.

"Good morning, Raymond," said Mickey as he walked up to the two men.

"Good morning, Mickey Ray. Your Dad and I were talking about the sewer lines. I think it's a bit early to sink them. If it rains too soon, they might get covered with mud before the inspectors see them. The inspector is a real stickler. If one grain of dirt gets on the pipes, he'll fail it."

"He can do that?" Mickey asked.

"Inspectors can do anything they want."

"Is that even legal?"

"Technically, no, but the code says every inch must be inspected, and if the inspector can't see a section of the line, then he doesn't have to pass it," Raymond explained.

"What do you do about situations like that?"

Ray rubbed his fingers together in the universal sign of "money".

"Isn't that illegal? I mean, that's a bribe."

"If what he's failing it for is in the code book, then it doesn't matter. What're you going to do? He can always be busy at another site, or he can't get to it for several days and hold up construction. Sometimes you don't have a choice."

Raymond continued, "Discretion, my friend. Discretion. Take him to lunch while you're there. Show him some plans to make it a business lunch. Give him a fifth of his favorite drink. Small stuff, but NEVER offer cash. Suddenly he finds time to make an inspection when you want it. Never ask them to pass something that's not correct. Then it'll come back to bite you. Sometimes you have to grease a few palms with small favors, but not cash to speed up the process."

Daniel was standing listening to Raymond give Mickey a lesson in construction politics. He spoke up as Raymond's lesson ended. "Ray's right, son. Don't ever try to get something passed that's not to code. It's not right or legal, but a few discreet favors for an inspector can speed things up."

"Sounds like bribery to me," Mickey said.

"It is, but it isn't. Consider it a bonus to the inspector to get at the top of their list, that's all," said Daniel. "It's part of doing business."

"I don't like it. Other than that, how's everything going?"

Raymond spoke up, "I've been watching the news, and reading the newspaper, Dan. I don't believe it at all but there are rumors that you may not be able to make your payments on time. I've got supply bills coming in, and payroll. I hope they're just rumors and no truth to them."

Daniel looked him straight in the eye. "Ray, we've done a lot of building together. Have I ever missed a payment to you?"

"No, Dan, but you've never taken on a job this big. All I know is what I hear. Some newspaper guy has been coming around the site asking questions. He talks, you know. He seems to know a lot about your business. He says that you are in financial trouble. That's all."

"I'll let you know if I can't make a payment. You have my word on that. I won't ask you to work if I don't have the money. Now, let's get this pipe in the ground and inspected."

Daniel and Mickey walked away. "Pop, things are getting worse, aren't they?"

"Yes, they are. We have enough money in the accounts for two more weeks, then we shut down work. I got here this morning and there was a message on the phone to call Claybourne when her office opens. I'm guessing her clients will be ceasing the scheduled payments."

"We need to put more security to keep that reporter away," Mickey said. "One of the new hires said he wanted to work in new construction. Maybe we could give him a security badge and a uniform. Let him wander around the site to keep unauthorized people off-site."

"I'll talk to him about it as soon as he comes in this morning."

"Great," said Mickey. "James and I'll be doing more research on the body we found. Is that okay, Pop?"

"Sure, Mickey. I've got it all under control. Hopefully, we'll have these lines inspected by the end of the week, and we can pour the footings."

"Thanks, Pop."

When Mickey got back into the truck, James, who had been waiting, asked, "How are things going with the construction?"

"Things are going pretty good so far. I learned a couple of things. To get things done, even in this business, you have to bribe people. Not in money but in small favors. It isn't right," Mickey said.

James sat as Mickey drove. "I know, bro, but sometimes you gotta go along to get along in any business."

"That guy you saw us talking to was the plumbing foreman, and he's heard the rumors that we might have to shut down work. It's getting worse, James."

When they got to the bookstore downtown, it wasn't open yet, so they sat in the truck waiting for Mike Reece to arrive.

"What did you think of going to church with the family, James?"

"It was okay. I still don't get it yet, but it was okay."

"What don't you get?"

"God! I don't understand God!"

"First, I have to say, no one understands God. You just believe and trust. That's all," said Mickey.

"That's what I don't understand. Even when I believed in him as a kid, I didn't understand. Why does he let crap like this happen to good people?"

"That's a question that's been asked since the beginning of the world. That's where the faith, or as you might say, trust, comes into the picture," said Mickey. "We don't understand God, but we trust that He knows what He's doing."

"Yeah…Hey, here comes our friend, Mr. Reece," said James.

Mike rolled his eyes as they walked up to him and opened the door to the store.

"I thought I was done with the two of you," he said as he allowed the door to close behind them. "You sicked the police on me, didn't you? I told him that you assaulted me."

James ignored his comment about the assault.

"We have a couple more questions to ask, then we'll be on our way, Mike," said James, following Mike as he turned on lights, fired up the registers, and booted up the computer system.

"Let's get this over with. I have a lot of work to do," he said standing behind the cash wrap counter.

Mickey stepped up to the counter, "How much were you sending to Betty to help her with your baby?"

"I don't even know if it was my baby. And even if it was, I told you, I offered to marry her, and she wouldn't let me. I did think about it and sent her some money hoping she'd consider marrying me, but that didn't work."

"How much did you send her?"

"Two thousand dollars. That's all I had. I sent her a hundred dollars a week after that until she quit cashing the checks, then I quit."

"When did she quit cashing the checks?" asked James.

"About two months ago. She didn't send them back. She just quit cashing them. I thought maybe she decided that someone else was the father, and he was giving her money."

"You may be right, but we'll check it out. Do you know who else she was dating?"

"No. Are we done here?"

"One last question. If you weren't sure you were the father, why did you send her money? No one does that without a reason," said Mickey.

Mike stood and stared at space for a few moments, "I don't know. I never had a real family growing up. Having a brother or sister and loving parents was kind of a dream of mine. I guess in a strange sort of way, I thought that Betty and I could have that kind of family. As I said, it was a dream. Now, looking back, it was a crazy dream. A dream that if we had gotten married and if the child was mine, we wouldn't have been happy. It's best it happened this way."

"You mean it was best she ended up killed?" James said.

"No, not that. I mean that we didn't get married. I probably would have been a horrible father. I'm sorry she's dead, but I didn't do it. Now can I go to work?"

"Yes, we have all we need. But, Mike, you are one strange man," said James shaking his head.

"And you can bite me, freaky man," he said from behind the counter. James started to move toward the counter but Mickey caught his arm.

"He's not worth an assault charge against you, James. Let's leave before someone ends up in jail."

Mickey turned to Mike. "Thanks for your help."

"Yeah, right," he said, turning from them back to the register to make sure it had booted up.

As they walked out of the store and back to Mickey's truck, Mickey said, "James, you've got to watch that temper."

"I know, but I don't like that guy. I kind of hope he did it so I can be here when he's arrested."

"We need to go back and talk to Ralph. Call Dee and see if she can find the two thousand dollars that Mike said he gave to Betty. The more we investigate, the more we see that the nice, sweet Betty we knew in high school changed a lot more these past few years," said Mickey.

"Yes, but who is the same person they were in high school, or even ten years from now?" answered James. "How was your date with Francine last night, lover boy?"

Mickey shivered when James said that. "Don't call me lover boy, James!"

"Whoa, I hit a nerve that time. What happened last night?"

"Nothing, just don't call me that. It makes me feel creepy when you say it like that. Nothing like that happened. That's all."

"Okay. I won't say that again. How did it go?"

"It went well. We went to a classical concert. I suggested it thinking that her father would have raised her a bit more refined. I loved it, but her, not so much. She fell asleep during the concert, but still, we had a good time. I like her," said Mickey.

"Watch yourself, Mickey. You know the rumors!"

"I know them, and there may be some truth in them, but you know rumors are just that until they're proven."

"I hope you enjoy yourself in the meantime."

"I plan to, James. Here we are at the garage. Want me to go with you or wait here in the truck?" asked Mickey.

"We're a team. We work together."

James pointed out Ralph, the mechanic when they got into the garage. "Hey, Ralph. How are you today?" started James.

"Great, and you?" he answered as he wiped the grease from his hands and put one out to shake James' hand.

James took it and, with the other, pointed to Mickey. "Remember the friend I told you has the Rolls Royce?"

Ralph nodded his head.

"I brought him with me to introduce you to him. Maybe sometime you can help him out."

"Glad to meet you, Ralph," Mickey said as he also shook Ralph's hand. They talked cars for a few minutes, then Mickey asked him about Betty. "Did Betty tell you she was pregnant?"

"Yes, she did, and she even asked me for money to help support it when it was born."

"Did she tell you it was yours?" asked Mickey.

"Yes, but I told her I knew it wasn't mine because I was always careful when we were together. I used protection. Always. Just so something like that wouldn't happen."

"What did she say when you denied it?"

"She got pretty mad about it and claimed that something like an accident had happened and insisted that I was the father. I humored her to get her out of my way. I sent her a few checks for a hundred and fifty dollars, but then I quit. She cashed the first two but not the last one. I don't know why. Well, I know why now. When James came by here and told me she was dead, that was about the last time she cashed a check."

James asked, "Why didn't you tell me when I was here last time?"

Ralph thought for a few moments, then answered, "I had my reasons."

"Okay, what were they?" asked Mickey

"It wasn't any of your business. I didn't kill her, and if I told you she tried to get money from me, that would look like a motive for murder."

"Yep, you pretty much summed it up correctly," said Mickey.

"Am I a suspect?"

"Now, you are. It would have looked much better for you if you had told me when I was here the first time," said James.

"You said you aren't the police. Are you going to call them now?" he asked.

"Correct. We won't do that unless we can prove you did kill her. Until then, we'll keep it between us. We can't guarantee the police won't find out the same thing and still show up here one day."

"I know. I've got a good job here. I don't want to spoil it with accusations that I killed someone."

Mickey and James turned to walk away when Mickey stopped. "Hey, Ralph, if you knew you weren't the father, why did you send her money?"

"Insurance. I didn't want her to tell people that I was the father. Also, I liked her, and I wanted to help her out. I planned to send her money until the child was born. Then I'd help her get onto some social programs. And I wouldn't support her anymore. I don't mind helping someone, but I'm not going to support someone else's kid for eighteen years."

"Good answer. I'm not sure I believe it, but it is a good answer." Mickey turned, and he and James continued to the truck.

When they got into the truck, Mickey told James to call Dee and tell her what they had found out from Mike and Ralph.

As James picked up Mickey's phone lying on the seat, he said to Mickey, "We spend more time on the phone in this truck than we do anywhere."

"Yep, but if you watch television, some shows they get in an elevator, stop it between floors, and talk. Even superman used a phone booth to change clothes. We use our vehicles to make calls. It is like our mobile conference room!"

James laughed and punched in Darcy's number. When she picked up, James told her what Mike and Ralph had told them. She said she would check their bank accounts also. While James was talking to Darcy, Mickey's other line buzzed through. James hung up and transferred to the other line.

"Caller ID says it's F. Braydon…who do you think that is?" he said smiling.

Mickey reached and grabbed the phone from James and answered, "Hello?"

James heard a female voice emanating from the phone as Mickey held it to his ear.

"Mickey, hello. I couldn't wait for you to call me. So, I reached out to you. When are you going to plan our next date?" she asked.

"I meant to call you. How about tomorrow? I have something very special for us to do," he said and looked over at James.

James grinned and smiled back at him and gave him a thumbs-up signal. "It's nothing fancy, but it should be a lot of fun. What time can you be ready to go?"

"You tell me what time, and I'll be ready for you."

"How about ten in the morning. Do you have a pair of jeans and boots?"

"Jeans, yes. Boots, no. Do you mean like cowboy boots or work-type boots? You aren't going to take me to a construction site?" she asked, laughing.

"That can be arranged too if that's what you'd like," Mickey said.

"You better not take me to a construction site. All that mess and dirt and nasty stuff. That's not my kind of fun," she added.

"Ha! Ha! Gotcha! No, it isn't that, but I guarantee you a good time. I'll be by in the morning to pick you up at ten sharp," he said and waited for her reply.

"I'll be waiting for you, Mickey Ray," she said and disconnected before he could say goodbye.

James looked smug as he said to Mickey, "I guess we're not going to be working on this tomorrow since you'll be out with Miss Braydon!"

"You got that right, James."

"What do you have planned for tomorrow with her?"

"I don't know. What would you suggest?"

James shook his head, "Hey, bro, that's not my problem, but whatever it is, you don't need to dress up for it."

"That popped out. I had forgotten all about her. We've been so busy interviewing Mike and Ralph. I've got to think of something."

"How about a picnic in the woods. You can take my ATV in the garage and ride out around the property of the main house. Take her to the lake at the back section of the property and have a picnic. It's nice, private, and a bit romantic to sit and talk by the lake. Do you have any fishing rods?" James asked.

"No."

"I do. They're also in the garage. You can drop a line in the lake. I bought a couple of bamboo poles to take the kids fishing there. There aren't many fish, and they're small, but maybe you can catch a few. It might be fun. She might find it's fun. Then again, maybe just being with you, she'll have a good time."

"Sounds better than anything I could come up with. Will you help me get the stuff ready for the morning?"

"Sure, now let's go see Mr. Wallace Cunningham," said James. "We should probably go to his office since we talked to his wife, and she gave us nothing."

"Mr. Cunningham, here we come, ready or not," said Mickey, as he turned and headed toward Wallace's office.

When they walked into Cunningham's office, they saw a secretary sitting at a desk talking on the phone.

"Would you tell Mr. Cunningham that Mickey Ray Christianson is here to see him, please?"

"Do you have an appointment, Mr. Christianson?" she asked as she reached for the intercom.

"No, we don't, but we need to see him. Please let him know we're here," said Mickey.

She picked up the phone and said into it, "Mr. Cunningham, a Mr. Christianson, and Mr......Oh, I'll bring them right in." Then she placed the phone back on the receiver.

She began to rise, and Mickey said to her, "Thank you, miss, but I know his office. We can go on back."

They knocked on Wallace's office and heard a voice say, "Come in."

He was sitting behind a desk loaded with papers, a computer screen in front of him, holding a pencil. He looked up from his work and began to stand until Mickey held his hand in a stop motion.

"Don't bother to get up, Mr. Cunningham. We won't be here long. This is my partner, James, and I'm sure you remember me," said Mickey.

"Why, yes. Of course, I remember you. We're selling stock in your project by the blocks. People really want to be a part of your business," he said, sitting back down.

"Great to hear that. May we sit down?" Mickey asked.

"Of course, have a seat, both of you," he said, moving the monitor aside so he could see them while sitting in his chair. "How can I help you?"

"We're investigating the death of Betty Duncan, and we hoped maybe you could tell us about her?" said Mickey.

"My wife told me you came by to talk to her the other day. Why do you need to talk to me?"

"We're talking to everyone who had contact with her," said James.

"I don't know what you mean. I didn't know her very well. She was my wife's friend. Not mine. I didn't even know Betty was dead until you told Laurel, and she told me. How did Betty die? I can't tell you much. I only met her a couple of times." He kept rambling so quickly that James and Mickey knew he was in deeper than they both suspected.

"Hold it. Slow down a bit. We haven't asked you anything, nor are we accusing you of anything. We just want to ask you a few questions. That's all, then we'll be on our way," Mickey said as he glanced over at James with a questioning look.

"Let's start at the beginning," said James.

"Okay, I didn't know her very well and…"

"Stop talking, please," James spoke firmly and sat back in the chair.

Wallace Cunningham stopped and looked alternately at James, then back to Mickey.

After a few moments of silence, James started again. "Let us ask the questions, and you give us simple answers. Okay?"

He nodded his head.

James continued, "If we don't understand, we'll ask you for an explanation. Got it?"

He gave another nod.

"Did you know Betty Duncan personally?" James started again.

"No," he said, looking down at the desk.

"Wallace, tell me the truth. Did you know Betty Duncan?"

"Are you a policeman?" He looked up at Mickey. "Is he a policeman, and do I need a lawyer?"

Mickey shrugged his shoulders. "No, he isn't a policeman. As I said when we came in, we're investigating Betty Duncan's death. She was murdered about two months ago, and we're questioning everyone that may have known her. Do you need a lawyer? I don't know. Do you?"

"Do I have to answer your questions without a lawyer?"

James spoke again, "Wallace, you don't have to answer our questions even if a lawyer's present. You don't have anything to hide if you didn't kill her, and talking to us won't hurt you. Did you kill her?"

"No, I didn't kill her. I didn't even know she was dead until Mickey said it when you came in here."

"You said that Laurel told you," commented James.

"Yeah, okay. I did know her but knowing her isn't a crime," said Wallace.

"You're correct. Knowing her isn't a crime. We told you we're investigating her death. We already know quite a bit about her past, but we want verification from you. We haven't found anything detrimental about you. Now, will you talk to us?" asked Mickey.

"I guess so, but I didn't kill her. You have to believe me."

James cut in, "No, we don't have to believe you. At least not yet. Maybe if you tell us more, we'll be more inclined to accept your word. We'll tell you this. We went to high school with her, and so did your wife, Laurel."

"We've found out that, like many people, they change when they graduate and move on with life. Betty was a sweet girl in school, but after school, she changed. When she died, she wasn't the sweet, innocent girl in school. She blackmailed some people. What do you know about this?"

"How did you find out about that?"

"Find out about what?"

"That she was blackmailing me."

"We didn't say that. I said that she was blackmailing SOME people. You said she was blackmailing you. Now we know, would you mind telling us why?"

"I don't have to tell you anything. I want you to leave my office now!"

"No. We won't leave until you answer all our questions," James added.

"I'll call the police and tell them you're harassing me and accusing me of murder," Wallace said.

"Go ahead. Call them. The police are looking for Betty's murderer also. We'll tell them about Betty blackmailing you. That's a pretty compelling motive for murder," said James calmly.

"I didn't kill her, I tell you! I didn't do it!" he said, raising his voice.

"Keep your voice down. You don't want everyone in the office to know, do you?" Mickey said.

He calmed down and said quietly, "No, I don't."

"We'll tell you why she was pressing you for money. She was pregnant, and she told you it was your child, didn't she?" asked James.

"Well," he hesitated.

"Go on. You might as well tell us. We already know, so don't deny it now," said Mickey.

"I don't feel comfortable talking about this with either of you. It's personal."

"We understand," commented Mickey, "but you can talk to us in the privacy of your office, or in the police station downtown. We don't care where it is."

"You said you aren't the police."

"We aren't, but if we think that you killed Betty, we'll call the police ourselves, and they'll come here and take you downtown for questioning."

"But you said that you won't tell the police."

"No, we didn't say that, but we won't call them if you talk to us. We aren't here to get you in trouble with the police or your wife if you didn't kill Betty Duncan. If you did, yes, we'll call them. Now, do you want to talk to us or the police?" asked James.

"You'll keep quiet?"

"Of course. If you're innocent, we have no reason to notify anyone else," said James.

"Betty told me that the baby was mine, but we only slept together one time. It was when Laurel went to visit her mother for a month. Betty called, and we talked on the phone, then met at a restaurant. We went out to dinner a couple of times, and once, just once, I took her to a motel. A few days later, Laurel came back home, and we never saw each other again."

"Can you give us the dates when you and Betty had this affair?" asked James as he continued to take notes on a small notebook he took from his pocket.

Cunningham thought for a couple of minutes and opened his calendar on his desk. "Let's see, it was the month before last, from this Tuesday to the end of the month. We spent the night at the hotel on route 60. It was the Maple Tree Inn. On the 16th of the month. Laurel left that Tuesday and got back on this Friday," he said, moving his finger across the calendar.

"So, you see, it was only for a few weeks, and we never went out again. I didn't even hear from her until she called and told me she was pregnant and said the baby was mine.

"She threatened to tell Laurel if I didn't give her five thousand dollars. I couldn't take it out of savings because Laurel would know and confront me. I went to another town, took out a loan, and gave it to Betty. I never heard from her again. I swear. I didn't kill her."

Mickey leaned forward in his chair and looked straight into Wallace Cunningham's eyes. "I can't say whether we believe you or not. But you do have a compelling motive for murder. We'll do this. We're going to continue trying to find Betty's killer. If we find out it is you, we'll report everything we know to the police, and of course, your wife will find out. If we conclude that you aren't Betty's killer, then your secret is safe with us. What you told us stays in this office. Deal?"

"Yes, I'll agree to that. Please don't tell Laurel. It was only one time, and I have regretted it ever since it happened."

James and Mickey got up to leave. As he reached for the doorknob, Mickey said, "The police are looking for her killer also, so they may come to you with questions, but they won't find out from us."

"Thank you so much, Mr. Christianson. Thank you so much. I didn't do it!"

When they got to the truck, there was a note under the windshield, and Mickey took it out and unfolded it.

The note was printed in large bold print:

She deserved to die. Do NOT pursue.

They looked at each other and got in the truck.

"What do we do, Mickey?" James asked.

"Have we ever backed down from a fight?"

"No."

"And we aren't going to start now! Damn the torpedoes, full speed ahead!" Mickey said, starting the truck.

As Mickey drove, they talked and agreed that Wallace Cunningham was innocent or he also gave an Oscar-winning performance. Neither thought he was guilty, but as they promised, they would keep him on the suspect list until they found the real killer or until they proved he was innocent.

"What do you say? We go home and get things ready for your fishing date tomorrow. After we finish, we can have a murder board meeting. I suggest we not tell Dee or your father about this note."

"What note?" Mickey said.

"Good answer, Mickey Ray," said James as he turned on the radio. "We need some good country music."

"Why not some good oldies rock?"

"Because you're driving, and I'm controlling the radio. Shut up and drive!"

They got James' ATV out at the main house, started it, and took a couple of trips around the backfield to check it out. James rummaged around and picked out a couple of small fishing rods and a shovel to dig for bait. He also found a wicker basket so Dee could fix a picnic lunch for Mickey and Francine to take on the ride.

"Your dad said he used to stock your lake so you could fish in it when you were little. Do you think there are any fish still in it?" James asked.

"I don't know, but we'll try our luck tomorrow morning. Let's go inside and talk murder!"

As they were walking in, Daniel walked out. He motioned for them to follow him back outside. "I renewed the truck license plates today. When I was putting the new registration in the glove box, I found this lying on the seat. What's going on now?"

"It's nothing, Pop. Really. A prank, that's all."

"It doesn't look like a prank to me. It's a warning, and I don't like it."

"We'll be careful," said James. "We promise. It's nothing serious."

"You better. James, you have a wife and two kids to live for, and Mickey, you have all of us. Don't do something stupid. And whatever you do, DON'T tell Darcy!"

They made a motion like a child crossing their hearts, "promise." Then made a zipper motion across their mouths.

In the house, the murder board was set up. Daniel, James, and Mickey Ray pulled up chairs as Darcy stood in front of the board.

They went down the list of suspects again.

Mickey spoke first. "We talked to Mike again, and he asked Betty to marry him, but she said no. We don't know why, but it could have been she wanted to keep her options open to reel in as many potential fathers to give her money. If she married Mike Reece, she would only have one source of income or blackmail. He should stay on the list.

"Ralph was out. He took precautions so she wouldn't get pregnant but sent her some money to help her out and keep a good reputation at his job. His motive is minimal at this time."

Darcy said, "I don't buy the reason Ralph gave for giving her money. I don't care who you are, why would you give a person hundreds of dollars for no other reason than to be nice? Especially someone that is sleeping with you and several other guys. That doesn't add up. Ralph has some secret that he isn't telling us about."

"We know that. We just don't know what it is yet," added Mickey.

"Yes, but there was a reason for that, and it doesn't factor in the reasoning in this case. Darcy's right. We should keep him on the list and dig deeper to find out what that secret happens to be before we eliminate him," said James.

Daniel had sat quietly until then. "Who has the most to gain by her keeping quiet, or the most to lose if she spreads the news that person X is the father. Blackmail is different to every person. One hundred dollars may be a lot to one person, and pocket change to another. Remember that one hundred dollars to Betty isn't a lot of money, but pennies make dollars."

"What do you mean, Pop?" asked Mickey.

"I mean, one hundred dollars from one person may not be much but if she got a hundred dollars from several people, that amounts up to a nice sum total each month. She wouldn't get rich for that piddling sum but it could make life easier for her. And we don't know, she could use something like that to increase the payouts at a later date. Criminals, especially blackmailers get a taste, and then they want more. You need to expand the suspect pool. So far, she is small potatoes, but it could have been the start to something bigger if someone hadn't killed her."

"I never thought of that," Mickey said.

James took over from here. "Wallace Cunningham is still up there. He had motive, means, and opportunity to kill her. Betty threatened to tell his wife. And she conned him out of five grand. As with many blackmailers, the first payment is only the beginning. He acted very upset about her death, but he's still number one on my mental list."

"What about Francine, Mickey?" asked Darcy.

"I know she's still up there, and we've been seeing each other, as everyone here knows, but I don't think she did it."

"You like her, and that's why you don't think she did it," said James.

"Yes, I like her. She doesn't have any motive. And the more I'm around her, the more I don't believe all those rumors about her. She's a fun and funny person to be around."

"And quite easy on the eyes," said Daniel.

"Yes, Pop. She's pretty."

"Beautiful, you mean," said James.

Darcy put her hands up and spoke out, "Okay, now that everyone here has had their chance at drooling over Mickey's new girlfriend, do we keep her on the suspect list or take her off?"

Mickey said, "I say take her off. No evidence and no motive."

James chimed in, "Leave her on. We need to keep checking her out just like we're doing to everyone."

Darcy turned to Daniel, "What do you think, Dad?"

"I agree with Mickey. You have nothing on her, but maybe we should keep her on the list until all the dust settles. Darcy, you keep on digging for data on the entire family. What about the other couple that Betty fired? Have you checked them out deeper?"

Darcy spoke up. "No, Dad, I didn't look any further. Mickey and James said they were fine, so I didn't look anymore."

"Take a deeper look at them. Everyone has something to hide. I know you said that they're happy sitting around on unemployment, but check them out anyway," Daniel said.

"I'll do that. Until we find out more information, I'll keep searching. Meeting dismissed."

Mickey got in the truck and went home and crashed. He was excited about his picnic with Francine tomorrow, but there were many unanswered questions about Betty's murder. His mind raced as he tossed and turned. Finally, he drifted off into a fitful sleep.

CHAPTER 14

Fishing at the Family Lake
with Francine

Mickey got up and dressed in his normal work clothes, a flannel shirt, denim jeans, and work boots. He went by the construction office to see Pop and check on progress like he did each morning, but today, despite his restless sleep, there was a spring in his step he hadn't had in months.

He called Detective Reynolds and told him what they had found out.

Reynolds agreed that they should keep in the direction they were going. The detective told him to keep digging into Ralph's past. He couldn't say more about Ralph, but he was high on their suspect list. He warned Mickey to tread softly with him. Reynolds added to question Howard and Riley more. There's more than meets the eye. Maybe they didn't have a motive to kill, but they also had secrets. He did say to keep a low profile because there were things about most of the suspects that were hidden, and he didn't want anyone to be alerted and bolt out of town.

Mickey was seeing a whole new side to Detective Peter Reynolds. And he admitted to himself, it was a good side.

He had a date with Francine. Yes, they had a few dates this past week, but today was different. It was on his terms and his turf. It wasn't going to be around a lot of prominent people with a tuxedo or three-piece suit. It was plain, simple, down-home, relaxing pleasure.

This date was not to impress or to be impressed. He was happy. He still had feelings for Valerie, his old girlfriend, but she had chosen to leave him. She needed to find herself after what had happened. She needed to heal. He still missed Valerie, and his heart ached for her company at times. Valerie was the only girl he had ever dated and loved.

Francine was different. She was vivacious as well as beautiful. To him, she was a breath of fresh air. She was something, no, someone he had never experienced in his life. Yes, there were rumors about Francine, but the more Mickey was around her, the more he knew they were awful rumors of jealous and selfish people.

After checking in at the construction site, he headed for the regular morning breakfast with James at the diner.

He walked to their table. James was already there and sipping his coffee. Pauline had also set a cup filled with coffee in anticipation of his arrival. When he sat down, she came over with her order pad.

"Good morning, Mickey Ray. You're all smiles today," she said. "What can I get for you?"

"I think I'll get my usual, but I'll have a side order of pancakes instead of toast."

She wrote on her pad and turned to James, "And you, dear?"

"The same for me, Pauline," he answered.

"I'll put the order right in, and I'll be back to refill your coffee," she said, walking away.

"I agree with Pauline. You're all smiles this morning. Does it have anything to do with Francine?"

"Yes, it does. I admit, at times, I miss Val very much, but there are times when I just want the company of a woman."

"I understand completely. Until Dee came along, I thought I was going to spend the rest of my life living in that apartment all alone with only the company of a bunch of veterans of a war I never fought in. I thank the Lord daily for Dee," he said.

"Do you? I mean, we talk about it, but do you really thank God for her?"

"Yes. You know my feelings about God, but I make exceptions, and I pray almost daily in thanks for her and those wonderful kids. I know they aren't mine by blood and that their biological father is out there somewhere, but in a way, they're mine. Dee, Joel, and Cyndi are a package deal. I love them like they're my own. We're two lucky men, Mickey Ray Christianson."

"When you look at it that way, you're right," said Mickey thoughtfully.

"Do you think she would let me adopt them?" James asked.

"I don't see why not, but you better ask her, not me."

"I think I'll do that. Hey, are you ready for your picnic today?"

"Yes, I am."

"After you left yesterday, Dee cooked some fried chicken, made some potato salad, and packed an old-fashioned picnic basket for you and Francine. You know, Dee doesn't do a lot of cooking, but she was so happy for you. When you come back to the house, she'll put the food in the basket for you."

"Wow, that girl is looking out for me, isn't she?" Mickey said.

"Hey, what about Ralph? I know what he said, but there's something off about him. Like Darcy said, no one just sends money to someone if they don't need to," James said.

Pauline brought their food and refilled their coffee.

Mickey cocked his head and look at James. "Of course they do. Look what we did last year for Janet and Bobby and what we're doing for Betty's mother!"

"True, but that's different. Helping someone out like we did and sending money to a girl like Betty, just to be nice isn't the same," he said, taking a bite of sausage.

"We should agree to disagree on that point. Maybe Dee can dig a bit deeper into his past and see what turns up."

"That reminds me. We'll pay for Betty's funeral as we promised, but since Betty had extorted so much money from her former lovers, there's money in Betty's bank account. We can help Alice get access to it and stop any more payments we are making to Alice's account and that pre-loaded bank card we gave her. We can help Alice invest the money that's in Betty's bank account, and that'll help her a bit."

"Okay, while you are spending the day with Francine, I'll look into that. I think I'll ask Darcy about adopting Joel and Cyndi while I'm at it," James said.

They finished breakfast and went back to James' house so Mickey could pick up the Rolls to drive to pick up Francine.

When he pulled up to the former mayor's house, several men in the front yard were trimming the bushes and landscaping the yard. Mickey walked to the house and rang the doorbell. Again, Mr. Braydon answered the door and invited Mickey inside.

"Come inside, Mickey Ray," he said with a broad smile. "Francine will be down in a minute. Come on back into my library." He moved toward the library like he did the first time Mickey was here to pick up Francine.

As they entered the library, Mr. Braydon moved to a side table in the corner of the room. "It's too early for a cocktail, but it's always a good time for a good Irish coffee. How about it, Mickey?" he asked, pouring steaming hot coffee into a stemmed coffee mug.

"No, thank you. Remember, I'm driving precious cargo today," Mickey answered.

He threw back his head and gave a short laugh, "Yes, you are! And I might say, Francine, is quite smitten with you. Now, don't you tell her I told you! She'd be very upset with me for divulging that secret. As you know, lawyers are supposed to be a tight-lipped group. Have a seat, son."

"Francine is quite the lady. I like her also," said Mickey as he took a seat and accepted the coffee from Mr. Braydon.

"Don't break her heart now. That would upset me tremendously."

"There's nothing serious at this time. We're just enjoying each other's company. It may or may not be anything more than that."

"Fair enough," Franklin said as he lifted his mug in toast fashion, then lowered it and took a long slow sip. "Dang it, this coffee is hot."

"Good morning, Daddy," said Francine as she made an entrance. "Good morning, Mickey Ray."

Mickey turned and looked at her. She was dressed in tight-fitting jeans, also wearing a flannel shirt. Instead of work boots, she had on cowboy boots. She had on a cowboy hat to match the boots.

Franklin smiled at his daughter and said, "Now, aren't you two a cute matching couple. You look like you're going out to be in a rodeo or something."

Mickey stood up and walked over to Francine, and arched his brows in obvious approval. She leaned over and gave him a peck on the cheek. Mickey hoped no one noticed that he blushed at her gesture.

"You are dressed perfectly for our outing today, Fran."

She wrinkled her nose and looked at her father, then she looked back up at Mickey and smiled.

"Go have fun, kids," he said and waved them off.

As they drove away from her house, they talked like two school kids getting to know each other for the first time.

"I must say, I never thought I'd ever see you in jeans and flannel," said Mickey.

"Why not?"

"I don't know. It doesn't seem like your style, but you look great in them," he added.

"Where are we going?" she asked.

"We're going to the old home place where I grew up."

He turned into a long driveway that led to a large white colonial-style house. Francine looked around at the land that surrounded the house.

"Your family owns all this?"

"Yes."

"Do you live here with your parents?"

"No. My sister and her husband live here. My father has lived in a small area downstairs since his recovery from that car accident."

He drove around to the back and stopped in front of the garage. He got out and opened the door for Francine. As they got out, the large door of the garage rolled back, and there stood James pushing the ATV out the door.

"Good morning again, James," Mickey said. Francine looked at James' scarred face but said nothing standing behind Mickey.

Mickey reached behind him, took Francine's hand, and pulled her toward himself. "Fran, this is James, my brother-in-law. My sister's in the house. Let's go inside and get our lunch, and we'll be on our way."

They turned toward the house with Mickey in the lead. Inside, Darcy was packing a wicker basket with food and accessories. She looked and smiled at Francine and put out her hand.

"Hi, I'm Darcy Jean. Mickey's sister. I assume that he introduced you to James already?"

"Yes, he did. It's nice to meet you, Darcy Jean."

"Oh, how about Dee. That's what close friends call me. Mickey's got a nice day planned for you. I hope you enjoy yourselves. As you can see, I've taken the liberty of packing a lunch. If it was up to Mickey, he would have stopped at a local fast-food drive-thru and ordered a burger and fries to go!"

They all laughed at that, and Darcy motioned for them to go and have a good time. When they got back outside, James showed them what he had packed onto the ATV for them.

He had strapped two small collapsible fishing poles on the luggage rack and a small bait package. He put the lunch basket on the frame and put bungee cords to hold it down.

"Are you ready, my lady?" Mickey asked Francine.

"Whenever you are, my Lord," she laughed in response.

Mickey climbed onto the seat. She climbed on in back, slid close to him and put her arms around his waist, and pulled him tightly to her. He started the machine, waved goodbye, and pointed the ATV across the field behind the house. At first, he drove slowly so she could get the feel of the machine. As they rode on, he got a bit faster. As they approached the other side of the field, he turned the four-wheeler and took off back across the field, bouncing as it crossed the small hills and depressions. He felt her body rising from the seat to let her legs cushion the ride. He could hear her laughing with delight as he drove on. After two laps around the field, he headed the machine into the woods and slowed down as they wove around trees and bushes. After several minutes, they came to a small dirt road, and Mickey turned onto it.

He picked up speed as they went down the road. On and on, they went until he pulled into a small clearing surrounding a lake. Driving to a small flat area, he stopped, shut off the engine, and helped Francine get off.

She laughed and said, "Wow, that was a wild ride. It was like a carnival ride."

She stood there looking up at him, then she pulled him close and gave him a quick kiss. She pulled away and started running across the clearing around the lake. He took off after her and tackled her to the ground.

They both lay there on their backs, looking up at the cloudless sky, breathing heavily from their run and laughing with delight. Mickey turned and propped himself up on one elbow, looking at the sensual lady next to him. He silently looked into her crystal blue eyes for what felt like an eternity to Mickey. He took in every feature of her face with its soft, radiant skin that glowed against the backdrop of the blondness of her hair spread over the grass framing her face.

Finally, he got up, extended his hand, and helped her up. After dusting himself off, she let him dust her off. His heart raced as he patted her down, carefully avoiding all inappropriate areas.

They continued walking around the lake, holding hands as Mickey told her about himself. "Dee and I were just little kids when Pop built the main house. This lake was initially used to provide water for milk cows. Pop stocked it for a few years to have a place to fish.

"The old building over there," he said, pointing to some rotting wood on the lake's other side, "was the original barn. It was used for a while when Darcy got into horses, and Pop bought us each a horse. When I got older, I moved from horses to cars."

"What happened to the horses? I didn't see any around."

"Life moved on. I got interested in cars, Darcy got married and had kids. Pop sold the horses and built that huge metal warehouse-style garage where we got the ATV. He started buying old classic cars, and I helped him sometimes with the restoration and maintenance work."

"I saw into the garage when James had the door open. I only saw a couple of cars in it. What happened to all of them?" she asked.

"My aunt took all of them and sold them. That's a long story for another time. My father was in an accident which killed my mother. Pop was in a rehab facility for months, and when James and Darcy got married, they moved into the main house. Pop recovered and moved into the guest area. Then I moved into Darcy's townhouse. I don't have a garage, so I keep all my cars here. I keep the truck at my townhouse. That's my whole story. Now, you tell me about yourself."

"We'll talk about me later. I've never fished before. Will you show me how?"

"Goodness, girl. You're in for a treat. James gets credit for today. He had the idea of bringing you here to this place," Mickey said as they held hands and walked back to the ATV to unpack everything. "We can enjoy each other's company without any distractions."

He took the fishing rods out, snapped them together, baited the hooks, and threw them into the water. After a few short minutes, Fran screamed in delight. "I think something got my string," she said.

Mickey laughed and said, "It's called 'line,' not string. Next time he nibbles or bites, do this," he said and showed her by snapping the pole upward.

"Why do you do that?" she giggled.

"It sets the hook, so he can't get away." As soon as he said this, he saw her pole bend downward toward the water. He dropped his pole and stepped over behind her. He reached his arms around her waist and grabbed the rod just in front of her hands.

"He's just nibbling right now. Wait for him to bite."

As they stood there waiting for the fish to bite, she backed herself tightly against his body. He felt her against him, and again his heart raced with desire. He liked it, and he stood his ground.

Finally, the pole dipped sharply, and Mickey quickly snapped the rod upward to set the hook. Francine once again giggled.

As the fish pulled the pole back down, Mickey let go of her and backed away. "Okay, girl, now reel it in slowly. It'll fight, but don't worry, you got him hooked good."

At that moment, Mickey's fishing rod that was lying on the ground started to bounce around on the ground. He jumped over to it and knew that the fish had set the hook when he took the bait. They each reeled their fish in at the same time. Mickey again laid his pole on the ground with the fish flopping around the edge of the lake. Fran's fish was bobbing in and out of the water as Fran just watched it. Mickey took the pole from her and brought it up and out of the lake.

"Okay, girl. You caught it. You gotta take it off the line," he laughed.

"No, no, no. I couldn't touch it. It might bite me," she said as Mickey stood with the fish dangling on the line in front of her.

Laughing, Mickey handed her the pole and took out his cellphone to snap a picture of her and her first fish. She roared with laughter as he snapped the picture, then took it off the line and put it on the ground. He took his own line and unhooked the fish from it. He then put the fish side by side on the ground and snapped a picture of Francine kneeling on the ground beside them.

"I'll send them to you later for a souvenir of the day," he said.

"What do we do with them now? We don't skin and eat them, do we?"

"No," he said as he threw them back into the water. "We'll come back another time and catch them again."

"I hope we do, Mickey Ray. Let's eat. I never realized know how hungry a person can get fishing."

They opened the basket and began taking things out. On the top was a gingham cloth which they placed on the ground. Next was a bottle of wine, complete with two wine glasses. At the bottom was a container of fried chicken, potato salad, dinner rolls, and two pieces of pie for dessert. They ate, they laughed, and they talked. They were having a wonderful time.

"Look at this, Mickey. Did you tell Dee that Cherry pie is my favorite dessert?" she said with delight.

"Yes, I did. And believe it or not, she doesn't like to cook, but she made the pie herself from scratch!" answered Mickey.

"Wow, Mickey. She's a special sister, isn't she?"

"She is, Fran."

"Are you making any progress on finding Betty's killer, Mickey Ray?" she asked.

"Yes, as a matter fact, we are," he answered between bites of food.

"Do you have any idea who it is?"

"No, but we're eliminating suspects. It's a step-by-step process."

"Am I still on your suspect list?"

"You're not on my suspect list."

"What do you mean by that? Not on YOUR list. Who's list am I on?" she questioned.

"Not now. I don't want to talk about it. Let's enjoy this moment," said Mickey trying to change the subject.

She sat up. "You don't really think I had anything to do with killing her. I told you she was a low-life slut, and I wouldn't give her the time of day. I find that extremely offensive that you would even consider me a suspect, Mickey Ray!"

"Whoa, Fran. I told you. I don't believe you had anything to do with it. We just haven't actually eliminated you yet. That'll come soon enough."

"You haven't 'eliminated' me yet? I shouldn't even be on that list. I want you to take me off that list. Do you hear me? I want to be off it now!"

They were sitting on the cloth on the ground across from each other over the food. Mickey leaned over to kiss her, but she backed away.

"I mean it, Mickey. I want you to take me off that list."

"Done. You are officially off the list. Now, don't let it spoil our day."

"Are you going to keep trying to solve it?"

"Yes, I feel a bit obligated to do it now. Remember I told you about that reporter?"

"Yes."

"Well, he keeps writing stories and saying we're involved in her murder. Maybe we killed or had her killed," Mickey said disgustedly.

"I know you didn't kill her, Mickey. Why is he saying that?"

"To sell newspapers," said Mickey.

"We need to get him to back off right now. He's doing more damage to us than anything that might concern Betty's death."

"How's that, Mickey Ray?" she said, sitting up with sincere concern in her voice.

"If he keeps pounding on us, we'll lose the funding for the construction project, and we'll be forced to shut down. If we shut down, we'll have no choice but to file for bankruptcy."

"You mean like go broke?" she said. "Can't you make him stop!"

"No, he doesn't make direct accusations. He just presents the facts like they are true, and people believe that they are. People pull their money out when that happens, and banks call the loans."

"What would happen then?" she asked, appalled at what Mickey said.

"We'd lose everything, and I'd start looking for a job, but with a bad reputation hanging over me, I'd be lucky to find any kind of job."

"That's horrible, Mickey. I'll ask daddy and Francis to see if there's anything they can do to stop it. I'm so sorry."

"Don't feel sorry, Fran. You didn't do anything. I'm sure it'll all work out. We have our lawyers working on a few things also. I just hope it happens before we lose our funding to continue.

"Let's enjoy this day together. Don't let my business trouble spoil our day," he said, stroking her hair.

She leaned over and kissed him passionately. "I think I'm..." stopping in mid-sentence.

"You're what, Fran?" Mickey asked softly.

"Nothing. I was just thinking out loud. Really it was nothing. Things can't be changed now if we want them to. I'll see what I can do," she said wiping away her tears. "Why don't you let the police handle it?"

"It happened on our land. We have a good name, and we want to keep it that way," he said. "I hope they find the killer in time to salvage the project and our family name," Mickey said thoughtfully.

"I understand. We feel that way about our family. We want to keep the Braydon family name unsoiled. It isn't any reflection on your family. You should let it go and let the police handle it. Whatever happens, I can tell daddy, and he can arrange a press release or a public announcement that your family wasn't involved."

"Don't worry about us. We'll handle it. Have another glass of wine, my beautiful lady," he said as he filled her glass. "Are you going to the festival at the fairground this weekend?"

"I haven't been to it since I was a little girl. Are you going?" she asked.

"Why don't you come with the family and me? Pop, Darcy and James, and the kids. It'll be fun. We do it every year."

"Sounds like fun, and I could get to know your family better."

Mickey looked at his watch, "We better be getting back. This's been fun, but I have a few things I need to get done this afternoon."

She made a fake pouty face and stuck her lower lip out, "Aw, Mickey. I was hoping we could spend the entire day together."

"Not today, Fran. I have to work sometimes, but we'll see each other again before the weekend. How does that sound?"

"Sounds wonderful, Mickey," and she leaned over and kissed him. "Are you busy Friday morning?"

"Why do you ask?" he said, kissing her back.

"You rode me on a dozen or more horses today. That's your ATV, so I'll return the favor. Did you know that we have a stable behind our house?" she asked.

"No. Do you really?" he answered, surprised.

"You can't see it from the house. We don't access it from our house but an access road from the other side of the property. Daddy raises racehorses. And Francis and I have one each to ride. We'll go horseback riding. I'll ride mine, and you can ride Francis'. You're under a lot of stress right now. You need time off."

"I know where that is, but I never knew it belonged to your family. I've seen it from the road. It has a white rail fence around it, and it must be a hundred acres!"

"It's a hundred and fifty acres, to be exact. And it has a pond right in the middle. It's not as large as your lake, and it doesn't have fish. It's just for watering the horses. He has two trainers and boards horses for other people. If you ever get a horse, you can board it at our stable, and I'll make sure you aren't charged any boarding fees. Let's go riding."

"It's been so long since I rode. I don't know if I can ride now."

"It's like riding a bike. You'll pick it up again in no time. Meet me at the stables at ten o'clock! We'll have another wonderful day."

"We really do have to go. I have some important things to get done today." He stood up, and they packed the basket and rods.

When they got back to the main house, James came out and helped unpack the ATV and told Mickey they needed to talk after he took Francine home.

When they pulled up to the front door of Francine's father's home, she leaned over and kissed him on the cheek and said she had a wonderful time. Mickey left the house feeling like he was floating on air.

When Mickey got back to James' house, he saw James, tinkering in the garage. He pulled into the garage.

Walking over to James, they gave each other a high five. "How was your day, bro?"

"Fabulous. I haven't had such a day in years. I loved Valerie, but we didn't go out and do things like this. I felt like a giddy teenager. Maybe if I had taken more personal time with Val, she wouldn't have left."

"Yes, she would have, Mickey. She was broken. It's nothing you did or didn't do. She did what she needed to do to heal. She's moved on, and now, so are you. Don't feel bad, and don't feel guilty. You're young only once. Enjoy your time with Francine. If it works out for you, great. If not, move on from this and never look back," James said.

"I guess you're right. What did you need to talk to me about that you couldn't say in front of Fran."

"I got a call from Irene at the library. She wants me to come back and give another talk to the book club. She again mentioned that she would love to help with some of our research," said James. "Dee got a call from the law firm she worked for, and they need her to help almost full-time for a few weeks. We need some help, and I thought Irene could help us do background checks on some of our suspects."

"Who should we have her start on first? I thought we had checked everyone," Mickey said.

"Everyone except, you know who. Since we decided to put Howard and Riley back on the suspect list, I can ask her to run checks on them also."

"You mean, Fran! No. I told you, she had nothing to do with Betty's death. It has to be someone else, but NOT her. I'll not allow Irene or anyone else to go digging into Francine's past. We know she had two bad marriages, and in my opinion, they got whatever they deserved. Francine's a wonderful girl!"

"Hey, hey, now," James said, holding his hands out in a defensive position. "I'm not implying anything. I'm sure you're right, but we need to check all the boxes on this one, and…."

"NOT her boxes. She doesn't have any boxes that need to be checked," Mickey protested.

"How about this, we check out her family?"

"You can check out her family, but leave her out of it. Got it?" Mickey said.

"Got it. She's out. Just check the family. We'll see Irene tomorrow morning and give her the files and all the information we have so far, so she can start with them. Then she can go back over the other suspects and see if she can find something that Darcy overlooked. Calm down, Mickey Ray. I didn't mean to accuse Francine of anything. You're right. You know her. All we know are the rumors floating around, and we know how unreliable those rumors can be. She's a nice girl," said James trying to calm Mickey Ray.

"I'm sorry. I didn't mean to jump on you like that. I know you're looking out for me, but she's gotten under my skin. I guess at this point; I'm a bit protective of her because, well, you know."

"I know," James said.

They both stood there for an awkward few seconds, then James spoke. "Hey, come back here, take a look at what I'm trying to set up for us. Remember, a long time ago, we talked about setting up a small home gym?"

"I remember, but it got lost in the turmoil of current family events."

In the back corner of the garage, James had begun installing exercise equipment. He had a treadmill and several types of body-building machines, including a rack of free weights. He had put down rubber mats on the floor.

"What are we going to do for heat in the winter. Don't forget cooling in the summer. It gets hot and cold in here depending on the weather," cautioned Mickey.

"I haven't gotten that far yet. You can work on that part of it. Maybe we can put a partition wall and add AC and heat," said James.

"I'll think about it," laughed Mickey. "See you at the diner in the morning?"

"Yep, Mickey Ray, I'll get there and order for you. What do you want?"

"The usual," he said and walked through the open garage doors to his truck.

He went back to the construction site, walked around the area, and talked to some workers to check on progress. He made some calls to verify the deliveries of materials to the construction site. After spending time on some paperwork, he called Sam, his maintenance foreman, concerning preparing some of the vacancies to get them ready to rent.

Back at the trailer, Pop was working on scheduling for the coming week. "Hey, Pop. Did you talk with the attorney?"

"Yes, I did. He is going to draft a petition of cease and desist and or a gag order, whatever he needs to stop those stories in the paper. I should hear from him in a day or so. He understands the importance of getting something done soon. How did your date with the Braydon girl go?"

"It went pretty good, Pop. I like her. Like her a lot. She's smart and takes time to listen to me. Valerie was great, but she never did that. Listen to me, I mean."

"Sounds like Valerie is finally in your rearview mirror, son," Daniel said.

"I don't know yet, but she probably is, no matter how things work out with Fran and me."

Daniel came over and gave his son a manly hug and said, "All I want for you and Dee is happiness with whatever or whoever you have in your life."

"Thanks, Pop."

Daniel got his briefcase, as he closed the door, he said, "See you later, son."

Mickey decided to call it a day, continue the work, and finish the paperwork tomorrow.

CHAPTER 15

Irene and the Explosion

Mickey arrived at the diner the following morning, and when he sat down, Pauline was bringing their orders.

As they ate, Mickey told James about Fran asking him to go trail riding on their horses.

"I knew he raised race horses. How did you not know, Mickey?"

"I just didn't know. I'm not into horseback riding. I've been by that place many times, but I never knew it belonged to the Braydon family. I don't understand how you did know. Can you ride a horse?" Mickey asked.

"Nope, never been on one in my life. I keep up with the news. Some of the horses his stable trains have won some minor local races," said James. "You can even go there and rent a horse, guide, and take trail rides," he added.

"I never knew that. What will be the topic of your book club talk next time?"

"Poe, again. We didn't finish the first time, and I'm going back to finish it. I'm glad she called. I'd forgotten all about her. Irene will be a huge help for us. She has time and experience in looking up records and being right at the library, it's easy for her to get local news from the archives. She'll have knowledge of things that we don't even know are available. We lucked out on getting her on our side."

"You really know how to change the subject. You switched from Poe right into Irene researching for us."

"Yep, I do have a knack for that, don't I?"

"Just remember what I said about Francine," insisted Mickey.

"I will, but she is part of the family, so in some areas, she'll be a part of the research. We can tell Irene not to focus on her," James stated.

"Okay. I'm once again leaning toward Ralph and Mike. Is there any way you know of we can get DNA on some of these people?" Mickey wondered out loud.

"I took pictures at Betty's funeral. I'll print them out, and we can go back to each suspect and show them the pictures. Then when they hand the picture back to us, we send them to a lab for testing," said James.

"Can you handle that for me, James? I need to get some work done on the construction project. Pop's been very patient with me. He's been taking the lead on the construction since this whole thing started."

"Sure, Mickey. We're working on this murder together. I'll take it for a while. You go to work. I've got to go see Irene and then get back home and work on our gym."

They finished breakfast, and each went their own way. Mickey headed to the site, and James went to see the librarian.

As Mickey climbed the steps to the construction trailer, he heard voices inside. He recognized both of them immediately. He opened the door, and Peter Reynolds looked straight at him. He pointed a finger at Mickey.

"You, Mickey Ray, have been doing a great job. Every person I've talked to has told me they told you all they knew. I have to give you credit, some of the things you told me are gold. They wouldn't tell a cop most of what they told you. I'm sorry I can't give you public credit."

"We're continuing the interviews, but we have some personal things we need to get straight," Mickey said.

Mickey looked at his father, who was standing behind his desk in silence. He looked at Mickey with a blank face.

"Will you give us a list of your suspects, Detective Reynolds?" Mickey asked.

"I'll do that verbally, but not in writing."

"Then we'll know who we can talk to and who we must stay away from?"

"Can you tell me why you intend to find this young lady's killer, Mickey Ray?" he asked.

"Betty was a friend. I went to school with her. My sister Darcy and her husband also went to school with her. We have some of the same friends. The wife of one of our sales agents is a friend. My sister's husband is giving a series of talks at a local book club, and Betty was also a member. Everywhere we go, we run into someone that's a mutual friend. We don't know if they are on your suspect list or not. Right now, I am dating the former mayor's daughter, who was at Betty's funeral. We all knew Betty."

Mickey took a deep breath and said, "I need a cup of coffee. Do either of you want one?"

Daniel shook his head, "No."

The Detective nodded, "I might as well drink a cup. Black"

Mickey took down two ceramic cups, filled both, handed one to the seated Detective, and sat down at his desk. He took another deep breath. As he talked, he told Peter Reynolds everything they had uncovered. He also gave him their opinions of who was guilty and who may not be guilty. It took him almost a full hour and two coffee refills to get to the end of their progress.

When he finished, he leaned back in his chair. There was silence in the room for almost a minute while each person pondered the facts, results, and the Detective's reaction.

Finally, the Detective spoke to Mickey. "I hate to admit this, but while I can't tell you what we found out, I can say that you, James, and your sister have found out more than our entire department. You have run circles around us. I can't condone what you did because that's our job, but you have done a great job. From what you've told me, I agree with your initial conclusions, but as of yet, you have not a bit of proof of anything. Can you get proof?"

"We have some ideas on how we can get some."

"Will you tell me?" he asked.

"No. We don't plan on anything illegal, but you have plausible deniability if we do something not quite right.

"Can you get us a complete copy of the autopsy report?" asked Mickey.

"No. Not officially, but somehow, you could get a copy by accident."

"Fine, we'd like to get it as soon as possible," said Mickey.

"I'll do what I can if you continue to share what you find with me."

"I'll do one better. If we find out who killed her before you, we'll notify you so your department can make the arrest and get credit. We want justice, not credit."

"I appreciate that. Now, why is this reporter slashing you in the papers?"

"Believe it or not, it isn't personal with him. He's doing it for the glory and money?"

"How's that?"

"Carter Evans met with James and me the other day. Carter openly admitted that he wants to get a job in a bigger city, and he doesn't care how he gets it. We're just collateral damage. He doesn't care who lies beaten to death in his path. It's all about climbing the ladder."

"He told you that?"

"Yep, and James and I have it recorded, but we can't use it, as you know," Mickey exclaimed. "Freedom of speech. As long as he makes no direct accusations, he's in the clear."

The Detective stood up to leave. "I'm sorry, Mickey. Since we are also in his sights, we can't cut you any slack as far as investigating. We'll be forced to bring you in if you even slightly look guilty. Captains orders."

"I get it, Detective. We'll try to help you and keep out of your way," Mickey promised.

Detective and Mickey shook hands, and he left.

Daniel hadn't said a word since Mickey had poured the coffee. He grinned at Mickey and said, "Pete's a pretty good guy and honest. He'll work with you the way he can, as long as it isn't putting him or his job in the crosshairs."

"Thanks, Pop. I hope he doesn't cause us problems."

"He won't. Especially if you give him credit as you promised."

"I'll keep my word, Pop. Now, what's on the agenda for today?"

"We need to do a thorough walk around the project. There are some work orders and invoices that you need to take care of."

"Let's do it, Pop." They headed for the door.

It took them an hour and a half to walk the entire project and talk to the various foremen on each portion of the job.

After all this, Mickey went back to the trailer to catch up on paperwork.

When the desk phone rang, he was relieved to see James' name show up on caller ID.

"Hello, James. How did it go at the library?"

"It went great. Irene's going to do a deeper dive on everyone. She said there are a lot of newspaper articles about the Braydon family that haven't been uploaded to the internet or archive files yet.

"It should've been done a long time ago, but someone put a hold on it for some reason. No names or signatures are listed on 'work' or 'stop work' orders. Irene has to go to the archives, physically look them up, and make paper copies."

James continued, "Most of the other names she can get in a couple of hours, but she will work the Braydon name first. She says that there were a lot of shady things happening in the town back in the day. Scandals and people making accusations just disappeared. In some court cases, evidence was destroyed or missing."

"I don't doubt any of that," said Mickey, "but that's all past. Even if the stuff came to light today, the statute of limitations is surely past. All we're interested in is something that may have a bearing on Betty's death, and that only goes back two or maybe three months."

"That's what I told her, go back three months. She's going to work on personal information first, then go deeper. I told her to add Howard Hudson and Riley Gentry to the list."

"That doesn't make sense to me right now, but I don't care. Let Irene look to her heart's content," said Mickey.

"She said the best way to run checks is to do a basic background check, then continue filling in blanks until something fits."

"I understand that. It's almost quitting time. I'll talk to you later. Pop left a few minutes ago. Let me get my truck keys and start my truck, so the air conditioning will cool it down before I leave." As he talked, he began looking through his desk drawer and picked up the keys. He pressed the remote starter button.

A second later, a loud boom rocked the trailer and blew his office window inside where he was sitting, and sprinkling shattered glass all over the room. He dove for the floor while pieces of metal tore through the thin walls of the trailer like shrapnel. He looked up and saw the flickering firelight through the open hole where the window used to be.

He heard a disembodied voice calling him from the phone lying on the floor across the room. He waited, not moving until he was sure there wasn't another explosion, before crawling out from under the desk. As he moved on hands and knees across the floor, he brushed aside glass and items that were blown off the desks in the room. There was a ringing in his ears now, and he felt dizziness from the pressure wave that had followed the explosion. He became nauseated and felt like throwing up but choked down that impulse.

He shook his head to clear his mind and headed for the door as he crawled. As with most trailers, this door swung out, and he tried to push it open, but it was misshapen and wedged tight into its metal frame. It didn't budge. The ringing in his ears seemed to get louder, and he sat up against the wall and fought off unconsciousness. He kept hearing the small tinny voice but couldn't make out what it was saying over the ringing in his ears. He closed his eyes as the world closed in around him and went black.

CHAPTER 16

Explosion Aftermath

Someone was shaking him. He felt like he had little men running around in his head wielding hammers and banging them against the wall of his brain. They were screaming over the sound of the constant ringing resonating inside his head.

They were calling out, "Mickey! Mr. Christianson! Are you okay? Can you hear me?" They kept shaking him. He wanted them to stop. He wanted to go back to sleep to get away from the little men in his head. His head hurt.

"Go away," he said. "Let me sleep."

They continued shaking him. They kept talking, but he couldn't understand what they were saying. He heard noises all around. Men were yelling out orders. There were flashing lights all around. Loud engine noises resounded inside his head, along with the little men with hammers. That incessant ringing. He wished it would stop.

He opened his eyes. He saw a man standing over him. He raised his head and looked around. He was lying on the ground, on a stretcher away from the construction trailer and a pile of burning metal that used to be his truck. He saw the whole side of the trailer dented and peppered with the shrapnel of flying parts thrown against it when the truck exploded. It was also black with the heat of the burning truck.

The man beside him pushed him back down on the stretcher, and Mickey saw his mouth move but still couldn't understand him over the ringing in his ears. All he could understand was "Mr. Christianson."

He laid his head back down and again closed his eyes, but the voice called out, "Stay with us, Mr. Christianson. Don't pass out. Wake up!" Then the man shook him some more.

"I'm okay. I'm not going to pass out." The ringing began to subside but was still there. "I want to sit up."

"You need to lay back down," the voice said.

"No. I need to sit up," he said, struggling to sit up.

Finally, the voice backed off and helped him sit up and look around. He tried to stand, but the voice again objected.

Mickey pushed the man away and said, "I want to get up. Now let me stand."

"You need to stay down for a few minutes longer."

"I need to stand. Help me to a place where I can see what's going on here."

The man with the voice helped Mickey stand and walk to sit on the back of the ambulance. "Thanks for your help."

He sat looking around. He saw men dragging hoses from two fire trucks and dousing the trailer to keep it from burning. Water and foam were dripping from the charred hulk of what was once his truck. He looked down at the ground and again fought off a wave of dizziness.

Mickey realized what had happened. When he pressed the button on the remote starter, it had started the truck and set off a bomb. The fog was lifting from his mind, but the ringing continued, but at least it was softening enough he could hear and understand most of what was being said. He looked up and saw a familiar face. It was the face of Detective Peter Reynolds.

He looked genuinely concerned. "Are you okay, Mickey Ray?"

"Yes."

"When the call came in, I called Daniel. He'll be here in a few minutes. Can you tell me what happened?"

"Later, I'll tell you everything. Right now, my head hurts, and I can barely hear."

"I understand. Let the EMTs take care of you."

It was almost dark now, and many first responders were still around, making sure there were no casualties and the fire was completely out. Mickey knew a crime scene investigative team would also be arriving on the scene.

He heard Darcy calling his name. "I'm over here," he answered to no one in particular.

She came around the side of the emergency vehicle and saw him. She ran over and grabbed him and hugged him close. "Are you okay. You aren't hurt, are you?"

"No, big sister. I'm a bit rattled but fine." He looked up and saw James with Joel clinging to him and Pop holding onto Cyndi.

"Looks like the whole gang's here," he said weakly.

Detective Reynolds had backed off when Mickey's family showed up. He stepped over to Daniel and asked to speak to him. Daniel told Cyndi to stay near James while he talked to the detective.

They stepped aside, and Peter said to Daniel, "I'm sorry this happened, but this is one of the reasons I wanted Mickey Ray and James to be more discreet. I don't want anyone hurt."

"I know, Pete. I'll talk to Mickey about it, but I can't make any promises. He has a mind of his own. I hope he'll back away also. He's my only son."

"Fine. I don't want to get in the way. I'll give you a call later. Maybe he can come by the station. If you want, I'll meet him somewhere so we can talk."

"I'll do that as soon as possible. Let us get through this. He'll meet with you soon. That I can promise," answered Daniel.

Peter walked back to his squad car, and Daniel rejoined Darcy and James.

Daniel pushed through to Mickey and knelt down in front of him, "Son, tell me what happened."

"I don't know, Pop. One minute I was talking to James on the phone. The next, I was lying on the office floor with shattered glass and papers all around me."

"That's enough right now. When you feel like it, let's go home. You don't need to talk to anyone else until you feel better."

The EMT moved forward and said to Mickey, "We need you to go with us to the hospital to get fully checked out, then if we find nothing, you can go home."

"I want to go home," he said.

"He's right, son. Go with them. We'll meet you there," Daniel said.

After helping Mickey inside the ambulance, it pulled out for Bridgeton General Hospital. Daniel and the rest of the family followed the ambulance. At the hospital, they waited in the emergency room for test results. As they waited, Francine walked into the waiting area.

"Oh, Dee, where's Mickey? Is he hurt badly?" she asked, sounding very upset.

"No, he'll be fine. He's a bit shook up, but he'll be okay."

"That's good. I was so worried when I heard what had happened. I don't know what I would have done if Mickey had been seriously injured," she said walking over to give Darcy a hug.

James and Daniel were sitting across the room from Dee and the kids when Francine arrived. James leaned over and quietly said to Daniel, "She could win an Oscar for that performance."

"I noticed," he answered.

"A bit of overacting, don't you think?"

"I do," Daniel said as he thumbed through an old magazine he picked up from the waiting room table.

They all sat for about two hours when Francine said she had to leave and asked Darcy to give her a call with Mickey's test results.

Finally, a doctor came out and said that test results and scans for internal injuries seemed okay, but they wanted to keep Mickey overnight for observation. Daniel and James decide to stay, but Darcy needed to get the kids back home and put them to bed.

The following morning when Mickey was released, Daniel and James took him back to the main house to rest for a couple of days.

When they brought Mickey home, Darcy had made Pop's bed and told Mickey to get in it and rest. Daniel insisted for the next few days, he would sleep on the couch.

As Mickey sat up in bed, he pondered over what happened last night. He had the gut feeling that they were on to something. He couldn't quit now. He still had a headache and ringing in his ears, but the doctors insisted that it would all go away in a few days. He needed to get back out there.

Pop had been in earlier and told him that the Crime Scene Investigative team had found nothing that would give them any clues to who set the bomb. All they determined was that it was a bomb and not a malfunction of the truck.

He thought to himself, Well, duh! He knew that. He didn't need a degree in forensics to determine that! He got up and moved to the room where the murder board was still set up. He sat and stared at it. He had no clues as to who could have done this. Ralph gave Betty money and didn't need to do it. He had no obvious motive. Mike didn't seem to have a motive since he was willing to marry Betty. Wallace. Nope. He had the strongest motive. But did he have the opportunity or means to do it? He doubted it, but one never knows. Howard and Riley seemed okay, so they were out of the suspect loop at this time.

He walked into the area that Dee was using as a home office now. She was at her desk typing on the computer. Dee stopped typing and looked up at Mickey.

"Are you okay? You look spacey. Can I get you something?"

"I need to call Fran. We were supposed to go horseback riding today," he said.

"That was Friday. It's Sunday. You slept almost all day Friday and most of the day yesterday. The doctor said you have a slight concussion, but you should be fine in a day or two. Dad went in and talked to you several times, and you were lucid for a while. James has been in and out too," Darcy said.

"Where is James?"

"He took the kids to church. He should be back in a little while."

"He took them by himself?" he asked, surprised.

"Yep. He's been reading the Bible a lot more lately. I'm so proud of him. We have a lot more information about the Braydon family. I'll let James tell you about it. Very interesting stuff. Francine knows about the bomb. She's called here every day to check your progress. She came to the hospital shortly after we arrived Thursday night."

"Wow, how did she know so fast?"

"Don't know. She didn't say, and we didn't ask. She left after a while. She made me promise to call her the next morning with a progress report."

"What do you think of her, Dee?"

"I don't know. She's okay, I guess. Are you really falling for her?"

"I don't know yet, we've only had a few dates. She's fun and beautiful."

"Don't let her beauty cloud your judgment, Mickey Ray."

"I know. You're right. I need to get out of this house. I need to get some fresh air."

"When James gets back, you can both get away from the house. How's your head feel?"

"It still hurts a little, but other than that, I feel fine. My mind is clear if that's what you're getting at," he said.

"I was kind of. I don't want you wandering around unless your mind is completely clear. And let James chauffer you around for a couple of days.

Why don't you go and sit on the porch if you need fresh air? That might do you some good."

"I can drive, but that sounds like a good idea. I'll let him drive. We needed to buy a new truck anyway," said Mickey thinking out loud. "Can the company afford one right now?"

"I don't think we have a choice, do we?" said Darcy.

"I guess not. Insurance should cover most of it."

"When James gets home, and before you boys go out again, we need to have a serious talk."

"Oh, no. Here we go again," he sighed.

"Yep. You heard me. We'll talk BEFORE you leave this house! Understand?"

"You're going to treat us like kids again with 'The Talk.'"

"Now, go before I start now instead of waiting until James gets home."

Mickey walked out of the room and out of the house to get some fresh air.

CHAPTER 17

Continuing the Investigation

Darcy called Mickey and James into her office, where she was still working. When they came in and sat down, she started, "Okay, you both know where this talk is going. Before I start, does either of you have anything to say?"

They each shook their head, No.

"Mickey, you've been out of it for the past few days, and you don't know what has happened. We, the family, and the construction project are still front-page news. Now, Carter Evans is insinuating that you bombed your own truck to throw suspicion off of us. The insurance company is withholding payment until the police conclude their investigation of the bombing. More investors are pulling out. Daddy has asked me to go over the books to see how long we can keep construction going. As of yesterday, we have only enough cash to last for two more weeks, and we shut down," Darcy said while drumming a pencil on the desktop.

She sat quietly and patiently as Mickey and James looked at each other.

"I'm sure that you think you know how I feel about this 'case' as you call it. You think you know what I'm going to say, right?"

They each silently nodded their head.

"Whatever you think, you're wrong."

"I'm asking you to let the police take over from here," she said.

"Dee," said Mickey, "You know we can't do that. We're closing in on something or someone now."

Darcy took a deep breath, clasping her hands together on her desk, and looked from one to the other. "Can I do or say anything to stop you?" she said calmly.

"No," Mickey said.

She looked at both of them and said, "Right answer! If someone doesn't solve this murder, we'll all be living in the street soon. We'll lose everything Momma and Daddy worked their whole lives for. I can't believe I'm saying this, but get out there and find Betty's killer, and this whole thing will be solved, and the family name will be cleared!"

Mickey and James just sat motionless and silent.

"Leave my office. Get out now, and I hope and pray to God that He'll look after both of you. I love both of you, and I lay awake at night praying for God's protection over you," she said softly. Then she shooed them away like waving off a fly.

They silently got up and walked out to the garage.

"Dee says you have to drive me around for a couple of days. Will you do it?" Mickey asked.

"Sure, Mickey," he said calmly. They got in the Humvee and left the house.

James drove around back roads. They rode in silence for nearly half an hour. Finally, James spoke up. "Mickey?"

"Yeah?"

"Dee was very patient with us. I don't think I've ever seen her like that. She's worrying more about this than she is showing," said James.

"Yeah, she is."

"She's telling the truth when she said she lies awake at night worrying about us. She tosses and turns in bed. She gets up and goes downstairs in the middle of the night for hours at a time. She doesn't get much sleep. And it's beginning to wear on her. What're we going to do?" James asked.

"Keep on doing what we're doing. Try to find the killer."

"I think we should turn it over to the police. I'm not afraid. I've faced far worse than this, but you haven't, and I don't want to lose my best friend."

"I don't want to lose you either, and you could have been the target instead of me," Mickey said, looking straight forward out of the windshield.

"So, we agree. We'll let the police take it over?" James asked.

"No, she said for us to get out and find the killer. The killer is trying to stop us from finding out who he is, right?"

"Yes," said James.

"To stop him, we MUST find him!"

"I hate to admit it, but that has a strange logic to it. We have to find him before he kills one or both of us," James said.

"Now you get it. So, tell me what you found out the last two days," demanded Mickey.

"We should still keep quiet about this. Dee won't be happy until it's over."

"I know, so we need to step it up. What did you find out?"

"First, I did what we agreed. I printed out the pictures I took at the funeral and went by to talk to each suspect. I handled each picture carefully and handed it to the suspects to look at in a way that they took the top right corner. Each took the photo and handled it. When I took it back, I was careful where I touched it. When I got back in the Vee, I bagged and tagged each one. I did Mike, Ralph, Wallace, and his wife Laurel. Even went by to see Howard, that worked at the grocery store, his girlfriend, and Susan at the realty office. I think I covered all the bases. Then I took the prints and mailed them to an independent lab out of state. They have the equipment to get DNA."

"You know a lab that can get DNA from fingerprints?" asked Mickey.

"I called a friend at the police department in that city. He gave me the name of the lab."

Mickey rolled his eyes at that statement. "Why am I not surprised."

"We should get the results in a few days. That took me most of the day Friday. I talked to Irene yesterday. She found a lot of public information and a ton of dirt on the Braydon family and some on Howard Hudson. A lot is just ordinary background stuff."

"Don't keep me in suspense, James."

"The old man, Franklin, made his money in some dubious business transactions. Nothing blatantly illegal but shady. There were many insider stock trades but not enough evidence to charge him. Apparently, he knew when to buy and when to sell certain stocks.

"As you know, both kids are twins. The brother, Francis, went to Harvard Law School, and Francine got a degree in Social Event Planning."

Mickey thought for a few moments and said, "I didn't even know there was a degree in that."

"That's like a degree in 'adult recess,'" continued James.

"My thoughts exactly. Anyway, she and her mother plan expensive fundraisers for rich people."

"Tell me something I don't know."

"Their father owns the horse racing stables, as you know, and they all know how to ride. Francis has an airplane titled in the law firm's name and a pilot's license. No record of any other family member having a license to fly. He also owns two barbeque restaurants in Raleigh, North Carolina. He flies there for long weekends with the cover of taking care of business. Scuttlebutt is, that's where he takes his girlfriends."

"I heard about the restaurants and affairs, but not the plane. What kind is it?"

"Her report says it's a Piper PA-28 Cherokee model."

"Okay, moving on."

"Francine didn't want children, so she took care of that at the hospital to avoid accidents. She didn't want to be tied down with kids."

"I said Francine was to stay out of this, James."

"It's just general family information, nothing that would even be remotely personal. All this is public knowledge."

"Her ability to have kids is public knowledge?"

"Yes. When you're in public life, even just a mere mayor, everything you do is public knowledge. You know that, Mickey."

"Okay, I guess you're right."

"Because they were public figures, their fingerprints and DNA are on file with the proper authorities. Do you want her to find them?"

"No, we don't need their DNA. They aren't suspects. When will we know about the other suspects?"

"In a few days. The lab will run the prints and extract the DNA for analysis."

"What do we do now?" asked James.

"There's nothing we can do until the DNA comes back. I guess I'll go back to work tomorrow."

"You need to get a new truck unless you plan on driving to work in a Rolls Royce every day."

"I need to go truck shopping tomorrow," Mickey said.

"Are you going to call Francine and tell her you're okay?"

"Yeah, I guess I better call her. Home, James," he said, flipping his hand like giving an order.

"You do that again, and I'll throw you out of this car," and they laughed.

When James dropped Mickey off at his townhouse, Mickey went inside and called Francine.

"Hello, my lady," he said into the phone.

"Oh, Mickey Ray, how're you feeling?" she asked.

"I'm doing great. My head still hurts a little from the concussion, but other than that, I'm doing fine."

"I'm so glad."

"Hey, I need a new truck. Would you like to drive me around to pick out another one?"

"Sure, but can't you drive one of your other cars?" she said, concerned.

"The doctor hasn't cleared me to drive yet. I can get up and get around, but I'm not supposed to drive. If you don't want to, I understand. Since we didn't get to go horseback riding or go to the fair, I thought shopping for a truck might be fun."

She hesitated a few seconds, then said, "I'm sorry, Mickey, but I have a few things I have to do tomorrow. Mother and I are working on another fundraiser for next month, and I need to find a venue for it. Maybe you and I can get together in a few days. In the meantime, shopping for trucks isn't really what I would be interested in doing. Maybe you and James or your father could go to pick one out."

"Sure. I understand. We can see each other in a few days. I'm behind in my duties at the site also. Pop's been filling in for me. I guess I should go back to work."

"Okay, call me in a few days, Mickey Ray. We'll have some fun. Thanks for calling," she said politely.

"Yeah, I'll call you in a few days, Fran," he said as he hung up the phone. He felt a bit down. He missed her and hoped they could spend some more time together. He wasn't holding his end of the workload, but Pop was so understanding, and Mickey enjoyed being with Francine. This was a big project. He needed to be there if there was a problem.

He called James and asked if he would come by and pick him up so they could go to breakfast and shopping for a truck. James said he would be there first thing in the morning.

CHAPTER 18

More Bad News, New Information from Irene

The phone on Mickey's bedside table rang, and Mickey answered once again in a fog from sleep.

"Good morning, Mickey Ray. Time to get up and get the latest news," came Dee's voice out of the phone.

"What is it with you and your propensity to make pre-dawn calls, Dee?" he said, rubbing his hand over his face to wake up.

"Would you like to hear this morning's headline?"

"No, not really," he said yawning.

"You're going to hear it anyway. It says, 'Newspaper reporter shot to death in his apartment this morning,'" she said and continued reading. "Let's see. It says that a neighbor heard the shot around two A.M. but didn't call the police until after three when she was sure it was safe to go out into the hallway of the apartment building. Want to guess who the reporter was?"

"Who? No, wait. Was it Carter Evans?" said Mickey now sitting straight up on the side of his bed, wide awake.

"Yep."

Mickey's phone beeped, signaling that the other line was ringing. Mickey looked at it. It was the Bridgeton Police.

"Dee, I have to go. The police are calling on the other line. Get Pop up and get him down to the police station with a lawyer. I don't feel good about this. Bye."

He switched over to the other line and said, "Hello."

Peter Reynolds was on the other line. "Mickey, can you come to the police station. We need to talk, or do I need to send a patrol car to pick you up?"

"I'll be there in half an hour," Mickey answered. "No, wait. Detective. I don't have anything to drive."

"Okay, I'll send a squad car to pick you up. Sorry about this, but it's protocol."

"I know. I'll be ready."

Mickey dressed and waited for the knock on the door. Detective Reynolds walked in when he answered, followed by two uniformed officers. He handed Mickey a piece of paper and informed Mickey that it was a search warrant and he was under arrest for the murder of Carter Evans. Then he read him his rights.

"Do you have any firearms in this house, Mickey?" he asked.

"Yes, in the drawer of the bedside table in my bedroom."

"What kind is it?" he asked.

"A Walther PPK."

The Detective was taken aback. "Are you serious, Mickey? You really own a gun like James Bond carried?"

"Yes. Why not? I've never shot it, and it's quite a conversation piece. I don't even have ammunition for it."

The Detective nodded for the men to start the search.

"I'm sorry to have to do this, but I have to take you in for questioning. I don't believe you had anything to do with Carter Evans' murder, but I must follow protocol and due diligence. You know, cover all the bases as well as my behind."

In a few minutes, one of the officers returned and handed a sealed evidence bag with the small handgun inside. He handed it to the Detective.

The Detective held it up and looked at it. "You know, Mickey. It isn't all that big. You'd think that the famous James Bond would have carried a larger gun."

"I just have it as a toy," Mickey said, standing in the middle of the room with his hands cuffed behind him.

"We didn't find anything else, Detective," said one of the officers walking back into the room. "No other firearms or ammunition of any kind."

"Do you have a permit for this gun, Mickey Ray?" Reynolds asked.

"No, I didn't think I needed one. I don't carry it. As your officers confirmed, I don't even have any bullets for it."

"Okay, I had to ask. You can ride with me down to the station, Mickey, and we can get all this sorted out. Want me to call Daniel?"

"No, he'll meet us there, probably with my lawyer." Reynolds led Mickey out to the car.

When they got to the station, Daniel and James were already there. They waited while Mickey was photographed, fingerprinted and led to an interrogation room. He sat there while waiting for his lawyer to arrive. Mickey waited for almost half an hour, and finally, a man carrying a briefcase entered the room.

Reynolds followed him inside. Reynolds sat on one side of the table. Mickey and Mr. Rosenbaum sat on the other. They had taken the handcuffs off and, to Mickey's surprise, did not re-cuff him to the bar bolted to the table.

Reynold's nodded to Mr. Rosenbaum and smiled weakly at Mickey. He started by placing a recorder on the table between them.

Reynolds pushed the record button and announced his name, Mickey Ray's name, the time, date, and added that Mr. Christianson's attorney is present.

"Mr. Christianson, have you ever met Carter Evans?"

The attorney told Mickey to answer only the question asked with yes or no.

If he signaled to Mickey, he was not to answer at all. Mickey nodded. "Yes, I met Carter Evans. We met in the park and..."

"Mickey, you don't have to say anymore. Just yes or no," interrupted the attorney.

"Excuse me, Mr. Rosenbaum. I understand you're trying to help me, but I didn't kill anyone. Let me tell you everything I know. Then Detective Reynolds can ask me questions to clarify."

"Mickey, that isn't the wisest move here. Answer the questions directly with yes or no, please," he told Mickey.

Mickey ignored the attorney and began with him and James meeting Carter in the park. He explained that that was the only time he had had any personal contact with the reporter. For the next hour, Mickey, Peter Reynolds, and the attorney talked with objections from each one at some point during the interrogation. After that time, the attorney told

Mickey that he had said enough and announced that the interrogation was complete. Peter Reynolds agreed.

Mickey felt exhausted. But after they had finished, Detective Reynolds concluded that they didn't have enough evidence even to hold Mickey. So, they would release him.

"Mickey, I told you I didn't think you did anything, but I was ordered to bring you in. I must still say, don't leave town. I never know when something else will surface." Reynolds took Mickey to the waiting area, where he talked with Daniel.

"Detective, when can I have my PPK back?" Mickey asked.

"Sorry, but we have to keep it for a while until the investigation is closed."

Francine was waiting for him also, and she looked horrified. "Oh, Mickey. I was so afraid you had done something crazy. I had to come and find out I was wrong."

"I'm okay. I didn't do anything, and they picked me up because I was the only one that had a strong motive to kill Evans. I was the most obvious. I'm still on their watch list, but it'll be okay," Mickey said.

She sighed, "At least now you don't need to continue this insane obsession that you have to find Betty Duncan's murder. Now you can let it go and let the police do their job."

"No, now there are two murders out there. Let's get out of here and get some breakfast. Let's all meet at the diner." After meeting at the diner, they all went their separate ways. James and Mickey headed to buy a new truck for Mickey.

The salesman said the truck wouldn't be ready until late afternoon, so they left to go to the jobsite. The police investigators were taking down the crime scene tape when they got there. He saw the same person that had taken samples of Betty's remains at the first site last week.

Mickey walked over to him and spoke. "Hello, Baker. It's Clyde Baker, correct?"

"Yes, that's me. I'm surprised you remembered. Most people don't. You're Mr. Christianson, aren't you? We talked when you found the dead body, didn't we? Someone doesn't like you."

"You're right, Baker. Someone doesn't like me a LOT. Can you tell me what you found?"

"Yes. I've finished here. I haven't written my report yet, but I'm sure you're correct. It was a bomb. The main ingredient was RDX."

James was standing beside Mickey, and when the young man said that, James shook his head. "What you mean is it's most likely a C-4 bomb."

Mickey looked at James with a look of awe, "Why am I not surprised that you know exactly what he's talking about?"

"Sure, I know. RDX stands for Royal Demolition Explosive and Research Development Explosive. The other ingredients are dioctyl sebacate which makes it pliable like plastic, and minute amounts of Polyisobutylene and motor oil. It's most commonly known as C-4," said James, matter of factly.

"How in the world do you remember crap like that?" Mickey said sarcastically.

James shrugged his shoulders. "I don't know."

"Yes. He's right. That's most likely what it was. The power set off a blasting cap that exploded the bomb when you started the truck. It was straightforward, really, and it probably only took 5 minutes to hook it up. The bomber knew what he was doing," Baker responded.

"Where would you get something like that?" asked Mickey.

James spoke again. "Where do you get anything illegal? Prescription drugs, illegal guns, anything like that, you can find."

"They tell me you had a remote starter, and that's why you weren't in the truck. You're one lucky guy!" Baker said as he continued taking down the barrier around the truck. "Okay, it's clear now. You can do whatever you want with it."

"Thanks, Baker. How can I get a copy of the autopsy report on the woman we found last week?"

"I don't know. You'd have to check with the Detective in charge of this case. That would be Detective Peter Reynolds. I can give you his number if you want."

"Thanks, but I have it. Let's go, James," Mickey said, turning back toward the Humvee.

As they got into the truck, Mickey said exasperatedly, "Where do we look now? We've checked everyone out on the suspect list. All we know for sure is that someone thinks or believes we're getting close to exposing them."

James sat silently in the driver's seat. "We haven't checked everyone out, Mickey."

"Francine has no motive for killing Betty," said Mickey.

"We didn't check out Carla Briggs, the manager of the store where Betty worked. Also, we didn't check out Howard Hudson and Riley Gentry, the two people she fired. Maybe we should look more closely at them," suggested James.

James' cellphone rang, and he answered it, "Yes. We can come right over. We'll be there in half an hour."

When disconnected, Mickey asked, "That was Irene?"

"Yes, she has a lot of information, and she asked me to stop by and go over it with me. Of course, you're coming with me."

They parked in the library parking lot and went inside, straight to Irene Blalock's office.

When they entered her office, she was bent over her desk, signing some papers. She looked up, smiled at them, and motioned for them to sit down.

"Hello, Mickey. You two boys have been busy, haven't you?' she leaned back in her chair.

"Yes, we have, and I understand you've been busy helping us."

"I've been busy, but helping you, I don't know. Let's look at what I found," she said, rising from her chair, walking over to a locked filing cabinet, unlocking it, and removing a stack of papers.

Mickey picked them up and rifled through them. "You did a lot of work on this," he exclaimed.

"That's what you're paying me for," she answered.

"We're paying you?" Mickey said in surprise.

"No, silly boy. I was just kidding. It's all pro bono!" she said, laughing out loud.

"You got me on that one," Mickey said, then looked through the papers. "There must be a hundred pages of documents and plain dirt on the Braydons."

"Yes, every time I'd look at one thing, it would lead me down another road. I just followed the dirt, as you could say. Frank was a good mayor. He did a lot of good for this town, and sometimes he bribed, threatened, and even blackmailed someone into doing what he wanted.

"And at the same time, he got a bit richer in the process. In the end, the town prospered as a result. You have to decide. Did he do bad things for good reasons or good things for wrong reasons?

"There's an article where a local doctor was intoxicated during an operation, and the patient died. The family filed a lawsuit against the doctor. The doctor funded the hospital's new trauma unit, and the charges were dropped. The doctor continued to practice until his death five years ago. Frank negotiated the settlement. The family got nothing."

"I understand that, but isn't that what lawyers do? They sue and sometimes get guilty people off?"

"I said, you decide, Mickey. The doctor was his brother," she said.

"Another example. You know where that nice park is located at the edge of town? It was initially farmland, and the family lived on it for generations. Mayor Braydon convinced the tax assessor to raise the taxes to an enormous amount. The low-income family barely scraped out a living on the crops they grew, and they couldn't afford to pay the additional taxes. After a few years, they lost it to the city for unpaid taxes.

"Our wonderful mayor bought the land from the city for the balance of the unpaid taxes. Suddenly, out of the blue, he decided that the town should have a nice park for all to enjoy. He sold the land to the town for a very nice profit. Of course, another brother of Mayor Braydon got the contract to design and build the new park.

"That beautiful concert hall we have in town. He spearheaded the project, and again, his brother got the contract. It was the highest of five bids submitted. I could go on, but you can read it yourself. He's a crook, but a good mayor, and the people have paid the price for it.

"The next time you go to the hospital, remember the person who died for the funds that built that trauma unit. The next time you go to the park, remember the family that lost everything for you to enjoy it, and the next concert you attend helped pay for the mayor's vacation home in the Blue Ridge Mountains.

"There are some things about the other family members, but I'll let you read that for yourself. Sealed court records show a history of date rapes before Francis turned eighteen. The mayor had them sealed. Francine claimed a boy got her pregnant, and she had it aborted, then had a tubal ligation to prevent future pregnancies. The mayor also had those records sealed."

"What about Mrs. Braydon?" asked Mickey.

"As far as I could tell, she's clean. She overcharges for fundraisers and takes a hefty percentage cut, but other than that, she's legal. People attend her functions knowing that their tax-deductible donations go mostly in her pocket, but it makes them look good in the public's eye, so they go along with it."

"Wow," said James. "If we need something else, would you mind helping us again?"

"Oh, my, James, I haven't had so much fun in years. I'd love to help you again!"

"If those records are sealed, how did you find what was in them?" asked Mickey, impressed with her skills.

"I said they're sealed. I didn't say they were destroyed. Any more than that, I can't say," she said apologetically.

Mickey rolled his eyes and looked over at James, who was smiling like a Cheshire cat. "Where have I heard those words before?"

"I worked for a law office years ago, and I know how to do legal research. I know when and when not to keep my mouth shut." She laughed and added, "I know how to do research and find information that many lawyers can't find. Now, James, you called and added the names of Howard Hudson and Riley Gentry and asked me to check them."

"Yes. At first, we thought that they were clear, but we want to be thorough, so I added them," said James.

"It is a good thing you did. They aren't so squeaky clean either," she said, shuffling through her papers.

"The girl, Riley. I didn't find anything on her. But Howard's a different story. He has a record. It's mostly all small stuff, but the implications are for the two of you to decide. He has been arrested a couple of times on drug charges and public intoxication. No big deal there. That's a misdemeanor. That last one, arrest and conviction, was possession with intent to distribute. In plain English, he was dealing. He didn't serve any time, but he is on probation. Losing his job could impact his probation. If he didn't tell his probation officer, he could go to jail. And if he's arrested again for almost anything, he could serve time. You said he was fired for sexual indiscretions with the girl in the store's backroom?"

"That's right," said James.

"Well, you two are the detectives here, but let me put this scenario to you. What if Betty found Howard and Riley using together in the back room, or he was her dealer. Instead of reporting him, she made up the story of their sexual escapade. She needed to get them out of the store but not land them in jail. Also, it would give her motive to collect money from one or both of them," Irene said. She sat looking at both Mickey and James, waiting for a response.

In turn, they looked at each other and back and Irene. "Wow," said Mickey. "You're pretty good at finding information, and you've put out a pretty plausible cause for a motive. We need to give another visit to Howard and Riley."

James sat nodding.

"I hate to rush you out the door, but I have work to do. But if I can help you again, please let me know," she smiled and handed James all the paperwork she printed out on the people she had researched.

They got up and thanked her profusely before they walked out the door. "Do you think my truck is ready for delivery now?"

"Sure, let's go by there on the way back to the house," James said, pulling into traffic.

They went by the Ford dealership and took delivery of Mickey's new truck. He knew the doctor didn't clear him to drive yet, but he wanted to drive it home. He decided to go by Darcy and James' house to show it off. Everyone came out to look at the new truck.

Darcy stepped up to it, looked inside, and asked Mickey, "Did you get this one with a remote starter also?"

"You bet I did. I never realized how handy it would be and never thought it would save my life. It'll be part of every new vehicle I buy from now on!"

After looking at his new truck, they all went into the house. James and Mickey went into the office to talk to Darcy for a few minutes.

"Hey, would you like to see what we found that former-mayor Braydon was involved in?" said James.

Dee sat down in her office chair. "Not really, James. I don't care anymore about what either of you is doing. I want you to find the person that killed Betty Duncan and Carter so we can put an end to this."

Mickey, standing behind James, moved around beside him and said, "The killer will keep after us until he succeeds. The only way to stop him is to find him first. We can't stop."

"You're right," she said. "I just want it to be over."

"Hey, we need to reinterview these people," Mickey said as he handed her the list of names and the papers that Irene had printed out for them.

"It's Betty's boss, the grocery store manager, and the employees she fired. It's just three people. It shouldn't take too long to do it," he said.

"Irene got a lot of legal background on Howard, Riley, and Carla Briggs, but she didn't get into their bank accounts. Maybe you and Digger can find out more about that for us. They could be like the others. If they have unexplained money going in or out of their accounts, that will tell us something."

Darcy sighed and picked up a pencil, "I'll see what I can do. I'll do it, but I need to do some legal work the firm sent to me. I need to bring in enough money to pay some bills before the bank seizes our bank accounts until this thing is settled."

"We hear you," said Mickey, then walked out of the room, followed by James.

Mickey's phone rang, and when he answered it, it was Daniel, "Mickey?"

"Yeah, Pop, what's up?"

"You remember that guy you hired then we transferred him to this site for security?" Daniel asked.

"Yes."

"Guess who hasn't shown up for work since the day of the bombing?" Daniel said.

"Pop, why didn't you say something earlier? We could have been looking into him also."

"I did tell Pete, and they are looking into it. I know that you and James are working on this case, and I didn't want to add to your worries, so I thought the police could take that load off."

"Thanks. But I wish you had told me," Mickey said to his father. "When I talk to Detective Reynolds, I'll give him the employment form he filled out for us when I hired him."

"Good, Son. Now I called you because I just got a call from Detective Reynolds. He said they just arrested Wallace Cunningham, and you hold off with your investigations for a while."

"Pop, Cunningham didn't do it!"

"Pete says they have enough evidence to arrest him. I'm passing the information to you and James. Are you going to turn the rest of the investigation over to Pete?"

"I can't do that yet, Pop. We need to talk to Howard Hudson and his girlfriend again. Then we can call Detective Reynolds."

"I lost your mother to some crazy people. I don't want to lose you or James also."

"Wallace didn't do it. We can't back off now. We're getting close," Mickey said into the phone. "I've got to go. I need to talk to Reynolds. I'll talk to you later. Have you gotten a new trailer set up yet?"

"No, it'll take them a few more days to get one and get it hooked up," Daniel answered.

"Fine, Pop. Thanks for letting me do this," he said, then disconnected.

"Hey, James, the police arrested Wallace Cunningham. I'm going to the police station."

"Want company?"

"Sure, hop in the truck, and you drive."

They pulled into the police station and found Detective Reynolds talking on the phone in his office.

When he finished and hung up, he looked at Mickey and James, rolled his eyes, then motioned them over to the desk.

"Well, boys, it looks like we got it wrapped up. Cunningham is down at booking as we speak. You'll have to find someone else to sell the stocks in your company. I am glad you weren't hurt in that explosion."

"That's what we came to talk to you about. We don't believe that Cunningham killed Betty Duncan."

"Can you give us a few more days to ensure you have the right man?"

"We're sure, Mickey Ray!" he said, "He has a motive."

"What was his motive?" asked Mickey.

"She was blackmailing him."

"Can we talk to him?" asked James.

"No."

"Come on, Detective. Let us in the interrogation room. You can be right there with us. We found more information, and we need to talk to a few more people, and we'll give you everything we have."

"He's lawyered up. He won't say anything without his lawyer present."

"Then it won't hurt to speak to him."

"It's against the rules," said the Detective.

"Can you put him at the crime scene? Or maybe find the murder weapon?" asked James.

"I don't have to. We have a motive, we'll continue until we have more evidence, but we don't want him disappearing while we continue to look."

"We agreed to share everything we had and everything we found out. We're working on this together."

"The only reason I agreed to share is maybe to save us some time. So far, you've helped us a lot, but we can take it from here."

"You admitted that even you don't have anything concrete."

"We're working on this case too. We have our sources, just like you have yours. We found out that Betty got pregnant about five weeks before Cunningham killed her. She told him it was his and blackmailed him, so he had a motive. We can probably get a conviction on that much alone," said the Detective smugly.

"You mean 'allegedly' killed her!" said James.

"Whatever! We appreciate your help. Now, if you don't mind, I have work to do," he said as he opened a drawer in his desk and took out a form to begin filling out.

"One more thing," said James. "What about Mickey's truck getting blown up?"

"What about it? You can't connect it to Betty's murder," said Reynolds. "But we are looking into it, Mickey. We'll do our best to find whoever did that also."

"It has to be connected. Especially after the note and the bombing of Mickey's truck."

"I agree, there may be a connection, but we have to have proof. It could just be a disgruntled ex-employee or someone that doesn't like your new project. Look at the people who came out against your project months ago when they had that open council meeting. There must have been 50 people that didn't want it. They felt it would destroy the quaintness of this town. They don't want this town to change or grow."

Mickey sighed, "We know all about that. We were both there but protesting and attempted murder is two different things. I don't think anyone there would kill over a new housing project. And I don't think you believe it either.

"I told Pop that I would give you our workman's employment application so you would have information on him to check him out."

"Good, that might help us to track him down. Your Dad gave us his name. It was Jesse Clayton if I remember. As far as Betty Duncan, I follow the evidence. And don't forget the rule, 'follow the money.'"

"Right, and someone gave her twenty-five thousand dollars, did you consider that? Cunningham didn't give that to her because he didn't have that much. Someone else had a much bigger reason to kill her than Cunningham had," added Mickey.

"When we find that person, we'll question them also."

"You promised me a copy of the autopsy report. Can we get it while we're here?" asked Mickey.

"Oh, I did promise you that," he said as he pulled open one of his desk drawers. "Here it is. I don't know where or how you got it if you're asked. I'll vehemently deny giving it to you or allowing you access to it. Do you understand?" he said as he laid the papers on the desk.

Mickey said, "Yes."

"Now, I'm going to the restroom, and when I get back, these papers will be sitting here on my desk, undisturbed," Reynolds added as he got up.

Again, Mickey nodded in understanding.

"When I get back, both of you will be gone! And I meant it when I said I appreciate your help. If it helps, we'll continue to investigate and find the person that bombed your truck. We don't take things like that lightly. We consider that attempted murder."

As Reynolds walked away, James took out his phone and began snapping pictures of the report. He did so as Mickey attempted to block the view of anyone that might try to see what they were doing. When James finished, he straightened the report as they found it.

Mickey and James looked at each other and agreed. There was nothing else they could do here, so they turned and left.

When they got into Mickey's truck, they sat silently with their private thoughts.

Finally, James asked his brother-in-law, "I've been sitting here watching the cogs turn in your head. What're you thinking?"

"I've been putting together a timeline. We need to check out where every person on our list was when Betty got pregnant," he answered.

"Why, what good does that do us?" asked James. "Now we have the reporter. What do we do about him?"

"I don't know. Right now, I'm the prime suspect for his murder."

"No one, even Reynolds, thinks you had anything to do with that."

"True, but he has to follow the evidence."

"Yeah, but there isn't any that points to you other than motive."

"That in itself is huge. And to the people in this town, it makes my family look even worse. If we find out where everyone was when Betty got pregnant, that could eliminate several people," Mickey said thoughtfully. "Also, we need to go back and confront Howard."

Mickey's phone rang, he saw it was Francine. "I've got to take this," he said as he pressed the answer icon.

"Hey there, Mickey. Are you busy right now?" came Francine's voice over the phone.

"Yes. I'm always busy. What's up?"

"I want some barbeque," she said. "Can you meet me at the Bridgeton airport in a couple of hours?"

"I don't know if I can get there that soon. I have some things I must get done today," Mickey answered.

"Can't it wait until tomorrow?"

"No, we need to do this today," Mickey said.

"James is with me. We have to interview more people and take James back to his 'Vee.'"

"What's a Vee?"

"It's what he calls his Humvee. I can be there in say about two and a half hours. What do you have in mind for barbeque?"

"You'll see, Mickey Ray. I'll see you in two and a half hours. Just drive on back to hanger 14-C," she said and disconnected before Mickey could object.

James asked Mickey what Francine wanted.

"I don't know. She said she wanted barbeque and asked me to meet her at the airport."

"By what I heard, we're going to interview Howard and Riley now?" James asked.

"Yep," Mickey answered as he drove to Howard and Riley's house. They pulled up and noticed that both cars were home. When Riley answered the door, she asked why there were back.

"We got some more information, and we want to talk to you about it," said James.

She held the door tightly against herself and the frame so they couldn't see inside, but they could smell the sickeningly sweet odor of Marijuana wafting from inside the living room. "We told you all we know," she said with a distinct tone that indicated that they had interrupted a private affair.

"We need to talk to you some more," said Mickey.

"Come back later," she said, "and maybe we can talk."

Mickey narrowed his eyes and said sternly, "Riley, get Howard. We'll talk NOW."

"Umm, I don't like your tone," she said and started to close the door.

Mickey stepped forward and put his foot in the door, blocking it from closing. "You'll get Howard and talk with us or we'll call the police. If you talk to us NOW, you can come outside and talk to us on the steps. If we need to call the police, they'll come inside. I'm sure you don't want any authorities inside now, do you?"

"No, but we're…"

"Call Howard, and both of you come outside now. As you can see, my partner, James, is dialing 911 as I speak." Mickey pointed to James standing there with his phone in his hand.

"Don't call anyone, please," she turned and called out in the darkness of the room behind her, "Howard, we need to go out and talk to the guys that came here a few days ago about Betty Duncan."

Inside, a voice called back, "Tell them to go away!"

"Howie, they won't go away. They insist on talking now."

"Tell them, I said to leave," came the voice again.

James stepped around Mickey and slammed his shoulder against the door. It flew open and slammed against the wall behind it, sinking the knob into the wall.

James called back to the voice, "Howard, don't make me come in there after you. If you do, I'll call the police and make sure that we talk through bars at the town police station. They will be charging you with drug charges when that happens, and you won't be coming back to this house for many years. Do you understand me?"

"Hey, man it's legal inside my house," the voice said.

"It depends on the amount you have. Anything over that amount can be interpreted as intent to distribute," James called to Howard.

"How much can I have?" came the voice.

"Why don't we let the police decide that when they get here?" answered Mickey.

"Last time you were here, you said you weren't the police!" Howard answered.

"We aren't, but if we call them, they will be here, and when they enter this house, they will find drugs. You know the rest of that story. Do you want to test my patience?"

"No, man. Don't call the cops. Hold on. I'll be right there."

Mickey and James could hear noises from the room, and James bolted off the steps and ran around toward the back of the house. Mickey stood waiting for Riley to run. She stood without saying a word as more smoke billowed out the door of the house.

"Why do people run?" said Mickey.

"Because Howard's an idiot, that's why," said Riley swaying slightly as she tried to clear her head of the fog of the drugs.

As they waited for James to return with Howard, Mickey looked at Riley standing in front of him with nothing on but a lacy bra and a pair of men's brief underwear. He tried to act casually, but he felt a bit uncomfortable.

On the other hand, Riley seems perfectly at ease, scantily dressed in the doorway.

After a couple of minutes, James came around the house with Howard, dressed only in a pair of white briefs. It was apparent what was about to happen if they hadn't interrupted Howard and Riley as they smoked the weed that Mickey could see lying on the coffee table.

When James came back up on the porch, he shoved Howard into the room past Riley, still standing in the doorway.

James told Howard to open the window to let some of the stench and smoke out. He told Mickey to watch them as he went back through the house to open the back door and allow a crosswind to clear the smoke further. When James got back, he shoved Howard down onto the couch and motioned for Riley to join Howard on the sofa.

"All we wanted to do was ask you a few questions, but since you gave us such a rude greeting, we want the entire story of why Betty fired you. We want the truth, or we will call the police, and you can tell them downtown," said James.

"Listen, man. We don't want any trouble. We didn't know what you wanted. We thought that maybe you came back to rob us or something."

"That is a stupid excuse, and you know it. You were getting ready for… umm…you know, and you didn't want us to interrupt," said James.

"Okay, I admit that, but why didn't you just come back like we asked?"

"If you had been more polite and not such a butthead, maybe we would have, but when you ran out the back door, and in your underwear, no less, that's when we decided that we definitely would talk now. I don't care what you do in the privacy of your own home. I don't care if you burn your brain up with weed, but I do care about the lie you told us. Now, talk, and it had better be the truth this time. I swear I'll dial 911!" James said with finality.

"Okay. Okay, I'll tell you. But you swear you won't call the police?" he pleaded.

"No, I'm not going to promise you anything. Tell us the truth, or else!"

"I did tell you the truth. We were in the stockroom of the grocery store when Betty came in and..."

James turned to Mickey, "He's starting with the same lie he told us before. Hand me the phone."

"No, wait. What do you want me to tell you?"

"We want you to tell us about the drugs you were dealing. Do you think we're stupid? You were selling drugs out of the back room. Weren't you?" James asked.

"Okay. Yes. Riley wanted a joint, and I agreed to give her one if she would... you know...let me..."

"I see the picture now," interrupted James and held his hand palm out to stop Howard from talking. "Betty caught you in the act, correct?"

"Yeah, we had just finished smoking one, and Betty came in just as we started..."

"I got it, skip that part, what happened then?" continued James.

"Well, she fired us. She agreed to say it was for 'bad conduct' and wouldn't report me to the cops for the drugs if I gave her the rest. So, I gave it to her. When I filed for unemployment, she kept her word on not reporting the drug part, and she gave us a good reference. The rest is just like I told you, honest."

Riley spoke up then, "That's not the whole story. Tell them the rest, Howard."

Howard turned to Riley and glared at her.

James said to Mickey, "They aren't telling us everything. Give me the phone, Mickey."

It was Howard's turn to hold up his hands in a stop gesture. "Wait, she told us that we had to give her half of our unemployment checks, or she'd call them back and change the good reference to a bad one. That's one of the reasons we moved in together, to share the rent. She wanted the money in cash, so we met her every week. Then she just stopped showing up to get her money."

"You were duped by her. Once the papers are filed with the state, she can't go back and change it. That would indicate that she lied on the first report. The most she could do is give a bad reference to a future employer," explained Mickey.

"What else could we do? If she had called the police and told them what happened, I would have gone back to jail. You said so yourself when you first got here," said Howard.

"We don't know what you could have done, but now you have a Class A motive for murder!"

"I didn't kill her. All we wanted was to be left alone. We didn't hurt anyone. I swear. I didn't kill her. We had nothing to do with her death."

"Where were you between six and eight weeks ago?" asked Mickey.

"How should I know where I was? On what day? What day of the week was she killed? Even if you could tell me that, I wouldn't know what I was doing on that day. Do you know where you were on the exact day and time she was killed and…" Howard rambled on.

"You can shut up now. We don't want to hear anything else you have to say. You lied to us. All promises are null and void," said Mickey. He motioned for James to leave.

As they walked out, James said, "He has a point. We don't know the exacts of anything in this case. What do we do now? We promised Howard we wouldn't tell the police what we found out."

"We promised that when we were here the first time. Howard now has the strongest motive of any of our suspects. I think we should call and tell Detective Reynolds what we know. And, in time, he'll run a background check on Howard and will come to the same conclusions we did. So, we'll get on Reynold's good side if we call him first," said Mickey.

Since James was still driving, Mickey dialed the phone and asked for Detective Peter Reynolds.

CHAPTER 19

Raleigh, North Carolina

After dropping James at home, Mickey drove to the town airport and to the hanger number that Francine had given him. As he drove up, he saw a pretty little low-wing airplane.

The little Piper plane was a single-engine plane. It was painted two-toned, white on the top and dark blue on the bottom half of the fuselage with tricycle landing gear. There were teardrop-style fairings around the wheels, and the entire plane had very smooth lines. It was as clean and shiny as a brand-new car.

Mickey saw Francine talking to her brother. She turned as he walked up and smiled, "Hey, Mickey. Do you remember my twin brother, Francis, from school?"

"Yes, but it's been many years since then," he said as he shook Francis' hand.

"How are you, Mickey Ray."

"Beautiful airplane you have, Francis," Mickey complimented.

"Thanks. It's old but well taken care of. I keep it in top shape. They first came out in 1960 and have been such a popular plane they're in production even today. Come on over, and I'll show you," Francis said with pride.

They walked over, Francis continued pointing out the features of his plane as though he was a salesman, and Mickey was looking to purchase it. "I had the engine rebuilt last year. As you can see, it has dual controls and four seats. I've added autopilot and more instrumentation so I can even fly at night."

Mickey shook his head in admiration. "So you're an IFR-rated pilot."

"I got my 'Instrument Flight Rating' last year, while it was down for the engine rebuild, and at the same time had the new equipment installed."

"Do all the Cherokees only have one door? I notice that the one door is on the right side?" Mickey asked.

"Yes, and I don't know why they didn't have one on the pilot's side, but I guess it keeps the cost down a few dollars. Francine said you wanted to come with me to take a ride down to Raleigh this afternoon?"

"No, I never said that. She called me and said she wanted some barbeque and then said to meet here," said Mickey as he looked over at Francine, who had a huge smile on her face at her mild deception.

She came over to Mickey, grabbed his arm, and said, "I said I wanted barbeque. I didn't say where I wanted to eat. Francis is flying to Raleigh to take care of some business at the restaurants he owns down there, and I thought we could go along for the ride and have a wonderful evening."

"That sounds like an enjoyable evening, but when are we coming back?"

"Tomorrow afternoon."

"Fran, I have a lot of work to do. Can't it be another time? We have some inspections in a couple of days, and I need to be onsite to ensure everything goes smoothly," Mickey said.

"Oh, Mickey. Would you please go with us? We'll have a good time. I promise," Francine pleaded.

"You have people that work for you. Can't one of them fill in, or maybe you can postpone those things for a couple of days?"

"Fine. Let me make a couple of calls to see what I can do," Mickey said, pulling out his phone. He pushed some buttons on his phone and put the phone up to his ear.

Francine and Francis walked over to the plane and put their luggage inside. After making several calls, Mickey went over to them and announced that he could take a day or two away from the construction site.

"Both of you have luggage, but I didn't come prepared to spend the night!"

Francine wrinkled her nose and smiled, "That's okay, Mickey. We'll go shopping and buy anything you need when we get there. Now, let's get inside and get in the sky. Francis' a great pilot."

After getting into the plane, with Mickey and Francine in the back seats and Francis in the pilot's seat, they taxied onto the runway and took off. As they climbed into the sky, Francine pointed out various landmarks on the ground.

"See over there, Mickey? That's Williamsburg, and in a few minutes, we'll see Hampton and Newport News as we turn around. We'll head a bit inland, but we'll see Norfolk in the distance.

"When we get on target for Raleigh, Francis, would you dip the wing a bit so we can see over the water before we go too far inland? Maybe we can see a ship leaving the port of Portsmouth," she said. "This low wing plane makes it harder to see the things directly below the plane."

"Have you ever been in a small plane before, Mickey?" asked Francis.

"Yes, I have, but only a couple of times. I thought I might want to learn to fly when I was a teenager, but I got into cars instead."

Francis turned back to the controls, "I understand. Cars are okay, but I feel completely free when I'm flying. I'm above all the stresses of the world."

"That's the way I feel when I'm driving around some country road in a car."

"What made you get into Rolls Royces instead of muscle or sports cars. Most young kids, and even guys our age like fast cars instead of luxury vehicles?"

"Good question, Francis. I don't know. Pop always liked exotic cars, and I guess I got the bug from him. That's all."

Francis occasionally reached up to one of the controls, flipped a switch, and looked around to make sure everything was fine and the skies were clear. Fran reached over and took Mickey's hand. She squeezed, and Mickey returned the squeeze as he looked at her smile with her eyes closed and her head laying against the headrest.

They sat in silence as the engine's drone permeated the inside of the cockpit.

Finally, Francis spoke again, "Hey Mickey, Francine tells me you're trying to find the person that killed Betty Anne?"

"Who?" asked Mickey.

"Betty Anne Duncan. The woman you found at your construction site. Francine says you're trying to find her killer."

"Yes, we have a list of suspects we're checking into," Mickey explained.

"It was a nice funeral she had. Francine also told me that your family paid for it."

"Thank you, Francis. We felt we owed her mother that much. I don't remember seeing you there."

"Yes, I kind of hung back. I didn't want to be in the way. You know what I mean."

"Yeah, I understand. Did you know her very well?"

"No. I didn't know her at all. I met her a couple of times, but that's it," he said. "Are you making acceptable progress?"

"We are. We've been checking on our list of people. The police have made an arrest, but we are certain he didn't kill her," Mickey said, looking out the window.

"Who did they arrest?"

"Wallace Cunningham. They picked him up this morning. He doesn't fit."

"The police must have evidence if they took him in," Francis said.

"The evidence they have is weak. I don't think the district attorney can make a case against him stick. They say it's because Betty tried to blackmail him, but that isn't enough to convict him. They're trying to find more evidence, and so they'll keep him locked up until they can build a case."

"You think they can do it?"

"I don't know, Francis. My gut tells me otherwise. Anyway, James and I have a few things up our sleeve, so we'll keep looking. Earlier today, we interviewed a couple that worked at the store with Betty. She fired them for bad conduct, so they have motive also. It's a mess, but James and I will work it out. Howard and Riley are rock solid. It could still be someone else. You never know."

Francis flipped a few more switches and said, "Francine told me someone put a bomb in your truck. Do you have any clues who did that?"

"No, not yet. I'm letting the police work that part of the case. They think it is someone that is trying to stall the construction. What bothers me is that someone killed the reporter that was writing all those derogatory stories in the newspaper. Those stories are doing a lot of damage to our company."

"In what way, Mickey?"

"People think that we had Betty killed. There is no reason we would do that. Anyway, people are pulling their financial support. Now with Carter Evans dead, people might blame us for that."

"Why would they think you killed him. He is just a reporter, Mickey," Francis said.

"Since his front-page stories were hurting our business, the police say I have a motive to kill him," Mickey answered.

"You didn't kill him, did you?"

"No. Of course, I didn't. If I did, you don't think I'd tell anyone do you?"

"I am an attorney. If you hired me as your attorney, I couldn't tell if you did confess to me."

"Francie, I wouldn't kill anyone. I don't know why you would even ask me that question."

"Don't get offended, Mickey. I was just talking. I certainly wasn't making any judgments about anything," Francis said condescendingly. "We'll be making our final approach in a couple of minutes. Wake up Francine so that she can get ready for landing. Make sure her belt's fastened."

Mickey gently awakened Francine. She shook her head back and forth as she woke up, rubbed her eyes, and looked out the window.

"We're almost ready to land, Fran," said Mickey as he reached over and checked her seatbelt.

Francis landed the plane and parked it. They all got out, checked into the airport terminal, rented a car, and went to a hotel.

When Francis stepped up to the counter, the Front Desk clerk said to him, "Good afternoon, Mr. Braydon. How are you today?"

"Fine, Arnold."

"Would you like your regular room, sir? I think the executive suite is available."

"That's fine, Arnold."

"If a young lady is arriving later, I could have some flowers sent to the room, or maybe a box of chocolates?" he suggested.

"No. Nothing sent up," answered Francis.

"So, you're alone this trip?" he said.

"Yes, I'm alone today," Francis said. He got his room key, and started for the elevator.

Francine stepped up to the counter and asked for one room, one king-sized bed, for two people.

Mickey moved up beside her and corrected her. "Make that two rooms, with one person each, please."

Francine glared at him and walked away with her bag. Mickey filled in the check-in paperwork, paid for both rooms, and took their key cards. Walking to her standing by the elevator, he handed Francine a key card.

She snatched the card from his hand and said, "You can be a real killjoy sometimes, Mickey Ray Christianson."

When they boarded the elevator, the door slid closed. Mickey grinned at her, pinned her against the wall, and kissed her. "Hey, at least we're on the same floor," he whispered.

"Big deal!" she said, turning away from him.

He backed away and laughed, "We need to go shopping. I'll let you pick my new underwear."

She turned back toward him with a mischievous smile, "Can I help you take the old ones off?"

"Well…" he said as the elevator doors opened up on their floor. He took her bag from her hand and led her to her room.

He took her card and waved it in front of the lock, and when it clicked, he opened it. Leaning inside, he placed her bag on the floor, gently pushed her inside, and backed outside again. As he allowed the door to close, he said, "I'll go wash my face and hands and see you in the lobby in thirty minutes, and we'll go get that barbeque you said you wanted."

He quickly went to his room and washed his hands and face to freshen up, and went back downstairs to talk to Arnold at the check-in counter. As he walked up to the counter, Arnold was shuffling papers.

"Is your room acceptable, sir?" Arnold asked.

"Oh, yes. It's fine. I have a couple of questions," he said, holding up his phone with a picture of Betty Duncan. "When was this woman in here last with Mr. Braydon?"

"Our patrons expect us to keep their personal information private, and he tips me very well to keep his 'indiscretions' very private."

"Most assuredly, Arnold. I'd expect nothing less. I'm an employee of his, and I'm following orders. If I don't get this information, I could be fired. I need this job. You understand, don't you?"

"You could be fired for not getting this information?" Arnold said questioningly.

"Yes, Mr. Braydon can be a real pain in the neck to work for, you see. Look, let me tell you the truth. The woman in this picture is trying to say Mr. Braydon got her pregnant and wants him to take responsibility and support his child. He isn't the father, so if we can prove they weren't here when she got pregnant, he's off the hook. I'm trying to help Mr. Braydon.

He wants it done discreetly, you know, below the radar. That's why I'm here instead of him."

"But, Mr. Christianson, he has brought several ladies here. He should be more careful," Arnold said.

"I couldn't agree more, Arnold, but this one time, he wasn't, and now it may come back to bite him. I'm trying to protect him, that's all. Will you help me, please?"

"It'll take me a few minutes to find the records," Arnold said.

"That's acceptable. Will you be here later this evening?"

"Yes, sir. I have the evening shift. I get off at midnight."

"I'll pick up the information before you get off at the end of your shift. Don't let them see you give it to me. When this is over, I'll let Mr. Braydon know, and he'll make sure you are well taken care of. Deal?"

"Deal, sir."

Mickey thanked him and walked over to an upholstered armchair, picked up one of the magazines off of a table, and began to thumb through it. Just then, Fran stepped out of the elevator. While in her room, she had changed into a black crocheted crop top that showed her midriff and low-rise skin-tight jeans.

She was naturally beautiful with her hair in a ponytail and her touched-up makeup, but these clothes made her look especially young and sensual. He noticed Arnold and gave him a thumbs-up as they walked out the door.

"I called Francis' room, and he said he would take a cab so that we can drive the rental car. We'll go to his barbeque restaurant and have dinner first. Then we'll get you some clothes to wear tomorrow," said Francine.

Francine drove and pointed out some landmarks until they got to the restaurant, and then she parked in the "reserved" spot that was obviously for Francis. They were greeted and seated at the best table near the back to have privacy. As they sat down, Francine ordered a beer and the same for Mickey Ray.

"I don't see you as a 'beer' person, Fran," said Mickey taking his seat.

"I'm not really, but wine doesn't go with barbeque. This place is loaded with rednecks, so I try to fit in," she said. "I much prefer a nice glass of merlot."

Mickey laughed, "Hey, don't put down rednecks. I know a lot of them, and they're good people. As a matter of fact, I consider myself a redneck of sorts."

She smiled, leaned over the table, looked into his coal-black eyes, and said, "You're definitely no redneck, Mickey Ray." She took his hand into hers and patted it gently on the table.

He grinned at her for a few moments. "As you remember, I started at the bottom of Pop's real estate business. I've had my hands in more toilets and sewers than some plumbers. I can relate to the average working man, and I'll get right down in the trenches with them if I have to."

"Eww," she said and pulled her hand away. "Okay, don't get so testy over a bunch of worker bees, Mickey."

He reached over the table, took back her hand, and squeezed it. "I was just kidding, Fran. I didn't mean anything by it. But if it weren't for those 'worker bee's,' this country wouldn't be what it is. I didn't take any offense to it.

"What do you suggest on the menu, pretty lady?" he asked.

"I think they have the best ribs in the state right here, but they're messy."

"Which ones, the baby backs or St. Louis style?" he asked.

"They're both great. I like the baby backs because the meat falls off the bone, and I don't have to pick them up with my fingers."

"Okay, you get the baby backs, and I'll dig into a pile of St. Louis style. I don't mind getting my fingers dirty. If I do, I'll just lick the sauce off them," he laughed.

She smiled back at him. She cocked her head and said, "I'll lick them for you."

They both laughed and placed their order when the server came to the table.

"What made Francis buy a restaurant? And a barbeque one at that?" he asked.

"He likes barbeque, and he wanted a tax-deductible reason to get out of town. Francis likes to fly and get away from it all sometimes. He bought that plane, and it's pretty expensive to maintain. Since Francis owns a business, every time he needs to get out of town, he flies and stays in the same hotel we're in, and he can count off the entire trip from his taxes."

"So, this trip is just a tax deduction for him?" Mickey asked.

"He needed to check on a few things this time. He's interviewing some new employees, and also, he's thinking of remodeling the entire place, so he came to go over some plans with the architect. We literally came along for the ride."

"Does he count it as a business trip when he brings his mistresses here for a weekend?"

"How insulting, Mickey Ray!" she said with contempt.

"He does bring them here. We both know that. You don't need to get upset about it."

"You make it sound so tawdry. His wife, Helen, is a cold little witch. He's asked her for a divorce, numerous times, but she refuses. So, they live in peaceful coexistence. She says she's refusing to leave him for the sake of the kids, not to mention her status with the community."

He reached over and took her hand in his. "Look, Fran. I don't care about your brother. I only care about you."

"I care about you too, Mickey, but why are you saying such nasty things about Francis?"

"I don't mean to be nasty. I'm just stating facts, that's all. While you were asleep on the ride here, he asked me if I killed that newspaper reporter."

"Why would he ask that?" she questioned.

"We were just talking, that's all. Just like when I said he brings his mistress here. Just conversation. As he said, no judgments."

"I don't know why he would think you would do something like that!" she said.

"He didn't mean anything. He's a lawyer. He asks questions. That's what lawyers do. Like detectives."

"You're right. I agree. How's your investigation into Betty's death coming along?" she asked.

"My, my, dear Fran. That's not pleasant, but to answer your question, we are making progress."

"How do you investigate a murder?"

"I don't know. I'm not a detective, but James and I made a list of suspects, then began eliminating each one. The one that's left is the killer."

"But what if no one is left?" she asked.

"Then you start all over. Sometimes you never find the killer. We won't give up until we find the person. They arrested Wallace Cunningham yesterday, but I don't think he did it. We're working on that."

"Who's Wallace Cunningham?"

"He's a financial planner and is also one of the people helping us by selling shares in this new project we're working on. Every share he sells, we have more funds to complete it. He admitted to having a brief affair with Betty and says she tried to blackmail him into giving her money for the child."

"Am I on your suspect list, Mickey?"

"No. Of course not."

"Good. I don't like people rummaging into my personal life."

Mickey picked up the bottle of beer. Francine did the same, and they clinked their bottles in a toast. As they dug into the meat, Francine used her knife to cut the meat off the bones, and Mickey picked his food up with his hands and grinned at Francine as he took a huge bite of a delicious barbeque rib.

She laughed, "You are an incorrigible redneck, Mickey Ray Christianson."

"Why I take that as a compliment," and he took another bite, getting sauce on his face.

She took her napkin and wiped it off, and for a few moments, all was well with the world. They finished their dinner, went shopping for a change of clothes for Mickey, and headed back to the hotel. Mickey took Francine to her room, and they kissed goodnight. He refused once again when she invited him to spend the night in her room. After leaving her, he went downstairs and got the copies of Francis' stays in the hotel for the last few months. Arnold, the desk clerk, had circled the dates that Betty had accompanied Francis.

When Mickey got back to his room, he dialed his phone, and James answered and said, "Hey, bro. What's happening in Carolina?"

"Not much, but I do have some more information."

"Tell me. I've got some to report also. Irene is phenomenal and super fast at digging up stuff," said James.

"First, we need to do a deep dive on Francis Braydon. While we were in the air flying here, Francis mentioned that he was at Betty's funeral, and he referred to her as 'Betty Anne.' No one ever called her that. When we checked in, the front desk clerk asked him if he wanted his regular room and did he want flowers or chocolates for when someone arrived later."

"He admitted to you he had an affair with Betty?" asked James.

"No, he said he had only met her a couple of times. I took a shot in the dark when I asked Arnold, the desk clerk, about her coming here with Francis. I told him that she was trying to get Francis to support his child," Mickey said.

"You 'kind of' told him the truth. You just didn't tell him that you're trying to solve her murder, and he is a suspect," James said.

"That's pretty much it. What's your news?"

James took a deep breath and started, "We didn't find anything new on Mike, but Ralph Clark's a different story. Remember, he spent time in prison for car theft. There's an open warrant for his arrest in Georgia. Pretty much the same thing. Car theft. They had his DNA on the car when they found what was left of it."

"I guess he didn't learn from his first experience in jail."

"Do you think we should notify Detective Reynolds of what we found?"

Mickey thought for a moment, then said, "Definitely, but I'm sure they already know it. They chose not to tell us. They can run searches and checks and get that info in minutes. I don't know why they haven't talked to him yet."

"Maybe they did, but Ralph didn't tell us."

"Possibly, but I doubt it. As I said earlier, before I left, we should report Howard. He's first on my list right now, but that could change when we reinterview others again. And if the police keep digging, they'll find out on their own."

"True. Since they've already arrested Cunningham, they probably won't look any further," added James.

"I agree. When the police get a suspect, they quit looking for anyone else. They move on to another case. It is the typical situation of the overworked and underpaid. The police mean well, but they're working on deadlines, underfunded, pushed by their bosses and media to close a case. It's not entirely their fault."

"Have you heard anything on leads to Carter Evans' murder?" said, Mickey.

James hesitated, then said, "No, but the stories have stopped, and the newspaper is keeping quiet about it. It's like the stories never started. It seems like they would have put someone in his place to continue what he started."

"I caught your hesitation. What are your thoughts on it? The total blackout of his case?"

"The paper doesn't have any more information and possibly doesn't have the inside sources that Carter had, and if they say the wrong thing, they could be sued. Carter was meticulous in how he reported his information.

He did it as inuendoes, not accusations. It's always possible someone with influence made the paper stop printing the story. What're we going to do?" James asked.

"You could be right on all points. So, we keep looking until we're sure we have the correct person. We still have people on our suspect list. That's Cunningham, Ralph, and now Howard. He goes back to the top."

"What about Braydon?"

"Francis is now on the list, but very low. It seems his wife is aware of his affairs and doesn't care as long as he stays out of the public's eye and she keeps her social status. He gets to have his cake and eat it too."

"That's a sad way to live, Mickey."

"Yes, it is, but some people thrive on that stuff."

"When are you coming back?"

"Tomorrow. We can start on that timeline I mentioned earlier. I have Francis' timeline here. We'll look at Cunningham's, Ralph's, and Howard's to see who comes together."

After disconnecting, Mickey took a long cool shower. It had been a long and stressful day. There was new information on Francis and Mickey's conflicted feelings about Fran.

The following day came way too early. Mickey had spent a fitful night tossing and turning in the king-sized bed. He awoke to the ringing of the phone in his bedroom. When he answered, it was Francine.

"Hey there, lover boy. Time to get up. Meet me downstairs in the hotel restaurant. We'll have some breakfast before we go to the airport."

"Okay," said Mickey as he hung up the phone.

They all met at the hotel restaurant, had breakfast, and Francis flew them home without incident. Mickey thanked Francis for letting him go with them, and he and Francine agreed to get together again soon.

CHAPTER 20

Ralph Takes Off

It was almost noon when Mickey left the Bridgeton airport. He called his father and went by the construction site to check on the construction progress and the new office trailer.

"Hey, Pop. Wow, the new trailer is nice but almost a carbon copy of the old one," said Mickey as he came inside.

"Yep, they're pretty much all the same. I'm still trying to arrange the files and get the paperwork in order. Fortunately, the main fire wasn't in here, so we didn't lose much. How was your trip?"

"It was good. Francine is a lot of fun, but, well, Pop, she can be pretty aggressive, if you know what I mean," Mickey said.

"No, I don't. I chased your mother for months. It was a real cat and mouse game," and they both laughed.

"I guess a lot of things were different back then. Still, Francine's beautiful, and we get along so well. Sorry I've not been much help lately. Between Fran and trying to find Betty's killer, I haven't been around as much as I should."

"Yeah, you haven't had your head in the game, or at least in this game. Remember, you can't do everything. Don't spread yourself too thin, son, but I know things will settle down when this thing with Betty Duncan and that horrible Carter Evans is cleared up."

"I haven't dated anyone since Valerie left. We talk every week or so, and I still miss her, but talking to her and having her here isn't the same."

Daniel put his arm around Mickey's shoulder, "I know, son. You've heard the old saying, 'time heals all wounds.' You'll eventually get over Valerie, and you'll find someone else. Maybe it'll be Francine Braydon, but if not her, God will send someone just right for you. I know He will."

"You're right, Pop. Sometimes it just hurts."

"I know. I can't help you with that. You have to go through that alone. Until then, let's see if we can get a new apartment complex built," Daniel said as he backed away from Mickey and walked over to some prints spread out on a large table in the corner of the room."

"Has Detective Reynolds called you about Carter Evans' murder progress?"

"Yes, he called this morning. He could tell me that Carter was shot from close range with a small-caliber handgun. They dusted his apartment for prints, and they're running them through the database. He said to say thanks for the heads up on Howard and Riley. They picked both of them up but think that they will probably drop the charges against her. She probably wasn't aware of the extent of his dealing, and she has a clean slate, and they don't want to ruin her life. If they don't drop the charges, she'll get probation. He admitted he had more but couldn't tell me. And he told me you could come by the station and pick your PPK handgun. They fired it, and it wasn't the gun that killed Evans."

"I could have told them that, Pop," said Mickey. "I wish they hadn't fired it. It was brand new, never fired. By firing it, it lowers the value. I only had it because it was the brand of gun carried by James Bond in the original books."

They talked about the progress of the basic framing of the buildings and the upcoming plumbing inspections. Mickey said he would do a pre-inspection to ensure it would pass before the city inspector came out. If he failed something, it would hold up construction. As they were concluding the progress check, James came in.

"Hey, Bro, you're back," he said to Mickey.

"Yep. Are you ready to check out our suspects again?" asked Mickey.

"Anytime you are," he answered.

They said goodbye to Daniel and left in Mickey's new truck.

"How's your father taking it that you're spending a lot of time 'dating' and running around trying to find a murderer instead of working on the construction project?" asked James.

"All in all, Pop's taking it well. I feel a bit bad about not being at the site as much as I should. After all, he put me in charge of the project. Are we going to check out Ralph first?"

"Yes, we need to ask him some more questions," answered James.

Mickey turned into Carlson's Garage. They saw Ralph on a creeper draining oil from a car as they pulled up. When they walked up to him, he rolled himself out from under the car and looked up at them.

"Can I help you guys?" he asked.

"Ralph, remember me? I'm the one that asked you about Betty Duncan a couple of weeks ago," said James, although he knew Ralph remembered him. James knew that he was a difficult person to forget.

"Yeah, I remember you," he said, sitting up on the creeper.

"We need to ask you some more questions."

"I told you all I know about Betty, if that's what this is about," he said. "I've been reading in the paper about you, Mickey Ray Christianson. The paper said that you killed her."

"No, it didn't. You need to learn to read. It said I had motive and could have done it. It didn't say that I did it. Get your facts straight," Mickey said defensively and moved toward Ralph.

James held up his palm on Mickey's chest to stop his advance. "Cool down, Mickey. He doesn't know what he's talking about."

Mickey stopped, took a deep breath, and let it out. "Yeah, you're right."

James looked around and lowered his voice as he spoke to Ralph, "Why don't we step away from some of the other people here to talk?"

As Ralph was getting up, Mickey said to him, "Why are you laying on your back doing that when you have a lift in the next bay?"

"Because the other mechanic just let it down and took a car off of it. He's bringing another one to put back on it. I can wait all day to do this oil change, or just get down and do it from the floor and move on to a customer that'll make me some money," he said.

"What do you look for?" Mickey said, trying to control his rising blood pressure as they followed Ralph into the office.

"We look for worn belts, worn tires, maybe a brake job. Simple stuff like that."

James stepped up and started, "Ralph, we did some more checking on you. Did you know there is an active warrant for your arrest in Georgia?"

"I don't know what you're talking about."

"Yes, you do. And when you're caught, you'll go back to jail to serve out the rest of your sentence. We know you got out of jail early on your first conviction, but you didn't learn. You did the same thing again. You came here to a small town to hide," stated James.

"I didn't do it. I was framed!" he said.

"Sure, that's what they all say," said Mickey.

"No. Really. I was framed, but you're right. I did run. I came here because I thought I could get a job and keep my nose clean. No one would ever find me."

"Well, you're wrong about that, weren't you? We found you, and I suspect that the local police will find you also."

"You think so?"

"We did, so why wouldn't they find out?" said Mickey.

"Oh, man. This is bad. I mean, really bad. I'm not a bad person. I didn't mean to shoot that guy years ago. It was an accident," he said as he sat down in a chair behind the office desk.

"We don't believe that garbage, but why don't you tell us anyway. I don't understand how you accidentally take a gun to commit a crime and accidentally shoot someone."

"I didn't take a gun…."

"Why don't you start from the beginning and tell us the whole story," suggested James.

Ralph sat staring at the desk.

"Talk, or I'll call the police and report you myself," said Mickey.

"Fine. As a teenager, I did small stuff. I'd steal radios out of cars. But then security systems became popular, and it got harder to steal. Then one night, I was inside a car pulling out the radio when this guy came out and caught me. It turned out he was the head of a local gang of car thieves that stole entire cars and stripped them for parts. He told me he wouldn't hurt me if I stole for them to pay for the damage I had done trying to take the radio out of his car.

"They had me steal to order. Someone would come to their shop and need a part that was hard to find or very expensive. I would steal it for them. I stole high-end stereo systems. I got a partner, and we could jack up a car, and steal the tires in less than thirty seconds, and be gone with the car on blocks while the alarm was blaring over the entire neighborhood. Once I stole an entire door from a caddie. Another time, I took out a complete rear end and differential in fifteen minutes. We were good. And then…"

"Now you're just bragging. Skip past that crap and tell us how you 'accidentally' shot someone," said James.

"Oh, yeah. Well, I was stealing this custom steering wheel. You know a custom steering wheel can cost a lot of money. Anyway, I was taking it off the car when this guy came out with a gun. I didn't know it, but he had a silent alarm on the car. We got into a struggle, and the gun went off. It didn't kill him, but he's paralyzed. In court, they didn't even consider that he had the gun and was about to shoot me! So, he got shot while I was defending myself."

"Sorry, but I don't agree with your 'self-defense' case," said Mickey. "If you hadn't been stealing the man's property, it wouldn't have happened. Don't cry to me about that. You were guilty of all charges."

James interjected, "That doesn't explain the part about you being framed. It sounded like when you got out of jail, you picked up where you left off. That is stealing cars or parts again."

"When they found out I had gotten out of jail, they wanted me to work for them again. They told me if I didn't, they would see that I went back and served the rest of my term. I refused, and they framed me for another theft."

Mickey shook his head, "That story doesn't fly. They found your fingerprints all over the stolen car, right where you left it."

"That's the part where I was framed. They put my fingerprints on the car. They can do that."

"No, they can't do that, Ralph," Mickey said.

James spoke up, "Yes, they can, Mickey. It's a simple process to plant fingerprints."

"Really? They can do that?" Mickey said in surprise.

"Yes, they can," James said. "I'll explain later."

"They told me if I didn't come back and join them, they would frame me, and that's exactly what they did. When I found out that there was another warrant out for me, I booked out of town."

Mickey pulled out a small card with a calendar printed on it and laid it on the desk. "Where were you on these dates?" he asked, pointing to a two-week period circled on the small calendar.

"How would I know what I was doing on those dates! That was months ago."

"Ok, you can tell the police where you were. We don't care."

"Hey, come on guys, I've told you everything. Don't hassle me. I didn't hurt Betty. You have to believe me!" he pleaded.

"We don't have to believe a word you said, Ralph. Come on, let's go, James," said Mickey as he motioned for James to follow him out the door of the garage office.

As they walked out of the office, Ralph called after them, "Hey, you guys. I went to jail for something I did, but I will NOT go to jail for something I didn't do!"

As they got into the truck, Mickey said, "Do you believe his story?"

"It sounds reasonable. Things like that happen more than you'd think. And by the way, you can put fingerprints on things just like he said."

"How?"

"It's a process that was developed years ago. It's a simple process. You etch a piece of plastic or rubber with a fingerprint and place it on an object. There's your print."

"Isn't the print itself just oils from your body. That has your DNA on it, so wouldn't it be detectable?"

"Yes, but it's extremely rare that the police go to the trouble of running DNA on a print. The police usually dust for prints and use what they have in court. Yes, the guys Ralph was talking about could have set him up," explained James.

"But did he kill Betty?" asked Mickey.

"He now has the motive to kill her."

"And that is?" responded Mickey.

"We know that Betty wasn't the sweet little schoolgirl she used to be. She was a cold-blooded blackmailer. If she found out about Ralph's past, she could have threatened to turn him into the police. The possibility of going back to jail is a pretty strong motive. I say he goes to the top of the list," said James.

"Are we going to turn him in?"

"Nope. At least, not yet. We don't have any proof Ralph killed Betty. But he did give her money, and he knew he wasn't the father. That could have been blackmail also. It doesn't add up. We promised to report our progress to Detective Reynolds, but we didn't tell him when we would. After we make some more checks, we can tell him," said James.

"We need to have another murder board meeting," said Mickey.

"No, we don't. Let's keep working on it for a while longer and then we'll report to Reynolds."

"But we don't want to cut Darcy and Pop out," added Mickey.

"We aren't cutting them out. We aren't keeping them up to date on what we're doing. We should no longer involve them, especially since someone blew up your truck. We don't want them hurt."

"I guess you're right. We go on without them," conceded Mickey. "We need to keep an eye on Ralph. I don't trust him."

"We still need to check out the alibis. Ralph didn't have an alibi for that time period, and Wallace's already in jail," said Mickey thoughtfully. "Hey, what's Ralph doing? He's packing up his tools. James, it looks like we have a runner!"

They sat in the truck at the end of the garage's parking lot and watched as Ralph put some tools into a small tool bag, gathered what looked like some personal items, and put them into another bag. He then put the bags in the trunk of a car and drove off the lot.

"Does it look like he's taking a lunch break to you?" said Mickey.

"Nope. He's running. Hang back so he doesn't see us, and we'll follow him," answered James.

After Ralph drove out of the parking lot and down the street, Mickey pulled out far behind him. He kept his distance so Ralph wouldn't realize he was being followed.

Mickey looked over at James and said, "Now, it's time to call Detective Reynolds."

Mickey stayed behind just far enough so that they wouldn't be seen.

Suddenly Ralph veered off into a grocery store parking lot. When they got to the lot, they saw Ralph jump out and duck behind his car. Mickey slammed on the brakes, and the truck skidded sideways into a broadside position a hundred feet in front of Ralph's car.

They both jumped out of the truck and called to Ralph, "What in the world are you doing, Ralph!"

"What does it look like? I told you. I'm not going to jail for something I didn't do," he answered. "Don't come any closer. I'll shoot. I have a gun."

"We're not the police. We can't arrest you!" screamed James.

"You were going to tell them, and then the police would come to the shop to arrest me."

"We weren't going to rat you out, Ralph. We told you we're investigating Betty's murder. We didn't care about your past. As you said, you did your time," said James.

"I don't believe you!" Ralph answered. "Let me go. I won't hurt anyone. I just want to get out of town! I'll shoot. I mean it."

They saw something metallic in Ralph's hand and ducked behind the truck.

"We can't do that, Ralph. Not until you get your name cleared," Mickey called back to him. "You're still on the suspect list. You need to clear your name."

"Clear my name? They didn't clear it when I was framed. Why should they do it now?"

"I can't answer that, but if you are not guilty, we can help you," Mickey called back to Ralph.

"You're just saying that to make me give myself up!"

"You keep him busy talking while I work my way around behind him. If you distract him long enough, I should be able to take him down. Oh, and now would be a good time to call the police!" said James, quickly putting his head up to see what Ralph might be doing.

"I won't go back to jail," Ralph called out.

"No, you won't, Ralph. Come on out. We're not going to hurt you. I promise," Mickey said as he cautiously raised his head above the hood of the truck.

"Yeah, but you could call the police, and they'd arrest me. I didn't kill Betty, and I didn't steal that car. I told you I was framed."

Ralph laid something long and shiny up on the hood of his car. "Let me go, or I'll shoot."

Mickey ducked back down behind the car. "We believed you. Now I don't know what to believe. Put down your gun, and we can work it out."

"NO. It's too late for talk. I have to go. I've got to leave this town."

Mickey couldn't see where James was, but he hoped he was working his way around behind Ralph. Mickey popped his head up for a quick look.

He saw James coming up behind Ralph and called out for a final distraction. "Yes, Ralph, it is too late now. If you had not run and tried to shoot us, we could have proven you didn't kill Betty and maybe even helped with those other things."

He heard some grunts and scuffling coming from Ralph's direction as he was talking. Then he heard James call out, "It's okay now, Mickey, you can come out now. I've got him."

Mickey carefully looked around his truck and saw Ralph lying on the ground like a turtle trying to run away. James had Ralph's gun and saw it wasn't a gun. It was a shiny new wrench that could look like a gun barrel.

"I was only trying to scare you. I wasn't going to kill you. You were going to report me to the police. Get this crazy freak off of me!" he said, referring to James, who was still standing there with his foot on Ralph's back, holding him down.

"We weren't going to report you, but we are now! And if you ever refer to my friend as a freak again, I will personally rip your face off and hand it back to you. Do you hear me, Ralph Clark?" screamed Mickey.

"What happened to his face anyway?"

"He got wounded in Afghanistan. He's a genuine war hero."

Mickey bent down and said to him, "If you were innocent, we would have helped to clear your name, but not now. You're going to jail."

They could hear sirens in the background. James turned Ralph over and sat him up to lean him against one of the light poles in the lot.

"Cut him some slack, Mickey. He was scared he'd go back to prison," said James.

"Yes, he is now. We both know, if we thought he was innocent, we would have helped him."

"True, but he didn't know that. He's not a tough guy. He's a weak little weasel who can't handle another stint in the big house."

Mickey called to Ralph, "Hey, Ralph, did you blow up my last truck?"

"No. I don't even know that it got blown up. Why would I do that? I thought everything was fine until the two of you showed up today and told me about the warrant. I thought you were going to the police to report me. That's why I tried to leave."

Mickey and James looked at each other, "Do you believe him, Mickey?"

"Yes, he didn't bomb my truck. He's too stupid!"

Several police cruisers pulled into the parking lot, and uniformed officers jumped out of the cars with weapons drawn on Mickey and James. James slowly put up his hands.

An unmarked car also drove up, the door opened, and out stepped Detective Peter Reynolds. He waved for the officers to lower their weapons as he walked over to the three men.

"Well, well, well. If it isn't Mickey Ray Christianson and his sidekick, James Bower. Who is this guy sitting against the light post?" Detective Reynolds asked.

"It's Ralph Clark. That's his gun on the ground, Detective," Mickey said.

"What gun. It looks like a wrench to me," he said.

"It is, but he told us it was a gun and threatened to shoot us," James said.

"Do you want to press charges for making death threats to you?" the Detective asked.

Reynolds looked around and directed some of the officers to take the names of some of the witnesses in the parking lot while he spoke with Mickey and James.

He turned back to James and Mickey, "Okay, is someone going to tell me what happened?"

James started telling Detective Reynolds what had happened.

"We knew about the warrant, and we were waiting to clear the murder up first, then we were going to arrest him. I guess we'll do that now so he won't disappear again. Both of you need to come back to the station and make your statements official, and you can pick up that little pea shooter that you call a gun. Why in the world did James Bond have such a small gun? It's almost a lady's gun," said Reynolds when James finished the story.

Mickey sighed, "He carried it because it was small and easy to hide in a shoulder holster. He was a spy, not a soldier. If he needed to shoot someone, he would do it up close, not across a battlefield. And since that gun has been fired, it has lost over half of its collectible value."

"Sorry about that, Mickey Ray, but we had to check it out," Reynolds said, shrugging his shoulders.

"See you at the diner in the morning, and after a bite of breakfast, we can give our statements to the police at the station," said Mickey. He took James to pick up his Vee.

He called Francine on the way home. "Hey, there, girl!"

"Hey, Mickey Ray. What've you been up to today?" she answered.

"It's been an exciting day."

"Why don't you come over to my house and tell me about it?"

"Is your father home?"

"No, silly. Not my father's house. My house. I told you I'm having mine remodeled, and I was only living at my father's house while the work is being done."

"I remember that, but you didn't mention that you've moved back into your house."

"I haven't. I stopped by here to check on the progress. They almost have the kitchen complete. I can check out the new stove and whip up something to eat if you want to come by."

"That sounds good. I'll be there in half an hour," he said and disconnected.

Mickey pulled up in the driveway of Francine's house within minutes of when he told her he'd be there. He had never seen her house. He always remembered her as a beautiful girl in high school and entirely out of his league. Even in school, she was popular. She won the Bridgeton beauty contest and was the Queen of the annual county fair. And because she was the mayor's daughter, she was always in the local news to participate in some beneficial event to help the less fortunate. He couldn't believe he was dating this fantastic lady. Sure, he knew her past, but many celebrities have sordid pasts. Her last two husbands must have been real losers and only after her for her father's money and to use his influence to get ahead. Well, she found out about them too late. He didn't need her father's money or power. He felt that he might be falling in love with her.

She had told him about her house, and he was looking forward to getting the grand tour. He got out of the car, walked up to her front door, and rang the bell.

In a few moments, she answered the door. A glass of red wine was in her hand, which she immediately handed to Mickey, then invited him into the house. She was wearing a pair of skin-tight jeans and a blouse that accented her petite size and hourglass figure despite being loose-fitting. Her long wavy blonde hair hung loosely around her shoulders, perfectly framing her face. She closed the door behind him, put her arms around him, and gave him a slow and passionate kiss.

He stood there unmoving but almost shaking, holding onto the wine, trying not to spill it.

She backed off, looked up at him questioningly, "Mickey, you're kissing like a stone statue!"

He was as nervous as the first time they had met at the fundraiser a few weeks ago. "I didn't want to spill the wine," he said.

"My, my, then put the glass down right here," she said, taking the glass from his hand and placing it on a table right next to the door.

"Now, let's try that kiss again."

Again, she embraced him, and he returned it by wrapping his arms around her and kissing her with enough heated passion to raise the temperature in a banquet hall.

"Now, that was a kiss, Mickey Ray!" she said, fanning her face and taking a deep breath. "You've never been to my house, have you?"

"No, I haven't. Will you show me around?"

"Of course. Follow me," she said, turning to lead him. As they went through the house, she explained what she had done to it. Most of the work was being done in a new addition to the rear of the house.

"Here is my new entertainment area. As you can see, we have a large fireplace with a raised hearth and a complete wet bar in the corner over there," she said, pointing. "We took out that wall, which now opens to the kitchen area with long peninsula cabinets to serve the guests."

He looked around the room with a vaulted ceiling, stone fireplace, and large kitchen area.

"That wall," she said, pointing to large glass panels, "is my window wall to what will be an outside dining area. A landscaped garden section surrounds the heated swimming pool. Next year at this time, I will have it fully landscaped with colorful plants and greenery, with a fountain in the middle of a small Koi fish pond."

"Wow. It's awe-inspiring," Mickey stated.

"Last is over here," she added. "I'm adding a very large garage. It'll be large enough to hold three cars. I know you like cars. If things work out between us, you will have room for a couple of your cars. We'll see how things go. Okay?" she said with a smile.

Mickey smiled back at her. "We'll see, Fran."

She moved over to him and leaned against his chest, and hugged him close. "I sincerely hope it does. I think we'll make a wonderful couple," she said.

He stepped away from her, took a deep breath, and asked, "What's for dinner?"

"I'm not exactly a gourmet chef, so how about something simple. I can throw a couple of hamburger patties on the stove, open a container of store-bought potato salad, and a bag of green salad and pickle spears."

"Sounds fine to me," he said.

"While I'm doing this, why don't you start a fire in the fireplace?" she said, taking items out of the refrigerator.

"Fran, it isn't cold enough for a fire!"

"A fire will be more romantic. You can start a fire, can't you? It is a real wood-burning fireplace. Wood is so much cozier than those fake gas ones, don't you think?"

"I guess so, but won't it get hot in here?" he said.

"I'm counting on that, Mickey Ray," she said with an impish smile and a quick wink at him. "We can always turn on the air conditioner to cool off."

"Everything looks finished here to me. Have you moved back home now?" he asked.

"No. There are some things in the garage, and one of the bedrooms still needs painting and some trim work here and there, and of course, the entire backyard needs the landscaping I mentioned."

"You can move back in, in a couple of days. If you haven't moved back in, why did we meet here tonight."

"I wanted some privacy. This way, I have you all to myself, without Daddy butting in and taking your attention from me," she smiled. "Come over here and take our plates over to the fireplace area, and I'll get the wine bottle to refill our glasses."

They ate their burgers sitting in front of the fireplace, and Mickey told her what had happened.

"Oh, Mickey, why don't you let this thing go. Let the police handle it."

"I can't. We're getting so close. I can feel it," he said.

"You said the police had arrested Wallace Cunningham. So, it's solved."

"No, Wallace didn't so it. It's someone else."

"Then maybe Ralph did it!"

"I don't think he did it. I guess he could have, but my gut tells me he didn't do it either. He was trying to run so he wouldn't be arrested for that warrant in Georgia."

"Sure, but didn't you say that Betty might have tried to blackmail him because of it. He didn't get her pregnant, so she could have threatened him with the warrant."

"I guess she could have, but we're going to look more closely at that. In the meantime, we're putting together a timeline for each suspect. That'll tell us a lot," explained Mickey.

"Timeline? What do you mean by a timeline?" she asked.

"That's a simple question to answer. Let's say, for example, a person tells you that they are at a particular place at a specific time. Now, you have a tracker on their phone. Then later they tell you they are at another place. And on the lie goes. When you pull up the tracker app, you see where they've been. Then you have a timeline of their actions. See?" Mickey said.

"I see, but you don't have trackers on everyone on your suspect list," she said with a bit of concern.

"Correct, but there are many different ways to track a person. You can look at the time and place of charges on their credit cards. Sometimes just talking with people they've come in contact with. Those people may tell you they saw someone on a particular day or specific time. As I mentioned, there are phone trackers. Even new cars now have connections to the manufacturers and dealers and tell everything done to the cars. So, you know that the owner was at the dealer to drop it off at a specific time. It's a giant puzzle that we pick up pieces and connect them to make a picture, or timeline, if you will. Then you overlay the timeline with the event timeline of when something happened, and you see the overlap.

"You see, with Betty, we know the approximate date of her death. In the personal effects found with the body, she was wearing a broken watch. So, we have an exact time of death or TOD. We also had estimated the day when she was buried, and that, with the time of her insemination, we can determine who got her pregnant and possibly who killed her," explained Mickey, as he took a sip of his wine.

"Have you put it all together yet?" she asked.

"Not yet, but as soon as I get with James tomorrow and another person we're working with, we'll be able to eliminate suspects and find the one who fits all the criteria and event times. Then we'll know exactly who killed Betty."

"How much longer do you think it'll take?"

"A couple of days. We should know by week's end. I've never enjoyed a burger so much," he said as he leaned over and kissed her.

"At least that reporter isn't writing those horrible stories about you," she said.

"True, but even that has come to bite us. Some people around town think we did it or had him killed to shut him up. So, despite the stories not being written, we look guiltier than ever."

"Oh, no, Mickey, I never thought that would happen!" she said sadly.

"Don't worry about that. It's not your problem. As soon as we find Betty's killer, we find who killed Evans, and construction will start again."

She laid back on the floor, looked at the ceiling, and took a deep breath.

Mickey turned, propped himself up on one elbow, and looked at her. Once again, he looked into her deep blue eyes and silky, smooth skin. Her hair fell open around her face. "You look worried, my love," he said.

She turned her head and looked back at him. "Yes, love, I'm worried about you. It hurts me that you might lose everything you've worked your entire life for." A tear ran down the corner of her eye.

Mickey reached down and wiped away the tear. "Please, don't cry for me. It's only money. It will all work out. You'll see. We're young. We have a long life ahead of us, and if we find out that we are right for each other, we can build it together."

"But I don't want you to lose it. Mickey, I think I'm falling in love with you," she said softly and turned away.

"Don't say that. We've only been dating a few weeks. We can't fall in love that quickly," he said, but he felt the same way in his mind. He didn't want to admit it. He was falling and falling hard.

He gently rubbed her cheek as she turned her head to look back at him. Slowly, he brought his face down to hers and kissed her plump, inviting lips. He felt her tongue slide between his teeth. His heart pounded inside his chest. She reached up, closed her arms around his shoulders and pulled him firmly and closer, and returned the fire in his kiss. They burned with the comfort of their embrace.

He moved his mouth down her cheek to her neck and continued with gentle kisses as he moved. She began taking deeper breaths as his lips explored the silky softness of her neck. She arched her back and slid her hands down his back, taking in the gentleness of his kisses.

She whispered to him, "Mickey, I want you. I want you to take me now, right here. Please."

"No, my love. Not now. Not until the time is right," he said breathlessly, pulling away and sitting up.

"When will that be?" she asked, also breathing heavily now.

"We'll know. We'll both know, Francine." He sat back up and looked around the room to stifle his desire. "I need to go now. I don't trust myself to stay here any longer tonight. I have some things I need to take care of tomorrow."

"Don't leave now, Mickey. Don't leave me like this!" she pleaded.

"I have to go," he said.

They got up, and Mickey helped her take the dishes to the sink, and they said goodbye at the front door. Mickey drove home feeling elated. She had actually said, "I think I'm falling in love with you." He was excited. His excitement and the heat of passion kept him from falling asleep for hours that night.

CHAPTER 21

Early Morning Plane Ride

He and James met at the diner the next morning as they did almost everyday.

"Okay, you called me and told me you were going over to see Francine's house last night. What did it look like?" James asked.

"It was large with four bedrooms. The master bedroom was like a suite area," said Mickey, continuing to describe Francine's home.

James sat drinking coffee and dutifully listened to Mickey talking. Finally, he held up his hand in a stop motion.

"Enough of her house. I don't really care about it. Tell me, how was the date. You don't think she invited you over there to show you her house, do you? Especially since she showed you her master bedroom. She wanted something you weren't willing to give her."

"I know what you mean, and you're correct. We spent the time sitting on the floor in front of that gorgeous fireplace. She said there was enough room for me to park my cars if things worked out between us."

"What did she mean by 'If things worked out between you?'" said James warily.

"What do you think she meant? She's really into me, and I admit, I'm falling for her also, James."

"You mean, you're falling in love with her?"

"I think so," Mickey said, looking sheepishly at his coffee.

"Come on, Mickey. You know what kind of person she is. She's a shark. She'll eat you alive," said James.

"Don't talk like that about her. You don't know her like I do."

"I know what I've heard about her."

"Yes, and that's all you know. I've been out with her. I feel giddy. My head just spins around. I think I love her, and she loves me!"

"You've only known her for a couple of weeks. You and Valerie dated since high school, and it took you years to decide you loved her."

"Fran is different. You can't compare the two! We've both known Francine since high school."

"Yeah, we saw her walking down the hall. We didn't know her. And besides, she's a different girl now than she was then," reasoned James.

"She was way out of our league back then, but not now. I've grown, James. And so have you," Mickey defended himself.

"Fine. Whatever. What's going on with our suspects. Which one killed Betty?"

"Shouldn't we get the team together and discuss it around our murder board?"

"We talked about this also. No more murder board. It was fun and interesting until your truck got blown up. Now, your dad and Darcy are out. We're on our own. We better talk about it here and not at home."

Mickey thought for a moment and agreed. He took out a tablet and began writing names across the top. He wrote Mike Reece, Wallace Cunningham and his wife, Ralph Clark, Francis Braydon, and the newest Howard Hudson. Then he drew lines between each one to write common events and a timeline.

"Starting with Mike. He tried to marry her, and she turned him down. That doesn't look like a reason to kill her to me. Have you talked to Irene Blalock about getting a timeline on each of our suspects?" asked Mickey.

"Yes, Mike doesn't fit. He doesn't have an alibi and no motive. At this time, he doesn't fit, but we can't count him out. Wallace admits to giving Betty some blackmail money to keep her from telling his wife, and he's still in the running.

"Oh, yeah, another thing. When I talked with Irene yesterday, she compared the baby's DNA to Wallace and Francis. Wallace Cunningham was the baby daddy, not Francis Braydon," continued James.

"Wow, look at the repercussions of all this. We have one marriage that'll be destroyed, one person will go to jail again, and another person dead," said Mickey shaking his head. "Why did she have an affair with two married men?"

"Money, maybe. Who knows?" shrugged James.

Mickey was making notes and checking off things he had written on the paper. "How about Ralph. He looked pretty high on the list. I know he denies killing her, but what sane person would admit it. He has a motive because of the open warrant for him. Maybe we're looking at the blackmail angle, and it turns out to be he killed her to keep from going back to jail."

"Yep, I think Ralph and Howard are tied for first place position on our list right now. They both had motives and means. Now, all we need to do is check out their alibis," said James.

"Exactly. Neither one has an alibi to remember. They both admitted they didn't know what they were doing during that time. Either way, they look pretty guilty to me. Not to mention that Ralph tried to leave town," said Mickey.

"Ralph and Howard look pretty good for it right now. What about Franklin Braydon?" queried James.

"I don't know anything about him. He piloted the plane to Raleigh. He seemed okay to me. He did take Betty there for a weekend romp. But we don't know if she tried to blackmail him or not. So where is his motivation?"

"He has enough money to pay her off, and most blackmailers don't stop at one payoff. They typically come back for more. If Betty did approach him, he would have more money than all the others put together. I'll bet the twenty-five thousand dollars was from him. That gives him a motive. All we need to do is get a timeline check on him. Then we'll have motive and opportunity," said James.

"Killing someone, moving and burying the body, and cleaning up the mess isn't an easy thing to do. Francis doesn't seem like the kind of person that would want to get his hand dirty like that," Mickey said.

"He could have paid someone else to do that."

Mickey shrugged his shoulders. "Let's eat. I've got an extensive inspection to get through today, so I need to get to work and go over a few things before meeting with the inspector."

They ate in silence, each left with their private thoughts, and then they left to go their way. It was still early, but Mickey detoured through downtown Bridgeton and stopped to do some window shopping at a local Jewelry store. He looked at wedding rings. He wasn't big on flashy jewelry, but he was sure that Francine would want something to show off to all her girlfriends, so he peeked at the high-end diamonds through the window. For himself, he quickly looked at simple wedding bands.

He knew James was right. He didn't know Francine well, and she had a reputation as a gold digger, but he couldn't believe she was that kind of person. Around him, she was funny and fun-loving, always seeing the beauty of everything. He didn't know what to do. Even though he had seen Fran in the halls of Bridgeton High, he had only dated her for a few weeks, so he didn't know her. James was right. James was his voice of reason. Mickey got in his car and drove to work.

Pop was already there looking at blueprints when he got to work. "Good morning, Pop," he said, sitting down at the desk.

"Are you ready for the framing inspection on building three today, Mickey?" Daniel asked. "We need to get this inspected. We don't have a lot of cash to continue. At least since that reporter was killed, the stories have stopped."

"Yes, Pop, but so have the investors. We need to get this solved, including Carter's murder, before we have to shut down. How long can we continue construction?"

"Another week, maybe two. Then we shut down until we raise more money, and convince the banks not to call the loans," Daniel said.

"James and I are still working on some leads. We should know more in a day or two."

"I hope so. Do your best, son, and stay safe. The town is pretty much against us. Believe it or not, I got my first death threat last night."

"Really? What happened?" asked Mickey concerned.

"Darcy was fixing dinner when the phone rang. I picked up and someone asked for me by name. Then they said they hoped we rotted in hell for killing Betty Duncan, and they would help us get there."

"Did you check the caller ID?"

"It came up 'name unavailable.' I called Pete, and he said they would check into it, but there wasn't much they could do."

"James and I are the ones that have been asking questions all over town, I wonder why they didn't call me?" Mickey said thoughtfully.

"Maybe because to the general public, I am still the head and face of Christianson Company, and I am more well-known than you. There is also the possibility that they haven't gotten to you yet," Daniel replied.

"Maybe so. James and I need to step up our game."

"Don't go crazy now, Mickey. They, whoever 'they' are, has already tried to kill you. Don't accelerate the problem. Maybe you two should back off and let Pete handle it."

"No, Pop, if we go down financially or otherwise, we'll go down fighting. I need to get with James and work on this before it gets messier."

Just then, the phone rang. Daniel picked it up. "Speaking. Yes, sir. Why? We had this inspection scheduled over a week ago. No, this isn't, but that area's at a standstill without this inspection. Do you know when he can get out here? No, that isn't acceptable. I need it now!" Daniel slammed the phone back on the cradle.

Daniel turned to Mickey with fire in his eyes. "That was the secretary from the Inspectors Office. She said that our inspection would need to be rescheduled at an undetermined time. Something came up, and the inspector can't get here. She apologized for the inconvenience and said the inspector would call when he had another opening in his calendar. She has no idea when that will be."

"What do we do, Pop?" asked Mickey.

"We send some of the people home, and move the others to another area, and start work there. If we don't get some inspections, we may shut down by the end of this week."

"James and I'll get out there now and dig deeper. We need to wrap this up now to keep the men working and not end up in jail. Since I'm still the top suspect in Carter's murder, we should continue looking into that if we have time."

"There's nothing you can do here. After I move the crews, there's little I can do, so you and James do whatever you can do. Be careful, Mickey."

"We will, Pop. It'll all work out. We're Christiansons. We are survivors," he said, walking out the door.

James came by and picked up Mickey and they drove off to interview Laurel Cunningham.

"Mickey, do you think that when we talk to Laurel, she'll tell us more than she told the police?"

"I don't know, but Wallace didn't do it. I still put my money on Ralph Clark. While I was waiting for you, Pete Reynolds called and told me that they matched up fingerprints on the bomb fragments and Carter's apartment. They matched up to the guy that I hired recently. Remember when I told you that the guy I hired didn't show up the day after my truck was bombed?"

"Yep."

"The police went by the address he gave me on his application, and he had skipped out. So, he applied for work, then asked to be moved to this worksite, placed the bomb on my truck and killed Carter!"

"Why?"

"No clue. We keep talking motive, but I don't know his motive. Maybe he was somehow connected to the protestors that were against the construction from the start. That doesn't explain his motive for killing Carter. Carter was trying to shut us down. If our bomber wanted us shut down, Carter was or could have been one of his best allies. You don't kill your allies."

"Yep," agreed James.

After arriving at Wallace Cunningham's house, they got out and knocked on the door. Wallace answered. When he saw it was Mickey and James, he started to slam the door.

"I have nothing to say to you. Go away," he said sternly, as he pushed the door.

Mickey put his foot in the door and put his hand on the door to stop Wallace from closing it.

"Wallace, you will talk to us."

"No, you promised you wouldn't tell the police what I told you. You lied to me," he said, still trying to close the door.

"We didn't tell the police," spoke James.

"Then how did they know to talk to me?"

"They are the police. They have more resources than we have. They have an entire team that we don't have and access to a lot more informants than we have."

"Maybe so, but I still believe you told them," he said.

Mickey spoke again, "Wallace, you're our biggest stock promoter. You're working for us to get financing through your stock sales. We're on your side. We don't want to hurt you. Laurel told us you even bought some of our stock. We don't want to jeopardize that kind of relationship!"

Wallace stood in the door for a few moments digesting what Mickey had just said. "Well, okay. Come on it, but I'm still not sure if you're on my side."

He opened the door and allowed Mickey and James to enter. He led them to the living room and offered them a seat upon closing the door. Laurel came in and greeted them.

"Laurel," said Mickey, "I'm sorry to be back here. I know this's an extremely delicate situation right now. We're all suffering now. I'm sure that you've been reading the newspaper."

Wallace and Laurel shook their heads but kept silent.

"Our entire project may be shut down in a few days. I don't know if you heard, but the reporter who was writing those stories was killed, and I am the prime suspect in that murder and…."

"Maybe, but they didn't arrest you and take you to the police station in handcuffs. I may lose my business as a result of that," Wallace interrupted Mickey.

"Yes, they did, Wallace. They took me down in a squad car, fingerprinted me, and interrogated me. When my alibi checked out, they let me go. Now we're here to get more insight into Betty and her indiscretions. Laurel, you were good friends with her. Can you tell us more about her actions just before her death?" asked Mickey.

"I don't know any more than I told you before," she said.

"Can you give us any names? Even if they don't seem important. Anything that we can check out would be a help," pleaded Mickey.

"You already know about Mike Reece. He seemed nice, most of the time. Then there was Ralph. And another Betty wouldn't name. She said he was rich and important, but she never told me his name. I think he might have been something like a doctor or something. You know, she even went away with him a couple of times for a weekend."

"Do you know where they went?" asked James.

"No, but it was out of state, so no one would know about it. I guess you could check some of the airlines for that information, couldn't you?"

"No, we don't have those resources, but maybe the police could check that out for us," stated Mickey.

"Will you still let Wallace sell your stock, Mickey Ray?" Laurel asked.

"If we clear things up and we don't go broke, I don't see why not. Assuming that you are innocent, Wallace, you didn't break any laws."

"He'll need the money for alimony. Since I found out he got Betty pregnant, I'll file for divorce." She looked over at Wallace with contempt.

"I'll be moving out as soon as I can make arrangements for another place to stay. Until then, he's sleeping in the spare room."

Mickey and James stood up to leave.

"Maybe you can work it out. People make mistakes. I hope you can forgive him," James said as they walked toward the door.

"I doubt it," she added.

When they got in the truck, they both sighed.

"That was intense and unfruitful. We already knew that Betty was going out of town, and we knew it wasn't a doctor but Francis Braydon. Where to now?" asked James.

The phone rang, and Mickey answered. It was Detective Reynolds.

"Mickey, I thought I'd fill you in. Again, you didn't hear any of this from me," he added.

"We're holding Ralph Clark until he's extradited, and we'll be holding Howard until we can check out his alibi. It may take a while, but there's a good chance he'll go back to jail. We still don't have Jesse Clayton, the construction worker you hired that blew up your truck and shot Carter.

"Now, all we need to do is nail the actual person that killed Betty. I'll let you know as soon as I know something. I'm getting flak from the Captain about letting you work on this case. He wants you as far away as you can get."

"Thanks for letting me know what's going on, Detective. We'll keep you up to date also," Mickey said and disconnected.

They drove back to the construction trailer office so that Mickey could work on some paperwork.

When Mickey's phone rang again, and he saw it was Francine, he reached to pick up the phone and answer, "Hello, Fran. I've been waiting for your call."

"Really, Mickey?" came the voice over the phone.

"Yes, I've been sitting here in the office going over some paperwork, hoping you would call."

"Hey, have you been working on finding Betty's killer?" she asked. "I heard the police let Wallace Cunningham go. They didn't have enough evidence to charge him."

"Yes, we are still interviewing the suspects, and I think we'll have the answer by morning, and we'll take it to the police and lay it out for them. They're looking for the person that killed that reporter, and blew up my truck."

"It was the same person?" she said cautiously.

"Yes. He's on the run. It turned out that he was one of the new hires that started last week. I should have checked him out better, but when someone comes knocking on the door looking for a job, you're happy to find someone that wants to work. Little did I know."

"What was his name? Do you know why he did those things?" she asked.

"His name was Jesse Clayton. We have no clue, but the police will find him. James and I will wrap Betty's killer up sometime tomorrow after we look at more information."

"Hey, why don't we take a little plane ride?"

"I can't right now. I'm up to my eyes in paperwork. I had an earlier framing inspection, but was canceled until further notice. Where to this time?" he asked.

"Over the town. In the morning."

"Why in the morning?"

"Francis can take us up for a short flight. The sunrise over the horizon is beautiful. We can take off and watch it from the sky. You'll remember it for the rest of your life!"

"Okay, when and where do you want to meet?"

"How about four-thirty in the morning?" she answered.

He laughed, "Are you kidding. I don't get up before five."

"Darling, if we don't get out early, we'll miss the sunrise!"

"Fine, I'll see you at five A.M. at Bridgeton airport."

"I'll be looking forward to seeing you, Mickey. And don't tell anyone!"

"Why?" he asked.

"It'll be a special moment. For our memories alone."

"It won't be all that special if Francis is with us, dear heart," Mickey said jokingly.

"Oh, please, Mickey Ray. Could you do this for me? It'll be special. I promise," she said pleadingly. "You can tell anyone you want later, but right now, just let it be our special moment. Please?"

"Okay, for you, my dear. Mums the word, my lips are sealed. Now I have to finish this paperwork if I'm going to meet you before the crack of dawn."

"Thank you. It'll be special. You'll see. I'll meet you in the morning."

Mickey disconnected and placed the phone back on his desk. He couldn't imagine why Francine thought that having her brother with them would make anything they did together special. He bent back over the stack of papers and continued reviewing them for his signature.

He arrived at the airport the following morning at four-thirty, as she said.

When he parked his car, the large hanger door was being pushed back to reveal the pretty little plane. He got out, went inside, and Francine handed him a cup of steaming coffee.

She looked up at him and gave him a slow, lingering kiss on the lips, then backed away and said, "Good morning, Mickey."

"Now, that's a wonderful way to start the day, Fran. Francis is pre-flighting the plane, I see," he said. Many private pilots skipped this procedure on their own planes, but Mickey was glad to see Francis doing it. It was an added safety for all flights.

He squinted as he looked up at the bright lights shining from the ceiling of the hanger. Francis walked around with a clipboard in hand as he checked various items and control surfaces on the plane's wings and tail.

"Oh, Mickey, you'll love the view from the sky first thing in the morning. You'll see the lights over the city. As the sun rises over the horizon, the sun will spread little spears of light over the trees, and the lights will go out as the sun comes up. We'll be low enough to see the cars moving back and forth as people drive to work. It's a fascinating and thrilling sight."

"It sounds mesmerizing," said Mickey.

"It is. As I said, you'll remember it for the rest of your life."

When Francis finished pre-flighting the plane, he called out, "Come, you two, let's get this plane in the air, or we'll miss the sunrise!" He gestured for Francine to climb aboard the plane and get in the back seat.

"Mickey, you sit in the co-pilot's seat to have the best view of the sunrise," he said. Since the only door on the plane was on the aircraft's right side on the co-pilot's side, Francine had to get in first and move to the back seat.

Mickey waited until Francis got in, and he climbed in and closed the door. Francis moved controls, flipped switches like he did the last time they had gone up, and finally, the engine roared to life. They taxied out of the hangar and onto the runway, then Francis moved the throttle forward to increase the engine speed. They taxied to the end of the runway and lined up for take-off. Finally, as the engine roared, the plane began to move, and at the proper time and speed, the aircraft began to rise and finally cleared the end of the runway into the air.

They rose higher and higher for several minutes until Francis leveled off the plane. He turned it toward the sun rising over the horizon. Francine called from the backseat, "Isn't it beautiful, Mickey Ray?"

"Yes, it is Fran," he answered. He turned around, and Francine was holding a gun in his face. He saw tears in her eyes.

"I'm so sorry, Mickey Ray. I told you that you would remember this sight for the rest of your life, didn't I?" she said sadly.

"What's going on here, Francis," he said, looking at the pilot next to him.

Mickey quietly reached into his pocket and took his phone in his hand, and pressed buttons to start recording the conversation. He hoped he had pushed the correct ones.

"She'll explain, my friend," Francis answered apologetically.

Mickey again turned to Francine in the back seat. "I don't understand, Fran."

"Oh, Mickey. I was really falling in love with you," she said. And Mickey saw the gun shake slightly in her hand. "You wouldn't let it go. I tried to convince you to stop the stupid investigation into Betty's death."

"What are you talking about?" he asked again.

"I mean us, you weak little man. In the beginning, at the annual fundraising party, I thought it would be fun for us to date. You know, since you were single and available. We could have a good time together. Everyone in town knows that Valarie left you high and dry."

"Enough about Valerie!" he said. "What does she have to do with anything?"

"Nothing really, but that's why I approached you. We were having such a good time, but then I found out you were getting involved with Betty Duncan's murder."

"And?" he said, looking alternately from Francine to Francis.

As Francine talked, Francis just kept the plane pointed at the sunrise. As the sun rose, he turned the aircraft away to keep the sun from his eyes. Francine continued talking.

"Oh, Mickey Ray Christianson. You didn't get it did you?" she said wiping away the tears.

"No, not really, Tell me, Francine."

"As you told me, Betty was going from one person to another, telling each one that the baby was theirs. My stupid brother here also slept with her. She came to him, and he gave her twenty-five thousand dollars to keep her quiet and have an abortion. She said the baby was his and that if he didn't give her more money, she'd go public and destroy his marriage and reputation. You see, Daddy was grooming him to be the next mayor of Bridgeton. In a few years, maybe he could run for governor of Virginia, and a scandal like this could destroy all of that. Francis' and Daddy's plans would die. She had to die to stop all that.

"Then you came along and had to get involved. I tried numerous times to get you to let it go, but you wouldn't. Now you must go, Mickey. I love you so much."

"You must be insane, Francine! How could you feel love and hate at the same time?"

"I do love you, dear man. It will take me a long time to forget you, but eventually I will," she said.

"So, it was you who tried to kill me by blowing up my truck, Francine?"

"Of course not, silly. I didn't blow your truck up. Francis hired someone to do it. We didn't…I mean, I didn't want you killed. We just wanted to scare you. We wanted you to back away. Let it go, Mickey. I never wanted to hurt you personally! I was falling in love with you.

"It was me that killed that reporter. I wanted to protect you. I didn't want you to lose everything. I wanted us to be together, complete with our family's money and influence. The way that reporter was reporting, he would have destroyed you and the family fortune. You would have gone broke. I swear, I never wanted that. I did it for you!"

Mickey shook his head, "Francine, you are one sick woman!"

"That reporter was vile. I hated the stories he was printing about you and your family, so I had to kill him to shut him up. Francis tried to give him money to shut him up, but he wouldn't stop it. I went by that night to try to reason with him. He said he would never stoop so low as to take a bribe to kill a story. I took this little gun," she said looking down at the gun in her hand, "and shot him.

"I ran out of his apartment building that night. Jesse Clayton was with me. He is, or his body is somewhere at the bottom of the James River. And when you are out of this plane, I'll throw the gun out, and no one will be the wiser."

"Oh, girl! You have a strange way of showing your love!" Mickey said, shaking his head. "I didn't know all that, Francine. I just found out yesterday that the baby wasn't Francis' child."

"What do you mean, it wasn't mine?" Francis turned from the controls and looked at Mickey.

"They did a DNA test, and it just came back yesterday. It wasn't your baby. It was Wallace Cunningham's child. You're in the clear. Yes, I found out that you took Betty to Raleigh for a weekend, but you're not the father of her child."

Francis sat looking at Mickey for a few moments, then looked back out the plane's windshield.

Mickey said, "Scandals happen all the time to public officials, but since the baby wasn't yours, you could deny it. You could deny the entire affair. Since you took her out of town, no one here knows about it. You're in the clear."

Francis remained silent in thought.

"Betty was killed by a blunt object to the back of her head. Which one of you actually killed her?" asked Mickey.

"She did," said Francis, now seething with anger.

"How did she do it? What did you use as the weapon?" asked Mickey.

"My nine iron," Francis answered, shaking his head and looking out the small plane's windshield.

"You mean Francine hit her with a golf club?"

"Yes. Then she calmly put it back in the golf bag in the trunk of my car. We waited until the middle of the night, loaded Betty's body in the trunk, drove out to the site where you were to begin construction, and buried her."

"And how'd that work out for you?" Mickey said sarcastically.

"Shut up, both of you," said Francine. Turning back to Mickey, she said, "Now, I told you that you would remember the sunrise for the rest of your life. Now, it's time for you to leave. This is where you get off, Mickey. Now open the door and get out!"

"I loved you too, Francine and I never would have suspected that you would do something like this."

"Yeah, me too, Mickey Ray. I loved you too, but now you have to go. I'm not going to jail for murder. Now open the door!"

"Sure. Do you expect me just to open the door and step out? Nope, ain't gonna happen, lady," he answered, shaking his head.

"I said, get out Mickey Ray! Now!"

Francis looked over at Mickey. "Sorry, but the little witch in the back is calling the shots. If she had let me handle this, no one would be dead." He gritted his teeth as he continued to speak. "That little spoiled sister of mine has ruined our lives, and even you are caught up in it. I'm truly sorry, Mickey, but you must get out!"

"This is why we came out so early, while it's still dark. So, no one would see me falling from the sky?"

"Very perceptive, Mickey. Now get out before I put a bullet in your head and push you out," Francine said as she raised the gun to the side of Mickey's head.

"Nope. Not going to open this door. This is why you wanted me to sit here, next to the only door on the plane, right?" Mickey was talking, trying to buy time until he could figure out what to do. He needed time to think.

"Why did you bury her on my property?"

"We didn't know where else to bury her, and we didn't think you would dig her back up," said Francis.

"You have property of your own. Why my property?" asked Mickey as he tried to find an opportunity to disarm Francine.

Again, Francis answered, "I don't know why. Ask Francine!"

"Shut up, Francis. It's time for Mickey to get out now."

As Francine spoke to Francis, she turned her attention back toward him. Mickey, already turned, facing Francine, reached around and tried to grab the gun from Francine's hand. As he reached for the gun, Francine moved the gun away from Mickey to her left in the rear area of the pilot's seat. When Mickey grabbed the gun, it went off and fired through the seat into Francis. Francis immediately slumped over in his seat. As he did, he fell onto the plane's controls, and it began a nosedive.

Mickey and Francine also fell forward as the plane began to plunge toward the ground. As Mickey struggled to get the gun from Francine's hands, it went off again. This time it grazed Francine's upper arm, and she screamed in pain and let out a string of expletives at Mickey.

He pulled the gun from her hands, turned around, and pulled the steering yoke back to bring the plane out of its dive toward the ground. At the same time, he pulled the throttle back to slow down the airspeed.

Francine was screaming in the back seat, "You S.O. B., I'm shot. I'm bleeding all over the place back here!"

"Be quiet, Francine. Francis is bleeding all over the cockpit up here. You don't hear him screaming, do you? You witch!"

"That's because he's dead! You killed him, Mickey Ray."

"SHUT… UP… Francine. I don't know how to fly this plane. Let me think!"

"I don't care. My arm hurts, and I'm bleeding."

"Hold your hand against the wound to stop the bleeding and let me figure out how to land this plane….and for God's sake, SHUT UP and let me think!" he screamed back at her.

He pushed Francis' dead body back against the seat and tightened Francis' seatbelt, so he would no longer interfere with the controls and Mickey could see the gauges. He picked up the radio's microphone and keyed the button.

"Mayday, Mayday. Hello, is anyone out there?" he said into the microphone.

Immediately a voice came over the speaker, "This is the Newport News International Airport. What is your emergency?"

"This is Mickey Ray Christianson. I'm in a Piper, PA-28 Cherokee. The pilot is dead, and I need help landing this plane."

"We got you, Mickey. A few questions first. Are you sure the pilot is dead?" the voice said.

"Positive," Mickey answered.

"Do you have any experience flying a plane?"

"About ten years ago, I took the ground school and two flying lessons, but that's all."

"That's great, Mickey. You already have a good start here. You at least have a basic idea of flying and knowledge of the instruments. We need some time to find a pilot for your particular plane. How much fuel do you have?"

"Almost a full tank."

"Okay, that's also good. We can use that for a few test runs before you actually touch down. We have you on radar, so keep your present course while we clear the airways around you, so you have plenty of sky to maneuver. Do I hear someone screaming in the background?"

"Yes, tower. It's an injured woman. Her screaming is driving me crazy. She has a gunshot wound and is bleeding. It is a minor wound and not life-threatening yet, so please just get us on the ground."

"You're doing great, Mickey. Just keep calm, and in a few minutes, we'll have an experienced pilot here to help you down."

"While we're waiting, can you tell me what happened? You said 'gunshot wound,' correct?"

"Yes, and while we're killing time waiting for the pilot, let me play a recording I got. Can you record it from your end, just in case I don't make it to the ground in one piece?" said Mickey.

"We are recording, Mickey," came the answer.

Mickey took the cell phone out of his pocket and pushed the play button as he held it against the microphone of the plane's radio. After several minutes the recording came to an end with the gunshot sounds.

At the end of the recording, the voice came back over the speaker, "We got it recorded at our end. Now, we need to get you on the ground. We'll have an ambulance and the police waiting for the lady. An emergency ground crew will follow you down the runway if you have any problems with your landing. The pilot just came in, so I'm going to turn you over to him. He'll walk you through the process. Good luck, Mickey. We all have our fingers crossed for you. This is John Higgens. He's a great pilot. He'll get you down safely. Just stay calm. You'll do great."

Another voice came over the speaker at that time, "Mickey, I'm John. I've been flying Cherokees for years. I know them inside and out. I assure you, if you keep calm and do exactly what I tell you, I'll get you down safely. Do you copy that?"

"Got you loud and clear, John. I'll be honest. I'm a bit nervous here."

"You wouldn't be human if you weren't nervous, my friend. Now, they tell me you have almost a full tank of fuel. Correct?" John asked.

"Correct."

"Good. Since you have enough fuel, can we do a bit of flying around so you get familiar with the controls and how the plane reacts? We're in no hurry here," the man said.

"You're the boss, John."

"Good. They told me you passed ground school and had some flying lessons."

"Yes, but that was a long time ago, and I only had two lessons."

"That's a head start. You'll do fine. With those lessons, you had instructor-assisted landings, correct?"

"Yes, I just placed my hands on the yoke while the instructor did the actual landing," said Mickey as he alternately took his hands from the yoke and wiped his hands on his pants to clear the sweat from his palms.

"That's typical, but an important part of learning to fly. Now, I need you to adjust the throttle and gently turn toward the airport. Can you do that?"

"Yep, doing that as you speak," answered Mickey.

"When you get near the airport, I'll direct you to line up on the runway, and I'll observe you as you pass. Don't expect to be perfect. We'll do a few practice runs since you have the fuel and we now have clear skies. When you come down, I'll direct you if you're too high, low, or too fast. I'll tell you to pull up and make another pass. Can you do that?"

"You're the boss, John."

Mickey did a few passes around the airport with John's guidance and directions. Finally, after several runs, John asked Mickey if he felt ready to try to land.

"Sure, let's do this," said Mickey, much more confidently than he felt.

Francine sat in the back seat, holding her arm to stop the bleeding and silently looking out the window. Mickey turned the plane around to line up with the runway.

"Okay, Mickey, what is your airspeed now?" asked John. Mickey answered.

"That's a bit fast, throttle back just a notch. Lower your flaps. That's a turn wheel between the seats. Be sure to keep your nose up. Keep your eyes on the airspeed indicator. You don't want to stall. The slower we can get you, the better and easier to control."

Mickey lowered the flaps as instructed and saw his airspeed go down.

"Okay, you're a bit too high. Dip the nose. Just a bit, we don't want you diving for the ground. We want just a gentle glide. Yes, I see it. You're looking good so far."

Francine spoke up from the back, "We're going to die, aren't we, Mickey?"

"No, shut up, Francine. We're not going to die," he answered.

"You are a real son-of-a...."

"SHUT UP, Francine. I'm trying to concentrate on landing this plane," he said as he watched the runway and the instruments.

"Power up and pull up gently, Mickey," said John. "You were doing fine. Then I don't know what happened. Pull up and make another round. Concentrate, you'll do fine."

"Sorry, John, this crazy woman in the back seat broke my concentration."

Mickey powered back up and lifted away from his approach. He turned around and lined up on the runway again.

"Mickey, right now, I don't care if I die in this plane. Because of you, I've lost everything."

"Francine, will you please SHUT UP. We can talk about this after we land!" he said as he wiped the sweat from his palms and forehead again and tried to concentrate on his approach.

As he flew again toward the airport runway, John again gave him instructions, and Mickey did as he was instructed.

As he approached the runway, his wheels touched the pavement, and the plane did a slight bounce, and Francine screamed. He heard John say, "You got it, Mickey. Perfect touchdown, now just throttle back, and step on those brakes until you stop."

As the plane touched the runway pavement again and began rolling, Mickey heard a movement in the back. He didn't dare turn his head to see. At that moment, he felt Francine's hands grasp him around the neck and pull him back against the seat. When she did this, it caused him to pull back on the control yoke. The plane left the runway a few feet, bounced back down hard, and caused Mickey to release the control yoke. He struggled to grab the yoke with one hand, and with his other hand, he reached for his throat to remove himself from Francine's grasp. The plane tipped, and the left wing crashed into the pavement, and the plane began spinning around like a child's toy. Mickey grabbed Francine's hands and pulled them from his neck. He was still buckled in, but Francine had unbuckled her seatbelt when she first took out her gun. She was thrown around the cockpit like a ragdoll in a washing machine. Still firmly in the pilot's seat, Francis' dead body was held in place by his seatbelt.

The left wing broke loose from the plane, and the landing gear crumpled as the small aircraft continued sliding down the pavement. Mickey spread his arms, trying to brace himself inside. Finally, in what seemed like hours to the occupants, the plane came to a stop. Mickey took a quick check of himself.

Nothing was broken, but he had gotten a severe whiplash in his neck when the plane spun around. He looked at Francine in the backseat. She was alive and conscious, but she was crying like a child.

As Mickey sat there, he looked up and said a silent prayer of thanks.

Someone climbed up onto what was left of the right wing and opened the door. It was one of the emergency crew. Mickey reached down and unbuckled the seatbelt.

"She needs help in the back. I'll be okay," he said as the man helped him out of the plane.

He climbed down as men sprayed foam over the engine compartment to prevent any leaking gas from igniting. The man climbed inside and began attending to Francine's injuries while others started cutting open the other side of the plane to get her out.

Another EMT helped him over to an ambulance to check him out. As they did this, Mickey could see another vehicle approaching in the distance. Darcy, James, and Pop got out and ran over to him when it pulled up to the ambulance. Closely behind followed a police car. When it stopped, out stepped Detective Reynolds.

They all gathered around and hugged him. "Hey, guys, thanks for the hugs, but it's my neck that's hurt. So don't squeeze me there, please," he said.

They backed off. Darcy was crying, and James was holding her up. Pop was standing on the other side of Darcy, holding her hand. Beside him was Peter Reynolds.

Detective Reynolds walked up to Mickey and put out his hand to shake Mickey's. "They played the recording you made in the cockpit of Francis and Francine admitting to killing Betty Duncan. I'll be arresting Francine Braydon as soon as they get her to the hospital. You did a great job. I know I gave you a hard time, and I hope there are no hard feelings. In my book, you're a hero. I was genuinely concerned about your safety."

Mickey shook the Detective's hand vigorously and said, "Thanks, Detective Reynolds. Glad I could help. Always glad to help our men in blue."

"Mickey, you've earned the right to call me 'Pete.' Now, let me get out of here so I can follow the ambulance to the hospital to make that arrest."

As the EMT put a collar around Mickey's neck, he saw the other EMTs taking Francine out of the plane and putting her on a stretcher. As they rolled by, he reached out and stopped them.

The EMT told Mickey she'd be okay. She had a few broken bones, but she would recover.

She looked up at him and said, "Mickey Ray, with my dad's influence and your dad's money, we could have had the entire state of Virginia in the palm of our hands. We could have had it all."

Mickey looked down at her. He leaned over and whispered in her ear. "I didn't want it all, my dear Francine. All I wanted was you."

He stood back up and looked at the EMTs, "Thank you, gentlemen. Take her away."

CHAPTER 22

A Time of Grieving

After crash landing the little Piper airplane, he rode to the hospital in an ambulance and got checked out. He had an MRI and a CT scan. As determined by the tests, he had only a severe case of whiplash, and they sent him home with a collar around his neck and told him to rest for a few days.

He followed the doctor's orders to the letter. He sat in his recliner and looked at a blank television screen for hours. He didn't even get up to go to bed. He left his domain on the chair only for meals and bathroom visits. He would turn the TV on for short periods to hear the news and weather, then turn it off.

His phone rang incessantly. He didn't answer it. He didn't want to talk with anyone. He turned off the answering machine after the first day of unanswered calls. He didn't care. He didn't care if it was day or night. He slept only a few hours of each day, followed by a few hours of sleep each night. He sat. He prayed. At times he cried, but other than that, he did nothing.

There were empty boxes of delivery pizza, hot pockets, and TV dinners lying around his chair. Empty soda bottles and cans littered the room. It was a mess. He was a mess. He didn't care. He wanted to crawl into a hole and disappear.

There came a knock at his door. He didn't move to answer. It came again and again. Finally, a voice called out. "Mickey, open the door. I know you're in there."

He recognized James' voice. He didn't move from the chair.

"Mickey, I said, ANSWER THIS DOOR OR I'LL KICK IT DOWN. I swear to you, I'll do it. You know I will! I'll give you 'till the count of ten.

ONE…TWO…THREE…"

"Alright, alright, I'm coming," Mickey called out as he got up. He threw the door open and went back and sat down in the recliner.

James walked in and sat down on the couch. "Mickey Ray, this place is a holy mess!"

"I don't care."

"That's obvious," answered James. "Everyone has been trying to get in touch with you. You aren't answering your phone."

"I know. I heard it ring every time, and I didn't want to talk to anyone. Go away and leave me alone."

"We're not going to leave you alone. You're family, and family sticks together," James said.

"Right now, I don't care who you are. Leave me alone. Fine, I admit, you told me. Pop told me. Darcy Jean told me. You all told me she was evil, but I didn't listen. Are you satisfied now? Now go away. I don't need to listen to you gloat."

"Mickey, I didn't come here to gloat, and you should know me well enough now to know that. I love you as a brother. When you hurt, I hurt. We all hurt. You fell in love. You couldn't help yourself. We've left you in your pain for days. Now it's time to get up, shake it off, and move on."

"Move on where?" Mickey asked.

"Get back to the construction site. Help Daniel get that project done," James said.

"It's not that easy," Mickey added. "I really thought she was the one. Valerie and I have always been together. I loved her, but she was comfortable. Francine was fun and exciting. I never felt so alive as I did when I was around her."

"I know, bro. That's the way I felt when I met Darcy. If something happened to her, I would feel just like you feel right now. You have to get up and move on. We'll all be there for you. You know that."

"Yeah, I guess you're right. What's happened to everyone on the list since I've been out of commission?" said Mickey, finally raising his head to look at James.

James thought for a moment, then started. "I guess the best place to start is with Betty Duncan. Betty Duncan had started life as a sweet little girl, and that continued through high school. What happened to her to make her change into who she was that caused her death, no one will ever know. Her actions had killed marriages, destroyed families, and the death of several people. She left a trail of misery and destruction."

He continued, "Well, Wallace Cunningham has been released and cleared and all charges have been dropped. The sad thing is, his wife will probably be filing for divorce."

"That's a shame. He made one mistake, and his family is destroyed," said Mickey.

"I agree, but that's the price for cheating on your wife. Mike is one of the few that came out relatively unscathed. I guess he'll continue working at the bookstore.

"On the other hand, Ralph will be going to jail in Georgia to finish his sentence due to the open warrant."

"It's a shame that the gang set him up as they did, and now he'll do time for a crime he didn't commit. Hey, maybe we could help him out by getting him cleared of those charges," suggested Mickey.

James cocked his head at Mickey and said, "Hey, bro, don't even go there. Getting involved in things like that keeps getting us into trouble!"

"As usual," Mickey laughed, "yeah, you're right. Darcy would have both our heads on a platter."

"All Ralph wanted to do was leave town, and we both believe his story about being framed. Trying to get the charges here reduced or even dropped would be a sign of good faith."

"Okay, what happened to the rest of our suspects."

James continued, "Howard Hudson will go to jail for drug possession and dealing. Riley was charged as an accessory but will most likely be reduced to possession as it was her first offense. The police raided the house and found several pounds of weed and some prescription drugs, so their case is pretty solid."

James continued, "Then there is, or was Jesse Clayton. We don't have to worry about him anymore since he's dead. Maybe one day, his body will wash up on shore.

"You know about Francis since he was dead from a gunshot wound in the back. The bullet went in from the back of his seat, and that's where Francine was sitting. The evidence and autopsy corroborate your story. It's pretty apparent that she was holding the gun when it went off.

"The most important news of all, Christianson Company is alive and well. The true story was printed by our newspaper, retracting everything that Carter Evans wrote. Investors are again buying stock, and the banks have released your working capital and rescinded the order to call in the loans, so you're back in full operation. Your dad even got the inspections done and passed, so everything is moving forward."

Mickey looked at James and choked back his feelings. "I fell hard for Francine Braydon. Everyone warned me. She almost killed me, but I loved her. Her beauty, her charm, her open laughter captivated me. She mesmerized me like a snake before it kills and devours its prey. She was evil. If she doesn't get the death penalty, she'll spend the rest of her life in prison."

"Mickey, don't beat yourself up over her. First, she isn't worth it. She doesn't deserve you. I remember someone saying that you know you're over someone when you have no feelings at all for them. As long as you hate Francine, you have feelings. When you feel nothing, you'll be over her. Another old saying is, time heals all wounds."

"I guess you're right, James. Only time will tell which saying is true."

"You've also missed out on a lot of other stuff since you've been sitting around here feeling sorry for yourself."

"Like what?"

"Let's see. I've finished the garage gym. You gotta see it. It is as good as any professional gym. Each morning before breakfast, we can meet and get a workout to start the day."

"Okay, what else have I missed?" asked Mickey.

"Did you remember that in a couple of days, it's your dad's birthday?" James asked.

"Oh, yeah. I forgot. I didn't get him anything. I need to go shopping to get him a birthday present."

"Nope, you're covered. Remember that old Model A Ford you told me about weeks ago?" James said happily.

"Yeah, what about it?"

"We bought it for him," James said and leaned back and folded his arms in triumph.

"What do you mean, we?" asked Mickey.

"You said we could go in halves on it, so we did. I tried calling you, but you weren't answering your phone. The guy called me and told me he had several offers to buy the car. If you didn't come by and pay him, he'd sell it.

I bought it, and it'll be delivered on his birthday. Now, you owe me a lot of money for your half!" James said, grinning from ear to ear.

"Sometimes you surprise me, James. You're a good friend. I'm glad to have you as my brother-in-law."

"Same here, bro. You can't see what we bought your Pop for his birthday if you don't get out of this mess hole. Let's go look at it. Daniel's going to love it."

They both got up and walked to the door. Mickey turned around and looked at the mess in his living room.

As he closed the door, he said to James, "When I get back home, I've got to get this house cleaned up."

James put his hand on his best friend's shoulder and answered, "Yep, you sure do. And while you're at it, clean yourself up. You haven't bathed in days. You reek, bro."

James smiled even brighter as they walked to the car. "One more thing. I asked Darcy if she would let me adopt Cyndi and Joel. She said she would love it, and so would the kids."

Book one in the "Landlord's" series

Synopsis of "The Landlord's Inheritance."

Siblings Mickey Ray and Darcy Jean are informed that the automobile disaster that caused the death of their Mother and their Father's multiple injuries including brain damage was not an accident but an attempted murder. The local police seem ambivalent, and their aunt comes in with a forgotten Power of Attorney signed by their Father, Daniel, and tries to take control of the Real Estate holdings. The brother and sister team begin a power struggle and are physically threatened by unknown thugs which results in Mickey's girlfriend's disappearance which is presumed dead and Darcy Jean in hiding. James, Mickey's best friend, a disfigured Ex-Military Black Ops operative, assists in the hunt to put a stop to the "takeover".

Terry Joe's novel includes Simple Detective Work, Internet Research, Adventure, Action and Suspense with a Sprinkle of Romance, and a Fast-Paced, Explosive ending.

Book two in the "Landlord's" series

Synopsis of "The Landlord's Wheelchair Child."

Landlord Mickey Ray Christianson is walking the grounds of his apartment complex late one afternoon, and he sees a little girl in a wheelchair sitting all alone. He sits down beside her and begins talking to her. He then finds out that her mother left her, intending to return. When the child's mother doesn't return, Mickey has the gut feeling that something has gone awry and calls his sister, Darcy, to run a background check on her parents. After Darcy gets permission from the Department of Child's Services to take custody of the child Carrie, Mickey Ray, and his best friend, James, go hunting for Carrie's parents, assuming they were kidnapped. With help from some of James' past Black Ops teammates, a find-and-rescue operation takes place. After a suspenseful mission and a lot of action, Mickey reunites Carrie with her parents.

The author with one of his collectable cars.

The Landlord's Ex-Fiancée

Prologue

"You need to take care of her," Grant said as he loaded another bag into the back of the van.

"Why? She doesn't know anything. I agree she's curious," Amir stated.

"We can't afford for her to see something she shouldn't see. Get rid of her," Grant insisted.

"Okay, but I don't like it. If she knew something or threatened us, it would be a different story, but she's just an excited young lady that wants desperately to be a chef," Amir said sadly. "I like her."

"You like every girl that smiles at you, Amir."

Amir grabbed a bag, threw it into the van, and shut the door. "Can we have a drink before I pull out?"

"Sure, come on into the office. I'll tell you how to get her out of the way," said Grant. "We can't wait much longer. She just paid her tuition last week for the coming semester. If we can find someone to take her place, then we get another tuition-paying student."

"That doesn't give me much time to prepare."

"You don't need time to prepare just to crack her on the head," Grant said. "Make it look like a break-in gone wrong."

"Man, I can't believe you're making me do this. You have no heart!"

"And you do? I'm just protecting my business," Grant said calmly, "and so should you."

They sat there drinking a glass of Kentucky bourbon straight up, each in their own thoughts. Grant Littleton owned the school where Valerie was attending, trying to become a certified chef. He had started this culinary school over ten years ago with a reputation for training excellent chefs around the country.

Several years ago, he had started shipping some of the popular desserts around the country labeled as "gourmet" sweets. Some were ready to serve. Others were combined ingredients ready to add things like water, cream, and eggs, making a fresh, delightful dessert served by many high-end gourmet restaurants all over the continent. When the economy took a dive, so did their business. Grant had gotten into trouble when he took in some investors to help keep them afloat. As it turned out, the investors were, in fact, drug dealers looking for ways to distribute their products that regular government agencies don't usually scrutinize.

Amir had come to this country illegally to work for Grant. In his mid-thirties, he was already a cold-blooded killer. He was small, wiry, and could make almost anything he picked up a deadly weapon. He could shoot but preferred a knife.

They trained chefs by day and ran drugs and occasionally guns at night. Grant Littleton found it very profitable and had built a sizable network of distributors. He had curious students in the past but had taken care of them in a similar way that Grant wanted Amir to take care of Valerie.

"Grant, are you sure there isn't another way we can get rid of her other than killing her? I don't like killing a woman," said Amir. "Can't we just fail her, and she'll leave?"

"No, we can't do that. That in itself would look suspicious."

"What do you want me to do with the body? Bury it like I did the other two guys?"

"No, I said earlier, make it look like a burglary gone wrong. Now, go," Grant said, getting up and wiping off the glass and putting it back into his desk drawer.

"Fine. But I don't like killing a woman."

"I know. I'm not too fond of it either. I agree, she's a sweet girl, but we don't want anything or anyone to get in our way. A few more years of this, and we'll have enough to retire. Just wait until late at night, and knock on her door. She knows you, so she'll answer. When you get inside, do what you need to do and leave quietly," said Grant.

Amir got up and left. Although he had killed men before, but never a woman, he was Grant's hit man. If someone didn't follow Grant's explicit instructions, Amir would make him disappear. Reluctantly he would do the same with the young girl Valerie.

It was going to be a long night for Amir. One he would not forget until his dying moment.

CHAPTER 1

The Late-night Phone Call (excerpts)

The buzzing in his ear wouldn't stop. It buzzed and buzzed and buzzed. He put the pillow over his head, but it wouldn't stop. Finally, he realized that his cell phone was on the bedside table.

Mickey reached over and knocked it off onto the floor. He reached down, picked it up, and pushed the answer icon as he put it up to his ear.

"Hello," he said groggily.

"Hello, Mickey Ray?" asked the voice at the other end of the phone.

"Um, yeah?" he answered.

"It's me, Valerie," she said.

"Oh, Hi, Val. What time is it?" he said, turning to the clock on his bedside table and trying to focus.

"I don't know. I think it is around eleven-thirty, I guess. Oh, Mickey, I'm scared."

He looked at the clock and said, "Valerie, it is almost two-thirty in the morning here. What's so important?"

"Someone outside my apartment is just sitting in a car. They keep looking up at me in the window."

"Maybe they're looking at you because you're staring at them, Val. I'm sure it's nothing. You're on the second floor, looking out the window," he said as he sat up and tried to clear his mind.

"They aren't just walking by. They're sitting in the car looking at me, or at least this window. It creeps me out. I'm scared."

"Okay. Calm down. Call the police. Tell them they should send someone out to check out the area. Okay?" he said.

"Yeah, Mickey. I'll do that. Can I call you back if they don't come?"

"Sure. You can call me anytime, day or night. You know that. It'll be okay. I guarantee it."

"Thank you. I still love you," she said.

She disconnected, and Mickey got up to make a cup of coffee. He was wide awake now. After pouring a cup of coffee, he sat thinking of Valerie.

Valerie Green was his high school sweetheart. A couple of years ago, they were engaged to be married, but some human traffickers abducted her. Mickey and his best friend James Bower had rescued her, but she was traumatized by the event, which changed her. She left Bridgeton, a small town between Williamsburg and Richmond, Virginia, and enrolled in culinary school.

She called Mickey on a regular basis, and at times she would be on edge with stress. He'd talk to her and calm her down. He knew she needed some professional counseling, but she refused to go.

He had to go to work tomorrow, and he needed his sleep. After finishing a cup of decaf, he crawled back into bed. He'd call Valerie on his way to work.

A few hours later, Mickey got up and started getting ready for work. He looked in the mirror and realized he hadn't shaved for several days. He didn't care. He skipped shaving a lot. Heading for the shower, he passed the full-length mirror and looked at himself. At almost 6 feet, he was toned and fit, but he knew he needed to work harder. He was in and out of the shower in minutes and on his way to work.

He would meet James, his best friend later this afternoon for a much-needed workout at the gym.

When his parents were in an auto accident, he stepped in to help run the apartment management and construction business with his sister, Darcy. When his father decided to retire, he took over. He was now 30 years old, single, and the CEO of the largest construction firm in lower eastern Virginia. He dialed Valerie's number as he drove to work.

When there was no answer, he thought that maybe after calling the police, everything was fine, and she was no longer upset. He disconnected and threw the phone on the seat of the car.

He had a lot of office work today to keep him busy until after lunch. He had to meet with a finance officer from one of the banks. Then he had a staff meeting with the maintenance crew at one of the apartment complexes he owned. It would be a busy day.

When he got to his office after a late morning meeting with the bank, there was a message on his desk to call Detective Veronica Morgan with the Florence, Oregon police department. The phone number was written at the bottom of the note. He looked at his watch and shook his head as he dialed. Florence, Oregon is where Valerie lived. He wondered why the police were calling him. Valerie couldn't be in any trouble.

At the other end of the line, he heard a voice say, "Detective Morgan."

"Detective Morgan, this is Mickey Christianson. I have a message to give you a call," Mickey said into the phone.

"Yes, Mr. Christianson. Thank you for returning my call. Do you know a Miss Valerie Green?" she asked.

"Yes, I do. Why? Is something wrong?"

"What relationship did you have with Miss Green?" she asked.

"What's wrong, Detective. Is she in some kind of trouble?"

"Please answer my question, Mr. Christianson."

"I will as soon as you tell me why you are asking them!" said Mickey Ray.

"I'm sorry to tell you this, Mr. Christianson, but Miss Green is dead."

Mickey had been looking out the window at his desk as he dialed the phone. When he heard this, he immediately sat down and took a deep breath. He continued staring out the window as the voice at the other end of the line called to him.

"Mr. Christianson, are you still there? Sir? Are you on the line?" she called to him again.

"Um, yes. I'm sorry. I never expected to get a call like this," Mickey said into the phone.

"I understand, sir. No one expects to get a call like this. Would you like to take a few moments to compose yourself and call me back?" she offered.

"No. I'll be fine. How did she die?" he asked as he felt a lump swell in his throat.

"What relationship did you have with Miss Green?" she asked again.

"We used to be engaged. She broke it off and moved to Florence. What happened?"

"For now, I'll ask the questions," she said.

"Okay."

"Before she called the police, your number was the last one she placed before her death last night. Why did she call you at eleven-thirty last night?" the detective asked.

Mickey answered, "She called because she was concerned that someone in a car was watching her apartment."

"Why was she so concerned?"

"Val would get that way sometimes. She had something happen to her a couple of years ago, and she sometimes gets upset over insignificant things like people watching her. I told her to call the police, and they would send someone out to check it out."

"What were her reasons for the breakup?"

"I told you, something happened to her, and she had problems with it. When she could no longer deal with it, she left town."

"Was that problem you?"

"No. Look, Detective. That's a long story, and I don't have time to explain it over the phone. Now, if you don't mind, tell me what happened to Valerie," Mickey said, getting exasperated with the detective's questions.

"At this time, it looks as though it may be an accident."

"What kind of accident?" he asked, trying to calm himself down.

"She'd been drinking, fell, and hit her head on a coffee table in the living room of her apartment."

"No. That couldn't happen. Valerie didn't drink. She called me around two-thirty this morning. I told her to call the police, and she said she would call me back if they didn't come. When I didn't hear from her, I went back to bed."

"That's why I'm working the case. A glass was on the floor beside the table with a rum drink spilling onto the carpet."

"I'm telling you, Detective, Valerie didn't drink. One drink, and she would get violently ill. You need to check other reasons why she hit her head."

"We got your name and number from the building manager as her contact in case of an emergency. Also, as I said, your number was on her phone."

"Yes, we kept in contact. We'd call each other every few days to talk."

"Is there someone else we can call to identify her and claim her body when the autopsy is complete?"

"No. She was an only child, and her parents died a few years ago. Can I claim the body so I can bring her home and give her a proper funeral?" he asked.

"Since she has no other family, and you are listed as her point of contact, I'll do my best to make that happen for you. You'll have to come here in person to sign papers to release her body. We still need time to complete the autopsy and get the report. Give us a week or two," the detective said sympathetically.

"That long? It doesn't take that long to do an autopsy, Detective."

"True, but we have other cases pending. We autopsy most people that die in situations like this."

"Like what?" Mickey asked.

"When someone is found alone in their home, like Miss Green. We need to find out why. If you excuse me, I have other cases. If I need more information from you, I'll give you a call," she said curtly.

"Wait a minute, please. That seems like a long time. Maybe you can speed up the process if I come there to claim her body?"

"I don't know, but I doubt it, sir," she said.

"Will you call me as things progress on the case?" he asked.

"I'm sorry, but I can't give you daily reports. I can only say that some things about her death don't quite add up. I will call you when my report is complete, and you can pick up her body."

"I'll take care of a few things here and come out as soon as possible."

"That won't be necessary, sir. I'll call you when my report is complete."

"Thank you, Detective. I'll catch the first flight out," he said. He politely ended the conversation and began making other calls to clear his calendar for the balance of the week.

He called his sister, Darcy, and told her about Valerie. "Oh, Mickey. I'm so sorry. I'm sure you're devastated to hear that."

"Kind of. I'm not devastated, but I am down about it. I never thought about something happening to Val," he said sadly.

"She was around in some way or another, most of our lives. In school, around the house when you were dating, and then you were engaged. She was such a sweet person. I know you'll miss her," Darcy said.

"Yeah. I will, but I've moved on, and I think on some level, so did she. But I still cared for her. And it will take a while for my feelings for her to dissipate."

"I Know. Do you want me to make reservations for you to pick up her body and bring her home?"

"If you don't mind, I would appreciate it."

"Okay. Done. I'll call you back as soon as I can make arrangements for you," Darcy assured him.

CHAPTER 2

Arriving in Florence, Oregon (excerpts)

He looked out the plane's window, and the setting sun gleamed in as it descended over the horizon. He thought of the times he and Valerie had sat on the front porch of her little house and watched the sunset.

Mickey had eaten so many meals at her house that she would use him as her guinea pig for some special recipe she found in one of her many cookbooks.

Mickey thought of Valerie until he fell asleep. When he woke up, the plane was on the approach to the airport in Oregon. Even though he had slept, he was still tired, but he got off the plane, headed to the auto rental counter, and drove to the hotel.

The following morning, he dressed casually in khaki cotton slacks and a polo shirt. He stopped briefly at the hotel breakfast area, got some coffee, and made a breakfast-type sandwich to eat as he drove to the police station.

The police station was a modern building surrounded by a short wall with the words *Florence Justice Center*. On the drive, he perceived it as a lovely sleepy little town. When he got to the police station, he asked for Detective Veronica Morgan.

When she walked out, Mickey took a deep breath. He noticed that she was about his age, and her long auburn hair was tied up in a bun with clips to hold it up on her head. She wore a dark business suit perfectly tailored to fit her petite frame, and the sun shining through the window made the gold chain hanging around her neck glisten. She pulled the suit coat around her and buttoned it as it tightened around her tiny waist. Her dark brown eyes showed bright as she looked at him with approval and flashed him a smile.

Putting out her hand, she said, "Hello, Mr. Christianson. I'm sorry to meet you under these circumstances."

"Thank you, and please, call me Mickey," he asked with a smile.

"Won't you come back to my office?" she said, turning with her hand and directing him to the back hallway of the building.

As they walked down the hallway to her office, they passed pictures on the wall of officers killed in the line of duty. Most were old black and white pictures, and the last one he noticed was the name, Sergeant Alfred Morgan.

"Was the person in the last picture back there any relation of yours?" Mickey asked.

"Yes. It was my father. Killed three years ago," she answered.

"I'm sorry," he said sincerely.

"Thank you.

"Now, Mickey, have a seat and tell me whatever you feel may be helpful in our investigation," she said as she pulled out the chair to her desk.

Sitting down in the chair on the other side, he started with a question, "Why do you say investigation? Will you tell me what you have so far?"

"I'll tell you what I can. It's an…."

"Ongoing investigation. I know the drill," Mickey said, shaking his head, "Look, I'm not here to interfere with what you're doing. I came here to claim her body and take her home. That's all."

"I understand, but we can't let her go for a few days. First, we need to do a complete autopsy, and then when we get every bit of evidence from her, we'll let you have her body. You said that you were engaged to her?" she stated.

"Yes, but that was a long time ago. She left Bridgeton, and we both moved on. We were still friends. And we kept in touch. That's all."

"If you moved on, why are you here to collect her body?"

"Now, you're getting a bit personal, but she has no one else. I owe her that. We were in love at one time, but as I said, it was long ago."

"I see," she said as she took notes. "Do you know why someone would want to hurt her?"

"No? Why do you ask that?"

"Just covering all the bases."

"Can we go to her apartment so I can see it? Who actually found the body?" he asked, getting up from the chair.

"As you assumed, she called our department the night before last after calling you. It seems that she carpooled with someone named Janice," Detective Morgan said, thumbing through notes on her desk. "When Miss

Green didn't come by to pick her up, Janice called her. When Miss Green didn't answer, Janice called the building manager. The building manager noticed that Miss Greens' car was still parked outside, so she went inside the apartment. She found the body and called us.

"It's a crime scene now. You aren't supposed to be there until we release it."

"You go with me and watch every move I make so I won't contaminate anything."

"I guess we could go together. It shouldn't be a problem," she said, then closed her notebook. "Are you ready to go now?"

"Sure, I've got nothing else to do."

She said they could take her police car. Since, technically, no one but police and prisoners are supposed to ride in the cars, she had to stop at the captain's office to get permission.

By the time they got to Valerie's apartment, she had told Mickey that he could call her by her nickname Ronnie, instead of Detective Morgan or her first name, Veronica.

When they got to the door, it had a padlock and was crisscrossed by yellow crime scene tape. She pulled the tape off and unlocked the door.

"Okay, Mickey, you can look at anything, but you can't touch," she said.

Mickey walked around the room, stopped, and looked at the corner of the glass-topped coffee table with dots of dried blood. He looked up at Veronica quizzically.

"Yes, it's her blood, and a broken drinking glass was lying on the floor next to her. We think she may have been drunk, stumbled, and fell. She hit her head on the corner of the table, which caused her death."

Mickey shook his head. "I told you, Valerie didn't drink."

"Maybe she didn't drink when she lived with you, but people change," said Veronica.

"We weren't living together just because we were engaged."

"It's just a thought right now. We'll know more when we get the autopsy report," Veronica said. "You two didn't live together?"

"Nope."

"But sometimes you would spend the night together, didn't you?" she asked.

"Nope. Never"

"If you say so," she said unconvincingly.

"I say so. Can we go into her bedroom?" he asked as he walked toward the back of the apartment.

Mickey walked to the dresser, opened the top drawer, and took out a journal.

"Hey, Mickey, I said you couldn't touch anything!"

"I gave it to her just before she left Bridgeton."

"If you didn't stay with her, how did you know where she kept it?"

"Because she told me that she kept it in her top dresser drawer. For some reason, she thought it would be safer there."

"I guess that sounds reasonable. But you still can't take it."

"I know, but you can, and we can look at it together," said Mickey with a smile.

"I can take it to my office, and I'll look at it there," she said.

Mickey thought for a moment, then said, "Why don't we take it to your office and look at it together. Sometimes she used a code to write."

"A code? What kind of code? And why would she do that?" she mused.

"Long story, Ronnie," said Mickey as he smiled, knowing the entire story. He remembered the time they had to crack an email code.

"Have you seen enough, now?"

"Yep, let's get back to the station and figure out this code."

"You can do that? Figure codes and stuff?" asked the detective.

"This code I can figure out in minutes," Mickey said as he handed the book to her.

Detective Morgan stopped at a coffee and sandwich shop, and while they waited for their food to arrive, Mickey took the detective's tablet and began decoding Valerie's journal.

He had a section decoded in a matter of minutes, showing Ronnie the decoded messages. It said:

At school today, I saw something strange. I went to the back area to look for some flour for one of the classes. I was supposed to go to the supply closet, but I turned wrong in the hallway and went into the loading dock area. I saw some men dumping what looked like sugar out of cloth bags and replacing it with another white powder. When I asked them why they were doing that, they told me to get out and never return there again. It was strange that they wore rubber gloves and what looked like gas masks. I didn't get near them, so I don't know who they were.

Some journal areas were written cursive, others were printed, and some had coded messages. Mickey knew that Valerie would write depending on her mood, but never in code unless she was concerned that someone might read her journal.

"Why would she use a code, and where did she learn to do something like that?" Veronica asked Mickey.

"It's a long story, and right now, it isn't important. This code's so simple but many people couldn't do it. It's a simple two-step over solution," said Mickey.

"What's a two-step over solution?"

"It's a simple matter of moving over two letters in the alphabet. Think of it like this. Take the letter A for example, and substitute C. The letter B becomes D, and so it continues."

"What happens when you get to the end? What are Y and Z?"

"Then you start over. Y becomes A, and Z becomes B. It's simple. There are no capitals and no spaces or punctuation. Valerie told me she puts private things in a slide-over code. Trying a couple of different slide numbers was simple to get the entire code. Anyway. We got the message. Now, all we need to do is find a way to get inside that culinary school and discover what's happening."

"We can't do anything. And I can't do that without a warrant, Mickey," she said. "I can't get a warrant on your girlfriend's third-grade diary code."

"It's a journal, not a diary. There's a difference," he said.

"Not to a judge or me," she said.

"Okay, it's time to call in help."

"What do you mean, help?" she asked suspiciously.

"As my brother-in-law would say, don't ask."

Mickey reached over, took the journal and began turning the pages and snapping pictures of each page. When he finished, he handed it back to Veronica.

Veronica pointed out some landmarks and gave him information on the city on the way back to the station.

"Florence has a population of over fifteen thousand people and has miles of beaches, many little antique shops, and the most delicious seafood on the country's west coast," she said as she drove.

"You sound like a tour guide, Ronnie," as Mickey looked at the various places she pointed out to him.

"I was, for a while, when I was in high school."

"What kind of case was your father working on when he was killed?"

"I don't know. He worked on many cold cases. He had just started an in-depth investigation on a case when he was shot. The Department investigated it but found no clues, so it's now officially a cold case," she said. "But it was CIOF, the same school that Miss Green, I mean Valerie was attending."

Mickey hesitated momentarily and said, "I lost my mom a few years ago in a car accident. It was also sudden and unexpected. Pop was injured in the same accident, but he recovered and did well." Mickey didn't explain further.

They rode the rest of the way back to the station in silence except when Veronica pointed out another possible area of interest. When they pulled into her parking space, she told Mickey she would call the coroner and determine when the autopsy would be done.

"We don't have many cases involving possible foul play. Most autopsies are done at the hospital because the police department doesn't have a lab. They're done by a doctor on staff there. I did ask him to put her on top of the list since it was suspicious, but it still may take him a couple of days to get it done and get us the report."

"Thank you. I appreciate it. The sooner you close this case, the sooner I can take her home and have a proper funeral."

"Not a problem, Mickey."

"Hey. Ummm, I'm a stranger in town, and all I know about it is what you pointed out to me on the way. When you get off work, are you free to show me around a bit more?"

Mickey looked straight into her black eyes that, at that moment, sparkled as she blushed. He had embarrassed her by asking her out. He smiled at her knowing what he had done.

He tried to help her out by saying, "I'm sorry. Maybe you're busy or have a boyfriend."

She looked at the pavement to hide her blushing face. "Oh, no. I'm not busy, and I don't have a boyfriend. You just kind of caught me off guard, that's all. I thought that maybe you might feel awkward since you're here to pick up your girlfriend."

Mickey said, "No. She broke off our engagement when she left. Yes, I still had feelings for her, but as a friend. I would still ask you out if she were standing here beside us."

"Okay then. I know a great little seafood place downtown that caters to the home folks here. It's small, but the portions are large and delicious. Since you're here from out of town, it's my treat," she said, smiling.

"Sounds good. How and where should we meet?" he asked.

"I can pick you up at your hotel, and we can go from there. That's easier since I know the town and you don't. I get off at five unless a call comes in and I'm assigned to investigate."

Mickey gave her the hotel's name and his phone number, got in his rental car, and drove away.

When he got to his room, he phoned James.

"Hello, James?" he said into his phone.

"Hey, Mickey. What's up?" came the answer.

"I'm here in Florence. It's a nice little city, and I've met with the police. They're doing an autopsy and suspect foul play but won't know until that's complete. So, I'll be here for a few days. Can you have Dee run a background check on the school Val was attending?" asked Mickey.

"Sure. What's the name again?" James asked. "Dee should be able to do that first thing in the morning. I'll be there in a few hours. I'll catch the red-eye as soon as I can get one out of here tonight."

"You don't need to do that. I've got enough to keep me busy here. I'm having dinner with the lead detective in the case this evening."

"Dinner? I didn't know that detectives got that friendly with out-of-towners on a case," James said.

"The detective is a woman. It's just dinner."

"Uh, huh. What does she look like, Mickey?"

"Oh, she's attractive," Mickey said.

"Just attractive? Mickey, you've been there just a few hours, and you've already met a woman and arranged for a date with her. She must be more than just attractive," James chided.

"You've said enough in those words, 'possible foul play'. I'll be there as soon as I can get a flight out. No arguments. No more discussions. We'll be back home with her body soon enough if it's nothing. Until then, I'm sticking by you as a good brother-in-law should. I'll ask Darcy Jean to make the arrangements. Later, Bro!" James disconnected before Mickey could object further.

Mickey took a long shower, a hot shower. He let the warm water roll down his back and invigorate the tense muscles in his back. It was early afternoon, and he was exhausted. His former girlfriend and fiancée was dead, possibly murdered, he's here to pick up her body, and he's going out on a date. Nothing was wrong with what he was doing, but it felt strange, like cheating on Valerie. He wasn't, but it felt like it. He needed to get over that feeling. She broke up with him long ago, and she's dead now.

"How messed up is that?" he thought. He stood under the flowing water, thinking of his past with Valerie. After all, they had known each other for years. Those feeling don't just go away. He got out of the shower, lay across the bed, and dropped into a restless sleep.

The buzzing in his head went off. It stopped, then started again. He woke up and reached to grab his phone.

"Hello. Mickey. I'm in the front of the hotel, and I'm hungry. Let's take a ride before we get something to eat," Veronica said when he answered.

"Sure, give me five minutes," he said, still waking up. After disconnecting, he sat on the side of the bed for a few moments to collect his thoughts. He got dressed quickly, went downstairs, and headed for the front doors of the lobby area. Parked outside the doors in a fiery red corvette was Detective Veronica Morgan.

Again, upon seeing her, his mouth dropped open. He stood there, looked at the vision, and finally moved to the car and got inside. When he looked at her, he saw a completely different woman. This woman had long brown hair flowing down her shoulders over a skin-tight bright flower print shirt that was low cut in the front. She wore shorts that accented perfectly shaped long legs and wore a huge smile with glowing teeth and oversized dark sunglasses. Around her neck was a different gold necklace with a small cross hanging at the end.

"Hi, Mickey. I didn't think you were going to answer your phone. I was about to hang up and go back home," she said as she put the gear shift into drive and pulled out of the hotel lot.

"Wow, you don't look like a cop," Mickey said, returning her smile.

"I'm not. The second I clock out, I'm just a private citizen, like you," she said as she pulled out for a drive along the coast highway.

"How does a cop afford a car like this?"

"I told you that my parents died. Momma and Daddy left a little life insurance and a house with no mortgage. They had a few investments that bring a small amount of money each month. I have no house payments, and the investment account pays the taxes, insurance, and monthly utility bills, so my paycheck from my job is pretty much mine to spend on extravagances like this car."

"You're also one of the lucky ones, Mickey. I did some checking on you this afternoon," she said without taking her eyes off the road.

"You did a background check on me?" he asked, somewhat concerned.

"Sure. I didn't know anything about you. You fly in town and want to pick up a body and pay for a funeral out of your own pocket. Then you're so forward as to ask me out when your fiancée's body isn't even cold. I may be a woman, but I'm not stupid or gullible. So, yes, I checked you out. And if you didn't check out completely, I would have called and canceled this evening."

Mickey then laughed. "I guess you're right on all points. I called my brother-in-law and told him that you were pretty sharp. Most men detectives would have called Valerie's death a home accident and moved forward. I understand that the autopsy is protocol, but you gave Valerie the benefit of the doubt. I appreciate that. So, what did you find out about me?"

"You were very thorough. I'm impressed. You'll get to meet my brother-in-law James because he's on his way here as we speak."

"Is he coming here as moral support, or does he think he'll help with the investigation?" she asked.

"Whatever's needed."

"While you're here, I'll work this case. You may tag along, but you'll not interfere. Do you hear me? I don't need your help," she said emphatically.

Mickey looked at her profile as they rode down the road with the ocean on his side. Her skin was silky smooth, with just a whisp of makeup just enough to disguise a few freckles sprinkled across her cute little nose. She had pierced ears with little stud earrings the shape of a tiny cross to match her necklace.

She reached over and turned the radio on.

Out of the speakers blared some golden oldies. Old songs of the 1960s. Just his style.

"You like the old songs?" he asked.

"Yes, that's what Momma and Daddy played all the time, so I got used to it. You don't like it?"

"I do. My Pop used to play it all the time. We have a huge garage, and Pop would go to his 'man cave' and play that music and work on restoring old cars."

"So did my Daddy. He didn't restore them. He would buy them already restored, but he did maintain them. He said life was too short to spend restoring a car. He liked to tinker, but he loved to drive them. I have a couple in the garage behind my house. If we have time and you are here long enough, we can go by, and I'll show them to you."

"I would love that," Mickey said and turned back to the road. He liked this woman. She was already on the same page as him. After taking a ride down the coast, she turned around, and they went back to town for dinner.

He insisted that she order for him at the restaurant since she was familiar with the menu. She ordered him a large seafood sampler platter and a small one for herself. As they ate, they talked. There was so much that Mickey couldn't tell her. He couldn't tell her about Valerie's abduction or when he and James had rescued a little girl's parents because it had to be done without the help or knowledge of the authorities. He found it difficult to speak of his past without telling these dark stories.

"What's it like running a building empire?" she asked, taking a bite of fish.

"Goodness, girl, you talk like we have some global business or something."

"Well?" she said cocking her head to the side like a puppy dog.

I just kind of supervise and make sure it all gets done."

"And that leaves you free to jet around the country burying old girlfriends."

"You make it sound glamorous and a bit sick at the same time," he said.

"I didn't mean it like that. I'm sorry. I'm sure it's upsetting for you, even though you were no longer engaged," she added.

"Yeah. It is difficult on some levels, but I don't know. Life goes on," he said thoughtfully.

After dinner, they walked down the street window shopping, and Mickey bought some items for his sister Darcy's kids. They continued until the sun began to set. They stopped at a coffee shop and shared a dessert. As they talked, they both felt comfortable being together.

Veronica's cell phone rang, and she picked up the phone and pressed the icon.

"Hello, Detective Morgan here," she said into the phone. "Oh, hello, Tom. Aren't you calling a little bit later than your normal hours? Sure, I understand. Tonight is fine. I'll be over first thing in the morning to pick it up. Is there anything particular that I need to see in person? Thanks, Tom, for doing a rush job for me."

After putting the phone in her purse, she said to Mickey. "That was Tom Wineberg in the morgue at the hospital. He said he's just starting on the autopsy, and I can pick up the report tomorrow morning. He's doing it now as a favor to me."

Mickey said, "I've had a good time this evening, but I still have some jet lag, so I think you should take me home. Also, James should be here in a couple of hours. I want to meet him at the airport."

"I've enjoyed this evening. I've got an early day tomorrow. On my way to the station tomorrow, I'll detour by the hospital and pick up the report. If you can meet me then, we can go over it together. Is that good with you, Mickey?"

"That would be great!" he said.

Veronica took Micky back to his hotel and drove off with him standing in front of the hotel, looking at her drive away. He saw her lift her hand in a goodbye wave and returned the wave with a smile.

He got to his room, turned on the TV set, laid back on the bed, and promptly fell asleep.